THE MEXICAN ASSASSIN

THE MEXICAN ASSASSIN

HARTSHORNE

CHARLES SCRIBNER'S SONS
NEW YORK

Copyright©1978, 1977 Hartshorne
Library of Congress Cataloging in Publication Data

———

The Mexican assassin.
I. Title.
PZ4.B65745Me   [PS3552.L842]   813'.5'4   78-3693
ISBN 0-684-15567-2

One

DRY. THE DUST SWIRLING. A dirt street littered with garbage; shards of grimy glass; no warning glitter as they waited to strike at the bare feet of the old men, slump-shouldered, walking slowly in the sun. Old men resentful of the hot sun and of their burdens, of life too readily eaten by that cannibal, death. A young girl sat in a half-shadowed doorway. About eleven years old, her toes curling idly around a dried-up orange peel, too thin and no doubt hungry; yet her belly was full. Too full, and the girl resentful of her burdens; of life and the devil who caused her desire; irresponsible nature that sprouted so many seeds in the hot desert of Sonora and left the seedlings to compete or die. Irritable with pubescent pregnancy, the girl was such a seedling but would not die. Mother love had not invested her yet; the devil of desire was still licking her loins. She wondered how she would kill the baby when it came. If it came. The old Yaqui—half medicine man and half bandit—had given her an herb, artemisia; maybe it would work. Yes, maybe, and tomorrow. That trinity of hopeless lies. Only "no" was certain; that and her hungry loins and the cannibal death. For a girl of eleven, she was wise.

This rubbish-paved alley dribbled over the edge of the hill and down precipitously to the small plaza below, the town center where the flies caucused in their droning summer senate. Like those other two politicians in the square, those flies. Noisy, devouring, and, of course, nurtured on feces. Pedro scowled. The mayor himself was buzzing; black at heart as any fly, and a disease himself.

The mayor was talking to the police chief. Another disease, that one, deadly. No flies settled on him, for fear they'd catch worse than they gave. The police chief was fat. A bag of oil with a white pig hide stitched over it, a wind-up laugh played on an old record set inside, and dull eyes. Nature was very specialized. One eye for money and one eye for cunt. And a specialized nose. For blood. Like the flies, the chief loved blood. Money, cunt, blood, in any order, any mixture. All together, much the better, that was heaven for Moctezuma Garcia Flanagan. Pedro crossed himself at the filthy picture in his mind, ashamed that there was such a man as Flanagan alive. Pedro would squash him before the week was out.

It was good to mix business and pleasure. Five hundred dollars and the satisfaction of watching the bag of oil leak out and the wind-up laugh go quiet. Well, will the smell of your own blood excite you, my friend? Pedro posed the question to Moctezuma GF as the two of them, he and MGF, sat talking in his mind's eye, just like it would be before Pedro squashed him.

"Will the smell of your own blood excite you, my friend?" Pedro asked.

It was nearly midnight. MGF had come smiling out of the whorehouse. They'd pleasured him tonight with a nine-year-old girl. Amazing, the things you could do to a nine-year-old. MGF had had a bloody good time. That girl wouldn't forget him. No. "No" was a certainty in Sonora.

Out of the joyhouse and into his car. Not really his car—well, not earlier, but his now. A fine American car, new. Bigger than the government allowed. So if anyone asked it was a loan from a friend, his friend, the Yankee.

"Never do that again, my friend," the chief had told him when they'd brought the Yankee in. A boy's horse had run out of a field and hit the car. Not hard, not seriously, simply into the fender, but enough to hurt the horse. It had fallen down sideways, its body stretching into the other lane of the road. If you could say there were lanes on a dirt road. That produce truck was coming by just at the time and hit the horse and killed it. And the boy who owned the horse came out of the field chasing after it and saw it hit once and then twice and then die. The boy cried, of course; why not? His father would beat him bloody for not taking care of that horse. Who'd plow now? Where would food come from now? Who would lose the farm now? Who would have to take work in town now? And what family would be poorer now and nearly starving? The boy's, of course, and all his fault for not watching that horse. MGF could see it all as it must inevitably happen. After all, the boy was his second cousin and MGF knew the father well. Well enough to loathe him. But when the father came to him and brought with him the Yanqui at gunpoint, well, something had to be done. The Yanqui was clearly at fault, hitting the poor horse and causing a family to starve. "Never do that again, my friend." The chief had said that to the Yanqui clearly, a friendly warning.

Those damned arrogant North Americans. Protesting. Getting angry. Rights. Lawyers. Denials of guilt. This one had been unpleasant. Foolish. One hundred dollars would have settled the whole affair. A small *mordita,* only a nibble as those things go. But no, this colonialist was righteous. He had been driving safely. He was in control of his car. He was insured. He had never had an accident. He was on his way to do business in Hermosillo. Liar. Who, going to do business in Hermosillo, would drive there through here, La Madre Dolorosa? He wanted a telephone. He wanted a lawyer. He wanted! Imperialists. They all wanted and were used to getting and didn't have brains enough to know when the game was over. The imperialist had lost and was too cheap to buy his way out of defeat.

A good beating first. Illustrative, to explain to him how matters stood. Then the jail for a long, long time. That, too, was a lesson for colonialists. Some of the people there would not be friendly. Some would be too friendly, even if the Yankee weren't young and pretty. None of the insects were friendly, but then it was only in the States that jails were supposed to be palaces. The Yankee would rot. Well, not really, not in Sonora. In his own hometown, near Vera Cruz—there a man would rot. Here, in the desert, one dried up and disappeared, the dead faster and the living too fast.

So, a fine Yankee car at his disposal. A crushed fender, some horse's hair stuck to dried blood, his second cousin beating the boy, and now to drive home for some mescal. A fine day, tomorrow would have been.

Except that here he was, standing in the darkness beside his own home on the finest street in town, with the devil himself beside him. The gun pointed at the bridge of his nose, so close that it chilled his bones. Crazy to feel a sinus headache when this devil was standing there. Not masked, not whispering, just that thin, grim man, wearing khaki drill trousers, a plaid cotton shirt, and a clean sombrero, wide-brimmed, asking him that question.

"Well, MGF?"

The fat man began to quiver; the spasms in his throat and the dryness made it difficult to speak.

"Excited by your own blood?"

"No, no, what are you asking?"

The bullet, hard-nosed, humane, and efficient, instead of a soft-nosed, bone-splattering butcher, whistled through the bridge of his nose to punctuate MGF's last lie with wheezing and squeaking as the red oil leaked out of the pigskin bag. Crunch, and a cockroach is dead.

Pedro relaxed. MGF's contract had been executed. Moctezuma Garcia Flanagan. The Irish had been in Sonora all right; but Moctezuma—why that? What mother curses a son? Or how many don't? Pedro preferred initials; they were abbreviated images, short as the tenure of his clients, once a contract had been let. Short, not so clumsy as a whole name wriggling with life. Short, good for the epitaphs of those who weren't worth a cold steel chisel or a whole tombstone.

Pedro unscrewed the silencer, put his .38 in his belt, and walked quietly over the flagstones down the dark street. The drama, well rehearsed on the many stages of his mind, had been played well.

Two

JUST AFTER SUNRISE, AT ABOUT the same time that, half a mile away, a fat corpse lying on flagstones was about to be discovered by a housemaid, Father Camillo Teran opened the door of the rectory. It was situated in a small, walled garden next to the cathedral and overlooking the square of La Madre Dolorosa. Father Teran glanced at the dewless garden, well kept by José, the old man who looked after the church, and hurried down the gravel path that would take him to the front gate, the street, and then the great front doors of the cathedral. There was a side door, too, but he would not use it today. He surveyed the dirty street, not yet beginning to stir. The square shadows of the two corner bell towers extended out into the square, flanking the beginning triangle of the roof upon which was superimposed the shadow—for the rising sun was directly behind it—of the basilica dome.

The builders had planned to gild that dome once riches came to Madre Dolorosa, but, as the priest knew too well, the devil as well as God lends men aspirations. And the interest on such loans is usurious. As it was, the church and the dome were fortunate to be freshly whitewashed. But the dream of gold remained. It had a stronger lure than heaven, for men die reluctantly in spite of the promise of heaven, whereas they rush to the slaughter for gold. This land had feasted on such dreams and the lies and slaughter that embellished them ever since Coronado had sought the seven cities of gold. Cold fare for feasting; but bread could be rarer even than gold, and many folk less likely to believe in bread than in gold, so always there was talk of gilding the dome of the cathedral.

Father Teran glanced up to the bell towers and saw what he expected: two white towers and on each a vulture sleeping. Hulking, red-beaked, fat-bellied, black-caped protectors of the faith, waiting to breakfast on the dying church. It would not be long, Father Teran was sure of that. These were angels a man could count on. Obligingly, they required nothing of the soul, no rendition of virtues and

5

sins and no delays in the waiting rooms of Purgatory. Why was it, when a Mexican wanted something, he had to wait so long before the patient insult of the waiting rooms of authorities? Saint Peter, the governor, the mayor, all followed the same appointment schedule; let the ordinary man wait, while the favored few buy their way to successful audience.

Two men waited in the shadowed church. A few tapers remained, the offerings of the wealthier or more anguished supplicants of the night before, but most were guttered. Unwindowed except behind the nave, where there was a small extravagance of stained glass, such light as came in was through the massive doors, now closed, with entrance only through a port, small enough that a man six feet high would have to stoop.

Father Teran walked past the two men, both lounging on the benches in front of the nave. Neither he nor they nodded, nor did their glances collide to acknowledge shared intentions. The priest moved into one confessional. It was one of two, a sentry box where a priest stood guard over a man's sins. This one was of undecorated but varnished pine, the wood scarred by nearly two hundred years of voices jagged with pain, anger, and hate.

The man came to the confessional and knelt. Dressed in the simple white cotton trousers and shirt of a peasant, carrying a faded green poncho carelessly over his shoulder, he spoke.

"The contact is with me, brother. He calls himself Che."

"A good name. I trust he'll keep it alive longer than the one after whom he calls himself."

"This is not Bolivia, brother."

"Nor is it yet better than Bolivia, brother."

The young man nodded assent.

"He tells me he's arranged for the arms delivery soon. There will also be radios, currency, medicine."

Camillo looked at the young man's half face, the other side in the shadows, as unseen as the back of the moon. He was about twenty-two and spoke too well for a peasant. Education was no disadvantage to a revolutionary, but it would raise havoc with disguise. Well, there was no use mentioning it, the boy could do nothing about it except keep quiet. That was the goal in any event. Let them put their energies into something besides words. Camillo was sick of words, the various gospels. Two thousand years of promises and exploitation were sufficient. The next manifesto would issue from the gun barrels of the people of Sonora. It was theirs, the Plan of Dolorosa, and it would guarantee the people's welfare. It would be punctuated with bullets.

He asked, "What are the delivery arrangements?"

"I don't know. Che will tell you."

"How did he come to us?"

"Through Raoul."

"Raoul vouches for him?"

"Of course."

Father Teran was annoyed at his young follower. Mexico was a monument to betrayal. Ask Carranza, who deserved it, in his grave. Ask Zapata, undeserving, in his.

"Send him over."

"Yes . . ." The student bit his lip to cut off the rest; a lifetime of habit had him about to say, ". . . and thank you, father." He rose, crossing himself, and gestured brusquely to his companion.

The other one was older, about forty, and stockily built. His hair glistened black in the dim church; his face was immobile behind a week's beard. His hair should have been duller, Camillo thought, dirty to go with the beard, filthy clothes, and shoddy leather sandals. Too much grease, it seemed. Che moved to the confessional awkwardly, staring into the lattice panel, refusing to kneel. Father Teran found that disturbing. The student, of course, was Catholic and approached a confessional—even for a revolutionary tryst—respectfully. This one, Che, was insolent. Father Teran disliked the man from the start.

Che, born under quite a different name, did not like churches and did not like priests, though he'd not before been in the one nor met the other. He could not disapprove of the arrangements on professional grounds; these were, in fact, ideal. A church to cover meetings and a priest running a guerrilla band—well, why not, who better to fight the pigs than one who lived in the same sty? Che had been well trained over the years, as case officer and dispatch. Mexican-Spanish practice after achieving Spanish fluency, just to be sure the accent was right. The clothes, brown contact lenses, hair dyed black just one week before, and, of course, the right documents. He had milieu training as well, rehearsing potential scenarios, so that, as it turned out, very little had surprised and nothing confounded

him as he journeyed through the United States documented as a
Spaniard, into Mexico documented as a Yankee, and now, two days
ago, into the Sonoran hinterland as a Mexican. But the scenarios
had not envisioned early-morning confessional and a gaunt, fifty-
year-old priest, intense and hollow-eyed as an El Greco prophet,
parading the long corridors of Leningrad's Hermitage, a museum
Che had seen only once, some fifteen years before, under the com-
pulsory aesthetics of an aunt. His mother's side of the family had
always had a bourgeois cast.

Che stared at the priest and said nothing.

"You are welcome here," said Father Teran, more courteous
than the occasion demanded. The patrician mode he'd learned at
home as a boy.

"Stinking aristocrat," thought Che, still smarting under the
recollection of his own mother's hardly proletarian origins.

"I've prepared for the delivery of the materials."

"How do we get them?" asked the priest.

"They will be delivered across the border near Naco. There's
a road west of there that's not controlled by the North Americans . . ."

An odd usage, thought the father. *Control* was not the word a
Mexican would use for *patrol*, although a European might. Father
Teran had been sent to middle school in Switzerland in those days
when his family had expected him to follow his brothers into commerce and a cosmopolitan life.

". . . and I've arranged for two trucks to meet us in a mountain
pass about twenty miles south of the border once I flash the signal
to them." Che did not realize that one walk to the confessional and
two perfect sentences had marked him as a foreigner. It would have
upset him as a professional had he known. Had his superiors known,
it would have been worse.

"Shall we keep the trucks or do we provide our own?" asked
the priest.

"You provide the drivers and we keep the trucks. Get Jalisco
plates and registration for the vehicles and be sure the drivers have
the right licenses. And we don't need twenty men to do the job of
two."

Che was peremptory. There was no telling what kind of fools
these native revolutionaries might be and he, Che, was charged with

making sure this sector ran well. It was, after all, the first operations group to be running in the north, right under the Yankee nose. The border was to be a major source of supplies; had it not been so in most of the Mexican revolutions? Díaz, Huerta, Madero, Obregón, Villa—were they not all supplied by the capitalist munitions-mongers? Che's branch had been accused of adventurism in pushing for the Mexican operation. His generals against the army generals; the branch's staff against the foreign ministry staff. Comfortable and conservative, the foreign ministry types were enjoying the cushy posts abroad and all the money they made peddling the forbidden imports that they brought home. As for the army, well, they were tough enough but no sense of cunning; they were technicians, really —if they couldn't shoot a missile at an enemy, they were not interested. Besides, they were occupied with the Chinese and wanted to risk no confrontations with the Americans. Well, that was their province, not his. Che was a Spanish-American specialist and quiet combat with the North Americans was the stuff of which his career was made. Che was waiting for the priest to reply.

"I appreciate your concern for safety, comrade, and I share it. But tell me, do you think we are all still Indians with bows and arrows that you use such a tone with me?" Father Teran felt his nose twitching; it always did when he tried to control his anger. It had twitched when he was a boy in his father's house, when he was a novitiate in Mexico City, when attached to the bishop in Cuernavaca, the modern one who had turned the altar into modern sculpture and brought in the radio stars to sing at Mass.

"My apologies, comrade. I am a soldier and I'm used to talking gruffly. We've only just met. How was I to know that you, a priest, would think of these mechanical details?"

Che knew he'd been careless this time. One must be a machine to manipulate people; there was no excuse for any sentiment existing, let alone showing. Emotions were to be saved for one's friends. It had cost him nothing to make a bandage for the wounded pride of this bandit aristocrat. Their mothers spoiled them, making these Latins into self-indulgent peacocks. This was a peacock hidden in a cassock, and one to watch. Clever, obviously, and sharp with his tongue, probably vindictive, and a dramatist, like so many of them. That was also something he'd been warned about in Mexican milieu training.

"No pardon need be asked, comrade. Everything is forgiven in this house."

"This house? You confuse me, comrade. Are you still a priest thinking me some fool come to confession or are you here to talk with me about getting those guns? I've worked hard on that border setting this up and I don't want to see my revolution delayed by your metaphysics. I'm not here to argue with you or to join the Church. I'm here because I've been sent here through Raoul, to work with you and to see you get supplied and such as you need it to see you learn how to use those munitions. I'll fight with you and give you all the help I can, but I don't take priesting or orders, and if it looks like you're messing things up, I'll walk off and find someone else who knows how to soldier and how to win a revolution."

Che knew that it had to be settled now, this matter of who was boss. Everything got down to that, who had the power. Sonora was his operation and these natives, whatever it was they thought they were doing, had better get it straight.

"Who sent you?" asked Teran angrily.

"Raoul sent me."

"No, Raoul found you or you found him, but I want to know who you are and who sent you. Other men come here and ask to join me. They come as socialists, even if they don't know it; they want to be free from exploitation, they want this rotten government overthrown, they want power for themselves because they are the people. Most are good men; students, peasants, once in a while a worker or even a professional, and they share a dream. I'm their leader but there's no room for tyrants, not here and not anywhere in Mexico." The priest went on, "Clearly, comrade, you're not one of those. Maybe you've made some arrangements with Raoul no one's told me about. That's up to Raoul and that's all right; we've got to have arms and support and I'll be damned if I care where they come from. Cuba's helping us; once, at least, China wanted to help us; the southern group is getting its arms from Czechoslovakia via Belen; and maybe Russia wants to help us up here. Fine, they're all welcome. But it's our revolution. What I won't allow is some uncommitted foreigner looking over my shoulder. Without commitment there's no revolution. What's more, there's room for only one chief around here and if you're not prepared to commit yourself to me, I'll have to ask Raoul to find us another contact to go with us to pick up those arms at Naco next week."

Father Teran was tingling with fury. Che, head cocked and one eyelid squinting, appraised this clerical bomb that had gone off in his face.

"I don't think you understand, comrade. There will be no other contact unless I say so. I control that shipment, not Raoul. To me, he's just another buyer out looking for a good deal. So, have it your way if you want, but don't plan on finding anything up there in that desert next week except lizards."

The struggle for power, Che knew, was ceaseless, and a man who held the advantage only to give it away was a fool who deserved what would inevitably happen. He would be ground under.

Father Teran's nose twitched violently. For the first time, in the months since he'd been forming his movement, he'd found an ideological comrade whom he hated more than the landowners, more than the bishops, more than the leaders of the ruling party. Teran had earlier faced but rejected the possibility that even when making a revolution one had to compromise.

"I don't believe you. I'll ask Raoul."

"Ask him. But you're losing valuable time."

"I'll chance that. Now, tell me who you are," demanded Teran.

A man more sophisticated in the ways of the world would not have bothered to ask such a question of a man like Che.

Three

GROAT WAS A BIG MAN, SCOWLING, with brown-black eyes, a pasted-dough nose, and a heavy way with him. That was his style. A college footballer, wartime marine attached to the OSS in China, a short stint after the war in his hometown Nebraska police department, and then off to combat again, this time as a career bureaucrat in Washington, D.C. He'd thrived there, supplementing his natural combativeness with what he'd learned from his Omaha uncle, with whom he'd lived during his teens in order to go to high school in the big city. Uncle was in commodities, trading mostly in hog bellies. Groat had become a trader, too, but his specialty was influence, careers, and, sometimes, lives. Like his uncle, Groat sported an oversize gold watch chained across his vest.

He was leaning back in his leather swivel chair, inhaling a cigar. He moved his big hand over to an incongruously rose-pastel telephone and pressed carelessly on one of its eighteen buttons. The buzzer rang in his inner office, where three secretaries sat, one typing, one primping, and one on the phone, surreptitiously talking to her girlfriend. Groat was indifferent to their activities and, it followed, to them. There had been a time when secretaries had interested him, indeed, a time when some had reciprocated—to their later regret. He'd given them all up as a bad habit, for one homeless heart had tried to blackmail him. She'd been ineffectual but he'd learned then and there not to screw the help.

There stood before him now the subsequent replacement to that earlier victimized heart—Miss Spinner, thin, neatly featured, thirty, fastidious, and competent. Her plainness was capable of remedy, but Miss Spinner was indifferent to her looks. Pad in hand, she waited, chronic disapproval of Groat signaled in her thin lips and unrelenting eyes. He gave her the fish eye in return.

"When Barber comes, send the Tiburon file in with him."

"Yes, sir."

"And I don't want any incoming calls while he's here."

"Yes, sir."

"Now get the hell out of here."

Miss Spinner wheeled about and left, slamming the door behind her. Groat paid no attention. Outside, Miss Spinner went to the open safe, leafed through the files, past Operation Taco and Project Tenacillas, and found Tiburon. File in hand, she returned to her desk and sat down. The outer office buzzer sounded. Lee Barber had arrived.

"You're looking lovely today."

Elise looked up to greet the lean and smiling man who had come in. She'd known him since she'd joined the Bureau eight years before. Indeed, she'd worked for him for a few months that first year. He'd been thirty-two then and a wonderful boss. Now, the soft gray was creeping into his auburn sideburns, but he was as lively— and, she realized, as handsome—as ever.

"Something wrong, then . . . ?" Barber, his face serious as he sensed all was not well with Elise, let the words trail. An incomplete question beckons a reply.

Elise sighed and silently moved her angry eyes toward Groat's office door. Barber comprehended.

"Ah, the Neanderthal has done it again. The full weight of his charm or simply a little thing he hardly noticed doing, like a crocodile eating a child?"

"Right, just a little thing like that."

"Poor child." Barber put his hand over hers and squeezed it momentarily.

"Why doesn't somebody bite him for a change?" she asked mournfully.

Barber tilted his head back, opened his mouth, and brought his teeth together in a snap.

"One day, when God graduates from law school and learns about justice, then that day, I promise you, Little Red Riding Hood, someone will eat both grandmother wolf and the Groat. In the meantime, sad to say, we meek had better look after our inheritance."

"And," said Elise, no longer morose, "lest you forget, CYA."

Barber, his face more serious than Elise would have wished it to be, his blue eyes knowing, nodded. "By all means, Elise, when in the water with crocodiles, at the very least CYA, cover your ass."

"Well, you'd better go in, because your Neanderthal is impatient. And here, take this with you." She handed Barber the Tiburon file.

Barber opened the door. Groat, his desk flanked by the flags of the Bureau and the nation, and his walls covered with the inscribed photographs of the country's leaders, looked up from the pile of papers. Barber stood in front of him. Groat motioned for him to take a seat.

Barber remained standing.

Exhaling cigar fumes, Groat looked upward sharply. "Sit down, I told you."

"It's been six months since last we met. I think a formal greeting is in order."

Groat glared. He wasn't sure whether Barber was making merry, taunting him, or angry.

"What the hell do you want me to do, salute?"

"No. When wily Ulysses returns home, he expects Penelope to rise from shroud-making in profuse greeting. After all, I did just win you a bit of the Middle East, if not Troy itself."

Groat flushed, biting his cigar with fury.

"You son of a bitch."

Barber remained standing.

Glaring, Groat crushed his cigar shapeless as he took it from his mouth, slowly rose, and offered his hand.

Barber nodded, shook hands, smiled affably, and sat down, no hint either of the grim jousting just now over or of the scene in his mind, of a self-satisfied, bare-ass swimmer just having soundly bitten a crocodile.

Groat was back in his chair, his fingers fondling his gold watch.

"Those idiots down there can't find their asses with both hands," he said irritably. "We've got five men in Mexico City, one in Hermosillo, and ten on the border, and not one of them can draft a cable, let alone let us know what's going on."

Lee was expected to play the prompter.

"What *is* going on?"

"The third police chief in Sonora assassinated this month, that's what's going on."

"Any details."

"Yeah, he's dead."

"Oh. Was he one of ours or one of theirs?"

"None of them are ours, none of them are theirs."

"I meant, was he mostly working for the government or mostly for the traffickers?"

"The bastards are always working for themselves."

"I wouldn't go that far," said Lee. "I know a couple who are straight, at least as far as drugs. In the Federales, you know as well as I do that the special boys are as clean as a whistle."

"Well, let them blow it up their ass. I don't trust any of them."

"That's too bad."

Groat glared at him. "Sometimes, Barber, I wonder if you understand the intelligence business."

"Who does? But once you prove a man, then you trust him. You've got to."

"If you trust any of those greasers, you're crazy. But then that's your problem. I want you to go to Mexico and find out what the hell is going on."

"Okay, where do you want me to start?"

"Oh, for Christ's sake, you worry about that. I don't care. Just find out what stinks down there and what it means and what we can do about it. Then we'll do it."

"Okay on one and two, but what if we can't do anything about it?"

"That's garbage. We can always do something. What the hell are we, anyway, if we can't even handle something in our own backyard? Who the hell owns Mexico, anyway?"

"The Mexicans?"

"That's what they'd like to think. But I'll tell you something, buddy boy, they only own it as long as they don't step on our toes. Little spicks don't cross the big man without making a painful discovery about what the world is like."

"You're the captain of a gunboat that sank a long time ago," said Barber. "Uncle can't have it all his way these days, you know that."

Groat was disgusted. "How can an intelligence officer sound so damn naïve, or should I say pious? Christ, over the years you've seen it all done or done it all yourself: rigged revolutions, stuffed ballot boxes, invented national heroes, started civil wars, bought and sold prime ministers, blackmailed whole cabinets, dropped the opposition out of airplanes without benefit of parachute or clergy, turned off the spigot and watched a national party change color overnight, bugged a king's pillow while your whore set up the succession to the throne, and had a Communist general for your very own ventriloquist's dummy. And you have the gall to tell me we can't do what we want in Mexico. I say bullshit!"

"If it's dry in Sonora, none of us are going to make it rain. It all depends, Julius, it all depends, and as far as drugs, violence, and what-have-you are concerned, Mexico is a sackful of very autonomous jumping beans. So don't have your heart too set on social reform coming out of the barrel of a gun, the good chairman's optimism notwithstanding."

"The purpose of power, boy, is to use it. And the man who has it, and doesn't, finds he doesn't have it any more. And the man who took it away from him did and will." Groat gestured toward the manila file on Barber's lap. "In two months I expect that folder to be full and closed. And you close it."

Barber glanced at the red-typed marker, *Tiburon.*

"Shark?"

"Shark," Groat agreed. "That's the name."

"What was the name of our late lamented police chief?"

"Moctezuma Garcia Flanagan. The town was Madre Dolorosa."

"The mother of sorrows," said Barber softly. "Probably they originally called it Mater Dolorosa."

"Wouldn't you know? Anyway, start there."

"Any ideas on how you want me to go in?"

"Alive, same as you want to come out."

"And beyond that?"

Groat wrinkled his forehead and covered his upper lip with his lower one. He reached for another cigar from the box of Cubans on his desk. He shoved it toward Barber. "Have one."

"You've good taste in cigars, Julius."

"There'd be no use running the Western Hemisphere area if I couldn't get a good Castro cigar, would there?" He was silent for a moment and went on, "I'll let the office in Mexico City know you're there. They can help in an emergency and can handle the routine reporting. Specifically, I want to know if this last killing has anything in common with the batch we had last year in Mexicali. The folder there will give you the details. Those happened when the

Fernandez syndicate—I wish to hell we'd learn who they are—were moving in on Lopez's syndicate and trying to wipe out Lopez's protection. When we got a handle on that, we made some money —offered the Lopez bunch protection on the San Diego side if they'd snitch on the heroin routes up from Sinoloa and Nayarit. You remember that?"

"I remember."

"Well, it worked then, didn't it?"

Lee shrugged. Did any of it work much? As long as people liked heroin and preferred hustling to working, and as long as a poor farmer could make four times more growing poppies than maize, and with half a million people down the line taking their share off the top as the stuff moved up, over, and into the States—well, how was anything going to work? Put one bandit out of business and another took his place.

Groat was continuing, "Anyway, it's probably somebody muscling in; just find out who and where we can make points."

"Alternatively," asked Barber, "could it be a Federale operation wiping out some of the baddies, just for practice? You know, their president's got a reputation for honesty and he might just have gone ahead and started to make some rather telling police reforms without bothering us with the news."

"No chance. Their security down there is like a sieve. They can't take a crap without our knowing about it. Besides, if it were that kind of action, there'd be a stack of dead traffickers from Acapulco to Tijuana. Last month they reported only seven dead, just the usual business disagreements and hijackings. Of course, if Flanagan—I do wonder where the hell a spick got a name like that —if he wasn't kinky, then either the traffickers or his brother peace officers could have been blackballing him from their cozy little club. When you were working that area, did you ever hear of this Flanagan?"

"No, I never did." Barber cupped his chin, cleft in the center, in his hands. Under high cheekbones there would be faint reminders of dimples when he smiled. But there was no smile for Flanagan, not the one he'd known. The Flanagan he'd known was no newly laid corpse in Sonora. His Flanagan was the man who'd run over Barber's wife two years before, drunk, they said, as he was; and, therefore, not really responsible, they'd said.

"Well, you look like you know something." Groat was impatient.

"We spooks are well known for our deceptive looks, Julius."

The other eyed him sourly. The one thing Barber did not look was deceptive, which was, of course, very deceiving. He just looked ordinary to Groat—well, say intelligent-looking, decent enough and unbearably confident, like the world was his oyster and him a big, shiny-bright pearl. Lord knows, the women liked him. Groat's wife, Alice, for example. She insisted he was "cute" and "cultured." And the girls in the office thought he was the cat's meow, that was clear enough. What was there to him? He stood an erect five feet eleven, small beside Groat; he had a normal face, low forehead with a widow's peak and near-red hair falling to brush the busy eyebrows, hollow cheeks that gave him an austere look, for all the affability; his manners too formal for Groat and, of course, those Savile Row clothes—Poole's of Savile Row, to be exact, because Groat had once taken the trouble to look. Groat didn't cotton to that sort of thing, nor to Barber's Yale Summa Cum Laude, nor his classics major, nor his Phi Beta Kappa, nor his goddamn independence. Fuck him is what Groat said to himself, wishing there'd been no envy behind it. The man wouldn't play the game, not Groat's game. Since the only game in the branch was Groat's, not to play was to lose and, in Groat's book, Barber had long been a loser.

But Groat needed him. Like that biddy Spinner outside. Barber was trouble but, in the balance, Groat had to keep him. If Groat was to get to the top and stay there, he had to protect his flanks, make sure the work got done, good work that Groat could take credit for. In Groat's jungle, his Washington, there was hunt and be hunted and that was life, full-time. The work, whatever it was, only dictated the habitat of the animals. The Pentagon, Commerce, Agriculture, protecting migratory birds, calibrating measures, whatever, the jobs didn't matter once you understood that it was all jungle. A man on the way to the top had to look like he was working, Christ yes, all hours and forever, and he would be, too, but on the main chance. So, somebody had to look after what the taxpayers thought they were paying for—those goon congressmen were always yelling— just to keep the flanks protected and give a man a platform for the next jump higher. So, you had to have a couple of people, a couple if you were lucky, who knew what was going on and really did the work. Really did it. And, thought Groat, Barber is my boy for that.

As for the others? Groat figured, had always figured, that about half of them were just like himself, jungle creatures, hunting and being hunted. And the other half were out of the game, permanently, their insides eaten out and their remains stuffed all good and proper, sitting at their desks waiting to collect their pensions. Mummies. The Civil Service was the biggest taxidermist in the world.

So here was Barber ready to go and to do or die, maybe do and die, since that was the way it was played.

"Up yours," Groat said out loud.

"Thank you, Julius, you've always had a way with words."

"I have a few more, but I'll save them for later. Right now, I want you to go downstairs and arrange currency, documents, any disguises you need from the technical boys, and whatever other quick and dirty backup you need. We don't have time for anything fancy, no legends, no deep support covers, nothing that can't be done in a couple of days. Since I don't want to take anybody off the border or Hermosillo, you're going to need a partner to back you up, wire you when you need it, handle the drops and emergency commo—the usual."

"That's fine. I'd like to take along . . ."

"I don't care who you want to take along, I've got somebody."

"Oh?"

"Yeah, somebody new."

"Why a new man on this job? Operating out in the Mexican boonies isn't easy. What's his Spanish fluency?"

"He just got out of training. He only speaks training manual and that's a language nobody understands. That shouldn't matter; he can play tourist and use a dictionary."

Barber was solemn. "Julius, this is no time for jokes. I thought you wanted a professional operation, not one of the usual stand-up comedy routines that you people run here out of your basement. There aren't any tourists in that part of the country; he'd stand out like a parson in a whorehouse. With two of us going in at the same time, somebody's bound to put it together."

"Lee boy, do you or do you not bear the title of my special assistant?"

Barber eyed him carefully. "So?"

"And do I not give you, as my troubleshooter, all the cushy

assignments that keep you out of the daily grind of this bureaucracy that you loathe?"

"Wrong on cushy, right on the bureaucracy," said Barber.

"Well, cushy, maybe or maybe not, still some people like making trouble and wading about in other people's cisterns and that's you, you're that kind of people. Do I not, then, as your eminently fair-minded boss and head of this branch, feed and care for you? Do I not protect your peculiar little ego from all the insult and bother that everybody else who has to work here puts up with? In other words, Lee boy, are you not getting for what you're giving?"

It was not arguable. Yet, as Lee sat here being drubbed as Groat's slave for the reasons Groat gave—and Groat knew another one, too, the main one, which was that Barber, like everyone else in the service, loved the game and dedicated himself to it—he would have liked to kill him. Struggling, Barber quieted his irrational demon. He was aware of a slight muscle tic in his trigger finger.

"Yes, Julius, I agree. You're right," he said resignedly.

"Now that's being a good boy."

"Enough, Julius." Barber became menacing.

Groat changed the subject. "Okay. Parks downstairs will introduce you to your junior officer. Show him what life is like and be sure to get him back here safely. He's an obligation of mine."

"Ah, the truth will out then, will it? Who is he, Julius?"

Groat shrugged. "You'd have found out in two minutes, anyway, from anybody except the kid himself. He's the son of the big boss, that's who he is."

"Oh, Jesus," said Barber. "Billie Hickock?"

"You know him?"

"Yes."

Groat sensed something he ought to know but didn't. "How come you know him?"

Barber said offhandedly, "Met him when I lectured to the trainees."

"Well, can you handle him? I'm dead serious, Lee boy. I don't know a damn thing about him except they said he was so eager in training they called him Wild Bill. He's the kind who wants to jump out of the airplane without his parachute just to prove he's gung-ho. Anyway, they gave him to me and I'm giving him to you."

"He's a good kid, Julius, a very good kid."

"Good, glad you're happy." Now, if anything went wrong, Groat could blame it all on Barber. Billie Hickock was the hottest potato that had been handed to Groat in a long time. Badly handled, a thing like that could blow a man's career sky high. Groat was pleased. He smiled at Barber, saying, "And one more thing. Parks and his committee will run you in the field."

"Run me?"

"Well, just to keep it orderly. You know on a job this big we can't just run it between ourselves. It's normal to have a committee coordinating a new operation."

"Normal? Listen, Julius, the last time you had a committee coordinating an operation, the Mafia imported five hundred pounds of pure heroin right into Bureau of Customs Headquarters and got off home free and a few zillion dollars the richer. And the time before that, we lost three destroyers right out of the mothballs to some pirate who convinced them he was king of Sumatra. And before that—Jesus, you name it, the Bay of Pigs, the eruption of Vesuvius, the fall of Rome—Julius, I don't need a committee!"

"Anyone running an operation like this needs all the headquarters help he can get. What if it turns big and you need people? What if you have to get an assist for some big equipment? What if you need to run down five hundred names? What if . . . ?"

Barber interrupted. "We'd do it just like always, through the desk. That's what Parks is for. We're not running the Kurdish army into the Caucasus or wiring another Kremlin limousine, for Pete's sake, and you know it. Julius, it isn't me who needs the committee, it's you. You need the committee because you've got the director's son in your lap and you want a whole big army to blame if it goes sour."

Groat was irritated. "I've got you to blame, buddy boy, that's plenty. The committee just makes it all shipshape. Some of them are your best friends—they'll be rooting for you! After all, we don't want anything to go wrong, do we?"

That was true. However Machiavellian, Barber could understand. Once again, he quieted his hateful demon.

Groat went on, "And just to be sure nothing goes wrong, I want you to clear everything you do with the committee, you understand? Just like you were anybody else working here. You know anything, you hear anything, you see anything, you cable it back. You want to

do anything, you get clearance. Then, after you do something, you
tell them what you did and just what happened and what you want
to do next. And they'll clear that. Parks will chair it, he'll have no
other priority work but yours. I'll hold him responsible right down
to his toenails as your coordinator. Everything you say or do will
have red urgent smeared on it so if it makes sense you'll get it, be
it man or beast. But I don't want you screwing around out there
playing any solo games; that is an order. Do you understand?"

And once again Lee understood. He understood Groat, covering himself against any eventuality. He understood the committee,
stuck in the middle and no way to cover their asses but to say "no"
and hope he'd ignore it. Groat already knew he would ignore those
orders, which was why he had made him his special assistant, simultaneously indispensable and expendable. No rules as long as he
succeeded. Crucifixion without any defense if he failed. He understood the whole system, the same old one he'd quit three years
before out of depression and raging frustration. And been wooed
back out of despair and boredom and grief when Beverly had died.
The promise made, "Never a committee." And the promise broken,
"Here's your committee." The same old Groat and the same old
system—well, the same new system, for in the old days—before his
time and even a bit during his time—it had not been so. The dino-
saur had evolved from the whippet, the sloth from the fox, and the
rabbit from the tiger. Why not? Much was ludicrous in the intelligence business and why not, therefore, find Darwin reversed?

Barber, picking up the Tiburon folder, made ready to leave.

"Have a good trip, Lee boy, and make sure we get something
done."

"Yeah." Barber could only be terse.

"And, Lee, while you're at it, why don't you move Mexico
somewhere else and put Canada on both borders so we can have
white men for neighbors?" Groat was grinning malevolently.

Barber slammed the door behind him.

Four

PARKS, IN CHARGE OF THE MEXICAN desk, was three floors down and a world apart from the lushly carpeted kingdom of Groat. His desk, a section, was an enclave in the larger satrapy of Latin America, and that, in turn, a dukedom in the principality of foreign strategic intelligence, and the most significant part of the kingdom of Groat. Over all that, and far more, there ruled the unseen Emperor of whom Only Good Things were said. As the Furies were called beseechingly the Kindly Ones, so, too, was the name for the Emperor, the Good Man.

Oddly enough, it was true, for Lee had known him long and well; he and Emperor Hickock played tennis when they could—clandestinely, of course, lest hog-belly traders like Groat intrude with their ambitions. Lee and the emperor had a rule: civilized men at play don't talk about work. Lee's father and Hickock had known each other in school, his father older but their families closely acquainted. It had been that tie which had brought Lee to the Bureau. Where else was there an adventuresome life so close at hand?

Parks was speaking. "I hear the kid's been assigned to you."

"So I hear."

"Good luck." Parks, friendly but not a friend, because in that kingdom few men afforded the risk, was careful not to commit himself further.

"Thanks," said Barber, wryly.

Parks waited. The line of command had gotten murky. Barber was under the control of his committee for this operation but, as Groat's special assistant, had some unspoken freedoms, the rules for which weren't defined. Barber did outrank him. With the director's son attached to Barber, Parks could only assume that Barber would try to go around them all, using the junior officer as the route. It was what Parks would have done. Parks's job, of course, was to make sure there were no waves, nothing rippling out from the middle of Sonora that would make Groat look bad, because if that happened Parks would never see another promotion, not unless, of course, Groat got his while Parks stood clear. That would be all right because, with promotions so tight, there had to be vacancies upstairs or nobody downstairs could go up. That meant that if Parks could manage to control what happened, so that things went to hell in clear contradiction of his committee's orders, making it look like Groat had connived in something stupid that Barber had done, where they could catch Barber's tit in the wringer, with the director's son carrying the message directly upstairs, it all might work out. He'd have to hope Barber did something stupid; that was the best he could do for now. Control was the key. And the devil take the hindmost. Parks smiled deferentially at Barber.

"Well, as you know, it's my job to see you get everything you want. You can count on us for full support. The committee is at your disposal. I've told them we'd all meet as soon as you were finished upstairs. Let's see, it's three o'clock now. Why don't I pick up the phone and get them together right away? Afterward, if you like, come on over to my place for dinner."

Barber was foolish enough to like Parks, for all his reputation as a nay-sayer. They'd worked together in the field once, Hong Kong, and Parks had been good company and reliable. Cautious, but tough action brought out the best in him. Here at headquarters he was penned up and all the mischief sneaked out sideways. Parks had developed a reputation as a schemer. It needn't have happened. This operation, letting him chair a committee, made him too important. The Peter Principle. He'd been promoted away from and out of his competence. It was a shame. The dinner invitation was kindly, even if there was a scheme behind it.

"Thanks, that would be nice," Barber replied.

There were martinis before dinner, but Barber preferred Scotch, Laphroaig neat, soda separate. Marilyn, Sam Parks's wife, had brought the cheese tray and was with them. They would talk business in front of her. It was that way in the Bureau with wives. Whatever the rule books on security said, wives knew everything they cared to know. Nobody bothered seriously to clear them, no lie detector checks on them regularly, no electronic sweeps of the house for bugs, no locking the briefcase full of classified documents into the safe at night, for there was no safe and the briefcase would stay on the living-room table. It was all, as Barber had said to Groat, a matter of trust, once some initial appraisals had been made.

Marilyn was speaking. "Alice Groat told me yesterday you were going to Mexico this week."

"Well, she knew it before I did."

Marilyn grinned. "We run our own intelligence service."

"You'd better," Lee replied. "The one I work for is in trouble."

"Gets worse every month," Sam Parks affirmed, not without bitterness.

"Keep the faith, Sam, some day you'll get out of the Bastille and into action again," said Barber, reassuringly.

Sam Parks shrugged and drank.

"What," he said, "did you think of the meeting today?"

"Great. I like nothing better than twelve men, tried and true, every one of whom can't wait to get out of the jury room before he himself is convicted of the crime."

"What crime?" asked Marilyn.

"Being on a jury that might make a mistake," answered Lee.

"What mistake?" Marilyn queried.

"If they knew what it was, they wouldn't make it," said her husband dourly.

"But they do know the penalty," said Lee.

"God, yes, they sure know the penalty." Sam spoke strongly.

"You mean if something goes wrong while the big boss's son is in on the operation to tattle?" asked Marilyn.

"How did you know that?" Sam was perplexed. His wife said so openly what was a matter of dark conniving for him.

"An unidentified informant named Alice."

"What else did she tell you."

"That Neams Market is having a sale on roast beef. So that's what we're having for dinner, or at least you will if I get it served." She got up and went to the kitchen.

Sam looked at his guest. "Do you know what's going on down there in Sonora? I've had the analysts going through everything and none of them comes up with anything. I don't have a clue. That meeting this afternoon was hopeless, we blew smoke rings. All that business about Mexicali last year, the new opium crop going in in Sinaloa, the usual seizures on the border, the corruption and double-crossing and the usual heroin hijackings, you never know whether by the mobs, the bandits, the local competitors, the police, or the army—I don't see anything special there that ties up to those killings of the police chiefs. And I can't see why Groat's got that stuck in his craw—there's nothing to indicate it's anything but local. Why does he want to get us all excited about it?"

Barber shrugged.

Sam went on, "And why does he want you there? What the hell, we've got a dozen men down there working drug traffic, why send you down? It just doesn't figure. Why bother with a couple of dead cops?"

"Maybe Groat knows more than he's telling us."

"Why would he play games? Hell, if I'm to chair that committee, we've got to know everything. Besides, all the Mexican cable traffic goes directly through me, anyway, so what could Groat know about it that I don't?" Sam Parks's martinis had excited, not sedated, him.

Barber was silent.

"Look, Lee, we've been friends a long time, through a lot together, right?"

Lee nodded.

"Promise me something, then?"

"What?" asked Barber.

"That you'll come clean with me on this operation. I mean, that you'll cable us everything you get and not go around any corners. I smell trouble on this one and my fanny could be in a sling, especially, as Marilyn said, with the boss's son down there to pass it upstairs."

"Don't you trust me, Sam?"

"Hell, yes, I trust you, Lee, but I know how it is once you're in the field. Headquarters guidance is a pain that is well left behind."

"We all know that."

"So, you'll keep me informed of everything? Look, I'll make you a little deal. If it's something you don't want Groat to know, just slip it in sideways—you know, put an 'eyes only' on it for me. Nobody on the committee will hear it. How's that?"

Lee smiled gently. "Look, Sam, I lie a lot for business, but not to the people I work with. I'll do what I can but I can't promise you the moon. Sit tight, nobody who's ever worked with me ever got in trouble. You know that."

"Yeah," Sam said dubiously.

"Now, will you make me a promise, Sam?"

"Sure, absolutely, whatever you want."

"Don't let me down, Sam. I know what a committee is like and I know the spot you're in. Even so, you are my backup. I expect you to be on my side if it gets hot in Sonora, Sam."

"Absolutely, Lee, absolutely." Sam moved his whole body in assent.

The two men grasped hands, each with his own thoughts about the other.

The telephone rang and Marilyn answered. "Sam, it's for you. Don't be too long, dinner will be on in a minute."

Sam went to the phone. It was five minutes before he returned. Marilyn had finished pouring the wine and was calling them to the table.

"Just got a little news for you, Lee. It was the duty officer."

"What news?"

"The armory in Fort Huachuca on the Arizona-Sonora border was broken into last night. The thieves were on their way out before anybody knew what was happening."

"So?"

"The sentries got one of them. Found his body. The local fuzz made him as a Hermosillo boy working for Fernandez, who's supposed to be the dope *jefe* down there."

"What did they get away with from the armory?"

"I hoped you'd ask. Mortars, M60 machine guns, M16s, M79 grenade launchers, ammo, grenades, you name it. They could start a war."

"With that, *jefe* Fernandez could graduate to king," said Lee.

"And last seen—which they weren't very clearly—they seemed to be heading south."

The next morning, Barber was typing instructions in a borrowed office, one not far from Groat's, which he used on those designedly rare occasions when he was in the headquarters building. There was a knock on the door.

"Come in."

"Yes, sir."

Young Hickock, stiff as a ramrod, grinning from ear to ear, snapped to attention in front of the desk.

"Brother," exclaimed Barber, "you're in the wrong outfit. Better save that for when you make doorman at the Savoy."

"Right on, boss. How do I look now that I'm out of training and a fully fledged spook on her majesty's service? Look, new threads and a haircut." He patted the sleeves of a gray-and-red-plaid sports jacket and made his fingers into a scissors mock-cutting around his ears.

"A crew cut. Lord, I thought those went out with the flappers."

"Not on your life. They're making a comeback. Just wait. Once you oldsters watch me cut my swath out in the field, you'll all be asking who's my barber. Modeling through admiration. Learned that in psychology. Happens every time."

Lee leaned back in the typing chair, surveying his new partner, apprentice, and ward. Twenty-five years old, brown hair—what little there was left after the haircut—freckles that would never go away, a pug nose, green eyes, about six feet, mischievously good-looking, and, no doubt about it, with that salute, excellent doorman material for the Savoy, and not bad for the Bureau, either.

"You'll make it, dad." Lee spoke approvingly.

Barber gestured to his friend to sit down. For the rest of the day they discussed and reviewed the Sonora situation, travel plans, backup and contact arrangements, headquarters communication, local liaison, and their cover.

"You've got it all now, Bill?"

The young man nodded confidently.

"Okay, I'll see you in La Madre Dolorosa."

Five

THE AEROMEXICO PLANE bouncing down from Tucson off the tops of thunderheads was full: Mexican businessmen, families visiting their relatives either in Arizona or Sonora, a few middle-aged gringos in loud sports shirts with battered briefcases and gin-spiked jokes shouted across the aisle, a stringy long-haired couple in matching faded blue jeans, both extraordinarily thin, and a Protestant minister in full regalia—collar, summer cotton gray vest, and neat black suit.

His dark hair strongly invaded by gray, brown eyes, glasses, and an overly plucked moustache, he was about fifty years old. A book on mission architecture was in his hands. From the oversize black plastic carrier bag, obligingly crammed under the seat in front of him as the regulations required, other books—English and Spanish —cascaded to the floor.

The stewardess was near him in the aisle, carrying a tray of coffee, cola, and miniature bottles of tequila, vodka, Kahlua, and gin.

"A drink, padre?" She was short and a bit plump.

The minister looked up, smiling prissily. "Why, yes, thank you. Coca-Cola, if you please. I try not to indulge in coffee."

The Mexican woman in the faded flowered dress in the seat next to him moved her arm off their joint armrest, crowding herself even farther into the confines of the economy-class middle seat. The minister gave her a chilled smile. As the woman looked away, he beamed it farther on to the gin-drinking man in the window seat. He was an American, dressed in khaki, with clear eyes and the look of the out-of-doors. He was reading the Tucson paper but looked up as he sensed the divine's critical benevolence. He, too, looked away, out the window to the dry mountains below.

At Hermosillo, a town whose modern central buildings were ramshackle before they were even completed and the littered, crowded streets no pleasure to drive, about one-third of the passengers disembarked. The minister, the sports shirts, and the khaki-dressed desert man were among them. After a desultory customs and tourist card check in the hot reception area, they passed the barrier to the outside. The salesmen hailed a cab, the outdoorsman, his Tucson paper still under his arm, climbed into a waiting dust-covered jeep and sped off, and the minister walked sedately to the one rental car counter. Whatever the promises of speedy service that the advertisements carry, it was not so. Conversation, regrets that such and such was not available, no matter what Tucson had promised, a search for papers to put in the typewriter, a further search for keys, hardly a glance at the driver's license (Connecticut, Alfred York, age fifty-two, parish house, All Souls' Church, etc.), and finally he was outside. And then a search for the rental car, which was not to be found in its assigned stall. He looked at his watch with that public annoyance which intends a general repri-mand. It had taken forty-five minutes to find a 1974 white Ford sedan. It started readily enough but soon jerked, coughed, and stopped. The slovenly attendant was indifferent.

The Reverend York spoke in tolerable Spanish. "It doesn't work."

The attendant shrugged.

"You'll have to give me another. This time I want an Oldsmo-bile."

The attendant pointed back toward the airport building.

The Reverend marched back inside, sweat beginning to show through his vest and coat under the arms.

"I'm sorry, sir, we have no Oldsmobiles here today," said the girl.

"But you must. It's the car I drive at home."

"No, sir, they are all gone. Perhaps later."

"How much later?"

The woman shrugged.

"Please, miss, if you will look through your papers, perhaps another car is due in today."

"Perhaps."

"Will you please look?"

She shuffled papers without reading any of them. "You may, sir, have any one of three other Fords."

York shook his head. "I tried your Fords. I had a Ford at home once. It didn't work. This one didn't work. None of them ever work. I want an Oldsmobile Cutlass, like I drive at home. Tucson told me you had one."

"Try again later, sir, perhaps tomorrow."

Lips pressed tight, the minister began to pick up his bags from the floor—the book-filled carrier bag and a neat new one in charcoal gray upholstered aluminum.

A portly Mexican gentleman, well dressed and hurrying, arrived at the counter. "I rented my car in Mexico City, but they said I could turn it in here when I came to catch my plane."

"Yes, sir, that is correct."

"Good. Here are the keys. I've marked the mileage on these." He handed her the papers. "It's outside, a blue Olds Cutlass."

The Reverend York turned and said in Spanish, "An Oldsmobile, did you say?"

The Mexican businessman looked at him suspiciously. "So I said."

"I'll take it," York said to the girl. "Yes, that is just what I wanted. You have it serviced while I wait, all right?"

"As you wish." The girl wondered about the luck of the Yankees; things seemed to go their way.

The Reverend York went to the restaurant for another Coca-Cola. In only three more hours he was on the road.

Two days later, after stops at a dozen old churches in a dozen humble towns through which the road ran, sometimes paved and most often not, an Oldsmobile, once blue but now brown with fine dust, arrived in Madre Dolorosa (on the map, Mater Dolorosa). A still carefully attired Reverend York, having inquired of several citizens advice about the town's hostelries, stopped in front of the Palacio Grande, the one of the two hotels in town that was not in the red-light district. It was half a block off the main square, two stories high, constructed of adobe, with a broken tile roof and faced with a limping portico. Entering with his bags, he was pleased to find that in the darkness of the lobby it was somewhat cooler—perhaps eighty instead of ninety-five—and not dusty. Dirty, yes; dilapidated, yes; but dusty, no.

As he walked to the reception desk, next to a wide stairway, three men, sitting in the battered chairs of the lobby drinking beer from bottles, stopped their conversation to watch the stranger.

"I'd like a room—the nicest, cleanest one you have."

The implicit doubt was ignored by the desk clerk, a thin old man with cataract eyes and a shaking hand. "Surely, sir, we have several."

The clerk had debated, at first, whether to call the stranger padre or not, but thought better of it, the gringo being a Protestant and therefore, in his eyes, a man of erroneous faith.

"Good. With bath?"

The old man studied the register book. "No, sir, no bath."

"Then near a bath." The Reverend York was perspiring. The car had been air-conditioned and the contrast was unpleasant. "I *need* a bath."

The three men in the lobby, their faces immobile, laughed inside themselves. Imagine, this fish-colored *religionosta* making all that fuss over such a matter. Almost in unison they reached for their beers.

"Yes, sir, the water will be on tonight."

"Tonight?" Shock and outrage.

"I think so, yes, I think so, it should be tonight."

"You're not sure?" The tremor of near horror and then disgust.

"Oh, yes, yes, certainly, no question, there will be water."

The Reverend York, divining no water, paused and then shrugged.

After siesta, about four, he was glad to be on his way out of the room. Its sagging bed and clustering flies were not so bad after all, for he was grateful that the sheets were clean—he had taken the precaution of removing them even so and spraying the mattress heavily with a can of pesticide that he'd purchased in Hermosillo. He'd purchased five, in fact, the other four remaining in the car, but he had carried the one through the lobby as though it were a war club, to the further amusement of the lobby cadre. The number of regulars there had increased to seven upon the news of the strange padre in town. Now he was on his way, notebook in hand, to continue the research that he had begun in other towns. He stopped at the clerk's desk, asking, in his Yankee-accented Spanish, "I wonder if you could help me?"

"Yes, señor, of course, if I can."

"I'm here to do research on your religious traditions."

"Yes, señor, of course. We are very religious here. We cele-
brate the Day of the Annunciation, Easter, Christmas, there is Mass
in the cathedral . . ."

Father York interrupted with sugar-coated impatience. "Yes,
thank you, but what I wondered is if there is someone in town who
is expert about your folklore—you know, the festivals, the funeral
customs, the history of the town in relationship to the church, how
the town got its name, when the church was built, who built it—that
sort of thing."

The clerk shifted weight from one old foot to the other, trying
to see the stranger through the prisms and clouds of his failing eyes,
wondering about such foolish questions. "Perhaps, sir, you should
ask the mayor. He receives visitors to the town and knows about
such matters."

The Reverend York pursed his lips and frowned, nodding.
"Yes, yes, that's a good idea. Anyone else?"

"I don't know, sir. The priest, perhaps, but he is not from here
and does not know the town so well. And then there is Señor de
Lemos. He has books and is much respected as our leading citizen.
Perhaps he would see you."

"Where shall I find these people?"

The clerk absent-mindedly scratched himself in the crotch.
"Well, the mayor is usually in the square in the evening. Ask for him
there. The priest lives next to the church. You'll find that easily."
The clerk gestured vaguely in a direction embracing north, east, and
south. "And Señor de Lemos, well, his is the hacienda some way
from town—" Another gesture, this one vaguely south. "—and
perhaps the mayor will take you there."

It was evident to the Reverend York that access to Señor de
Lemos was a privilege that the clerk could not accord. Notebook in
hand, he walked out the door in search of religious history and
folklore.

By seven, he had walked the town, primly skirting the red-light
district, had spurned five shoeshine boys and the town's lone taxi
driver, had visited the church, drunk three Coca-Colas and two
orange sodas—being careful not to take ice and inspecting the offered glass to be sure it was dry—and had become the town curiosity, as any stranger so embarked must. He was now sitting in the
plaza, under the shade of locust trees. He observed that the town

must be grateful to some long-dead planner who had planted these undernourished trees. With lengthening shadows, more people came to walk and shop, to talk and look. Social life was beginning. He asked someone on the bench next to him—all other benches were crowded but no one had dared sit on the same bench as the Protestant religious—after the mayor. He need not have, for at that moment the mayor, having been widely advised of the stranger and his interests, was making his way toward York. On such an occasion the mayor wore his second-best suit. Aside from the black one used for state occasions, there was no other.

The mayor, about forty-five, balding, fat, cunning-eyed, sly, magnanimous, plopped himself down next to the Reverend York and offered his hand, speaking in Spanish.

"I am the mayor." The word *alcalde* reverberated proudly.

"I am the Reverend Alfred York, of Connecticut, the United States."

"Welcome to Madre Dolorosa. I understand you have come to learn about our religious life?"

"Not so much your religious life, mayor, as your religious history and folklore. You see, I am doing research for an article for a church magazine. I want to write about the religious features of special interest here in Sonora."

"Of course, of course, naturally. Yes, we are very proud of all that." The mayor, who had not been to church since he was a child and would not ever do so again, short of exquisite duress, lied smoothly. "What would you like to know specifically? Perhaps I can tell you?" The mayor was prepared to lie on any subject that could be addressed by mortals, especially when in conversation with ignorant strangers.

"Well, for example, when I was in San Ramon, just east of here, recently . . ."

"Yes, yes." The mayor nodded knowingly of San Ramon, twenty miles away.

". . . I had a chance to observe a funeral parade. Very interesting. Very different from our funerals in Connecticut. Quite marvelous, really."

"Oh yes, marvelous," the mayor said unenthusiastically.

"The way the body is prepared, the way the marchers carry the banners, the whole ceremony in church, the wonderful way the family carries out its part, the mourners and all, even the appurtenances of the hearse—why, did you know that in San Ramon the hearse is drawn by horses?"

"Yes, yes, of course, just like we do it here. The old ways are the best."

"Oh, you are certainly right, mayor, absolutely. Well, are you planning any funerals—tomorrow, for example—so that I might watch the ceremony? I trust, of course, that wouldn't give any offense—I mean, not be taken ill? All I would do is be as quiet as a mouse and sketch the hearse, note the kind of music sung, consider the ritual aspects of it, you understand."

The mayor smiled sickly. "Oh yes, no problem at all. I mean, of course, you're welcome, but, well, we don't have anybody dead right now. I'm so sorry."

The Reverend York looked crestfallen. "Perhaps later, then?"

The mayor stared at the Yankee vulture. "Well, I suppose, some day there's bound . . ."

"Exactly. It is inevitable, isn't it?" The minister rubbed his hands in delight. "Tell me, when was your last big funeral? Oh, I don't mean a little one with poor people, where there'd be no hearse or mourners, but a really religious ceremony—someone important, for example?"

"Oh, that. Well, I don't know." The mayor's voice was weak. "Perhaps—well, yes, recently we had one: a very honored citizen, uh, uh, he died. Our police chief."

"Oh, I am *so* sorry. Had he been ill long?"

"Uh, no, no, I wouldn't say that."

"Well, perhaps God was merciful, then."

"Well, yes, uh, no . . ."

The Reverend interrupted the mayor's quandary. "Would it be all right—I mean, no offense—if, while I'm mapping the cathedral and that sort of thing, I looked at the hearse and perhaps—well, I know I'm being obtrusive but still, as a man of the cloth I could perhaps bring them comfort, well, if I went to give my condolences to the family? I'd like to meet the pallbearers, too. Do you realize, in San Ramon the pallbearers march to a kind of ancient rhythm, not at all like Connecticut? Very remarkable. Well, if I could talk to the pallbearers, they could tell me how they learn to do all that so well, especially since they handle their grief so nobly. You do think of the pallbearers as grieving nobly, don't you, mayor?"

"Yes, yes, of course, it's the only way."

"Fine, then I'll not bother them but I will tell them that I came with your permission. Perhaps they'd be interested in receiving a copy of my article when it's published, but then again—well, probably not: it will be in English. Well, mayor, I can't tell you how pleased I am, you've been so informative. And now, I wonder if, so that I could get started on my writing, perhaps you would introduce me to the pallbearers right now? There must be some of them around the square, don't you think? It seems everyone in the town must be here by now."

Before the mayor was aware of it, the Reverend York had seized his arm, propelled him to his feet, and was guiding him toward the dirt walk of the plaza park. Anything to escape this Yankee madman, the mayor scanned the folk nearby, looking for those who'd borne the casket at the funeral of the chief. As was to be expected, they were sitting on benches in the park, drinking beer. Two were police officers out of uniform, one was the town hardware store owner, one the owner of the largest cantina, and the fifth a man of dubious occupation but obvious local stature. The Reverend York made appointments with each of them for the next day to discuss their honored role in the town's religious and funereal ceremonies.

By the end of that next day, the fast-moving pastor had visited each, learned of his role in the community, learned of his relationship to the chief, and learned—"Oh, how terrible, my goodness, how disturbing, yes, indeed, a terrible shock to you all, I'm sure." —of the nature of the illness that had brought Chief Moctezuma Garcia Flanagan so suddenly into the cold, cold ground. He had also met, commiserated at length with, and presented an English-language Bible (King James) to the widow of the chief. He had learned from the widow details of the death and shared with her, profusely, an utter inability to conceive of a motive for killing such a fine man. With that, the Reverend York was soon in the scullery with the maid. Explaining, in a repeat visit the following day, that God's grace required that he be generous to those smitten by misfortune, a hundred pesos and two earnest blessings passed from him to her. In return for his solicitude the Reverend York became privy to the fact that the chief had been (a) clearly no less corrupt than was to be expected; (b) rather more venal and cruel than was to be expected; (c) enjoying unexplained additional income, as inferred from spending, these last few months; (d) cagey, in that he had not been caught in any loathsome frolic; (e) and (f) most certainly nervous, irritable, and easily frightened the last few weeks, such that he drank even more than usual and took less pleasure than ordinarily in placing burning cigarettes on the buttocks of the maid before having anal intercourse with her, using, she said, some steel instrument to keep her cheeks spread, that being—as she further said—one of the less satisfactory parts of being a servant in the household. Still, she needed the money, having two illegitimate children to support and having to pay the doctor for treatment of a recurring disorder, otherwise unnamed but sometimes fulminating and certainly venereal. God, in his wisdom, had seen to it that the chief had been given to as well as been giving.

For three days in town, it wasn't too bad. York had, in addition, drafted the cathedral architecture—it was a lovely building—met the priest (aloof, probably hates Protestants), and become well known to the one police lieutenant pallbearer, Rosales, who constituted the total remaining administrative echelon of the four-man town force. The lieutenant, in turn, while uninterested in funerary practices or church history, was relieved to learn that the Reverend York had a brother in the police. The lieutenant was quick to perceive that there was a family understanding in Connecticut about sin, it being sinful not to take one's opportunities where one found them in order that the family fortunes might go forward. His brother, the Reverend had allowed, had done very well in the police, for which his mother and his brother and several dozen assorted children, nephews, and nieces were indeed grateful. The Reverend indicated he would like, in fact, to bring his brother to meet the lieutenant some day, there being matters of business that they might find in common. Or better yet, the lieutenant might wish to visit his brother in Jersey City, toward which the Reverend York, in a fit of international brotherhood, promised to contribute a substantial amount. By way of down payment, he pressed five hundred pesos in the lieutenant's modest hand. It was, therefore, no surprise to that officer when, sometime later, the generous padre offhandedly mentioned a personal interest in securing pre-Columbian artifacts for his devoted mother's collection. He asked idly how one might get them safely across the border. It was contrary to the law, of course, but were there not, he inquired, profound human considerations that transcended petty regulations? One's obligations to one's mother did come first, didn't they? Shortly afterward, the cleric had wished a most sympathetic lieutenant God's blessing and returned to the hotel.

As on previous nights, the good pastor drew the shades, pushed the bureau against the door before retiring, and then, removing his wig, glasses, brown-tinted contact lenses, and moustache, stretched out on the bed.

"Son of a bitch," murmured Lee Barber softly, as he dropped, fatigued, onto the knotty mattress. "I do hope, as the Commandment saith, that I do get to doeth unto them before they doeth unto me."

Six

LEE BARBER, A.K.A. THE Reverend Alfred York, had gone to see the hearse. It was a shiny black, massive, columned, fluted, gilt-edged rococo beauty, with glass windows and a high buggy seat. It was burnished to a shiny gloss, even though it looked to be a good century old. It was the only public object he'd yet found in the village that had been cared for tenderly over time. The town undertaker—also its pharmacist—was clearly devoted to this museum piece cum transport. He liked the rest of his job, too, as Lee inferred, listening to the story of the police chief's last journey. No detail of the bullet-ruptured disrepair of the skull of Moctezuma Garcia Flanagan was too insignificant not to have excited the undertaker's fervid interest.

Although Lee learned nothing more of value, there was an unexpected bonus. Having proved to be such a good listener, he was flattered to be told that, should he need it while he was in town —the undertaker said it guilelessly and with the best of intentions —the charge to Lee's family for the hearse would be half of the ordinary price. Lee mused that the accountants back in the Bureau would, no doubt, be pleased. With that bargain assured, they could hardly object to a minor extravagance now. Lee bought, from the undertaker, one of those narrow black rayon banners with the figure of the Virgin stenciled in silver, which the mourners in this region carried during funeral parades. Mounted on a gold-painted pole, it reached about six feet over his head. Hoisting it aloft as he stepped outside, it began to flutter above him in those dry eddies of wind that the whirling dust devils raised from the dirty gutters. He intended to carry it decorously to his hotel room some four blocks away. "When you can't be invisible, be so damn conspicuous that people will get tired of noticing you." One of his trainers, no doubt following Nathaniel Hawthorne, had once so advised him and had, in the past, been proved right. He wanted the townsfolk to be convinced, beyond the shadow of doubt, that the visiting gringo divine was earnestly, extravagantly, morbidly eccentric, if not totally bananas.

He had not gone fifteen feet from the undertaker's door, immediately becoming the object of wide-eyed stares and clucking tongues from the two store owners and three loungers whom he'd passed, when a grimy jeep came banging and jolting down the pot-holed dirty street, stopping at the undertaker's door. It was a Mexican army vehicle, its canvas top nearly shredded in frazzled disrepair. He turned to watch as two soldiers emerged. The one whom he could see best, exiting nearest the mortuary door, was sweaty, dirty, unshaven, and red-eyed. His khaki shirt was torn at the shoulders and there were bloodstains over his shirt and trousers. With his companion helping, the two were tugging and pulling at something in the back seat. It resisted and then gave way. A body came slithering out the door to slump onto the sidewalk, head lolling back into the gutter, exposing a dark red wound where the shoulder and neck had joined. The corpse also wore an army uniform. The two soldiers lifted it, one by the feet and one by the still-intact right shoulder, to carry it inside. Shortly they returned and again groped in the back seat; another body came slumping out onto the sidewalk. This one, too, had been a soldier; his forehead was missing to the crown of his skull.

Within a few minutes the soldiers had returned, gotten into the jeep, and driven off. Bystanders stood staring but did not move. A wise man in Mexico does not rush toward trouble. The Reverend York, however, banner still aloft, turned around to walk to the mortician's door and entered.

There was no one in the front room, which was simultaneously pharmacy and office. Behind it, Lee knew, was the middle room, which was both mortuary and pharmacy storeroom. The hearse was in the rear room, a garage facing a narrow alley. Lee walked into the middle room. The mortician was hovering over the two bodies laid on the large wooden table, tiled on top, which, along with storage cabinets, constituted the total appurtenances of the morgue. There was no refrigeration.

"Will you administer the last rites, padre?" the undertaker asked, perfunctorily, looking up only briefly, so intent was he on the bodies whose clothes he was about to remove. His hand was on a sponge in a bucket already bloody.

"I don't think I should. I am, after all, not of their faith."

"Will these care?" The mortician nodded toward the corpses.

"Perhaps. And their families might," answered the Reverend York.

"If they have families and if someone told them, only then."

"Still, it would be wrong. I'm a stranger here and a Protestant. I returned only to see if there was some small thing I might do to assist."

"Well, no, I can't think of anything—I've just got to straighten these cadavers out. The army should take care of their own, but what can they do? Their headquarters won't be paying any attention now to these poor devils. So I'll stuff them with formaldehyde and send them on their way to Mexico City on a truck tomorrow; I'll put a flower in their navels—a gift for the generals' breakfast table." The mortician was almost smiling.

"What happened to these men?" asked the pastor.

"Ah, these got eaten by the bandits."

"Bandits?" Reverend York was horrified.

"Yes."

"But I didn't know there were still bandits in Mexico."

"Padre, when there are no bandits, it will no longer be Mexico."

"But where, why, I mean this kind of thing doesn't just happen . . ." York's voice was squeaking a bit.

"Oh, come now, padre, you have lived, you study funerals, you watch graves swallow men, surely you know how men die? And here, well, very often they die violently. Don't you think I chose my work carefully, eh? Plenty to do, padre, plenty to do." The mortician was fingering through the thin, tattered wallet of one soldier which he'd found roped to the waist as he undressed him. He took out the money and counted it, continuing, "Three hundred and twelve pesos, not bad—a rich soldier, this one. Lucky he'd hid his wallet, or I wouldn't have found his money. This other one—" He nodded toward the other corpse. "—a foolish one. His companions found his wallet, so now this one must pay me for both." The mortician pocketed the money and casually but expertly flipped the wallet into the waste bin, some ten feet away, smiling. "Good practice, see? Like your basketball. Wallets, shirts, hearts, lungs, livers, kidneys, stomachs, they all go in there. I never miss."

The Reverend York appeared distressed but resolutely pursued his earlier theme. "Well, I mean, well; goodness, yes, still, do the bandits come into town? Could *they* have killed the police chief?" He paused, fingering his collar uncomfortably. "I mean, are *we* safe here?"

The mortician grinned. "The town, padre, is run by big bandits; the little bandits stay away. As for the chief, someone of them might have killed him, but why? He was a bandit, too. Why kill him simply because he was richer than they were? No point in it. He never carried his money with him. No, I don't think these bandits killed him."

"Well, goodness gracious, how many other bandits are there? I mean, that some others might have killed him?"

"Padre, the question is not where are the bandits; that is asking where are there sharks in the ocean. Where, indeed? No, ask me the harder question—where are the honest men?"

"Well, all right, where?" York was fidgeting.

"I don't know, padre. Not here."

"Well, it certainly is unsettling," said the pastor, nervously. "I wish I knew enough about these bandits to avoid them."

"To know very little about them, padre, is a very good way to avoid them."

The mortician was intent as his hands went about their work sponging the dirty bodies, preparing the large syringe with formaldehyde from a giant bell jar. With its opening, the smell of sweat and death was mixed with chemistry. "I shall try to put your Yankee mind at ease, padre. I do know the bandits, or at least some. Mine is a big family, many, many cousins. Not all received a patrimony and not all like to work, as I do. And, then, bandits, too, die and must be made pretty for the funeral. Sometimes, too, they need medicine and come to my pharmacy for that. Since I am your friend —did I not promise you a special rate on your funeral?—well, as your friend, I can tell you that the bandits I know will not hurt you, especially if you are sensible enough to leave your wallet in the safe at your hotel."

"But your cousins are killers—look what they did to these soldiers."

The mortician looked firmly at the pastor. "The ones who killed these here were not my cousins, padre, this is not their work.

These men were ambushed while they worked in their little vegetable garden on the hill behind the garrison. You probably saw the building as you came into town. There are only twelve men and a sergeant stationed there; they're nothing, a kind of useless police, that's all. But they do keep a garden and half of them were working in it when someone opened fire on them from ambush. They used machine guns. That is what the ones who brought the bodies here told me. Those ambushers killed only these two, but the others were wounded badly enough that I hear I'll have more business from the doctor before the day is over. The ones in the building shot back eventually, of course, but at nothing. And then they brought their comrades to the doctor and to me. A thing like that, shooting men working in the garden—well, that is not the work of the bandits I know."

"Who would do it, then?"

"Who knows? Maybe there are some new fish swimming hungry in our sea."

"I don't understand it at all." The Reverend York shook his head. "Anyway, there's no use fretting. Perhaps I'd best go and find the priest. What is his name?"

"Teran. I'd look for him at the doctor's, if I were you. That's where he ought to be, anyway, giving those devils the sacraments before they die. See if you don't find him there."

The Reverend York did not find Father Teran at the doctor's. Nor, someone in the small clinic cautioned, would he be in the church or rectory. The gardener there had said the priest had left early that morning to visit someone ill in the country and had not yet returned. No, the clinic aide didn't know where in the country —perhaps José, the gardener at the rectory, could tell him. So it was that the Reverend York, after visiting the cathedral garden, determined to take a drive in the country. Even though the gardener had been uninformed, the matter was, as the good parson told at least two dozen people whom he stopped on the pretense of asking their ideas about where to look for the priest, of such great importance that it was his Christian duty to do what he could to find the priest and bring him back to administer Extreme Unction to the dying.

"You do agree, don't you? I mean, a terrible thing like this— well, there should be their own priest and, well, it's the least I can do to try to find him." He was talking to the mayor, whose business, the town garage and filling station—gas was hand-pumped from fifty-five-gallon barrels—stood on the main street a few blocks from the square.

"Yes, of course. It is the right thing to do," said the mayor. "But still, it is not exactly the day I would choose to go for a ride in the country."

"But why not? I mean, if the priest is visiting the sick out there —perhaps near the de Lemos hacienda, someone told me—how else do I find him?"

"As you like, but for myself, I would stay home. I do not like the idea of bandits so close by, killing the soldiers. It is not . . ." He paused. ". . . propitious."

A few miles out of town, in that generally southerly direction which was all he could learn as to the whereabouts of the de Lemos place, Lee Barber, still in clerical attire, stopped his car on the side of the dirt road. There were no houses or people in sight. The day was beastly hot. He was grateful for the air conditioning. He slid aside a metal plate underneath the dashboard and felt, beneath it, a row of buttons. He pressed the one on the right that activated the radio unit concealed behind the wall of the rear trunk. The speaker and a high-sensitivity microphone were nested in with the speaker for the standard car radio, behind the dashboard. The arrangement allowed him to speak without need of a conspicuous hand microphone. The volume and frequency controls were under the sliding panel, invisible but easily manipulated.

Barber pressed a second button and held it down.

Outside the town of San Ramon, twenty miles over the hills from Madre Dolorosa, the buzzer in the cooking time clock on the little stove in the living area of the van began to sound off. It was a van typical of the long-haired young Americans who used them as homes, campers, and, sometimes, a traveling stash. This one, white and dusty, had a variety of ecological bumper stickers peeling off the front and rear bumpers and an astrodome neatly constructed on the top.

Outside the van a snub-nosed, freckle-faced, blond-haired American, about twenty-five, wearing a broad Mexican sombrero of red straw—made for the tourist trade exclusively—sat in his camp chair, easel in front of him. He was doing a preliminary sketch of a tumbling adobe house with a rotting cactus and thornbush sheepfold behind it. On the folding table next to him was a supply of watercolors, paper, and a glass tumbler full of charcoal sketching pencils. A fresh painting of the same scene, the red rocks of the mountains behind it standing out distinctly against the seared blue sky, was pinned, along with four others done in the last day and a half, on one of those lightweight wood dowel folding frames on which towels are hung to dry. Price tags of $19.99 and $24.99 were paper-clipped to the paintings. A charcoal portrait of an old Indian woman was also displayed, but without a price.

Hearing the buzzer, the artist put down his charcoal and walked to his van. An observer would not have detected his excitement. Once inside the van, which was curtained by a calico print behind the driver's seat and over the small rear windows, Bill Hickock scurried to the stove and switched off the alarm-set button on the clock. The buzzing stopped. He then tugged on a built-in bureau, slipping a latch underneath until it moved forward and sideways on hinges. Between its foreshortened backside and the external wall of the truck a large radio panel was revealed. Hickock switched it to "on," studied the signal direction dial, saw that he did not need to adjust the antennas by turning the astrodome on the truck in which its fine wires were located, and picked up the microphone.

"Whale answering minnow, over."

"Hi, there—how you doing?" Lee Barber's voice came through clearly.

"Fine, nobody here and no flak."

"Good. Everything's on course here. The connections are good and the smells are all downwind. I haven't located the skunk yet, but there's some action beginning, though I don't have a make on it. At least two lead injections that took were administered here today. Let me know if you read about it. My bet is that you won't. Have your friends tell you what they heard about it there. And, you can tell your friends that we at least know that our Celtic friend didn't die of sainthood, so they can rule out that worry. That's it from here. I'll keep in touch. Have you got anything for me?"

"Maybe. Last night, when I was at one o'clock from you, I heard an airplane flying northward and low. I'd say a two-engine job. That's it."

"Interesting. Try again tonight. I'm closing now."

"Okay, over and out."

It was unlikely that anyone would pick up on their special frequency. If they did, no Spanish monitor would comprehend and no one would be able to get a triangulation fix. Any English-speaking Mexican would likely miss the slang and misdirections. As normal low-risk radio commo, Lee knew his communication arrangements with Billie would work.

Barber slid the plate over the radio-control panel. Hickock's airplane might be a key. Things were picking up. He scanned the area around him. It was still deserted. He took time, therefore, to check under his seat for the 357 magnum secured tightly by a whip-spring release to its underside. He knew that under the back seat there was a submachine gun, ammunition, and sundry other utilities. The station in Mexico City had done a good job getting the car ready for him. And they'd done well in delivering it to him so quickly in Hermosillo. The office in Mexico City was probably not as fouled-up as Groat had said. That was typical of Groat, bitching about everything.

He studied the Sonora topographical map on his lap. There was a valley that would lead from about fifteen miles west of Madre Dolorosa, from there north-northeast, passing ten miles west of San Ramon. That valley roughly paralleled the one through which the road ran, connecting the two towns. There was a road leading west out of San Ramon that Hickock could have taken, placing him—as long as he was near, and west of, San Ramon—at one o'clock from Madre Dolorosa. They were generally east of Hermosillo and north of the coastal town of Los Mochis. *Mochis* indeed, given the neighborhood: *mochin* might be the better word; it meant "executioner."

Barber gunned the idling engine, turned around, headed back to the last turning he'd seen, a side road running west. He took it. After a few miles the road began to twist and slope as the hills of the valley side were reached. The gully became narrower as it climbed and the road, never more than a track, became a rocky, rutted, cactus-bordered trail. As he made a sharp turn, he was confronted by an aluminum gate, which was locked. A new "No Trespassing" sign hung on it. A crude barbed-wire fence snaked up the sides of the canyon on either side. There was room to turn around, which he did. Then he stopped the car, wondering what chance to take with the Reverend York's credibility. The decision was made for him.

He heard a car coming down from the hill on the other side of the gate. Looking in the rear-view mirror, he saw a jeep with two men in it, both Mexican, both in peasant dress, both carrying rifles, and—shades of Pancho Villa—both braced with cartridge belts, the old-fashioned *cartuchera.* To avoid suspicion, and not least to reduce the possibility of getting the rear end of his car shot full of holes, he got out and walked toward the gate as the jeep roared up to it. Both men piled out of their jeep and ran toward him, their rifles swinging in their hands. The Reverend York smiled.

"Well, I am certainly glad to see you," he said, holding his arm out to shake hands with the one who had been first to climb over the locked gate. "Can you tell me just where I am, where the hacienda of Señor de Lemos is, and where I can find Father Teran? It's terribly important."

The two men looked, first at him then at each other, frowning. The initiative had passed, as he had intended, to himself. He went on, "There is someone dying in town who needs the priest. I've been sent to fetch him. Where is he? I was told he was here."

The thinner of the two men stared at him sullenly and his fat partner belched.

"Well?" asked the pastor, this time with a more demanding note in his voice.

"I don't know him," said the thin one.

"Me, too," said the fat one.

"Well, you must. They said he'd be here, near the de Lemos ranch."

"Ahhh," said the thin one.

"Ahhh," said the other.

"Si, this is the de Lemos ranch?"

"Si," nodded the fat one.

"Well?" asked the divine again, sweat beginning to break out in the heat.

"You must go," said the thin one.

"Si," agreed the fat one.

"Where will I find Señor de Lemos?" asked the Reverend York, his face now stern.

"I don't know," said the first.

"Me, too," said the fat one, adding, "maybe at his house."

"Good. Where is that?"

The fat one pointed behind the pastor and waved his hand in a generally south-by-southeast direction. "A few miles the other way."

"Si," said the thin one. "This is just ranch land, the house is in the valley, near the trees."

"The trees?" asked the pastor.

"Of course, the trees, where else?" replied the thin one, impatiently.

"Well, why don't we drive there together? You can show me. I'll take you in my car or you can lead me in your jeep. Which do you prefer?"

The two men turned to look at one another, frowning, their rifles dangling from their hands. The fat one shrugged. The thin one turned to the gringo divine, still not quite comprehending.

"Good," said the Reverend York. "Come along. I'll drive you back here when we're through."

"No," said the thin one, suspiciously. "We'll lead you."

Soon the Reverend York was following the billowing, dusty trail of the jeep. He found himself humming a jaunty tune.

About ten miles later, first east on this side trail, then to the southward road he'd been on before, then, once again, west, toward the close-lying barren hills, he sighted the cluster of trees in the distance. As they neared them, a group of buildings became visible beneath their rare and welcome shade, but blocking the road was another gate. Encircling the compound was an adobe wall, about eight feet high, on the top of which was cemented jagged broken glass, a common practice thereabouts. The gate, of wrought iron, was attended by an old man whose quarters were a small, but well-kept, adobe hut, the sides of which extended from the stone pillar that supported the gate itself. The old man was opening the gate slowly as the Oldsmobile drove up. His escorts drove slowly through and York followed. A circular drive brought them to a magnificent old adobe house, two stories high, with well-tended bougainvillea and jasmine woven over its walls. The two men got out of the jeep and gestured him toward the massive carved front door. The thin one spoke in a low and suddenly respectful voice.

"Here, padre, this is the house of Don de Lemos. We shall wait here for you." The men had left their rifles in the jeep.

"Thank you, you've been very kind. I appreciate your help."

"Thank you, padre," said the fat one ingratiatingly.

The pastor knocked on the door. It was answered by a very pretty girl of about twenty-five, wearing a black rayon dress. The house was cool and the entryway was elegantly simple. A great Spanish chest stood in the hall, a tapestry behind it. The girl looked at him without speaking.

"How do you do? I'm the Reverend York." He handed the girl a calling card from his wallet. "I'm told that Father Teran may be here. He's needed urgently in town. And, if Don de Lemos is in, I would be honored to have the opportunity of meeting him. Is he here?"

The girl, her face noncommittal, took the card and, leading him into a reception room on the right, gestured for him to take a chair. She left without saying a word. This room, perhaps thirty-five by twenty-five, with a beamed ceiling, was furnished in the grand manner of old Spain. He sat on a wooden chair, lions' heads carved on the armrests and a carved coat of arms making up the back. The upholstered seat was intricately embroidered with flowers in red, green, and gold. The house was still. He waited ten minutes.

A door at the other end of the room opened and a man in a dark business suit entered. He was about forty, balding, and hard. His stride was quick and soft as he walked over the carpets laid on the old tiles. The Reverend York rose to meet him.

"Father York? I am the secretary. Please follow me. Don de Lemos will see you now."

They passed through a short hall and into a large modern office with one desk, a typewriter, and a number of file cabinets. The secretary knocked on the door opposite and entered. The room was also an office—spacious and simply furnished in excellent taste. A huge desk faced them. Behind it sat a man of about fifty-five. He was thin, with gray hair, and had penetrating brown eyes. He was wearing a black suit and, as he rose, gold and jeweled rings could be seen on the fingers of both hands. The secretary stayed near the doorway as York walked beyond him toward the desk. The rustle of cloth suggested, ever so faintly, that the secretary had reached into his pocket for something. York speculated on what it might be.

The thin man walked to the side of his desk, holding out his hand. "I am Don de Lemos."

"I'm the Reverend Alfred York, Don de Lemos, and I am very pleased to have this chance to meet you."

"Thank you. What can I do for you?" The Don was courteous but businesslike.

The Reverend York explained the circumstances of his mission and how he had got lost on a byroad, there to be met by the Don's ranch hands, who had been most helpful.

"I'm glad no harm came to you. Our roads are very bad and a man whose car breaks down in such country can become lost. We've had strangers die in this summer heat of ours before anyone found them."

"Oh yes, I can appreciate how that might happen. Still, I'm not very adventuresome myself. I prefer the main roads if I'm to travel at all."

"That's wise. Yet I'm not sure I would call the road to Madre Dolorosa a main road. Something adventurous must have brought you to this out-of-the-way region."

The Reverend York explained his interest in local religious history, and in funeral customs particularly, adding that he had undertaken to write some articles for a religious magazine on the traditions of Sonora. He added, modestly, that he was a contributing editor. It was great luck, he explained, that brought him to San Ramon and from there to Madre Dolorosa, where tradition seemed to have flourished to become, so to speak, a living museum and a monument to the religious past. It would be of no end of interest to the readers of the magazine.

"How interesting, father, yes. I can see why you would want to study here. What, by the way, is the name of the magazine? I've an interest in traditions myself—not, I confess, those of your country, but of mine. Nevertheless, if I ever chance upon your journal, it might be worth reading."

"Oh, you read English then?" asked York, happily.

"Poorly enough, I fear, but sufficiently for my needs."

"That's fine, just fine. One finds so few people down here who speak one's own language. Why, I . . . ."

"I said 'read,' father, not 'speak,' although I wish it were otherwise."

"Well, yes, that is a shame, isn't it?"

Don de Lemos picked up a pad and pencil from his desk. "So, if you'll tell me the name of your journal, I'll just jot it down here, in case I'm ever so fortunate as to run across it."

"Ah, yes, well, it's the *New England Magazine for Religious Studies.* I'm almost ashamed to recommend it; it doesn't have a large circulation and those of us who read and contribute to it are not great scholars, of course. We're simply interested in the byways of religious life, nothing denominational about it, you understand. Still, it gives us pleasure and makes some small contribution."

"I'm sure it must." Don de Lemos replaced the pad on the desk, remarking, "Your Spanish is rather good. You must have lived here in Mexico for some time, have you not?"

York prepared to settle down for a serious fencing match. De Lemos was clearly neither mark nor fool. Here was no simple gentleman farmer. It was too soon to guess why he was so suspicious. A successful man in this country had reason to be careful. Naïveté and trust were shortcuts to victimization. He could be fairly sure that there was a gun pointing toward his spine. Nothing extrasensory about it, simply a probability, given the wisdom of Mexico, the rustling of cloth, and the fact that his host himself had written down the name of the the phony journal. Ordinarily, a boss would have told his secretary to do it, but not if the secretary was holding a gun and was, therefore, not free to take notes. The test was easy: if he began to turn around to admire the Spanish swords hung on that wall left of the door as he came in, or to ask the secretary a question, well, either Don de Lemos would stop him with conversation or there'd be another quick rustle behind him as the bodyguard put the weapon back in his pocket. These would be the normal gambits. If he'd miscalculated totally, there would be a different response.

He returned to his host's question. "Well, I do visit Mexico as often as I can. In fact, a few years ago I was a delegate to a conference here. But the truth is, I learned Spanish in college and I get my practice in my parish. We have some delightful Mexican families living there and I visit with them as often as I can. Still, there's nothing like coming down for a study trip to polish it up, wouldn't you agree?"

"Of course."

"By the way, I noticed on your wall, as I came in, some splendid old swords—those . . ." He began to turn around, casually, swinging his arm to point. As he did so, he saw his host's eyes dart fiercely to the secretary behind. There was a rustle of cloth and York saw the secretary scratching his left shoulder, simultaneously pushing down a slight bulge underneath the jacket. Fast and professionally done, York thought.

"Now, about Father Teran." Don de Lemos said, after a brief explanation of the origins of the swords. "You were told he might be here?"

"Near here, yes. The people in town said you employed more people than anyone else around here and so it was most likely that you'd know who'd be ill for the priest to visit."

"Yes, that's true, I would. But I don't know of anyone who's sick."

"Perhaps someone whose mother died, or perhaps he's planning a baptism or christening or wedding. These things can keep a pastor busy."

"It's all possible. I just don't know. I'm afraid I can't help you."

"Ah, well, too bad."

"By the way—who is it that's so ill in town that Father Teran had to be summoned?" His host seemed to ask more out of courtesy than interest.

York, in vivid and occasionally excited detail, told the story of the ambush of the soldiers.

As he did so, Don de Lemos's face turned grave. "You're sure of all you told me?" he asked.

"I can only be sure of what I saw. And I saw two dead soldiers and I'm sure there were wounded at the clinic. But I've no reason to doubt what the mortician told me. Isn't it terrible?"

"Yes. I do hope you won't think me rude, but I shall have to excuse myself. This is very serious and I think I'd better meet with my foremen. Perhaps they will know something that will help the army find these murderers. And we shall have to take some steps to protect the hacienda from these bandits. My secretary will see you to the door. I do thank you for seeking Father Teran—it was kind of you to try." Don de Lemos shook York's hand, took his arm to guide him swiftly to the door, and quickly closed it behind him.

As York was ushered toward the front door by the silent secretary, there came into the hall that girl in the simple black dress. Moving gracefully, she looked at him directly, with bold appraising eyes. The secretary nodded to her brusquely, a gesture she did not return. Her eyes were on York and did not waver as the secretary turned his back on them both and strode silently away. His action was a remarkable discourtesy to a guest leaving a Mexican house.

York looked at the secretary's back and then at the girl, a question on his face.

"He has no manners," she said, firmly.

"No. Well, perhaps he is preoccupied."

"Ah, if you've given him something to think about, that may be."

"Oh no, not that I know of—I don't think we exchanged a word."

"That would be like him. It's no loss."

"I hope I didn't offend him."

"He does not offend easily."

"Good. I wouldn't want to have made a faux pas."

"I'm sure he would have let you know."

York, thinking of the automatic under the secretary's coat, could only agree with this direct and somber girl. Who was she? Self-possessed and her Spanish elegant. Another secretary? A daughter? He scanned her fingers for rings. None. So she was not de Lemos's wife. Well, now was the time to find out. There were several simple rules of inquiry in the game with strangers. You could ask almost any question at the beginning. You must ask it only once. You learned more if questions were flattering. And you must expect almost anything to be forgiven the foreigner if he makes it clear that he claims that privilege as part of being the fool.

"Are you Señora de Lemos?"

"No."

"Oh. Do you live here?"

"Yes."

"I'm sorry, I hope you don't mind my asking. But, well, I'm a stranger here and today has been a bit confusing to me, what with the frightful events in town and then being stopped by those fellows with rifles and now this fine house. It's not what a New Englander would call an ordinary day, so I'm just trying to get my bearings. I hope you'll forgive me."

"Of course, I understand entirely." This time she smiled and was lovely to behold. Straight white teeth; rich, warm lips; a superb pale olive skin; and such dark eyes. He wondered what it was she understood: that he found her beautiful, that he was pumping her, or that he was, in fact, surprised that his usual questioning technique was not working.

She moved toward the door to open it for him.

"Are you, then, perhaps the daughter?" It was taking a chance. The earlier rebuffs had been polite. She now could be offended.

Instead, she smiled more broadly. "Are New Englanders always so inquisitive?"

"No—well, by nature, perhaps, but we're told it's impolite to ask questions. I know I'm behaving badly, but I can't help it. After all, one doesn't chance upon such a lovely girl in the middle of the desert every day. I didn't want to offend if you were married."

"But you knew I wasn't."

"Why, what do you mean? How could I know that?"

"You looked at my hand for a wedding ring. I saw you do it." She was laughing at him now. A low, tinkling laugh, small camel bells swinging in the desert breeze.

"You knew I was just making conversation when I asked you?" The Reverend York was laughing at himself with her now.

"Of course. Why else should I tease you so?"

"Well, I deserve it. I'm not very clever with beautiful women, I guess. Ministers are supposed to be pious, not flirtatious. I've been caught out in sin."

"In my country, a priest does not flirt. So you are a Protestant, father. Are you married?"

"Oh no, not at all. I mean, if I were married, I wouldn't have brought it up at all."

"What?"

"Oh, I mean, well, your being lovely and my wanting to talk to you."

"I see. Well, New England ministers must be very proper, then, if they aren't even supposed to talk to girls."

"Yes, it can be that bad, I suppose. But it's almost as bad with me because it's not that I'm not supposed to, it's just that, as you can see, I don't do very well at it."

"You seem to be talking to me this minute."

"Well, yes, and I'm glad for that, but it's thanks to you."

"Ah, you're accusing me of being flirtatious."

"Oh no, no, nothing like that, it's just that you're letting me talk to you."

"What's wrong were I to be flirtatious—is that a sin, too?"

"Good heavens, no, hardly. Why, it's very nice, it's, it's—well, it's wonderful. But I didn't expect you to . . ."

She put her hands on her hips, rolled her head to the side, eyes downcast, and stamped her heel on the floor, pretending anger. "You're very young to be my father, sir, expecting me to be demure. You impose an immense obligation on women to hold them responsible for the honor of the family. Shall they all be dishonored, then, by my talking to you? Are you *that* bad?" She turned her eyes upward to him under long black lashes, sighing dramatically.

York was laughing loudly and it was no subdued pastoral chuckle, either, for she had tickled his funny bone. They laughed together.

"No, I'm not *that* bad," he assured her.

"What a shame. Here I am, surrounded by dangerous-looking *vaqueros* armed to the teeth, and they are all afraid to look at me sideways. Not that it matters; they can't read or write and they never bathe. There's that secretary you saw; he doesn't walk, he slithers like a snake. And now you, the stranger from the North, come on a visit, and you aren't a bad man, either. Where are there some bad men who want to flirt with me?"

"I like to talk to you, if that will do."

"Because flirting is sinful?"

York sighed. "I've been a minister too long. I think I've forgotten how to have fun."

She eyed him suspiciously. "You have no fun?"

"Well, I enjoy myself, but it's not very exciting. I have a hobby, studying religious customs."

"And that's fun?"

"I suppose. It's interesting, anyway."

"And you do nothing else?"

"Not much."

"No girlfriend?"

"No."

She pursed her lips and lowered her eyelids. "You are not one of those who likes young boys, are you?"

York tried to blush for her, averting his eyes a bit from her mischief. "No, I don't like young boys," he avowed firmly, slowly and in a strong voice. It was the voice of Barber and not of York.

"Thank goodness. And you do know something of women?" She was challenging him, half playful, half serious.

"Yes, I do know something of women. And I know, for example, that you're making mischief. And I like it."

"Good! That is a relief. I was worried about you for a minute."

"There's no need. Even though I wear a collar, I am a reasonably normal man."

"You were once married?"

"Yes."

"And?"

"My wife died."

"I am sorry. I didn't mean to tease you to the point of sorrow." Her face was somber again. He could see she was unhappy with herself. Her eyes said she was concerned for him as well.

"But you are really a padre?"

She was appraising him seriously and he realized that she had picked up the clues in his voice and manner that were not the York he'd been when he'd come in. In the play of it, the foundation of Barber had overpowered the mannerisms of York. It had been so simple; he was having fun and had been careless and she had scented something incongruous. She was a smart girl and a sensitive one. In this business one could live or die by that ability to detect the incongruous. And now she was aware of his pause as he appraised her perceptiveness in a new light.

"Are you really a padre?" she repeated. And he was mindful of his own rule: ask any question but ask it only once. She was asking twice.

He discounted her having penetrated his disguise. Only amateur liars were prone to interpret chance remarks as discovery.

"Yes, I am a minister."

"It would be, I think," she said, quietly, "a strange life." Her manner was suddenly subdued.

He kept his silence as he moved toward the door.

"Well, in any event, padre, perhaps you will return here again, one day?"

"Yes, thank you, that would be very nice."

The door closed behind him. Walking back to his car, he nodded at the two toughs who lounged against the fenders. They smiled fulsomely, with obsequious distrust. As he drove his Oldsmobile to the gatehouse, where the old man opened the great iron gate for him and waved him by, Barber wondered who the girl was and what it was she had on her mind. On the way out he knew what was on his mind: her.

Seven

THIS WAS AS GOOD A TIME AS any to get lost. It might be some time before he had as good an excuse, searching for Father Teran, as he had today. Wherever he went, his Oldsmobile would be seen.

Reaching the main road, he turned south. He didn't know the reach of the de Lemos ranch, but most likely it was big, bigger than the stretch of seven or eight miles that separated the first west turning he'd taken from the second one, which led to the de Lemos compound. He had to get to the top of those brush- and cactus-covered western low mountains. According to the topo map, the highest was no more than 3,500 feet. The valley through which the road ran was, he guessed, about 1,800 feet lower. Not much of a climb if one could keep out of the way of the rattlesnakes and those translucent white scorpions. Out of Durango he'd seen a man die in agony from a scorpion bite. Another eight miles south brought him to a track running west toward the hills, those not more than two miles away. He turned the car around so that it faced north, toward Madre Dolorosa. Pulling to the side of the road, he locked the car, leaving his coat inside, and stepped out to open the hood. He left it propped up, put on a narrow-brimmed black hat, and set out on foot for the hills. In three hours it would be sunset.

He walked slowly in the heat, enjoying the desert air, looking carefully whenever he heard a lizard scurry in front of him. Two hours brought the cooling dusk and found him partway up the hillside, along the meandering cart and cow trail. In less than another hour he was through the mesquite and had come over rocks and small gullies to the high point he'd sought, the top of this range of hills. Looking out over the narrow valley from which he came, he saw to the north the clump of trees that grew in the de Lemos compound. There was no traffic to be seen on the road he'd left; indeed, at no time had he seen any on it—not surprising, since it led nowhere, except to whatever holdings fanned out along the valley's stubby southern tail, backing up against a roadless spur of mountains running across it to the south. To the east he could see the high, forbidding range of the Sierra Madre, escalating slowly in a rising series of mountains and shadows, all higher than the ridge before him.

Immediately westward and below him, the valley he sought was narrow and, for the most part, inhospitably rugged, with gulches, worn mesas, and rock outcroppings. To the south the valley climbed quickly to join the same spur of mountains that terminated the road he'd traveled. A few miles or so north it flattened a bit, and it was this terrain that interested him. He wished that he'd been able to bring the binoculars, which were under the rear seat; but the risk was too great were someone to see him. Would there be any reasonable accounting for a man whose engine had stopped—vapor lock or overheating, he was prepared to ask in the manner of one totally inept mechanically—looking for help carrying binoculars? Hardly. Dusk fell and then the desert night, clear and star-studded. He waited, enjoying the smells and hearing the howl of coyotes. He knew they were harmless but was glad, as a city-bred man must be, to counteract the instinctive chill they brought upon him with the thought of the 357 strapped discreetly in his shoulder holster. He thought of the puma that prowled these hills and, likewise, rejected his foolish fear with the comfort of the gun. The half moon had come over the horizon and traversed the sky when he heard the distant noise. His luck was with him. It was unmistakably an aircraft starting: the deep coughs, as first one and then the other engine fired. Here in this stillness, with the valley acting as an acoustic corridor leading the sounds downward to reverberate back and forth across the mountainsides, he heard it easily. There were, of course, no lights to be seen. There had been, after all, no buildings visible. The facilities were either underground or camouflaged—the latter, more likely, since an earth revetment, covered with netting and vegetation, would thwart air surveillance easily and at low cost. As long as the land itself was guarded against trespass, as his experience showed him it was, discovery was unlikely. If, as he guessed, the de Lemos lands took in the whole valley in which the airstrip was situated, then potential trespassers would be rare in any event.

He listened to the engines as they warmed up. The pilot seemed to be in no hurry, but then why should he be? When the plane took off it would detour around the town, perhaps flying low to avoid radar all the way to the U.S. border. There was no need for

evasive tactics down here; the Mexican government did not main-
tain airspace surveillance of any kind. Private aircraft were checked
in and out of the official airports, but as a control measure that was
like making sure that only the "A" students in school didn't cheat
on exams. The planes that used official airports had nothing to
worry about. Hereabouts, isolation was security enough. That and
bribery, fear, and the passive indifference of the local peasants, an
indifference that protected them intuitively from dangerous knowledge. Moctezuma Garcia Flanagan would certainly have known
about the airfield; that was his business. How else would he deserve
to be bribed? Unless he had been part of the operation. But why?
What did an outfit with airplanes and big money behind it need with
a country cop? Conversely, why would it need to kill him? Was de
Lemos worried about something? Was it even de Lemos? After all,
there was no reason to believe that because the plane flew from his
land he knew of it. It wouldn't be the first time that a clever foreman
had made a deal with outsiders for land use about which the boss
knew nothing. That kind of thing went on all the time.

The plane took off to the north. In a minute it would be over
the area where Bill Hickock had seen it the night before. If it was
that regular, they may as well publish a schedule. With little else in
Sonora ever on time, wasn't it incongruous that the clandestine
aircraft would be so reliable? Ah well, such were the minor mysteries of life. York turned and headed back down the mountain.

As a precaution, when he was about a hundred yards from the
car he began a wide circle, which he narrowed stealthily and in a
crouch, slipping from bush to bush, listening. He was in no hurry.
Why should a man hurry into ambush if a little patience could
prevent it? His caution proved unnecessary. There was no one
watching or waiting, nor had anyone broken into the locked car.

The car started easily as he moved off in the night toward
Madre Dolorosa, driving slowly, for he wished no lights to reveal
him now. Were he to see lights coming toward him in the distance,
he would simply pull off the road and feign sleep. After all, someone
who'd spent a futile day looking for the priest, suffering an obstrep-
erous engine and fear of being lost, would have every reason to be
fatigued—should anyone ask. No one did. Arriving in town, the
Reverend York parked his car in front of El Palacio Grande, dragged
himself into the lobby, looking for all the world like a man who'd

been lost all day and night, and went upstairs to bed. His act was unnecessary. The lobby was deserted and no one saw him come in.

Barber slept until noon. He shaved in the tin basin in the room, filling it with water taken from a chipped yellow enamel pitcher. He brushed his teeth with cola from the cans he kept on the shelf. His dentist might disapprove, but a cavity five years from now was better than amebic dysentery this week.

Once on the street again—in fresh clerical attire, thanks to the one-woman, one-washtub corrugated scrubbing-board laundry service in the back room of the hotel which daily did his clothes—York headed toward the cathedral. The caretaker, José, was in the cool, dark building when he arrived, large sketchbook in hand.

"Good day, José."

"Good day, padre."

"I'll sketch the inside of the church today, if it's all right. You don't think Father Teran would mind, do you?"

"No, father, he would be pleased."

"And the inscriptions, too—I'd like to copy them."

"Of course."

"Where are they, José—the memorial epitaphs over the crypts of the old ones buried here, the plaques to the early patrons, that sort of thing?"

"They wear the blanket of time over them. No one has looked at them in years. There's an old crypt on the back of the south transept there. It's set in the floor near the saint. Then there are several along the ambulatory walls; you can see them from here. You'll probably find others, I don't really notice. My job is to keep the altar and nave clean, that's all."

"Well, I'll just go have a look. By the way, I never did find Father Teran yesterday. My, what a time I did have, too—out in the desert till I thought I'd never find my way back. And then my car broke down and I was sure I'd never get back. I'll never go out there again, José. That wild country is absolutely frightful."

José looked at him uncomprehendingly. He'd been born on an impoverished hacienda out there; it was his home. Ah, well, gringos —city people—what could one expect? "Yes, padre," he said, indifferently.

"Is Father Teran around today?"

"Oh yes, I think so. Perhaps he'll be in his garden later today. Perhaps you'd want to call."

"How nice, yes. Perhaps I would, if it wouldn't be an intrusion. But in the meantime—well, on to work." York brandished his sketchbook and walked to the ambulatory.

It was several hours later before he had sketched and copied his way along the west wall memorials and crypts to reach the transept. He had, in the meantime, attracted the eyes of the several dozen women who'd come into the church to pray, light candles, and occasionally offer ex-votos to a wooden statue of the Mater Dolorosa that stood in a niche in the wall next to the pulpit. The antique carving had her feet and pedestal woven with tin forms of limbs, bodies, babies, cows, and the like: representations of that which yearned for her curing power. Only one man had come in to pray, a young fellow with a walk ambiguously teetering between swagger and stealth. Quite self-consciously, it seemed to York, he'd clipped a large tin heart to the chain of offerings slung around the Virgin's feet, leaving hurriedly with the most cursory of genuflections. His manner struck York as odd, but who could say? Some youngsters considered religion a sin these days and could only practice it guiltily.

York moved into the depths of the transept, which was not lit and where no candles flickered; obviously this saint's statue was not popular, and singularly unattractive it was. Paul, perhaps? York could barely make out the contours of the wall, let alone any inscriptions. There was an old door in the wall. He guessed it would lead to the garden. Taking a candle and lighting it, being careful to deposit an offering before the flickeringly watchful eyes of the women at prayer near him, he roamed to the back of the transept while searching the floor with his eyes to find the crypt of which José had spoken. One had to be diligent in such matters; his notebook must be full of sketches, inscriptions, and his own pedantic notations. There was a table near the saint, and he had to crawl under it, candle in hand, to look for signs of the burial supposedly there.

It was odd. He'd been expecting the usual small memorial, or perhaps a boxlike structure for bones or at most an outline the size of a casket. There was nothing of the sort. What he did find was a grimy stone inscription nearly worn down; he would have to use a brush, acid, and latex poured over it to make an impression mold in order to get a legible reading. Yet there was a seam in the old tile floor that formed a rectangle about three feet by seven. The seam was clean and deep and the tiles edging it on the inner aspect were not as worn as those around it. The conclusion was inescapable. He was on his hands and knees over the center of a trapdoor, a door that someone had taken trouble to conceal by placing a large table over it. The door was in current use, otherwise there would be dirt in the seam.

He crawled out from under the table. He didn't mind if the old women in their shawls saw him there, but he suspected there would be some people he'd rather not encounter. Who they might be, he had no idea. José, the caretaker, would not be on the list; otherwise he would not have told him of the vault. Getting to his feet, he snuffed his candle and quickly made his way to the ambulatory on the other side of the nave and resumed his copying among the memorials there. Another hour passed before his attention was attracted by another man walking into the church in poor farmer's clothes. The man genuflected and then walked quickly toward the statue near the pulpit, now some distance away from York, who was near the narthex at the front of the church. Curious, York watched the young man as he drew an offering from his trouser pocket. It was difficult to discern what it was, but it might have been a heart. The man had turned his back on the few women sitting on a side bench opposite, as if to screen their uninterested eyes from him. In so doing, he had not noticed York standing in the darkness.

What York saw was a very crude job of servicing a drop. The young man clipped the ex-voto he'd been carrying to the chain on the statue and took away the one placed there earlier by the other man. Pretending nonchalance, he slipped it in his pocket, genuflected, and walked quickly out of the church; he never saw York at all.

José was just completing a very slow push of the broom on the other side of the church. He appeared to have taken no notice of the young man.

"José?"

"Yes, padre?"

"I've noticed the offerings given to the Mary near the pulpit."

"Yes."

"Does she work miracles?"

"Oh yes, many."

"I saw that young man who was just in here giving an offering to her. He looked so worried, so strained—I felt sorry for him."

"Yes, padre."

"Do you think someone in his family is ill?"

José, who knew the reputation, now town-wide and ineradicable, of this gringo religious as a crazy vulture who wanted to watch funerals, looked at the pastor suspiciously. "I don't know, padre, I don't know the man. Perhaps he is from out of town."

"Oh."

"But, padre, if it is someone in his family who does die, I'm sure you'll get to see the funeral." José said it with sour resignation.

"Yes, yes, of course, naturally. But, well, I will be sorry." The Reverend York, whose query had had another purpose, was brought up a bit short by this morbid reminder of his now fully established public image.

He allowed another hour of copying to elapse before he moved to the miraculous statue. He seated himself on the floor before it, sketchbook on his knees, and did a rough drawing of the statue and its ankle bracelet of ex-votos. He was only fair as an amateur artist but that wouldn't matter to anyone else going through his material. The seriousness of his endeavor would be genuine. After sketching, he got up and looked over the assorted tin arms, legs, and babies. There was only one heart. Dexterously, he ran his hands over it while appearing to be interested in a tin icon propped up on the pedestal nearby. The heart was hollow. His fingers found a snap on the back that upon being pressed released a spring lock.

It was an ordinary locket. His fingers swept the inside of the cavity without so much as stirring the heart on the chain; there was a piece of paper inside. He palmed it, opened it with the fingers of the same hand, glanced down to read the message, returned it to the hollow, closed the locket until he felt it snap, and continued his uninterrupted examination of the other pieces on the string. No one watching from any angle would have seen what he had done.

On his way back to the hotel, he considered the situation. It did not make sense. The covert aircraft flights were not a problem; that was a standard smuggling method and there was no reason to think it was more than that. The probabilities were high that the contraband was drugs; there was nothing else valuable enough to support the investment in planes and personnel. According to these same probabilities, Flanagan would have been involved in that operation and his death should be linked to it. He had either wanted too much

money or he threatened blackmail, or he was helping someone else
muscle in on the local boys. All well and good. But the attack on the
army barracks, the trapdoor in the church, and the drop that he'd
discovered at the Mater Dolorosa's ankles—these were something
else. The trapdoor might be irrelevant. For all he knew, the priests
for the last two centuries could have had their wine cellar down
there. But the drop could not be explained away, not to a professional who admired the choice as excellent but could only ridicule
the amateur way in which it had been serviced. The incongruity
suggested there was a smart mind at work who was not enjoying
professional assistance. And the message—again amateurs; no safe-
guards at all, just a simple commo system for men who clearly
thought it better not to be seen together. Perhaps they were overdo-
ing it—the melodrama of a bright amateur, after all. All the message
in the heart had said was, "At two, tomorrow, as agreed."

On returning to his hotel, the Reverend York got into his car
and drove off to the old, abandoned cemetery at the edge of town.
Near it was a tumbledown chapel, still used on the day of its saint,
which merited his study. It was also conveniently located, because
it was separated by an arroyo from the nearest mud huts, most of
which were windowless on the cemetery side.

He parked the car in front of the little church, reconnoitered
the cemetery and the building, returned to the front seat to prop his
notebook upon his knees, pen in hand, and sent out the signal for
Hickock. Twenty miles away, the stove timer buzzed and within a
few minutes his junior partner was on the air.

"Whale, how's it going?"

"Fine, what's new?"

"Lots, I think, but being a cautious sort, let me suggest we go
on to the scrambler for this and all future communications."

Both made adjustments with their radio dials to activate the
scrambler unit, one essentially like that used in telephones, except
that it was adapted in transistorized miniature for radio use instead.

"Reporting progress and confusion here," Barber said, giving
his young colleague all the details of events so far. "I think it's time
to get ready to bring in some more company. Tell headquarters to
groom someone to be my brother—a lieutenant in a New Jersey
police department. Get him selected, documented, and ready to
come down immediately. He doesn't need to know Spanish, but

he'd better know the various minor syndicate connections on the East Coast. I want him to look as kinky as a two-dollar garden hose and I want headquarters to be sure about the backup on that *New England Magazine for Religious Studies*. They'd better tell the editor to expect a subscription order from down here and my name had better be on the contributor's page of the special printing. And, for safety's sake, in case these guys are better connected than usual, start keeping a tally on every new subscriber to the magazine, no matter where he's from. Have them run each one down and see if he's known. If not, start a dossier on him for good measure. And be sure my parish house backup is solid. This isn't a political case, where we've got the other side doing a fine-tooth-comb job on backgrounds, but de Lemos, if he is in on it, strikes me as smart enough to run through a few quick queries. We don't want to under-rate him; this might be a bigger operation than we usually run into down here. Okay?"

"Okay."

"Now, what did you hear on the ambush?"

"Well, the branch in Mexico City sniffed around but didn't come up with much. There was nothing in the newspapers, which means the government is repressing it. The old hands tell me that's what the administration does whenever they think it's guerrillas, but none of the ministries seems to have the foggiest. They all say this part of the country is clean, no guerrillas since Carranza's time, Pancho Villa and those types. So maybe it's bandits, after all—you know, cutting up a little to keep the army types' noses indoors while the banditos keep the whole outdoors for themselves. Maybe the same guys hit Flanagan to intimidate the town cops. Who knows? Next, maybe they'll go around selling life insurance policies, the old extortion bit. What do you think?"

"Maybe. We'll see. Now, I want you to do something else. De Lemos needs checking and I think he has an eye for good looks. See if Mexico City has a female agent, good-looking, savvy, clean enough to stand being checked out, and ready to come up here with some cock-and-bull story that can get her into the de Lemos place. Maybe he'll go for bait and try to hire her, screw her, or something else worthwhile. Leave it to them to check out de Lemos, down to what's under his fingernails; there ought to be something that a man that rich and smart does that gives us a point where we can run

someone up against him. There was a lot of fine old furniture in the
place and some first-class tapestries; maybe she can be on a buying
trip out here in the boonies. He's got a first-class modern office
there, too; she could sell office equipment. It doesn't matter much
as long as she's got a damn good cover, takes her time in town and
doesn't make a beeline for his place, and can handle herself.

"Okay," said Hickock. "I'll get on it. Anything else?"

"Yeah. Something is going to happen at two o'clock tomorrow
when our friends at the drop proceed with the big whatever it is. I'll
be sticking around to see if I can get wind of it. I want you to stand
by and tell Mexico City to do so as well, just in case there's some
movement we want to follow. No matter what, keep liaison under
control. Until we've got some idea who's behind this mess, we can't
trust anybody in any of the government ministries, except the ones
we've vetted ourselves. Tell them, if any of their big mouths start
opening, all our effort could go down the tubes. Okay?"

"Okay."

"I'll talk to you tomorrow."

York slid the panel back into place, wrote copious notes concerning the chapel of Saint Theresa and its "simply exquisite font,"
and went outside again to date the graves in the cemetery.

Eight

IN THE EARLY AFTERNOON the Reverend York wrote letters to his mother and brother, telling them of the fine progress of his work in Madre Dolorosa. He was eloquent about the richness of the material for his forthcoming article, and he invited his brother to take that vacation he'd been talking about for so long. "Be impulsive," he wrote to Harold York. "You've not had a day off from that police department in four years. Come on, a bachelor like you doesn't have to be so much a stay-at-home. I've really met some fine people in the police department down here. You fly to Hermosillo, I'll come pick you up, and then we'll drive through Mexico together. I know Madre Dolorosa won't interest you for long, so we can take off for grander parts as soon as you get down here. Maybe we can find some reproductions of pre-Columbian antiquities to bring home to Mother." He wrote it all in a large, round hand, easy to read for anyone monitoring his mail. He sent it to a Connecticut address with a very special zip code; headquarters would get it without the letter ever seeing New England. He put down his pen, glanced around the lobby, walked over to the ancient clerk to ask for aspirin because, he said, he wasn't feeling well, and told the old man he would be taking it easy. "A cold coming on, perhaps, or something I ate." The clerk had no aspirin but told the Yankee that the drugstore might. York thanked him and walked out the door and toward the mortuary/pharmacy a few blocks away.

He walked slowly. It was dismally hot. Dusty. Dirty. A few people walked the streets on their way home to siesta; most were already there. The shops were shuttered. He knew the drugstore would be closed by the time he arrived, but that was inconsequential; he had needed an excuse to be outside.

Two o'clock arrived, and three. By four the town was stirring and by five the cantina was doing big business. How he would like a cold beer. Well, a cold cola would have to do, for appearance's sake. He went into the cantina near the plaza, which was crowded

with the local men. No woman could enter without losing her reputation. There were other bars elsewhere with women present but
they were in the red-light area. For a tiny town to boast a batch of
brothels seemed rather much, but then Madre Dolorosa was the
district center and old-fashioned. If bachelors and adulterers were
to get their jollies, it would be done commercially. Freebies and
liberal sex were not in style in the Sonora hinterland; neither were
drugs, except as items for export.

The cantina itself was a fine old building across from the police
station. It had a high, sagging, beamed ceiling, a great long bar—
mirrorless—and a high platform built out from the wall at one end.
On special occasions a mariachi band played there. By being on that
balcony above the bar, the musicians were easily seen and heard
and, when the inevitable fights started, out of harm's way. Had it
been otherwise in this brawling town, they would soon have deci-
mated their musical population. The drinkers were, on the other
hand, expendable and were regenerated from an inexhaustible res-
ervoir of thirsty men. As York entered, three men were slugging
away at one another until one, too drunk to continue, fell over of
his own accord. Another, pulling a knife, slashed away at his oppo-
nent but, too drunk to see, managed only to twirl himself about into
a heap on the floor. The third shouted his victory noisily before
falling back in his chair, heavy as a bag of sodden oats.

York took a seat near the door and ordered a Coke without ice.
Several patrons spoke to him, spontaneously now, for he was on the
way to becoming a town institution—odd, of course, but no longer
frightening. He chatted idly about the heat, their cattle, and his finds
in the cemetery and, in turn, encouraged them to talk about their
work and lives. He was enjoying it.

The explosion burst in upon them. The shock wave of vibra-
tions scattered the bar patrons as a tsunami hits a children's party
on the beach. For York, it was the same heavy sensation felt in
high-G acceleration—the pressure in the gut, the limbs powerless,
and the mind blacking out. He felt himself pushed against the far
wall tangled in a pile of tequila- and beer-washed, otherwise astrin-
gently sweaty, bodies. Curious how odors predominate in states of
shock; man's primitive brain comes to the fore to sniff death or
escape.

How long he had been unconscious he couldn't say. His first
awareness was that he couldn't see. Had he been blinded? He

strained his eyes as his heart grasped the cold fear of being sightless forever. No, there was something. He pushed and struggled upward and felt others doing likewise, worms in a dark tin can, all writhing. He could see. First, the outline of the body of the man whose stomach had been covering his eyes, then various legs, arms, and torsos above and beside him, then the swirling dust of the shattered room. As his eyes focused, he could see overhead the underside of a balcony; one of four pillars supporting it had buckled and with it the corner had come tumbling down. He could not think why he was under a balcony or in this room. What time was it? He tried to look at his watch, but his left arm was underneath a body, one beginning to move and grunt. Slowly he pulled on his arm and brought his watch close to his face. The crystal was cracked. Why? He tried to reconstruct the scene and found it impossible—retrograde amnesia. He fought his cloudy brain. Well, yes, he'd been sitting at a bar somewhere and his arm, his left arm, had been resting on the counter top. And next to him had been a man whose right hand was on the bar. A heavy oversize shot glass had been between the two. The man had been drinking tequila. Yes, the shot glass must have been propelled into his resting wrist, against his watch, like a bowling ball into a pin. Of course. If only he knew what place and why. He stared at his watch, wondering why he was doing so. Suddenly, he felt foolish: he'd wanted to know what time it was. It was five forty-five. Why wasn't it two o'clock? But why should it be two o'clock? Why did that stick in his mind? He shook his head as though that would clear the brain. Two o'clock—why? Ah, that was it: he'd been waiting for something to happen at two o'clock, but it hadn't, they'd been late. He should have known. Everything in Mexico was late. Ah, he was in Mexico. That was good to know. He struggled with his confusion. A picture of the street formed itself in his mind and he saw himself approaching a building. Across the street from the entrance to the building was a police station with a faded stucco doorway. And above the door was the number two. Of course, an address. Not two o'clock, but number two. Had his subconscious known it all the time? Had it brought him here to the street number it had known about but his conscious mind had not? Had it suspected that he was to wait at number two, not for two o'clock? Well, if his subconscious had been so damn smart, why did it let him get blown up?

He was trifling with bits and pieces of his mind, trying to coax them together. It was Colombia all over again, or was it Peru? Funny, he'd thought for a moment it was Mexico, but it was all going whirr in his head, so that he was sick as well as dizzy from the spinning. He could no longer focus on the watch face in front of his nose.

What was he doing dressed in black? Had he known he was scheduled for a funeral? What was that all about? A funeral. Yes, there'd been that. He caught a glimpse of his friend, the Reverend York, putting on his wig that morning in front of the hotel room mirror. What a prissy bastard York was. He'd first better re-create Barber—ah, so that was his name, good. Each moment he told himself he was feeling better and better. If he could keep his mind from wandering, he could get up out of this pile of stinking bodies and go to work. He owed this bunch of guerrillas one. At least he knew that and, by knowing that, he realized his mind was reassembling itself at last.

He felt two firm hands take hold of him under the arms and pull him gently outside.

"Just lie here for now, father." Barber looked up. The police lieutenant headed back toward the bar.

It was a much-littered sidewalk. There were, as best he could count without turning his head too much, because his neck muscles ached, several buildings across the street that had been turned to rubble. There were people milling about, some helping, including the police lieutenant and his junior, but many just looking, grave Indian stares from unrevealing eyes. The debris of faces was around him, some alive, some dead. Fifty bodies, maybe, or a hundred— mostly men from the bar, some from the store across the street or from among those who had been walking the street; none visible from among those who'd been inside the police station. They, too, had returned abruptly to dust. So, too, must have the inmates of the jail yard behind the station, enclosed with a high wall and a guard tower on top. They, too, must be dust and a high price it was to pay for having been arrested the night before for getting overdrawn on your quota of drunken brawling. Well, the clear air helped. He tried his limbs, like a novice puppeteer warming up: first the foot and then the leg, first the fingers and then the hand. Now, see if I can make the arm move; now, see if I can make the back move; and now —ouch, damn it—well, I can, but wisely will not, make that neck move.

He looked up to see the figure of Father Teran, bending beside him. The Catholic father was desperately pale. There was blood on his cassock and his hands. He had been holding bloody bodies as he administered the sacraments.

"Father York, are you all right?" The priest's voice was tense.

"Yes. I think I'm just resting."

"Well, thanks be to God. You do look like you could do with a rest, and a new set of clothes, as well. Do you want some of mine?"

"What a sly way to lead the heretics back to the path of faith, father, cloaking me in the garb of the mother Church." Barber, slowly becoming York again, summoned a tease and a smile.

"The Church be damned," said the priest intensely. "You need a rest and some clothes. This—" He swept his hand around him. "—this is terrible."

"Yes, it is a nasty bit, isn't it?"

"I had no idea a bomb could do so much damage."

"No. Well, the people who put it there must have known. That's their business."

"Yes. Still, we must forgive them. I'm sure that in their own way they intend only good."

"Your faith in man, father, surpasses mine."

"No, that it does not," said the priest, grimly, "that it does not. I have faith in some men, faith in what some men must do, but faith in men generally, never." His tone was bitter. "But now, what about you? Shall you move into my little house for the next few days while you get over this? José isn't a bad cook and I have a supply of restoratives—some good Malagas, Madeiras, even some Scotch whisky."

"That's a generous offer, Father Teran," Barber replied, shakily. "I do appreciate it. I am wobbly. I must confess a strong jolt of John Barleycorn might be just the thing. But I'm afraid I'm not much of a drinker. It would be good to stay with you, though, just overnight, until my sea legs are back. I am grateful. Thank you." He was touched by the anguished priest's kindness. "I think I can manage to hobble over to your cottage. I'll just get started now. I know you've got a lot to do still with these poor souls." He scanned the grisly scene which, with the completion of the immediate rescue work, comprised, besides the rubble and the dead, an assembly of groaning wounded, weeping women and children, milling helpers, and the impassive Indian onlookers, rocking on their haunches.

Father Teran nodded, his lips pressed together in suppressed psychic pain, and moved away. York pushed himself slowly up from the ground, bracing his back against the building against which he'd been leaning. Dizzy, he stood still for some moments. He noticed for the first time that his head hurt and he put his hand to his forehead. Where he touched was sore and wet; he looked at his fingers and they were red with sticky, drying blood. Well, that, at least, accounted for some of the weakness and confusion. He had a moment of panic. Was the wig still on? He felt again. Yes, thank you, Lord, for that. Oh, that head did hurt. The bastards had gotten him a good one. He bit his lips. It would be their turn soon. With the return of anger, there was also increased strength. He began to make his way, slowly and unsurely, through the people. No one noticed him. Others around him were surrounded by family and friends, the dead being mourned, the wounded being tended, and the unhurt survivors telling the tale.

In front of him a family group were putting a blanket around a badly hurt man, preparing to move him to a rickety automobile, which, like others now coming in and standing by, would do as ambulances to carry the wounded to the town's one clinic or to their homes. York tried to sidestep but, still weak, stumbled over a heap of bricks. He was falling in spite of his effort to right himself, when a hand was placed quickly under his elbow. A small shoulder, but supple and strong, was there under his sagging arm.

"I think you need some help," he heard a woman's voice say.

Looking left, he saw her, that beautiful girl he'd met at the de Lemos hacienda. She took his arm gently and placed it around her neck and over her shoulder. Her face was grave, her eyes deeply concerned.

"An awful thing, this," she said quietly.

"Yes, very bad," he agreed.

"Your face is bloody and you're pale as ivory. Are you sure you're able to walk?"

"Yes, I can walk, although not as well as I thought. I appreciate your help. How is it that you're here?"

"I came to town today to shop. Don de Lemos left the hacienda this morning and so I thought I'd drive in. I arrived a few minutes ago and heard about the explosion; I was curious. This is more than I bargained for."

It was only then he realized that, as amazed as he'd been to see her, and grateful for her help, he had not stopped to think that she was speaking English, not Spanish.

"My Lord, but you're speaking English."

She looked up at him.

"I went to school in the States—Oberlin College, in Ohio. I wanted to study music and English and my uncle agreed."

"Don de Lemos is your uncle?"

"Yes."

"So that's it. You never told me who you were."

"I was playing hard to get. It was a fair trade. I didn't know who you were. I'm still not sure."

The warning lights lit up inside his brain. She had moved in at the right time. He was too busy being alive to be on guard. And he'd been grateful to her—more than that, in fact. But now she was asking him the same question she'd asked before, but this time she was not teasing. She was inviting him to confess all. Was it because she was astute? Had he done something stupid to arouse her suspicion? Had she been tipped off? Did she work for an organization that had identified him and put her on his trail? Or was it simply her way of getting acquainted, of probing people for hypocrisy at the very outset? The sirens were ringing in his head, telling him he'd better be as clear as a bell or the next stumble he took might bring the whole operation down. Yet, Lord, how he hated to be coy, to fence with this girl at this time.

"Don't I look real enough?"

"Oh yes, I can tell from touching you that you're real. But there's something about you that's odd. Oh, please don't take offense. This is no time to talk about it, while you're not feeling well. It can wait. We'll have a lot of time together."

They would have time together. She had assumed that they were already together in their understanding.

"No, I don't mind talking about it, but I don't know what it is that we're talking about. I mean, I don't feel exactly clever right now and I'm sure I look an unholy mess, but 'odd'—well, I don't know."

"Aren't you aware that something is odd about you?"

"Maybe I am odd, but I think mostly I'm a fool."

"Why is that?"

"For going into that cantina in the first place. All that for one

Coca-Cola. I must say it's an argument for keeping away from bars and bad company; as Proverbs has it, 'Only fools make a mock at sin,' and 'The way of transgressors is hard.' "

She looked at him. "Maybe I'm the one that's odd."

"Oh, I can't believe that. I think you're wonderful."

"The way you talk, sometimes it's so superficial. And yet, when I look at you—I watched you back there when Father Teran was talking to you, did you know that? I watched you carefully, how your face looked and the way you moved. I told myself that I'd been right when I met you at my uncle's house, that there was some depth to you. Your eyes, that brightness touched with doubt—at least, that's what I thought was there. Then you turn false again, going on about Proverbs and bars and bad company. I thought you were more of a person than that. Silly of me, wasn't it? Well, no matter. There's my car. I can take you wherever it is you want to go."

She had dumped a bucket of ice water on him. He had it coming. She could be as cold and courteous as he was, as she withdrew her emotion from him. Perhaps she had been a fool, as she said, but to know it was only in trusting him to respond to her. What a rotten business he was in, rotten!

"Well, thank you very much. Father Teran invited me to stay with him for the night, in his house near the cathedral. I accepted and . . ."

"Of course," she interrupted him, no longer interested in his talk. He got in the car and she drove him in silence to the priest's bungalow.

"I do thank you, ah . . ." He hesitated, realizing he didn't know her name.

"Think nothing of it, father, I was glad to be of assistance. Can you make it on your own to the house?"

"Oh yes, I'm sure I can, but I would like to be able to thank you in person."

"What do you mean? I'm here. You just did."

"But I don't know your name."

She hesitated. After revealing so much of herself, now he guessed she wanted to yield nothing further to him, not even her name. "Dolores Calles." Her voice was uninflected.

"Not de Lemos, then?"

"My mother was his sister."

"Calles is a famous name."

"Yes."

"The same family as the president after Obregón?"

"It's a large family."

"Size makes it no less famous."

"Mexico has had many presidents, some more famous than others."

"I'm not competent to judge, Dolores. I only know it's an honored name."

She stiffened. He had let her first name slip. Given the distance between them now, it was an impropriety.

"If you are to call me Dolores, then I must know your name."

Lord, he had never told her even that. He felt himself blush. "Al —Alfred York, from Connecticut."

"You write articles, don't you?"

"Well, I try. Nothing much. Just little pieces that may interest a few New Englanders."

"I'll look forward to reading them."

"Oh, they're nothing, I assure you. Not worth looking at."

"My uncle doesn't seem to agree."

"Oh?"

"I mailed a postal money order for him today. It was for the *New England Magazine of Religious Studies.* You must have impressed him."

"Hardly. I imagine it's just curiosity."

"Yes, that may be it."

"Well, I suppose I should let you go on about your business. I am grateful, you know, very much so."

"I told you, think nothing of it."

"As you wish. I wonder, though—perhaps in a day or so, could I invite you to dinner here? It's the least I can do."

"You're not under obligation to me for anything, Reverend York." She stung him again with the proper name, rebuffing intimacy.

"No. Well, you don't think so and it's not that I feel obliged, but—well, to find someone so kind who speaks English . . ."

"No, I'm sorry, but I have a lot to do. My uncle returns soon and since I manage the house for him, well, I have to see to it that it's given a good cleaning while he's gone."

"Well, I am sorry."

"Yes, so am I."

He was sure that they were both sorry in their many ways as she drove off and he hobbled shakily through the gate and garden to the bougainvillea-covered cottage. Sorry or not, he had some thinking to do. De Lemos was checking up on him and this girl had told him. Was it out of naïveté, as it appeared, or was it a warning, some part of her still caring? Or was it another provocation, the howl of the coyote in the quiet night to frighten the hiding animals into the open? He might be her target, but now she must be his. She was his route into the house and into the de Lemos operation, if operation it was. He'd have no need of pretty little furniture buyers from Mexico City, stirring up the waters, with a potential agent like that in the wings. He would have to see her again, no matter what she had said. The idea pleased him. Now that she was gone and, he was reasonably sure, none the wiser and none the worse for what he'd said, or not said, he felt he could manage the affair. If an affair it was going to be. Was he recruiting an agent, planning a seduction, assessing an enemy, or playing dynamite with romance? When next he had Bill cable headquarters, he knew what the cable would say. Not much. It would be misleading; field reports always were. No competent case officer ever did tell all. Groat had known that all along.

Nine

THAT EVENING THE PRIEST CAME in late. York had gone to bed on a cot that José had made up for him in the small front room. José had been solicitous, finding clean sheets, a blanket, and boiled water and offering to cook food any time the guest desired it. York had cleaned himself up first, grateful to find a neat, modern bathroom in the cottage. The gash on his forehead—dead center—was deep but not broad; the flesh had been peeled away in a serrated flap, leaving the white bone exposed. There would be no hope of getting it stitched up here, with the town's one doctor up to his neck in the seriously wounded; well, it would be one hell of a scar to invent stories about. He had found no medicine chest so he'd washed the wound in Scotch. His clothes, shredded beyond repair, had been thrown away. A new set, Father Teran's, had been placed on the chair next to the bed. York wondered how he'd feel wearing a soutane. Finally, José offered him brown paste with water in a glass, "to help you sleep." It was opium, of course, widely used locally to quiet teething infants, relieve bellyaches, and the like. Well, why not? York accepted a tiny potion of the pain-killer. He needed sleep.

He resented his awakening. Ordinary voices would not have aroused him, but these angry tones, shuttered within whispers, alerted him. Drugged, he did not respond quickly, nor was there need—the sounds were outside and fading. He couldn't hear the words, only the tense hiss of fury, *sotto voce*, and the scuffling of feet on the gravel. Two or three people. Then they walked away toward the backyard and there was silence. Fatigue and drugs returned him to sleep until, he could not say how much later, the priest came in. He moved quietly, not turning on the light, but York woke up anyway.

"Hello," he said groggily.

Teran turned, a flashlight in his hand, greeted York, and turned on the lights. He was pale, haggard, still wearing the bloody cassock. He was an imposing figure, nevertheless, with his Old Testament

beard, deeply lined face, intense eyes, aristocratic bearing, and electric zeal. But there was something missing. There was no charisma
through inspiration. York had sensed that at their earlier meeting,
for the zeal was too personal.

"I'm sorry I awakened you."

"No, I'm ready to wake up, at least for a little while."

"Do you want some dinner? José's little cottage is down the
back alley from here. I'm going to call him. He'll be glad to fix us
something. Lord knows, I need a bite."

"Okay—a little something, not much," agreed York.

"Can I get you something in the meantime?"

"No, I'll wait a while. Besides, you look like death warmed over;
why don't you clean up, change, and rest a bit?"

"I will, but let me get José first." With that, Teran reached up
to a rope tied to a cleat on the wall near the front door. The rope
extended through a small hole drilled through the wall. He pulled
the rope heftily. "It's primitive, but it works. It rings a bell in José's
house."

"When I was a boy, we used two open tin cans and a tight string
for a telephone."

"Yankee ingenuity. We used bells on a rope."

"Mexicans are more musical."

"I doubt it. We simply stay in the seventeenth century."

"It was a good century."

"Not for Mexico. It wasn't then and it isn't now."

"Why don't you clean up? You look awful."

The priest looked at his robes. "Yes, I guess I do. I'll just take
a minute."

In about fifteen minutes he'd returned, washed and changed,
but his face looked no less tense and exhausted. "Is that better?"
he asked.

"Well, you're less like a surgeon after a messy emergency-room
operation, but you still look worn out. I bet you need a drink."

"You're right. And not a Madeira, either. I'll have a Scotch. You
want to join me?"

"No, thanks. I'd better not."

The priest took a bottle of Ballantines from the cupboard and
poured a water glass half full. "I could give you some soda," he said.
"But there's no ice. My little refrigerator is broken. Can't get it

repaired here and I won't get to Hermosillo for a while to get a new
one. Part of the penance of exile."

"No matter. I don't need anything. So you're in exile, eh?
Offend the bishop?"

"There are bishops and bishops. I offended several, but no
more than they offended me."

"The usual Church politics?"

"Hardly. I'm not so shallow as to care about that. My concerns
are of more consequence." He looked at York reprovingly. "The
bishops have betrayed the people, the Church has betrayed the
people, the government has betrayed the people, and the people
protest it. I protest it. That's why I was exiled here. They thought
they could punish me, but they are wrong. This is not a punishment."

"No, of course, a man of principle can do good works wherever
he is." York spoke very slowly. It would take extra care not to offend
this gaunt El Greco figure who flamed with righteous anger.

"Yes, in a way you might say that. Your idiom is different from
mine, but then we are very different. For one thing, you are a North
American." There was no flattery in his tone.

"Well, of course, yes. But we are neighbors, aren't we?"

"Like the cat is neighbor to the mouse."

"Oh." York was silent for a moment. Conversation was tricky
indeed. "Still, when men of goodwill are together, there is always
hope. And they can do wonders when they put their shoulders to
the wheel."

"Merde!"

Well, at least York now knew Teran spoke French. "I beg your
pardon?" he lied. "I don't understand." He said it with a show of
as much genteel stupidity as he could muster. Teran glared at him.
He went on blithely, "I'm sure you would agree, father, that most
men are good on either side of any border."

"I prefer not to be addressed as 'father' in my own house. My
name is Camillo, or, if that is too intimate, call me 'brother.' And
I do not agree. Most men are what their society makes them and,
if the ruling class constitutes an evil society, then it will bring out
the evil in men. For men to be good, they must be nourished by
good. Under feudal tyranny, under colonialism, under capitalism,
they are nourished by evil. Saint Thomas says that concrete attribu-

tion of authority is made by the people. The ruling class, including the Church, are in opposition. When there is authority opposed to the people, that is unlawful and it is tyranny. A Christian must fight against tyranny! Don't you agree, brother?"

"Well, goodness, that is something to think about, isn't it? I mean, no one can be in favor of tyranny, can they? But, still, what you say all sounds rather political, doesn't it? I mean, don't you think those of us who wear the collar ought to busy ourselves with our ministry, render unto Caesar and all that? I mean, there are so many spiritual problems to deal with, so much good to be done."

"I hope, brother, you're not as hopelessly stupid as you sound." Teran was impatiently angry, speaking rapidly. "Christ was a politician and he died for his revolution. Your Christian imperative, your apostolic mission, is that revolution. But the Church has joined the counterrevolution; it is the institution of the rich. We must make it poor again. That is the politics of faith, brother. The people have been tricked. They are always tricked. Your mission is to inform them, brother, not to mislead them. We face the same martyrdom today that our ancestors sought in Rome. Your country is Rome itself, my Mexico is your Judea, our president is your Herod. Your mission is the same revolution that was begun in Bethlehem. If you are not persecuted, brother, you are on the wrong side, tricking the people, being tricked yourself. Do I make myself clear?"

There was silence then between them, broken at last by Teran, who had finished his Scotch and went now to pour himself another, fuller than the first.

"Well, brother, at least you don't dispute me with bourgeois arguments."

"I guess not." York strove for deference in his voice. "But still, I don't fancy myself in a real revolution; I mean, not shooting anyone. That would be awful. Take today, for example. I don't know what happened, no one told me. Perhaps it was a gas tank that exploded—that happened in Connecticut last year in a filling station and it was brutal. So many people burned. I saw the children dying. Were there any children killed today, Brother Camillo? Was it a gas tank or what?"

Camillo's eyes clouded. "I am not sure what happened today, brother, but, as you say, it was terrible. I saw no children, but what does that matter? These people are all children, however old they are. That they were killed is grotesque."

"Isn't that the kind of thing that happens in a revolution? For instance, what if it wasn't a gas tank? After all, I didn't see any flames. What if it had been a bomb? If that's a revolution, that's an awful thing. I couldn't do anything like that, I'd never forgive myself, slaughtering innocent people in the street."

"No, there can be no forgiveness for such mistakes." Teran's speech was halting now. "Men who do that are beasts and must die. They betray the revolution by killing its children."

"Do you think it *was* a bomb?" Wide-eyed, York's face was all innocence.

"I told you, brother, I am not sure what happened today. But I will find out. If it is as you suggest, someone will pay."

"My goodness, I should think so. They ought to be arrested and sent to prison. Frankly, I'd like to see them shot, but since I'm against capital punishment, I oughtn't even to think anything like that."

"If it is as you say, there will be capital punishment."

"The police will catch them, then?"

"These police? Those corrupted butchers? What can they do? Besides, it was their station house that blew up. But two were away, so they lived."

"Yes, the lieutenant carried me out of the cantina. I owe the policeman a great deal."

"You owe them nothing. They are robbers of the people."

"Oh? But then who will catch the bombers—the army?"

"More exploiters. They can do nothing but suffer their miserable fates. They are a pestilence to be wiped out."

"I recall Pancho Villa destroyed Orozco's troopers, the Colorados—a plague they were called, too. Villa felt the same way about government soldiers."

"Yes. He was right. But Villa didn't live up to the ideals of the revolution. He became greedy, forgot justice, and finally allowed himself to be bought off to live in luxury."

"And get assassinated."

"Yes, and get assassinated."

"It's quite the thing down here, isn't it?"

"What is?" asked Teran.

"Assassination. I mean, your police chief here was assassinated only last month. And then those soldiers, and now the police. What do you make of it?"

"I don't know, brother. Who would kill Flanagan I cannot say, although he was no loss—a bad man. The others? Well, perhaps the revolution has begun. If so, you have come among us at a glorious time. You will watch the liberation." Teran gulped the whisky in his glass and poured another half tumbler for himself. He was beginning to show its effects: bleary-eyed, slurring his words, but not quite drunk.

"But what about dinner?" York asked gently.

"I'm not hungry."

"Brother Camillo, do you drink this much often?"

Teran glared at him with red eyes, knuckles white around the glass. "So, you think I'm a whisky priest, eh? A drunk, a raving maniac, perhaps. Is that it?"

"No, brother, I was just inquiring. You've had too much to drink and it's not good for you. You know that, too."

Teran shook the glass in his hand, staring at the churning Scotch. "Yes, I know that. But don't worry. Ordinarily, I don't drink. This is an exception. It has been a difficult day."

"I know, yes—a terrible day. What about dinner?" York reminded him.

"I've no appetite now. There are matters that I must think about."

A little later José came in, bearing a large platter of refried beans, tortillas, rice, and chorizo. York ate heartily and dropped off to sleep immediately afterward. Tomorrow would be time to add the new piece to the puzzle. Not that he knew where to fit it in; only that Brother Camillo, too, was part of the picture. To meet a revolutionary priest was in itself nothing new. There were many and this one had as good a heart as any, otherwise he wouldn't have taken the capitalist Yankee to his bosom—warnings and all—nor would he have been so outraged at the slaughter today. Yet, the downwind smell was odd. As Brother Camillo had said, there were many matters to think about.

The next morning he indulged himself. A late sleep, José bringing fruit, bread, and coffee for breakfast, and a morning dawdling, poking about the cathedral garden in borrowed clothes. His forehead hurt, his muscles ached, but the rest of him reasserted its vitality. Teran had risen early and had gone off somewhere before York woke up. So it was that York left José with thanks, wrote a note of gratitude to place on the kitchen table, and, before departing, made one quick sweep of the house. As he expected, there was nothing suspicious to be found.

That afternoon, parked this time in the shade of some old stables looking out from the edge of town over the desert—its situation such that it was free from undetectable surveillance—York got in touch with Billie Hickock, telling him the news of the bombing and asking him, in turn, to cable Washington and check with Mexico City to see what was known about Camillo Teran. The selection of a female agent to be run against de Lemos was to be called off. That agreed, he asked of news from headquarters and Mexican liaison about the status of his magazine backup and the selection of a man to pose as York's policeman brother.

"Everything's hunky dory, they tell me. They've done their homework, the special printing of the magazine is ready, subscriptions and requests are being monitored, and they've got some guy from New Jersey who works in the European section who spent a couple of years as a cop. He's ready to come down."

"Good," said Barber.

"Well, yes and no," replied Billie.

"What's wrong?"

"Headquarters told me they'd send him down when they figured the time was ripe."

"What the hell do you mean?"

"The cable said they felt you were 'too close' to the situation and—I quote—'weren't in a position to collate all the relevant data,' and further, and I do quote, 'you may want to move in too quickly whereas headquarters'—by which, of course, they mean Parks's committee—'will insist on prudence,' which I make out to mean they'll send the new body in when they get good and ready, regardless of when you need him."

"Yummy."

"I thought you'd like that."

"If they do that, we've lost control of the operation," said Barber.

"Headquarters believes it is supposed to be in control of operations."

"Like running a train from the caboose. Well," Barber sighed, "nothing we can do about it, except scream and hope for the best. Send them a screaming cable, will you?"

"They'll be mad, but I will. Hope you don't mind if I sign your name to it. I don't want to end my career yet. I'm bored here but not suicidal yet."

"By all means put my X on it. Now, what other news?"

"Well, for one thing, I got a hint from Mexico City about why they're pulling back there and playing cautious. Seems the foreign ministry is protesting, said they heard the Bureau had engaged in unilateral action down here and they would have none of it. Threatened to close the branch down if it was true and persona non grata everybody there."

"PNG the lot?"

"The lot."

"Great!" said Barber sarcastically. "Do you think someone spilled the beans to liaison on our operation?"

"Doesn't sound that way. I think maybe somebody just got too cozy with the wrong man and the Mexicans drew the inference. If they knew what was going on, they'd have ten Federales in on top of you by now, or at least so I was told."

"You were told right. Still, it puts our necks under the guillotine. If the wrong people in the ministry do find out, we could be deported tomorrow. And if the ministry people are tied in with the bad guys, we could be clay pigeons."

"That's comforting. Have you, by the way, any more thoughts on which ones are the bad guys?"

"Wish I knew. Did you get anything on your query about de Lemos?"

"Only what Mexico City told me: he's rich, well connected, and supposedly clean; his brother is deputy home minister, his sister married into an ex-president's family. De Lemos owns land here and on the border near Agua Prieta and also in Cuilican. He's taken a flier or two in the stock market, too. Headquarters hasn't said boo about him."

"Anything on Air Narcotics?"

"You mean the two A.M. special? Well, it came over again two nights ago, just after the takeoff you reported. The border people didn't pick up anything on radar, though, even though they were alerted. You know how those planes come skimming down the valleys; he could sneak in and out for months if he's got a good route and the weather stays clear."

"So far, we're drawing hearts trying to make a spade flush hand. Well, nothing for it but to keep digging."

"Sorry, boss. I'll keep painting. Any time you need me, yell and I'll be there to smother the enemy under my false beard."

"Good man."

"Luck, over."

York slid the radio control panel cover into place underneath the dashboard and considered his next step. It would be southward, candy box in hand, to pay a call on the lovely Dolores. Courtesy required him to telephone first, but he knew if he did that she'd tell him not to come.

Thirty minutes later, his bandage on his forehead adjusted turban-style to make him as presentable as the walking wounded can be, he drove the Oldsmobile to the gate at the de Lemos compound. The old man looked out of the gatehouse window but did not open the gate. York got out of his car and walked to the window. He was met by the ugly snout of an automatic rifle pointing toward his chest. Another one of those cartridge belt–encrusted cowboys was inside, moustached and grizzled, and no more friendly than the Bobbsey Twins he'd met the other day.

"I've come to visit Don de Lemos."

"He is away," said the old man.

"Well, then, I'll pay my respects to Señorita Calles."

"She has not left word that she expects anyone."

"It's a courtesy call."

"No visitors are allowed," said the old man vaguely.

"Oh, I'm sure she'll want to see me."

The old man was uneasy. He couldn't disobey orders, but he didn't wish to offend an important visitor. The *pistolero* clearly felt no such ambivalence; a mean eye followed the gun barrel's line to York's middle.

"Look," said York, "I've brought her candy." He displayed the box in his hand. The old man shrugged. "Telephone her, advising her I'm here," York urged him. The old man nodded and picked up the phone.

"She will see you," he said. The gate was swung open and York drove in. The door was answered by a maid, who ushered him to

the large parlor. Dolores appeared, dressed in light blue silk, a red
Hermès scarf around her neck. Fine features, dark eyes, glistening
hair in a pony tail, a light perfume—she was stunning and his heart
raced. It did not augur well for his management of himself. He
handed her the candy, a box that he'd spent two hours looking for
in Madre Dolorosa before finding it in a grocery store.

"It's probably ten years old," he said.

"Thank you." Her manner, her voice, were controlled. "I
thought I told you I would be busy."

"I know, but I have an excuse for my rudeness already made
up and rehearsed."

"Oh?"

"I wanted to see you. I was so confused—only half conscious,
really—yesterday that I can't remember whether or not I thanked
you for assisting me. You were like Florence Nightingale. How
could I not thank you?"

"You did thank me and it isn't necessary to repeat it."

"Oh, I know that."

"But you said you couldn't remember."

"That was my excuse. I told you. I rehearsed it driving down."

"Well, at least you're being honest this time."

"I thought you might like a picnic in the desert. I brought
everything from the grocery store: cheese, tomatoes, wine, bread,
a tinned Danish ham, tinned Danish butter, and in the dust of the
grocery store I even found a can of cactus worms. Quite a delicacy.
I love them."

"You must think we have no food in our kitchen here."

"I'm sure you do, but it's my pleasure to ask you to break bread
with me at my table, the whole desert."

"Well, I confess I've never been invited to picnic on my own
desert. And I've never been invited to picnic with a clergyman. I may
have a difficult time. My family, I fear, have made me anticlerical."

"Oh, we can be a sanctimonious, pasty-faced, precious bunch.
But some are really sincere, pious men; some are even spiritual. And
some have dreams, like Father Teran."

"And you?"

"I wear a hair shirt, flagellate myself every morning, and still
can't get over being on the sanctimonious side. That's why you
don't like me. I'm a natural-born hypocrite, even when I believe
what I say."

She smiled again. "Well, you must admit that is unsettling."

"It's worse—it's a curse. But its effects are moderated by my parishioners; they're such a fine group of people, they put up with me, anyway. They don't need me but I need them, except when I'm down here, pursuing my eccentric hobbies. Runs in the family, I suspect. Rumor has it there was a bishop in the family back in the second century who was martyred for collecting butterflies."

"But how could that be?"

"They were already in Caesar's collection."

They both laughed and York was pleased. "You will picnic with me?"

"I will if you want, but I propose the front lawn. What's waiting in your desert are scorpions, rattlesnakes, and, my uncle says, guerrillas. You saw our army at the gate. If the guerrillas attack, there's only the foreman as our general, and frankly, I don't think much of him."

"Why not?"

She tossed her head, "I think he's a bad man. I don't know why my uncle keeps him on all these years. He sneaks, he lies, he does not bathe, and I don't like him."

"Sounds a bad one, all right. Isn't your uncle's secretary here?"

"No, he went rushing off this morning to the border. Some big business to take care of. He takes himself too seriously. I'm glad he's gone."

"You really don't get along with him, then?"

"Like fire and dirty water, except I would like to put *him* out."

"He's another bad one, then?"

"Who can say? All I know is that I don't like him. My uncle is an intelligent man and knows what he's doing. His taste in employees isn't mine, that's all."

"Well, that can happen. They're probably all very efficient and that's what a man like your uncle needs."

"I suppose, but I'm not sure Guillermo is so efficient after all."

"Guillermo?"

"That secretary. He left so fast this morning after that phone call that he forgot his briefcase. Had to come rushing back for it. And then he'd forgotten to phone the airline in Hermosillo, so I had to do that. Lucky for him there was space on the plane."

"I'm surprised your uncle doesn't keep a plane of his own. Lots of ranchers do. The valleys are flat enough and it would save him time if he travels; you're a good way from Hermosillo."

"Yes, I suppose. There is an old airstrip about fifteen miles from here, over the hills. It was built when there was a mining operation, but that closed down ten years ago, when new machinery became more expensive than gold."

"Your uncle's mine?"

"Yes, it's his, but that's all finished, unless gold gets over two hundred dollars an ounce. At least, that's what he said to me."

"Well, still, with the airfield there—hasn't he ever thought about having an airplane?"

"I don't know. I've never talked to him about it. I suppose it's a lot of trouble—mechanics, pilots, all that. He doesn't mind the drive to Hermosillo and it's his secretary who has to travel to the out-of-the-way places, like this trip to Nogales."

"Well, your uncle is lucky to have gold mines in so many places."

"Oh, it's not gold. He has some cattle ranches up there and there's a terrible drought this year. Maybe that's what Guillermo went up to look after. I don't know."

"Well, I regret there's trouble for him. He must worry a great deal."

"He does. He seems very tense these days. Of course, I've only been here a few weeks. I hope it's just a passing problem."

"I see. This isn't your home, then? I don't want to pry."

"I don't mind your asking. My parents died when I was in my teens. My uncle is my guardian. Within the family he's very generous and kind. I come to visit each year. The rest of the time I live in Mexico City, at least when I'm not in the States or abroad."

"It sounds as though you travel a great deal."

"Yes, I like to. There's no career for me in music, I'm not good enough, but I do enjoy going to concerts and the opera, so I spend some time each year in New York, Milan, Paris—that sort of thing."

"Have you seen the Moscow opera? I heard a *Boris Godunov* recording made by them. I only have a tin ear, but I liked it."

"Moscow? Yes, I was there. I saw the Bolshoi, the opera, and the concerts. The music is superb, but it's a dreary city. Dictatorships bore me."

"Yes, I should think so. I gather you don't take any interest in Mexican politics?"

She looked at him suspiciously. "Is that a loaded question? Just because Moscow bores me doesn't mean I'm apolitical. Perhaps you, as a man, expect women ought not to be interested in politics, is that it?"

"Oh no, not at all, I'm not so old-fashioned. I think everyone should be interested—vote, you know, exercise his citizen's responsibilities. It just seemed, with your traveling and interest in music, well, you might not have the interest or the time."

"Well, I confess that's partly true. I am interested, but I can't do much. Our government is more paternalistic than pleases me. I'd prefer a real democracy, not one that punishes the opposition newspapers by denying them newsprint when they get out of line. No wonder we have guerrillas when decent people can't be effective in their opposition. I think everyone my age who's had a liberal university education feels the same way; we bring our idealism home from school and find that it's a plant prohibited from importation, just like new cars or appliances. People do a big business smuggling those in but I'm not sure the idealists have such a big market. That's why I'm not an activist. Most people aren't interested; it's only the contraband idealists, the professional agitators and the intelligentsia, of course, who are stirred up. There's always discontent when people are poor and badly treated, but their ideals are very simple: enough food, health, a chance to live, fair laws, that's all. That's what powered our revolution originally—the great names: Díaz, Madero, Carranza, Obregón, Zapata, Villa. They fell, some of them, from their heights, but those were times of greatness, bloody as they were. There's no one around like that any more, and no need, really. Things are very much better, just not good enough, that's all."

"So you think the guerrillas who've just opened up around here now are on the wrong track?"

"Good heavens, yes. How could you ever think I'd be in favor of massacres and ambushes and terrorism? It's awful. Besides, they're most likely bandits pretending something else. Who knows? They're animals. I hate them!"

He'd probed as far as he could. The way she said it told him that. She was either a consummate actress and no hired agent or hanger-on, but a real professional, in which case he'd never learn anything, anyway, in conversation; or she meant just what she said.

The odds were on the latter. It was more than a businesslike esti-
mate. It made him very happy. He nodded assent.

"I couldn't agree with you more. These days young people get
led astray so easily. One always worries."

"That I could be led astray?"

"Well, obviously not, but some people . . ."

"And do you think of me as so much younger than you?"

"Well, I have to, don't I? After all I'm fifty-two and you're—
well, I'd guess—no, I'd better not, people get in trouble telling a
woman how old they think she is."

"I'm twenty-seven and I think I'm old. But, Mr. York, you just
don't seem fifty-two, despite your gray hair."

"It's a long-lived family, blessedly so. My mother still looks
quite young and so does my brother. By the way, he may be coming
down to visit." York hoped he wasn't taking too much of a chance,
he couldn't know what the new man would look like if and when he
arrived. But he had to lay the groundwork, worse now that he'd lost
control of the timetable—and had to begin to get people ready now
to accept another stranger on the scene. But there was a risk: the
fellow might not resemble him at all. York added, "He's my half
brother, actually, doesn't look like me, but he's a good fellow and
needs a vacation, so on an impulse I wrote and told him to come
down."

"How nice."

"Yes. Now, what about getting ready for that picnic?"

Ten

AS THICK AS HUNGRY FLEAS on a fresh new dog, the soldiers were there. Sitting on the dirt street sides drinking beer; standing against the buildings with their weapons leaning haphazardly; some crammed into jeeps like a rolling pack of clowns in a circus act, raising gritty swirls of dust as they raced down the streets; others flirting with the few women who were out shopping. The army was certainly at ease. A sergeant and a lieutenant rolled slowly down the street in a dusty command car, shouting. As they did so, the troopers straightened up, eyes smartly ahead, rifles at parade rest. As soon as the officers passed, they slumped again into disarray. It could be no other than a provincial garrison drawn for the emergency from some nearby area. There ought to be heads rolling when the disciplined regulars moved in, as York imagined they must. When guerrillas hit the government, response was usually massive. These were the initial dribble.

The soldiers stared at him as he drove by in his grimy Oldsmobile. Most were impassive, a few sullen, none friendly. He reached his hotel. Two men he'd not seen before among the hotel lounge regulars were in the lobby. Hard faces, cold eyes, clean-shaven, poorly cut city clothes, black shoes. They had to be state or federal police. He recognized neither of them. He got his keys from the nervous old man at the desk, walked up the stairs, and heard their footsteps behind him. As he unlocked his door, they came up behind him. He went into his room to find the bureau drawers half open, the sheets rumpled, the mattress exposed, his suitcase closed but with pieces of shirt sticking out. His clerical garb hung lopsidedly on the closet hangers.

He exclaimed loudly, "Good heavens. What's happened?" Then, turning to the hard faces next to him, "And who are you? Do you know anything about this?"

"About what?" The taller of the two asked unsympathetically.

"Why, someone has broken into my room. I wonder what

they've stolen?" York bobbed about, agitated.

The tall one, surly and aggressive, ignored the query. "You're Mr. York?"

"Yes, I'm the Reverend York. And who are you?"

The tall one took a battered wallet from his pocket and pushed the red identification card of the state police into York's face.

"Well, thank goodness it's the police. You know about the thief, then. Have you caught him?"

"What are you doing here in Madre Dolorosa, Mr. York?" The voice was flat, sharp.

"Well, I'm a visitor, of course. I'm studying local religious customs—the church, funerals, you know, that sort of thing. But what about the burglar?"

"Let us see your papers, Mr. York."

York handed over his wallet with its tourist card and fished his passport from his inner coat pocket. First the tall officer and then the short one looked at them carefully. The short one ruffled through the paper currency in the wallet, counting it quickly before handing it back to York. He put the passport and tourist card in his coat pocket.

"But you can't do that," York protested. "You're taking my papers."

"They must be inspected. If they are in order, they will be returned tomorrow."

"But what if someone else asks for them while you have them? I'll need a receipt. I must have a receipt." York's hand, holding his wallet, gestured nervously. The tall man's eyes followed the wallet.

"We will take the wallet, too."

"But you can't. That's my personal property. And it has my money in it."

Mutt and Jeff gave him the fish eye. The tall one spoke.

"All of your papers must be examined. If they are in order, you will get them back. We must see if the money is counterfeit. There has been too much counterfeit money around here recently."

"Gentlemen," York spoke with exasperation. "It is improper for you to take my money or my wallet. If you insist on doing so, I demand a receipt."

"You will demand nothing from us. We will demand what we wish from you. If you are lucky, we shall not arrest you right away."

"Arrest me?" York's voice howled with a combination of shock, fear, and fury.

"Yes." The tall one leafed through the money in the wallet, counting it. "Seven hundred and twenty-five pesos. That is a lot of money."

"Well, what do you expect? I can't stay in Mexico without money."

"If we arrest you, the fine will be seven hundred pesos."

"Fine for what? I've done nothing. I'm a minister and an American citizen. You can't fine me; a judge would have to find me guilty of some charge."

"If you're a spy with these guerrillas, you will be shot. Right now your fine for resisting arrest is seven hundred pesos."

"But you haven't arrested me. I haven't resisted. There is no charge, no judge, no fine at all. This is all quite insane."

"You will be wise, Mr. York, not to make any more trouble for yourself than you already have. You are arrested, you have resisted arrest, you can choose between going to jail right now with us or letting us pay your fine for you. That way, we shall tell the judge that you did not intend to be so bad and then you will not have to stay in the jail for a year or two, as you would have to otherwise. Do you understand?" With that, the tall officer counted out seven hundred pesos, placed them in his coat pocket, and returned the wallet to York. "If you want more trouble, we can arrange it, Mr. York. As it is, I think you may have much more trouble, anyway. We do not like guerrillas here. We shoot them."

"Dear Lord in heaven, what kind of a place is this?" York looked miserable.

"This is Mexico, Mr. York, and we shoot terrorists. We don't welcome troublesome gringos, and we do not like people who resist arrest and then fail to appreciate it when we help them to avoid a worse punishment. Now, do you want your money back so that you can come with us to the jail or shall we do you a small service by paying your fine to the judge? Make up your mind; we are very busy men."

"Keep the money," wailed York, "and for goodness' sake get my papers back to me."

"Tomorrow, Mr. York, if they are in order, yes. Or the day after, perhaps. We shall see. In the meantime I'm sure you will not go too far away, eh? We will want to see you again." Both men turned and walked out the door.

York followed them to the door and closed it loudly. He then went to the basin, poured water from the old pitcher, and splashed his face. You bastards, thought Barber, you cheap, rotten, thieving bastards. Oh my, will you be surprised when this round is over and I bust your crooked asses. My, oh my, that will be my day.

Now the pressure was on but his own path was unclear; he still didn't know enough to move directly. Pushing developments at this point would be risky, but he would have to take his chances. It did not take him long to find the lieutenant of the local constabulary, the one who'd pulled him from the rubble, the one with whom he'd begun that promising discussion of antiquities for his mother. The lieutenant was in the city hall, that two-story building on the plaza. The building was alive with uniforms; the arriving military had made it their headquarters. He expected to see Mutt and Jeff there, too, but they were not about. The lieutenant had temporary quarters in a back office, sandwiched between an ancient file cabinet and a stack of overflow records stuffed in gunny sacks leaning against the wall. He did not look happy.

"Lieutenant, I had to come see you. I want to thank you for pulling me out of the cantina. I would never have made it on my own legs. I'm very much in your debt."

"It was nothing, padre, nothing. Well, I see you wear the marks of that explosion. When I saw your face all bloody, I feared the worst. I'm glad it was not too serious. Are you feeling better then?"

"Oh yes, fit as a fiddle, although I'll have a scar on my forehead to remind me never again to go into a bar, even if it is only for a Coca-Cola. That was all I was having there, you know. Even so, I guess it was unseemly of me. I was certainly punished for that sin."

"Others were punished far more for theirs, padre. You are fortunate to have such very small sins and such small punishments."

"Yes, yes, indeed. That was a terrible thing. Now I see the troops here. I suppose they'll find the guerrillas and put an end to the troubles?"

"I hope so. For myself, I am not so optimistic. The soldiers you see are conscripts stationed at the garrison over in San Ramon. They won't find the guerrillas by standing around town. They should be out scouting in the mountains; but no, they're having their beer and their women. Perhaps when the Federal troops come in, something will be done."

"I do hope so, yes, I certainly do. But there are some new police in town, too. They searched my room, threatened me with jail, took all my papers, and then stole seven hundred pesos from me. They accused me of being a foreign spy for the guerrillas."

The lieutenant sighed. "I can do nothing, padre. Those men are from Hermosillo, state police. I am only the local constabulary. I have no power over them. They, in fact, can command me. You have my apologies, padre. What else can I say?"

"Oh, nothing, nothing at all. I understand your situation. It looks to me like they don't appreciate you. That proves they don't know how to go about things. After all, here you are, the acting chief of the local police now, and they do things like that in your own town. I find it shameful that you're not in charge. You strike me, lieutenant, as a true leader. Some day you will be commanding them, I'm sure of that."

"Thank you, padre, I hope you're right. In the meantime, we must all live as best we can."

"Yes, yes, of course. Well, I just wanted to thank you and to say that I'll be leaving very soon—or rather, that I'd like to leave now. But now I can't go. They told me I had to stay here and they took my papers. Lord, what a situation to be in. I'm a peaceful man, I lead a quiet life, and now this, the explosion, the shooting—well, it's all just too much. You can understand that, why I'd want no part of that? Still and all, what am I to do? I know you can't do anything more than you're doing. My goodness, lieutenant, you've already done so much for so many people. You're my idea of what an officer of the law should be—saving lives, being on the scene in an emergency. That's real police work. Don't you agree?"

The lieutenant nodded. "We do what we can, padre."

"Exactly. Well, now I've invited my brother down here for his vacation—I think I told you that, that I'd meet him here and we'd go traveling, perhaps find some antiquities for Mother, if we could; she does love those pre-Columbian pieces. You know, of course, that there are some marvelous finds being made west of here, on the coast. If you could just get to the bottom of this, lieutenant, if you could just find out who these guerrillas are, I mean, I could leave and those soldiers would go and it would be safe and then my brother and I could try to find some art objects for Mother. Not that I care who they are at all. I just want them to go away and leave things in peace. I just don't understand it. It all had to start when they killed that poor man, wouldn't you agree?"

The lieutenant looked confused. "I'm not sure what you mean —what poor man?"

"Oh, your chief, of course. I don't remember his name, although it was quite a striking name, I do recall that. If you could find who murdered him, don't you think the rest would clear itself up?"

"Now that is a very big order. It may seem easy to you, padre —you're not a man of the world—but to a man like me, a policeman, well, I know how difficult these things are. Very difficult."

"Oh, I do understand, but who else is there to do it? Certainly not the soldiers and not those so-called police from the capital. There's only you left, isn't there? I'd be glad to help, if I could. I don't mean I'd do anything dangerous, but I could take notes or do little errands for you, if that would help. After all, I've got time on my hands now. I'm not so foolish as to show any more interest in funerals. Lord knows there have been too many, that would be bad taste. And churches—well, I've measured them and photographed them and have done all my work there—the material I need for that article I'm writing is practically on hand. So I have time, don't I? Aren't there any clues, lieutenant? I mean, surely all of this doesn't happen without lots of people seeing things? For instance, when your chief was killed, didn't anyone see what happened?"

"People are not always cooperative, padre. Sometimes they are afraid to come forward. These are difficult matters. Besides, when senior authorities are investigating, it is not up to junior personnel such as myself to interfere."

"Senior authorities? Who?"

"Well, the Justice Ministry, for example. Or, if state security is involved, the Home Ministry. Or, if it's guerrillas, well, the army."

"Yes, I see, of course. So when your chief was killed, what authorities came in?"

"Well, ordinarily, it would have been the investigators from Hermosillo, which is the state capital, and the Justice Ministry people from Mexico City."

"You say 'ordinarily.' Wasn't it ordinary? I mean, aren't they investigating, then?"

"No, these things are complicated. The Home Ministry took the case. I'm not sure why, but I understand the deputy minister took personal charge of it. They must have believed that some state security matter was at stake."

"But you don't think so?"

"Who am I to say? I'm just a junior officer, after all. But still, I don't understand it. I agree we had these guerrilla attacks several weeks after Chief Flanagan was assassinated, but such things need not be connected. Why should they be? The chief had troubles of his own."

"There was some reason he might have been killed, then?"

"Well, padre, not all men are saints. He had his enemies, more than a few, I think. He was, well, shall I say, a bit free with the girls —young girls, padre—and his amusements were, well, I don't like to speak about it to you, but let us say they were of a special kind."

"Oh my, well, yes, that is distasteful, isn't it? So you think some woman, perhaps, might have killed him?"

"Oh no, that is not so. He was executed in a very professional manner. Very efficient. The type of gun, the time and place. No cartridge was found, you see, which means that someone was being thrifty, probably someone who hand-loaded his own bullets specially for such work. We have such people in Mexico, padre, they are hired assassins. My chief was no fool, you know, he knew where to expect trouble and wouldn't have been so easily surprised, certainly not by a woman. No, this was not a woman's hand."

"Well, certainly the Home Ministry investigators could follow up on that. After all, there can't be that many hired assassins, can there?"

"Who knows? But it is odd, I would have expected to see the investigators."

"You mean you haven't seen anyone from the Home Ministry, they haven't even been on the job?"

"Well, these things take time. They're probably very busy."

"But you mean to tell me that there has been no investigation after all these weeks?"

"Oh no, padre, don't ever say I said anything like that. On the contrary, it has been very diligent, I'm sure, very diligent."

"But there have been no investigators from Hermosillo or Mexico City?"

"Oh no, padre, I'm sure there have been many."

"But you haven't seen them? They haven't talked to you to get your ideas, an important man like yourself?"

"Well, I am only a junior officer in the local constabulary. Why should they talk to me?"

"Why not? Who else could know more than you do about solving local crimes?"

"Well, I think I could have been helpful."

"Of course. I'm sure there's lots you could have told them."

"Yes, for instance, my chief was very knowledgeable, very knowledgeable, you know. Perhaps he knew something that others wanted him not to know."

"I see, yes, I can see how that would happen. It's perfectly natural, isn't it? He would know something about a criminal and someone would kill him to be quiet."

"That's possible, but he was also a man of great discretion, as I am. Discretion is very important, you know, especially in affairs of consequence."

"Yes, I'm sure it is. Discretion is the mark of a mature man, a diplomat, yes, one must know when to be silent. I mean, for example, if my brother and I were to find some antiquities for Mother, well, and if you were to help us get them back to New England for her, we'd all be discreet, wouldn't we? One doesn't want to hurt one's friends or get in trouble, does one? That's foolish. A wise man has to judge for himself whether the law really makes sense or whether it's just a bother. You see what I mean, don't you?"

"Yes, of course."

"So your chief was naturally very discreet. Perhaps someone feared he would stop being discreet."

"Who can say? Such things happen in this world."

"Well, lieutenant, do you have any idea what was so important that someone would kill a police chief to gain silence?"

"My friend—" The face of the lieutenant was grave. "—some things are better not inquired about. If it was such a matter and the chief was killed, well, there are always other bullets in the assassin's gun. You would be wiser not to be too curious, as would I."

"Yes, yes, I see what you mean. You do have a point." York's fingers fluttered nervously. "Well, I'd never thought about it that way, but you are convincing, very convincing—yes, well, yes indeed, my goodness. Why don't we forget the whole thing right now? As far as I'm concerned, neither of us even thought about it, don't you agree?"

"Agreed."

"Well, lieutenant, I won't keep you. Thank you again for being a lifesaver."

York was aware as he walked to his car that he was under surveillance. It had begun when he'd left his hotel. Mutt tagged along after him on the other side of the street. He quickened his pace, not to shake the tail but simply to discomfort him, for Mutt had a paunch and breathed heavily. Turning a corner, York glanced back to see Mutt sweating and puffing, his face glistening even in the cooler evening air, for the sun was dropping now behind the rooftops. York reached his car with Mutt well behind, staggering in an erratic trot. Good enough—that was but the first installment of a long series of repayments.

York got into his car and drove away, looking in the mirror for telltale lights behind him. Soon they were there. Dusk had fallen and a drive around town would be in order. York slid back the radio panel and pressed the contact button for Hickock, who soon replied. Briefly, Barber recounted the events of the day and gave Billie his assessment of Dolores, that the signs pointed to her as uninvolved. He would increase his efforts to use her as an unwitting informant and, if the signs were right, recruit her to work against Guillermo and the foreman. He would not tell her that the final target was her own uncle.

"I'll bet you won't," muttered Billie. "She'd hate your guts."

"As all women may, in time, come to do," replied Barber quietly, "but now is too soon. Besides, I could be wrong, de Lemos and Guillermo could be clean."

"You really believe that?" asked Billie.

"Hell, no. It all fits too neatly—de Lemos owning land in Cuilican where poppies grow, the landing strip, his holdings on the border at Agua Prieta, all of this activity? Hardly coincidental."

"What about Flanagan?"

"No one calls in a professional hit man to cull the innocent. Flanagan must have been blackmailing someone or threatening to join the competition. Who might want him wasted? Well, keep in mind that one of the most important events for us is a nonevent; the

Justice Ministry stayed out, the Home Ministry grabbed for jurisdiction, the Home Ministry has done absolutely nothing, and the deputy home minister just happens to be de Lemos's brother. Master stonemason for a fine stonewall job, and that means that good worthy has to know why Flanagan was killed. So does the good lieutenant or he wouldn't have been so fearful of retaliation, not just for my sake but for his own."

"You think the lieutenant is one of theirs?" queried Billie.

"One never knows for sure, but I'd guess not. He was too far down the line to be cut in on the profits; around here the little guys have to shift for themselves while the ministers, governors, generals, and the local elite all eat the pie. Anyway, Billie, tell headquarters that this is how I read it. It's only a guess but the probabilities are high."

"And Fernandez?" Billie reminded him.

"Ah yes, the big narcotics cheese, the arms heister, the invisible *jefe*. I'm in no position here to pursue that one; the only action I see here is air transshipment; the heroin labs are mostly over on the coast—Sinoloa, Narayit, and Jalisco; saves moving the heavier morphine so far. If Fernandez has a presence it will be near the labs or the border warehouses and not around here. Besides, Father York's inquiring long nose can only go so far; I'll need some help to push the narcotics investigation any further. It's time that the new man was brought down. Tell headquarters to get that 'brother' of mine in pronto. With the lieutenant warmed up I can duke my brother in and he can carry it from there, co-opt the lieutenant, back me up if Guillermo or Teran decides to move on me, all of that."

"I wish I could be there to help," Billie said.

"You're my man just where you are," Barber affirmed. "Besides, there's no emergency, at least not yet. With my cover I'm well but precariously placed. The cover's the thing; if anybody blows that I go down the tubes along with this whole operation."

"Cover or no, you've got a problem with the guerrillas there, dad, and those Hermosillo gumshoes too." Billie's voice held a serious warning.

"Those police clowns." Barber was irritated. "I'm convenient, the only foreigner around, who else can they shake down so easily for so much? But you're right, they'd like to see me in jail, or pushing daisies for that matter; tourists are fair game for those bastards. As for the guerrillas, I really have to keep out of that if I can. You know how sensitive the Mexican government is about unilateral operations; they take a very dim view of Uncle Sam poking about in their political stews."

"So what do I tell headquarters about that?" Billie asked.

"You tell them it's not my job to save the Mexican government from revolution."

If headquarters wanted him to enlarge his mission, someone would have to remind them that one man could hardly work both insurgents and narcotics at the same time, certainly not unilaterally with the one and in liaison with the government in respect to the other. Someone from Justice would surface him—or burn him intentionally—and then the foreign ministry people would erupt. "Why was he here in the first place?" they'd demand. They'd all be at his throat and each other's.

"Tell them I need backup as it is. If they move me officially on the political side it will blow this whole matter, Flanagan, narcotics, airstrip—and me—sky high."

"Okay, boss, your steadfast servant will convey."

"And while you're at it, find out what the air traffic surveillance has yielded, or their checks on Dolores Calles, Guillermo, and Fernandez."

"Okay, boss. Will do."

Barber began to drive his car slowly through Madre Dolorosa toward a fly-trap of a restaurant that lay on the outskirts of the little town. That was his destination, as far as Mutt and Jeff were to know.

"Sounds complicated down there," said Bill, "and rough."

"Worry thee not, everything is under control. You just keep our commo working and pray headquarters gets the new man down here and keeps my Connecticut cover strong."

"Roger. But I'd sure like to do something more than run radios and callous my fingers by keeping them crossed."

"You keep your sweet Picasso self over there, lad. Without you, I'm out of business."

"I'll be good."

"As I knew you would," replied Barber, glad for this one tie to safety, Bill waiting his lonely vigil for his sake. With a good thought for that young friend and partner, Barber closed down radio contact. He was, by then, at the little restaurant. He cleared his throat, summoned his pastoral self, and got out of his car, ignoring the rattling black Ford that had pulled off the road some distance behind him.

Eleven

THE REVEREND YORK CAME downstairs the next morning feeling chipper. He greeted the clerk and lounge lizards cheerily. His head wound felt better; he'd been able to replace the swathing turban bandage with a much smaller patch. He'd obtained the new bandage the night before, after dinner, for when returning home he had seen the pharmacy/mortuary open and stopped in. The proprietor had clucked sympathetically over the wound and dressed it for him with stinging alcohol, merthiolate, and sulfa powder. There was no sepsis and, although the hole was deep, it was also clean and sharp. Healing was well begun. York had complained bitterly to the pharmacist that he was now being kept in Madre Dolorosa against his will, because the state police had taken his papers and money. He would hardly mention that ample funds were secreted in his automobile, along with several sets of papers under several false identities, with disguises to match. Mutt and Jeff might well try to clout the car, but his supplies were sealed behind the equivalent of a strong box. If they worked hard enough—with torches, for example—they might make progress in opening it up, but anyone trying that would be sorry. The compartment had been booby-trapped with explosives and a special gas tank, rigged to explode if anyone tried to break in. A car clouter was expendable. A dirty trick, perhaps, but things were that way; not everything in the business was nice.

As he stepped outside, York saw a group of three soldiers moving slowly down the street, inspecting doorways. One carried a gunny sack over his shoulder. York stood until they were abreast of him. They pushed their way against and past him with intentional rudeness and asked the desk clerk if he had found any yellow pamphlets at the hotel door. The clerk had. Turn them over, the soldiers said, and the old man reached underneath the desk to come up with three yellow leaflets. The soldiers asked if there were more, the old man said no, the soldiers strolled out.

York went to the desk.

"What's that all about?"

"Nothing."

"I saw and heard. What was going on?"

"Oh, some little thing—people distributed leaflets during the night."

"Oh. What were they about?"

"Nothing." The old man spoke reluctantly.

"Well, I appreciate your position. I mean, something is obviously trouble and I don't want any part of trouble, either, especially after those policemen were in here yesterday. I'm sure that upset you, too, but don't worry, I have friends and they won't let those ruffians get away with anything; no, sir, they won't, I can tell you that. Something is going on around here, but nobody tells me anything and now they won't even let me leave here, because those thugs took my papers and ordered me to stay. So you can appreciate, what with my nearly being killed by that bomb—why, the least I expect is for someone to tell me what it's all about. You understand that, don't you?"

The old man looked at him with tired eyes and said slowly, "Yes."

York knew it well, that tired sing-song *"si."* He would learn nothing from the clerk.

York stepped outside. A short walk and a sharp eye revealed what the clerk feared to discuss and the soldiers had been too slothful to find: a derelict copy of the yellow pamphlet. It was jammed under the door of a tiny bakery which for some reason had not opened.

The pamphlet was entitled "The Plan of Madre Dolorosa." Well, that at least was traditional. Since the revolution of 1910, rebels had felt it obligatory to proclaim a doctrine. The Plan was simple. And it offered one certainty: power would be exchanged. The People would triumph.

Had there ever been sincere or unexploited revolutions? Lexington and Bunker Hill, Mao, Castro? Perhaps, but the Plan of Madre Dolorosa did not portend one of them. Why not? Hard to say. The manifesto was written in good, clear Spanish, the ideological syntax was predictably dull, the call to action stood out boldface, as it should. But there was also the alien smell of hack Politburo Marx. Someone, it seemed, had studied abroad and brought back more than vodka in his baggage.

York thought, To hell with headquarters. Reversing his earlier decision, he decided to go at least one step further on his own. Ten A.M., the garden refreshingly green in contrast to the desolate streets outside, and no José in sight. York knocked on the door of the little cottage and heard footsteps coming to answer. There was Father Teran, looking a wreck: bloodshot eyes, tension, a sag in the shoulders, doubt, anger, and a tic, a twitching of tiny muscles making his nostrils flare like those of a horse badly spooked, ready to rear or bolt. Camillo Teran looked at his visitor, hardly recognizing him.

"Good day, Brother Camillo. I came to thank you in person for your help and hospitality."

"Oh? Oh, yes—not necessary, not at all. I was glad, glad to do it, glad to do something for someone after that horror." He stood at the door, not inviting York in.

"Well, you did a great deal of good that day, you should know that."

"Good and evil, brother, they intermix, no one without the other. Quite different from what I want to believe. I prefer perfectibility, but some days I doubt."

"Oh, I am sorry. I can see you're not in the best of spirits. Is there anything I can do?"

"You?" Teran stared at him uncomprehending. "How could you do anything?"

"Oh, I don't know—just the urge to help, I suppose. You look so—well—so wretched."

"I do?" Teran looked down at his cassock, inspected his hands. "Yes."

"Well, it's not easy; no, this is a difficult time."

"I can imagine. Shall we walk about the garden a bit? Maybe a little air will help."

"The garden?" Teran looked at it as though for the first time. "Well, all right—for a minute, perhaps. I have things to do."

Leaving the door ajar behind him, Teran moved slowly into the garden, York at his side.

"It was a bomb, you know," said York.

"Yes, I know it was a bomb."

"In case you didn't know about it, I thought you'd be interested in what it's about. I found this this morning." York pulled the yellow manifesto from his pocket and handed it to Teran.

Teran's hand was shaking as he took the paper from York. He held it without reading it, his head nodding slowly.

"You've seen it, then?"

"Yes, I am familiar with it."

"I must say, as I read parts of it I thought of you. I mean, some of the language is not too far from what you were saying to me the other night. Please understand, I recognize a big difference between what you believe in as an idealist and what these terrorists write, especially when they say—here, may I borrow it back?" York took the paper and scanned it to find the lines he wanted. " 'The armed struggle begins now. The heroes of the revolution, Marx and Lenin, leading the world's people, have shown the way. Let your gun be your voice. Your voices will bury the enemy.' " York stopped reading to turn to his companion. "That's what they're about, Brother Camillo—killing."

"It's sometimes necessary to kill. Before peace, war; before justice, retribution; before perfectibility, failings; before tranquillity, struggle."

"But you can't possibly agree with this paper," York protested. "Not after what you saw happen the other day! Those poor innocent people all murdered by these fellows. Why, they don't care who they kill. You saw that yourself."

Teran stared at the ground. When he spoke, his voice quivered. "Believe me, brother, it is difficult for me to accept. I really do believe that the only way to achieve the revolution is through armed struggle, but I hate blood. It was easier for me before the bombing, before I saw the blood. You're right that those fools killed the innocent. They were supposed to bomb the police, not the people."

"Lord knows I'm no student of revolutions, Brother Camillo, although I've been doing as I promised you the other evening and have been giving it some thought. There is injustice and there are oppressors and they don't give up their power, that's true. But as I read this—" York shook the yellow paper. "—well, that Marx and Lenin, it has a Soviet flavor I don't like. Everyone knows the Soviets are tyrants. You're an educated man, you know that."

Teran looked at York. "You're right, this manifesto has a flaw." He paused, searching for words, speaking very carefully. "It's not exactly what I would write. So it has a foreign flavor to it, does it? If you can see that, the people can see that, too. I could have told them. Damn the imperialists. The revolution must begin pure. The Plan of Madre Dolorosa does not need Moscow—never needed Moscow, must disavow Moscow, and cannot be dictated to by Moscow. You're right. You come in your naïveté and tell me what I knew, had forgotten, and then had to learn again when the blood of innocents was on my hands. And that's my struggle now, to expiate my sins. May God forgive me. You say I'm not looking well? You're right, I'm not well. But I've resolved that I myself must purify the revolution, brother. My conscience and our destiny demand it." Teran's face was grim. His shoulders had straightened up, the twitch had stopped, but the eyes were gleaming. "I have already taken steps."

"Oh. I see." Perplexity and diffidence were on York's face. "Well, I'm sure you'll do what you can. But guerrillas—well, they have guns and I'm not sure they'd welcome a priest, if you don't mind my saying so. How could you hope to change them? Those men are ruthless. I'd be more comfortable if you'd not take this too far. You could get hurt."

For the first time since York had known him, Teran smiled.

"This is my affair," answered Teran, "and these are my people. I shall do what is necessary. And now, I'm sorry, but if you will excuse me, I have much to do." He shook York's hand absent-mindedly and returned to his cottage.

York passed from the garden outside and then to the street and into the cathedral. An aimless walk, thoughtful and curious and, once inside, more curious. He passed near the statue of Mary, looking at the ex-voto offerings hung about her feet. The tin locket was there. So, too, were several women, talking softly nearby. York palmed the heart, opened it, and was pleased to feel paper inside. He glanced down, read it, and closed the locket so that it hung no more disturbed than before. Then slowly moving along the wall, he reached the door and went out into the bright light of the Sonora sun, now climbing toward noon.

Where would it be, that "urgent meeting roses" written in that bold hand? Who was Che? For the message had said, "Che must attend." Who were the roses for that matter—or where were they? He'd seen no rose blooming in the whole of Madre Dolorosa. Could it be a wordplay on *rojo,* red, as in politically red, possibly the code name for the terrorists? It would bear thinking about; York wanted no more misguided searches. Neither his body nor his pride could take that again. Nor did he feel comfortable going any further without headquarters guidance. He'd pushed as far as he could with Teran, and still he was unsure. Teran had been upset, had agreed that the manifesto smelled of Moscow, and had been as fervently xenophobic on that count as he had been about the United States. As for his allusions to his sins, one couldn't tell what he meant. Teran was certainly no vocal Soviet supporter, but it didn't rule out his being a Soviet dispatch, a "mole," as the British called them, some Soviet case officer sent here long ago to live a life of deep cover, only to emerge like a butterfly frozen for years in its chrysalis when the Great Moment arrived. That was always possible, but statistically improbable. One saved such gems for capital cities and, when one was lucky, for top secret research or intelligence—the general staff or high public office. Second-order countries, client states, didn't rate that kind of preparation when one could buy locals cheaply or send in professionals on short order. The deep-cover boys were meant for the major opposition.

In any event, this business was too big for York on his own. He could not work on it without a headquarters say-so, if for no other reason than that he respected his own incompetence. Whatever the petty stupidities of Parks and committees, when there was action needed abroad the Bureau was usually competent. To keep things that way, they needed his compliance, and he needed their support. He would have to get in touch immediately. Mutt and Jeff had not shown up that morning, nor had anyone followed him. He hoped they'd keep off his back until he'd talked to Billie again.

He parked the car in front of the repair shop entrance behind the one and only filling station. It was closed, of course, because it was siesta. The onlooker would think the American needed gas or some repair and was waiting for the shop to open. The station had a high roof over its gasoline barrels and the Olds air conditioning worked nicely. He'd brought a newspaper—the Hermosillo one took only two days to arrive—and put his face in it much as a nearsighted reader might. No one could see his lips move but his eyes could look over the top of the paper: he'd be warned if anyone came in sight.

Bill came in immediately. A good man. Barber told him of the yellow pamphlet, his meeting with Teran, the smell of Moscow in the manifesto.

"Well?" he then queried Bill. "What's headquarters got for us."

"Negative."

"What do you mean?"

"Under advisement is the term they use. Too important to move quickly on, that sort of thing; but, pending a final decision, they agree you keep out of the guerrilla mess and stick with l'affair Flanagan."

"And the new man?"

"Under advisement. They don't want to arouse suspicion."

"Grand, just grand; oh, Parks is a great helper, indeed."

"Don't blame him; it's the committee," Billie remonstrated.

"Whenever you don't want to have anything happen, form a committee. When you want to ding something and don't want to take the blame for it, say the committee did it, even if you don't have a committee. Those guys drive me nuts."

"I guess I'll learn," said Billie. "But I do have something for you, in spite of them. I've been on the air to the branch in Mexico City and they've given me some preliminary stuff. Dolores is who and what she told you she is. Guillermo may be a nasty—did time in the States for narcotics conspiracy but then got his Bachelor's in business administration. Then back home to Mexico, never to show on a police blotter again. But some of the boys there remember he was in close to a hit man on the border. Guillermo—his last name is Perez—was mentioned in a debriefing last year. It was nothing much—he was in the background—but he has kept bad company. You like that?"

"I like that fine. The puzzle begins to place itself."

"I've got more from the branch. The deputy home minister is not de Lemos's brother, but his brother-in-law, through de Lemos's sister's marriage."

"You mean he's Dolores's father? A Calles?" Barber was stunned.

"Nope. He'd be Dolores's uncle by marriage—to de Lemos's other sister. His name is Hernandez. Hernandez has no daughter, just a high-living playboy son. The two men are close, though, de Lemos and Deputy Minister Hernandez. They've no idea how the Flanagan action moved from Justice to Home Ministries, but they say that sort of thing is easy. Unless Justice had a strong interest, they'd double on the case—let Home have it while they investigated

as well. In theory, that is. But, in fact, if an investigator thought
Home was working on it, he'd go do something else. Some guy way
down the ladder in Justice would never know that Home had
queered the action. Does that make sense to you?"

"Eminently. Why work when you can goof off?"

"It figures. And branch doesn't know beans about your guerrillas, but they say there is a big stir in the Home Ministry now.
Hernandez is all upset about that arms theft in Arizona, put ten men
on it, wants branch to pull all the stops working on it, too; says he
doesn't want those arms to get to Mexico. They say he's madder
than hell."

"I'm not sure that fits," said Barber.

"No?"

"If de Lemos and Hernandez are running narcotics, they'd
have no reason to be stealing arms. The deputy home minister isn't
going to do it, since it's his job to prevent just that. He's got as many
armories as he likes under his own supervision. Now, as I recall, one
of Fernandez's men was killed in that armory heist—not that anyone
knows who Fernandez is, but disregarding that—some cheap hood
in the narcotics business left his dead body with the U.S. Army in
Fort Huachuca. So, if that's the case, then someone tied to the
narcotics business is also ripping off munitions in a big way. Now
we don't know they went into Mexico, but it looked that way. Fact
is, there's no sense in their going anywhere else. Weapons are big
in Mexico and anybody can make money who wants to sell them. So
far so good. Hernandez in his official role has every reason to get
excited. The wrong people get those guns and they blow him out
of office, or, alternatively, the buyers waste a few prominent types
with smuggled guns and he gets his ass fired. But his asking our
branch to get involved is crazy if he, or he and de Lemos, have any
tie-up of any kind with Fernandez. Hernandez can control an investigation down here and if it gets too close to home he closes it up;
but once he's got us in on it he can't do that. And while we're not
always that good, we're not always that bad, either. He knows that.
If we get on it on both sides of the border, there's a good chance
we'll catch the baddies and there's nothing Hernandez could do to
put the old kwyeetus on it."

"Okay, I follow so far."

"Therefore, my good Watson, Hernandez has nothing to do

with Fernandez and is out to get Fernandez."

"Okay, I buy. What's wrong with that?"

"Only that, if he'd really wanted to get Fernandez, he could have done it long ago. There's no big operation going on down there that Home Ministry can't scuttle if it puts its mind to it. Those boys have guns and do travel. And they don't bother with arrest and trial if they're serious. No way. Just dead bodies blazing that old trail home."

"But what if Fernandez was no trouble till now? He could be a noncompetitor, couldn't he? Probably paying off Hernandez for protection, like any other businessman who needs a crooked patron. Then Fernandez gets too big for his britches and tries diversifying into arms. That's a real no-no and Hernandez has got to put him out of play; otherwise, as you say, it's his own ass."

"True, but if we were to bust Fernandez and Fernandez is as big as we think he is—remember we were all chasing him last year for all kinds of forty-five-caliber high jinks—and he's been buying Hernandez, then he can do Hernandez lots of damage. A big mouth singing sweetly to us is no music to Hernandez's ears if Hernandez is dirty. Because then we go to his boss and Hernandez's sweet butt hangs high. He might as well have stood in bed, because his boss will personally blow him away."

"Maybe Hernandez knows his boys will find Fernandez while ours won't. Corpses don't talk real well."

"Possibly, but why, then, is he so upset? Why is he telling branch all about it, and why is bother pushing branch to work so hard? He could get the same Brownie points for playing law and order through a routine paperwork request for cooperation, whereas the way branch tells it is that he really wants them to go out and play tough cop, right?"

"That's the way it sounds. So where are we?"

"Puzzled, just plain puzzled."

"I've got it!" Bill came through, speaking rapidly.

"Yeah?"

"Fernandez knows where the arms are going. It's a revolution that he knows is going to blow them all away. He's a real patriot at heart and is willing to sacrifice himself to save Mexico."

"Oh, come now."

"I was only kidding." Billie went on. "Well, how about this, instead, as a real smoothie? Hernandez is in on the clandestine arms business, after all, as long as they sell only to assured risks—you know, old ladies and orphanages. This caper was Fernandez's idea and Hernandez approved, but then someone hijacked their load. You told me yourself that they do that all the time down here. Imagine the poor innocent being the victim of some vile crook. Of course, he'd be all twittery about it and want justice done. Since Fernandez doesn't have the stuff any more, nobody has to worry about our catching the wrong guy. Whoever catches them, Hernandez comes out a public hero and privately has his revenge. Why not?"

"Watson, you interest me. Substitute an army procurement officer for your orphanage and it might go. Say if Hernandez had a deal to supply some Mexican division with stuff he had stolen from us—using Fernandez to make the sting—and somebody did hijack it, you're right, he'd be very upset, wroth you might say. It's far-fetched as hell but not totally impossible."

"Well, boss, do I get an A for trying?"

"An A even if you're wrong. Like Christmas, it's the thought that counts."

"Gee, thanks a lot."

"Think nothing of it. For a price, I'll note your diligence in your annual personnel evaluation. Of course, if you turn out right, as your superior I'll have to claim credit for the lucid exposition myself —privilege of rank and all that."

"Don't kid about stuff like that, boss. I've seen it happen."

"Sorry, I was carried away. Radio waves go to my head like nitrous oxide—I get quite giddy, in fact."

"Well, anyway, you keep your humor in the damnedest situations."

"I try. If I were a realist I'd probably shoot myself," said Barber. "As it is, there are enough other people around here who may want to do that, so I don't want to spoil their fun."

"Boss, you're kidding, but I'm worried about that. I'll tell you something. You're not going to get that new case officer 'brother' of yours from New Jersey. One of the guys in branch hinted to me on the QT. I cheated, talked on the public phone rather than the radio scrambler. I guarantee it had nothing to do with the operation or anything that could blow security. He actually wants to buy some of my paintings—they're getting better each day—he's my contact there and the call went in just like it's supposed to; you know, I call in from a phone booth for someone who doesn't exist and he calls back to the booth for someone who doesn't exist and I answer and all that; but, anyway, we were in training together and so I called because I was just getting damned lonesome. I'm not supposed to, I know, but I just did. I wasn't going to tell you, but really, with you sitting over there like a wooden duck on a pond, well, I worry and I can't not tell you. That's what you really will have to put in on my evaluation, and I know it, that I broke security making telephone contact when it wasn't an emergency. Anyway, we just talked— about girls we knew and stuff. But before he hung up, he made one of those veiled remarks I know he wanted me to know so I could tell you. Headquarters has been back and forth to branch all the time on this operation, trying to 'collate' everything, as they say. So their cables tell branch things they don't tell us. My friend said to me, 'By the way, you remember your friend from New Jersey?' I knew what he meant right away, because neither of us knows anybody from there, so I said, 'Yeah,' and he said, 'Well, he was supposed to go to that big party they're having, but his mother won't let him. Can you imagine, a guy his age and his mother being like that? The party won't be the same without him, but there it is, she's into astrology and thinks he shouldn't travel.' That's what he said, boss, and if you make out of it what I do, Parks is going to let this operation go hang."

Barber was quiet for some moments before he replied. "Look, my friend, you're over your adolescence, so you can do without those heartwarming telephone chats from now on. I'm glad you told me, though, because when I see you I'm going to curse you so blue you'll think you're a hydrangea. And that's it. I'll put it in your record if you do it again, but not this time. And thanks, thanks very much for telling me. From what you say, it sounds like we're screwed. Our friend Parks has got something stuck in his craw, he had it there before I left. Well, there's nothing to be done but scream for the record. You do that, will you, on each cable you send out of there? If it gets too frustrating or too rough, I'll just have to pull out, that's all. They can all go to blazes."

"I wish you would pull out, but I don't believe you would. You've never pulled out from anywhere. You've reason enough right now to get out, with all that stuff coming down around your ears. You've been hurt, you've been threatened, you're in a minia- ture war, and you've got no partner on the scene. Well, the Bureau wouldn't want to put anyone in that position. It's untenable."

"Groat would."

"Yeah, I guess he just did. So, boss, how about it? Why don't you just develop a splitting headache and leave the party? Oh, yes, that reminds me of something on the cable from headquarters I didn't bother you with."

"Christ, you're supposed to give me everything they send."

"Yeah, I know, but this was different."

"Oh?"

"Yeah, they said they were sorry you got hurt but since you are obviously still ambulatory they will not allow you any claim for compensatory sick leave when you get home. I didn't think you'd like it, boss—insult to injury. That's why I didn't tell you."

"Yeah, I see. That's okay. You were right, I didn't need to hear it."

Barber, as he closed down radio contact, pressed his lips to- gether in anger and despair. Insult added to injury; Bill was right. Out of sight, out of luck, those bastards at their desks were going to grind him down. If he got shot, or pulled out without orders, Parks would drink Champagne all the way to his next promotion. And Groat would break his jaw smiling, at least until he started to cry because he didn't have anybody left to do the crazy work. Parks and Groat deserved each other, but Barber wouldn't serve as match- maker for that little marriage. No, come hell or high water, he wouldn't leave Madre Dolorosa.

Twelve

THIS TIME, WHEN HIS GRIMY CAR pulled up in the early evening to the gate of the walled de Lemos compound, the old man opened the heavy gates without a word. Through the open door of the gatehouse York could see another *vaquero* sitting idly with a rifle cocked in his arms, two pistols on his belt, and a knife sheath strapped to his lower left arm. The big fellow, with a belly to match, wore a black sombrero, an immense moustache, an embroidered shirt, and bright silver spurs on sharp-toed, worked leather boots. Whether or not he had a horse was uncertain; what was sure was that he'd seen a Mexican western movie and was playing it to the hilt. Pity the guerrillas should they take on this extravaganza of a warrior.

York had called Dolores in advance this time. She appeared, smiling broadly. Yesterday afternoon's picnic had been a pleasant one for them both. He was pleased to see her, and especially pleased that she had invited him to dinner.

"Anything new?" he asked as they sat down in the reception room over a glass of sherry that a maid had brought in.

"Why, yes, my uncle returned, just an hour or so ago; his plane came into Hermosillo early this morning and his chauffeur made excellent time getting home. I'd hoped he'd join us for dinner, but he said he had too much to do. He sends his apologies to you. He does that sometimes, you know, works in his office and has sandwiches brought in. It may seem uncivilized, but it is quite customary, even in Mexico City, for men with heavy responsibilities; a light snack at seven P.M. with coffee and then they go out to dinner at ten or eleven. That's what he'll probably do tonight, have some great private feast while here I am feeling sorry for him, overworked and starved."

"Oh, my, there's no need to apologize for him," York interjected. "I admire hard work, I can even rouse myself to it from time to time. Besides, I came here to see you and that's not denied me. It was very kind of you to invite me to dinner."

"It won't be anything fancy. I told the cook to give you some local treats—I'm testing you to see if you can adapt. Goat wrapped in plantain leaves cooked in a charcoal pit, fried cactus worms, a few other goodies like that. There—does that frighten you away?"

"Oh, no, not at all. I like Mexican cooking. Besides, I like goat; I had it in Greece a great deal."

"Did you live there?"

"From time to time when I was younger. I had an interest in classics and dabbled in archaeology. I was a complete dilettante, you understand, with a bit of the pirate thrown in. I always kept hoping I'd stumble over some treasure that Schliemann had missed; some great gold rhyton from Ithaca, for example. If you want to know my true nature, that's it—a grave robber looking for treasure."

"So all that talk in town about your morbid interest in funerals is really a disguise for your grave robbing, is that it? You see, I knew there was something mysterious about you; haven't I said that all along?"

York was surprised at how quickly their conversation had turned to his dual role; unconsciously, he was revealing his cover to her and she, always perceptive, had picked up on it. He ignored her last question, replying, "I'd rather call it a sublimation. Can you imagine the trouble I'd be in if they really suspected me of grave robbing around here?"

"No. I don't suppose human nature has changed much."

"I suppose not. But I am a perfectionist, I think civilization is a progressive process. Every few hundred years our veneer of virtue gets glued a bit more firmly to our savage hides, discounting, of course, side effects like atom bombs and chemical warfare."

"That's a high discount rate," she said solemnly.

"True, but when you speak of it that way you talk like a businessman or a banker, rather than like a musician."

"Perhaps I do have a bit of business on my mind." Her face became serious.

"Oh? Nothing wrong, I hope?"

"I hope not." She looked at him, her eyes appraising his.

"Has it something to do with me?"

"It seems to."

"Well, I can't imagine what it is. Tell me."

"Reverend York, you told me . . ."

He interrupted her. "Please, it's Al. Yesterday we agreed to be on a first-name basis; there's no need to be so formal, is there?"

"I'm not sure," she replied. "Perhaps there is. If I can't trust you, then we shall be very formal."

"Trust? My goodness, what have I done?"

"When you came here the first day to visit my uncle, you didn't tell me what you talked about. It wasn't my business then and it isn't now. Later, you gave me to understand that you didn't know him. Oh, I know you said you came here looking for Father Teran and I believed you—why shouldn't I have? When you're with me, I get the impression that you don't want me to know what's going on between you and my uncle. I mean, you never make any reference to your business with him. That's all right. People have the right to confidential business and my uncle is a very private person; he rarely talks to anyone about his business, except for an odd remark now and then, like the drought affecting the cattle or when they had to close the mine because of high operating costs, that sort of thing. But, you see, it's not that I want to pry, or that I feel shut out, but because I wonder why you pretend there's nothing between you and my uncle when there obviously is. And, if that's so, then I can't help wondering if you might have lied to me from the first. I know I'm bringing up something that's very delicate with you; you've always ignored it when I've brought it up. It makes me feel as though I'm crazy. Yet I have to trust my own judgment, my intuition; it's the only anchor I've got for judging the world and so far it's served me very well—except now, with you. I respect you, you can see that for yourself, and—well, I'll be very improper for a well-bred Mexican woman and tell you that I like you—oh, I don't mean any confession of romance, but there is something about you that I find very appealing, even if you do cover it up with chitchat. I suppose that's just the manner of a New England clergyman. After all, I've never met one before. Anyway, I've just ignored the intuition I had after that ugly scene between us when you were hurt. I know you may not call it that, but that's what it was. But now, well, when I heard my uncle talking on the phone to Guillermo this afternoon just after he came home, I realized I had been right, there was something going on, with you involved, that you were keeping from me. Please understand, I wasn't eavesdropping. I was just walking down the hall and the two doors were ajar; Uncle never does that, but he came home in a great hurry and seemed upset and so I guess he just rushed into his office and forgot about the doors. Well, I heard him talking, only a few words, and he mentioned you and some business."

York's eyes were wide. "He did?"

"Yes, he did." She spoke firmly. "And this time I won't have you evading me."

"I'm not evading, cross my heart and hope to die. I don't know what business your uncle was talking about. I've only met him that once. We talked no business and I'm not a businessman, as you can plainly see. The only thing we mentioned that had to do with me were my studies and my minor role as an editor of my religious studies journal. So there has to be some misunderstanding. What was it he said, exactly?"

"Well . . ." Dolores's forehead furrowed. "I know he said your name—just 'York,' no title, and I heard the word 'matter'; I guess I assumed he'd said 'business matter,' because then there was something about your 'contract.' I distinctly remember hearing that word, but I don't remember exactly how it went, I think he said something more, I really don't know; something like 'letting it' or 'processing it' comes to mind, but I'm not sure. And that's all. I didn't stop to listen, that would have been very wrong of me. I actually hurried to pass by faster so that I wouldn't eavesdrop. Now I'm absolutely sure of what I've told you. Do you deny now that you have some arrangement under way with him? Please don't lie to me, Al—please. I don't want to know what it is, but if you lie to me, in the face of this, I'll simply have to ask you to leave now and never to see me again. I'd be sorry to have to do that, but I can't be with you if you're lying to me, no matter whether or not you are going to do business with my uncle."

York's face was very serious. He was silent for some moments before he spoke. "I'm going to speak very carefully to you, Dolores. I'm going to choose every word carefully, so that now or later there'll be no misunderstanding about what I said or meant. I want you to listen carefully. Afterward, you can throw me out or not, as you please. What I say will be the literal truth." York paused, his eyes not on her face but on the floor as he concentrated. "What I just told you is true. I have never met your uncle before and we have no commercial dealings together. I'm not a businessman, never have been. I have no interest in trade or moneymaking for itself. I know very little about your uncle, in fact nothing more than what you've told me or I've seen for myself, although he appears to be an interesting man and I would like to know more about him. I do know a little bit more about Guillermo, because after we talked, I asked an acquaintance about him. You remember you said you didn't like him? I didn't, either. So I asked and a distant acquaintance in Mexico City provided some information—not much, just a little, and on the face of it, it would appear that Guillermo deserves some disliking. But I don't know him, either, except for that one meeting here, and he's certainly not a person with whom I would ever want to have business dealings. Now the phone call is very important to me, because it suggests that your uncle and Guillermo intend to have some dealings with me. I don't know exactly what it is that they have in mind, but I have an idea. And now, before I say anything more, I must extract a promise from you. It's that you'll say absolutely nothing about what I'm going to say next. If you can't give me that promise, then you don't have to throw me out—I'll have to leave on my own. It's very serious. I know it's improper for me to ask you not to talk to your own family about something that concerns them—in this instance, to promise me you won't tell your uncle what you've told me or what I've said or am going to say. You love him, you have an obligation of trust to him. I'm a stranger whom you can't trust and have no obligation to. It is quite wrong of me to make this request. But it's come to this, Dolores, and I'm sorry. You'll have to make the choice. Were I you, I think I'd choose not to make that promise and not to violate my family obligations. And you are not choosing for or against me. If I leave now it doesn't mean I'm walking out of your life or that I won't see you again. It simply means that, at this time, there are things I can't say to you that I otherwise would. To make a promise to me is to choose to be in some small way disloyal to your uncle, to gain nothing for yourself, except a little worry, and to gain nothing from me, because I can promise you nothing. There. I think I've put it as fairly as I can."

Dolores, beautiful, calm, serious, clasped her hands on her lap and appraised York carefully. She lifted her head to gaze at the ceiling, then examined a ring on her little finger, turning it carefully. Finally she spoke.

"I believe you. In fact, it's the first time I've really felt comfortable with you. Do you know, your voice dropped a key lower while you were talking and your intonation level changed? That's quite remarkable. Somehow, the new voice fits you better."

York smiled but said nothing. Dolores went on, "If you have anything unkind to say about my uncle, I don't want to hear it. I won't promise anything that implies I'd listen to any kind of criticism or insult. If you have that kind of thing to say, then, as you say, you'll have to leave and we'll both be sorry. Even if you do leave, though, I promise I won't tell my uncle what we've said so far. I say that because you and I also have the right to our private conversation. Our talks, yours and mine, are my life, not his. I can feel that something very important to you hinges on what we've already said, even though you are right in saying that, without my promise, you can't reasonably ask me not to tell him about it. I don't trust you —not just because you are a stranger and not family, not just because we've only recently met, not just because you come from a different culture, but because my intuition tells me that you've not been frank with me—not that you are under any obligation to be, unless we were to be friends. But I do believe you now. I will, therefore, give you my promise, providing you don't step beyond the bounds I've set. I'll have no scurrilous remarks, even from a minister—no conspiracies, no attempts to convert me to your faith, should that be on your mind, no petty gossip. In a word, nothing reproachable."

York paused. "All right," he said, and then, speaking slowly and with concentration, "The promise that you've made, not to talk about what we've said so far, is very kind. You're right, it has become important to me, but only because of what I guess the telephone conversation to be about. I won't tell you what that guess is. I think it involves your uncle's plans and Guillermo's but in no way mine. It's nothing they would talk to me about. On that basis alone I would have to conclude that I cannot trust them. Naturally, if I do see your uncle here, I'll be courteous, but because what you've told me comes as something of a nasty surprise, you'll forgive me if I'm cautious, too. There—I've said all I can and I've told you no lies, and I've tried not to put you in a bad spot. What do you think?"

"I think you would make a good diplomat. I don't mean that disparagingly, either. All right, I'll settle for what you've said, but I won't stop wondering what's going on."

"Curiosity is the spark plug of the mind," York said lightly.

"Good. I'll try to keep my mind lively. And whatever it is, I can see that it bothers you and I am sorry. But don't worry about my uncle. He may be a bit harsh and suspicious, but he's a very fine man. For all we know, he could be worried about me, not wanting me to become involved with a Yankee devil. Can you imagine what he'd think of that? He's probably just checking up on me. I hope you don't have any dark secrets."

"Me, too. Still, I'm flattered that you even think we might become 'involved,' as you say. For an old bachelor that's exciting talk. Who knows if I'm up to it?"

Dolores blushed and stared at the floor. "Good heavens, don't take me seriously. I'm terribly embarrassed. I was just teasing, trying to think of what Uncle was up to. It could be that he's very protective of me."

"I'm glad he is. You deserve the utmost cherishing, dear Dolores. In my own poor way, I, too, want to see you protected."

"What, from you?" She laughed.

York smiled. "Yes, perhaps just that, from me."

He excused himself immediately after dinner, about ten P.M., and drove speedily back to town. There were three things on his mind, two that he wanted to think about and one he couldn't help. Dolores was the latter. The meeting of, at, by, or with Che and the roses was one. Admittedly it was out of his bailiwick, to be pursued no further, but his interest was aroused. The other was the contract that de Lemos had out on him, no doubt with one of Guillermo's little friends up on the border—perhaps even the same one who'd executed Flanagan. The question was, how had de Lemos identified him? Had York blown his own cover somehow? Or was de Lemos simply taking no chances on any strangers, letting his intuition be his guide? It was an intuitive family, if Dolores was any example. Bless Dolores. She might not have saved his life but she certainly had given him a fighting chance, insofar as any sitting duck on a strange pond has a chance when the hunters know him but he doesn't recognize them.

Circumstantial, the prosecutors would say, not an iota of hard evidence, and they'd be right. He had no airplane, no heroin, no marked bills, no witnesses, no transactions, no tapes, no movies, not a thing for a prosecutor to put on the table in front of the judge. Not that it mattered, because as long as de Lemos and his brother-in-law were running things, there would be no judge and no trial, just lots of lost evidence, disappearing witnesses, and *mañana* promises, the tomorrow that never came. This case required that one start at the top. York had done so almost by accident, and now the top was starting on him. They were likely to have more success than he would, the odds being what they were. There were times when it was good to be a childless widower; one could mourn oneself in advance without worrying about the mourners one left behind. But he could sleep easily tonight and start mourning tomorrow, for it would take Guillermo and his new hired hand at least a day to get down here from the border. Be grateful for small things. When York got to the hotel, his room was undisturbed, Mutt and Jeff were nowhere in sight, the desk clerk was awake, and his room key was not lost. Door bolted and blocked, his wig off, his wound healing and dressed, Barber fell into a sound sleep.

When he came downstairs the next morning, it was late, about ten A.M. There'd been no reason to hurry, and when life might be very short the little luxuries were sweet. The desk clerk stopped him. That old man always looked exhausted, and no wonder: he was on duty twenty-four hours a day, sleeping in a little cot in a cubbyhole just off the reception area.

"Mr. York. I have a message for you."

"Thank you, may I have it?" York put his hand on the counter top.

"From Lieutenant Rosales."

"Rosales?" York was sleepy, he couldn't place the name.

"Our police lieutenant, sir, the acting chief. You know him, I'm sure."

"Oh, yes, of course." And it was "of course"; more than that, perhaps, it was—aha—*rosales,* meaning "rose bushes." Were his the roses the drop message mentioned? Could it be that friendly young man so willing to help a silly, smug pastor smuggle antiquities to his poor old mother up in the U.S. of A.? There must be one Rosales among every twenty Mexicans, like the Jacksons or Robertses back home; but why hadn't York at least considered it before? The answer was partly because he wasn't supposed to be thinking about it; headquarters had agreed with him that it was not his business. Partly, it was because he had only been introduced by name once to the lieutenant and that in passing. And partly it was because he must be just plain dumb. Puzzles could seem so simple once they're solved, like two o'clock and number two on the station house. Was it an odd coincidence that Rosales had missed the bombing, turning up quite safely, while all but one of his brother officers spiraled up to heaven? His chief, Flanagan, had been the first to go. That left the young lieutenant quite by himself, in charge of almost nothing. There would at least be no internal opposition. If it were so, Rosales would simply have to wait for Mutt and Jeff to go back to Hermosillo, as they must, and law and order in town were his. Well, not quite. There was the occupying garrison; there would be disciplined Federal troops in town by now; and as long as the guerrillas were about, these would stay, and the chance for Home and Justice investigations, as well. There would be no free hand for rose bushes, and anyone would have known that in advance. He could be a sympathizer, a partisan, an insurgent leader, for that matter, but he wouldn't control the police for the foreseeable future. Later, come the triumph of the revolution, he might, but most cops were squarer than that. It was an improbable group from which to recruit terrorists—which made it all the more attractive if it could be done. York brooded. No, this was no key to the puzzle, this rose bush, just another possibility to be considered. In the meantime, what was the clerk saying?

"Lieutenant Rosales would be pleased if you would come by his office this morning, sir, with his compliments."

"Oh, yes, of course, glad to. I'm on my way. And thank you." Pressing a ten-peso note in the old man's accustomed hands, York walked quickly out the hotel door.

"Thank you for coming, padre. Here, let me have someone bring you coffee."

They were seated in the tiny, makeshift office, the lieutenant compacted between his desk, the wall, and the gunny-sack records system and York squeezed on the folding chair in front of the desk, next to a locked case with four shiny rifles in it, the remaining armory of the local police. The lieutenant yelled a coffee order through the door to a passing charwoman, who said nothing, turned not, and continued her slow pace down the hall.

"Coffee will be here soon," said Rosales. York, thinking of the charwoman, could imagine how soon. "I am sorry it's not more comfortable here. My apologies."

"Oh, think nothing of it, nothing at all. You have to make do with what you've got," York reassured him.

"Exactly, exactly my point." The lieutenant seemed pleased. York had obviously struck on the theme for the morning. "Yes, when one has so little one must make do, wouldn't you agree?"

York nodded agreement without any notion of what was going on in the lieutenant's head.

"I am, let me put it bluntly, padre, in something of a predicament. I'm alone here now for the moment. Your two friends from Hermosillo have gone back for instructions. I regret that they've taken your papers with them; they told me that much, but tomorrow perhaps the papers will be sent back. Yes, that is possible. Soon, a new investigator is supposed to arrive, a senior man from the Judicial Police, a Federal officer. And, as you may have noted this morning, new troops are here—trained men, for a change. I think there will now be some progress on that unfortunate business of the terrorists."

"Well, that's good. I certainly hope they find them in a hurry. Then maybe I can get my papers back and leave here. I don't like living on a keg of dynamite."

"Exactly, padre. That is exactly what you are doing. It is very dangerous. I'm glad you understand. I think you know that I want to help you all I can."

"Yes, of course, I appreciate that. You've already been a great help, practically saving my life and being so kind."

"It is nothing, nothing at all. I do my duty. But, as you can see, I am nothing, just a junior officer, and I am a poor man. My poor wife and children, they care nothing for my job. What can I do for them on my salary? Did you know that they pay us so badly that it is only the equivalent of one hundred dollars a month? Can you imagine? And my expenses, always expenses—sometimes I wonder what I shall ever do."

"Terrible, just terrible. A man of your worth, too. They shouldn't allow it."

"Exactly. I couldn't agree more."

York reached in his trousers for his wallet, "You know, when those two from Hermosillo took my money, they didn't get all of it. Thank goodness for that. I had some in my mattress and when they searched they missed that. It's an old-fashioned place to hide money, but it worked. I'd feel very much obliged to you, lieutenant, if you would allow me to buy a gift for your children, out of gratitude to you for saving my life. It would bring our families closer together, don't you think?"

"Padre, I couldn't take your money, not even as a gift for my children, not unless I'd done something special for you, something out of the line of duty, you might say." Rosales paused dramatically. "Yet, if I think about it, I might be able to do something like that. My children would be so happy. My wife would be so happy. I can see their smiles now. Let us see, how could I deserve your generosity? Yes, I think there is one thing. You must be very discreet about it, padre, very discreet. It could cost me my job if anyone knew I told you."

"My goodness, I wouldn't want that to happen. No, perhaps you'd better not tell me. I would never tell, but I still wouldn't want it on my conscience." York began to return the wallet to his pocket.

"Oh, no, padre, think nothing of it. For a friend, one makes sacrifices; for a friend, one trusts; one must expect to be trusted in turn. That is the world of honorable men, padre. I'm sure you, a religious man, would be discreet. We've discussed that before."

"So we have," said York, his wallet remaining in midstroke, halfway between his pocket and the lieutenant's desk. Lieutenant Rosales went on rapidly, eyeing the wallet.

"So we understand one another. You know I'm ashamed to admit it, but we Mexicans are not so trusting, especially these days. There are many who are jealous of you Yankees. Even when a kind man like yourself comes to visit us, there are some who have only bad thoughts, for they hate foreigners, no matter if they are priests or little children or old ladies. Maybe it is worse if the foreigner is a Protestant priest. You can appreciate that. If they are foreigners, they hate them and speak bad things. If others believe those bad things, the foreigners feel bad. Worse, even, they can get in trouble for things they've never done. Do you understand me, padre?"

"I think so, yes. People are easily swayed and sometimes aren't kind."

"Exactly. This morning, padre, we have perfect understanding, you and I. It is just one of those things, a gift. Now, in regard to this business, as you know, everyone is very upset about the guerrillas. No wonder—dead soldiers, dead policemen, dead citizens, buildings blown up, everyone afraid to go outside or to stay inside. Then those pamphlets calling for revolution. It's very upsetting."

"Yes, I'm as upset as anyone."

"I'm sure you are. The people here are ignorant, simple people. They do not think clearly. Their troubles give them bad thoughts, just like too heavy a load day after day makes sores on a burro's back and eventually breaks his bones. Now, to the point, padre. Someone has spoken ill of you. That's why those Hermosillo policemen were so rude. They'd heard the rumor and it was their duty to check up. If they'd believed it, they would have arrested you. But they weren't so bad as you might think, because they didn't arrest you, after all. They knew the rumor was just an evil thought. After all, padre, we both agree that it is utterly ridiculous for anyone to think that you are a Russian spy who has brought a battalion of Russian soldiers here to make war on Mexico. Have you ever heard of anything so stupid?" The lieutenant smiled broadly and began to laugh. "Isn't that the most stupid thing you ever heard?"

York, not smiling, nodded. "Yes, indeed, that is probably the most stupid thing I've ever heard."

"Of course. Don't worry, no intelligent person believes it. The Hermosillo police don't believe it. The soldiers don't believe it. The Federal officers won't believe it. The mayor doesn't believe it. I, I would never believe it, not in a thousand years. But I thought I should tell you, out of the line of duty, you understand."

"Of course, and I am grateful. Although, dear me, it is frightening, isn't it?" York counted bills out of his wallet and handed the lieutenant two hundred pesos, a fairly large *mordita*, large enough to express thanks, small enough to deny the charge. The lieutenant took the money, smiling.

"You are very kind, padre, very generous. My children will be so happy. I will do everything I can, you understand, to stop this stupid rumor."

"I'll certainly appreciate that, lieutenant. It's bad enough practically being a prisoner here because of those orders not to leave and now, with this awful gossip—well, I'm quite upset."

"Of course, of course. But we'll do our best to protect you."

"Protect? What do you mean?" There was the show of fear as well as distaste on York's face.

"Yes, it's unfortunate, but, you know, when the guerrillas made so much trouble, it was natural for the government to do all it could. Naturally, they posted a reward for the guerrillas, dead or alive. Sometimes, though, that is not such a good idea, because the people around here are violent. Why, do you know that in this little town we had over seventy killings last year? A lot of bad blood, too much drinking—you know how it is. Sometimes, when there is a reward out for someone, people use that as an excuse to settle old scores. They shoot some fellow they don't like and say it was because he was a guerrilla. If they can make the judge believe that in court, then they get a reward, too. If they can't—well, then, we send them to jail instead. Now, with everyone so upset and so many carrying guns again—you and I know that the president has outlawed carrying guns, but in a little town like this so far out of the way—well, laws take a while before they sink in, anyway, and people have itchy trigger fingers. Some will make some foolish mistakes."

"Oh, goodness, that is dreadful."

"Oh, yes, terrible. We don't even have a jail to put them in now if they do get out of line, so we shall just have to kill some of them if they misbehave too badly. But that is how it is. I'm sure you understand."

"Well, I'll try. But the police killing people instead of putting them in jail—it does seem, well, a bit excessive."

"Exactly. Yet what can we do? So we shall kill them. Take heart, padre, if anyone kills you, thinking you are the guerrilla leader, we shall kill him immediately and he will not get the big reward."

"The big reward?" York's voice quavered.

"Oh, yes. For the leader of the guerrillas, five thousand pesos. That's more than any honest man in this entire town earns in a month. You can see how interested they are in that money."

"I can see."

"Dead is so much easier than alive. There are no arguments and there are no risks and, although I hate to say it, some of the people around here enjoy killing. Life here is so simple, I suppose, there's not much to do—it's a kind of entertainment."

York sighed deeply. "It's not a very happy picture, is it? I mean, not for them and not for me. What can I do?"

"Pray, padre, and trust in the police. We shall do all we can."

"There's nothing else I can do but wait here until my papers come back? Just wait here until someone shoots me?"

"Oh, no, don't be so upset. It's not absolutely certain that you will be shot, not at all. They might miss."

"That's reassuring."

"You see—" The big smile was fixed on the lieutenant's face. "—I knew I could make you feel better."

"Thank you, lieutenant, thank you very much." York, his hand appearing to shake, reached in his wallet and gave the lieutenant a fifty-peso note.

"Oh, you are generous, padre. I promise you that my men will do all we can. So will the soldiers. You can count on us."

"I hope so."

"Just rest easy. By the way, padre, do you know how to shoot a gun?" As he asked, the lieutenant reached in his desk drawer.

"No, I shot a twenty-two pistol when I was a boy, but never since. It's not exactly the sort of thing I'd be interested in."

The lieutenant had pulled out a .32 snub-nosed Belgian Saturday night special from his drawer and was filling the chamber with cartridges. "This came from someone who was killed last week. The other man shot first. But we let him keep his gun, because he will be out of jail next week. It was self-defense. But the dead man doesn't need this. I think you should keep it, padre, just for safety's sake."

"No, thank you, lieutenant, absolutely not." York's voice was horrified and adamant.

"As you wish, but it would be wiser to keep it." Slowly the lieutenant returned the gun to the drawer. "There is one other possibility . . ."

"Yes?"

"I think it's a good idea. You should employ a bodyguard."

"Me with a bodyguard?" York was incredulous. "A minister with a bodyguard?"

"Why not? The good God guards your soul and someone walks beside you, guarding your body. That way, your soul goes to God without being full of bullet holes. I think God is offended by souls that come to him in such poor condition."

"Good heavens, lieutenant, are you serious?"

"Very serious, padre. There is something you must understand. I have told you the truth today. I did not have to do that. True, I have accepted a gift from you for my children, but in return for that, I have told you shameful things about my countrymen and this town. The money you gave me is not worth the trouble I would have if anyone knew about this talk we've had. You Yankees think we are all lazy, backward people here who only want to be bribed, that we have no human feeling for strangers. That is not so, padre. I do not want you to be hurt. There would be another investigation, it would be bad for our reputation. But that is not the real reason I have told you this painful truth. I do have a human feeling for you, even though you are a gringo and a Protestant and not so much of a man as I would choose as a friend. I tell you this from my heart, padre, being too frank with you. If you leave here without taking my advice, I don't want you thinking, as you die, that no one cared about you. I do care, with or without your money. That is the truth." The lieutenant was very serious.

"I believe you, lieutenant, and I thank you. Where do I find a bodyguard?"

"Good. You have sense. I will look around. There is no local man I would want for you. They are bad shots. Sometimes they have to shoot five times before they kill one another. That's not sportsmanlike. I will ask around to see if there is some professional we can find nearby—perhaps some former policeman, perhaps someone who is not. Perhaps God will send someone along, who knows? I will let you know when I find someone. In the meantime, good luck, and do not go outside too much." The lieutenant got up from his chair and offered his hand. His grip was firm, manly, and he held it longer than necessary, as though saying good-bye.

York walked slowly toward the town square. He didn't bother to look sideways, let alone over his shoulder. In this business, he told himself, you're supposed to be paranoid as a professional trait, but as with paranoids one's suspicions were often fantasies. When faced with the facts of a tight spot, it was a waste of energy to play hide-and-seek. One tried to lay things out, figure the odds, and stick to a heads-up plan. Win, lose, or draw, there was no more than that to be done. He was in a ridiculous situation. The Bureau was at its best in running organized operations in the field, teams of men backing each other up, specialists at every turn, no man with his flanks exposed. Operations meant that people knew what they were doing before they did it, anticipated what the enemy would do and moved in unison, whatever the task. And here was he, in a situation that was the antithesis of every rule in the book. It had all developed more quickly than anyone had expected. Headquarters had dragged its feet and they had all failed to comprehend the evolving problem, with its two unrelated but merging facets, drugs and insurgents. That the narcotics smuggling case was essentially solved was irrelevant. Until they got Hernandez, nothing would happen, and Hernandez was to be had in Mexico City, not here—and probably not there, either. The Flanagan killing had become moot; it didn't matter whether he'd been killed on de Lemos's orders or by the guerrillas, whether or not Rosales was with the latter, with the former, or just watching. That, too, was just a technicality. If York lived a day or two longer, he'd know that, too, for what it was worth. One or the other had taken care of Flanagan; the best bet was still probably de Lemos. Rosales didn't talk like an insurgent and neither did he act like one. The rose bush was not a rose. York's job had just begun, now that he had the picture, Hernandez-de Lemos-Guillermo and the insurgents. As for the insurgents, they probably had some bright-eyed, Muscovite-trained, dogmatic youngster and sadly, Brother Camillo was probably involved, in some stupid, idealistic way.

It was time to report the good news. But Bill wasn't there. Twenty button presses and twenty silences. The monitor light told York that the sending unit worked. That was all it could tell him, unless the monitor light was on the blink, too. The last straw. Bill's receiver was out or Bill was out buying groceries; hope for the latter. Read the paper in the shade on the veranda of the hotel. Chances are no drunken crazy will shoot you there. They'll wait till dark, till they're good and drunk and the witnesses will all swear to shadows and Russian voices. There. Thirty minutes. Try again, Monitor light on. Contact button pressed. Do it once a minute for ten minutes. Done. No answer. Try again later; nothing to do now, anyway. Paper read, pull out a book. *Middlemarch*, George Eliot. Eight hundred intensive pages; one hundred and fifty read so far—read the remainder on the way to salvation, Camillo-style. Read. And every hour the car, pretending it won't start. Don't screw up the battery by turning it over too long with the ignition turned off. The radio battery is different, you can't drain that. What does it matter? Five P.M. and no Billie. Seven P.M. and a tasty enchilada next door to the hotel, with beer. The Mexicans make excellent beer, enjoy it. Eight P.M.

and no Bill. Darkness soon and the crazies out, guns in their belt and drunk, looking for that Russian gringo to kill. What irony, to be shot as a Soviet spy. And any time now, Guillermo and friend would arrive, enough time for them to take the ten A.M. plane to Hermosillo and the long drive over here. Unless, of course, they flew back here in their own plane. Why not? Why book passage—there are witnesses on public carriers—when Air Narcotics has empty space up front on the homecoming run? No one to see Guillermo with his unusual friend. That means the heavy won't arrive until the wee hours. That nonsched airline prefers the darkness. Would Guillermo bring the new hand to the hacienda next morning? Would he be introduced to Dolores as a new accountant? Would her intuition be good enough to tell her he had only one account to settle? Would she ever let herself come to a conclusion she'd forbidden York from suggesting to her—crime in the bosom of the family, her beloved uncle a skunk in the world outside, even if a good-natured shepherd at home? It would be tough on Dolores, either way.

Barber had only three advantages. One was his 357 magnum in its shoulder holster and a small armory under the car's back seat. Second, no one expected that silly prating lamb, York, to be hunting them. And third, he knew more about the guerrillas than anyone else. The army was garrisoning the town but scouring the hills, because every Mexican revolution of the past had used the cover of country, at least until they'd captured the towns. Only Barber knew that this one was different. There would be no artful drop in the cathedral if the operation weren't housed in town. He wouldn't have to travel far, no farther than the church: a long trip in the dark all by himself, with a town full of too many crazies, looking to scalp his face to hang on a ring from their nose.

Thirteen

CONTRARY TO POLITICIANS' instincts, there were times when it was better to be nobody than somebody, thought York, with a hearty "amen." He had finally managed to rent a shed to garage his car, one on a back alley a few blocks from his hotel and accessible from at least seven unfrequented passageways and several streets. York had entered the old stable and, again in his car, found once more that Bill didn't reply to his radio call. With a grunt rather than a flourish, he played Houdini, making the Reverend York disappear. The kit, sheltered by the thick steel plate underneath and behind the rear window, helped. A swarthy Mexican with dirty black hair emerged, wearing dirty cotton peasant clothes, an ugly unbandaged but healing wound in his forehead, partly hidden by a forelock. The man padded via the alleyways toward the square, made a beeline for the cathedral, and soon slipped into its canyon of shadows. He waited for a few minutes, leaning against the side wall until his eyes were accustomed to the darkness. It was nine P.M. and the church seemed empty. "Seemed" wasn't good enough. The unsavory-looking fellow, a half-empty bottle of rum protruding out of the side pocket of a light cotton jacket, made a circuit of the place. There was no one inside. He checked the ex-voto drop at the statue's feet and found it empty, as well. Then he made for the trapdoor over the crypt. The heavy table stood partly over it, blocking it from any view but not, in fact, preventing the door from being raised. Saturnino —the worn papers in his bedraggled wallet showed that was his name—was careful not to jostle his rum bottle. He smelled powerfully of the stuff, for his clothes had been soaked in it and his mouth washed in it. It was nothing an ordinary man dare drink. He put his ear to the trapdoor and listened. He held his position for fifteen minutes, hearing nothing. He pulled his 357 magnum from its holster under his armpit, took a pen-size flashlight from his rear pocket, and felt for the cooperative tile he expected to find centered at one end of the trapdoor or the other. It was there. When he pushed it, it slid outward, revealing an old iron ring. He pulled the ring slowly upward and lifted the door.

It was a large room, no doubt once a crypt but later enlarged, for two walls were of old stones carefully laid and two of more casual masonry. A steep stairway led down to the dirt floor, about twelve feet below. High in the wall on the side paralleling the church foundations was a crude ventilator pipe with a hand-operated, rusty ventilating fan. These living quarters might very well date back to Obregón's time. The smell of cigarettes, stale beer, and sweat wafted up to Saturnino as he began quietly to descend the stairway. There were three cots in the room. One was made up very neatly with hospital corners, its blanket as taut as a trampoline. The man who slept there either had had a top sergeant for a mother or was military. The other two beds were lumpily unmade. About twenty empty beer bottles, a half-filled bottle of mescal, a half-filled bottle of Mexican vodka, six unopened bottles of Moctezuma beer, and a large crock of water stood on the floor in one corner. On two beds lay worn popular magazines in Spanish. That was all, except for an aging footlocker against the wall. Saturnino opened it. In it were two clean sets of undershorts, socks, and t-shirts, all one size, an unopened pack of chewing gum (made in Mexico), a hand mirror and a toilet kit with a U.S. brand of toothpaste, razor, blades, and shaving lotion, plus a comb, locally manufactured aspirin, iodine-base water-purifying tablets, U.S.-made hair tint, to "take away the gray," antacid pills, and an unmarked vial with pills that appeared to be antidiarrhea lomotil.

Saturnino scratched his dirty head but the itch didn't go away: it was beneath the wig. His guess was that two of the men who stayed here were Mexicans and the third had come in from the United States. None of them lived here, but for one it was more often home than for the others. There would be another hideout elsewhere that would be better stocked for living. The foreigner's stomach—was he an American?—wasn't enjoying its stay in Mexico, for the lomotil and antacid bottles were nearly empty. Saturnino emptied the two bottles further, leaving only a few pills in each. The chemical toilet in one corner had recently been emptied, probably a very good thing for all concerned.

Saturnino finished his search quickly, climbed the stairs, cautiously opened the door to the fortunately still dark and silent church, and hurried out of the transept into the nave. There, built out from a massive column, standing about fifteen feet from the floor, was the pulpit, like a crow's nest on a mast. It had a good view of the entrance, the trapdoor transept, and, behind it but invisible in the dark, the small door that led into the garden where stood Teran's cottage. Saturnino climbed the circular staircase. Once settled in his nest, the carved wood sides of which were about four feet high, he found he had room to sit on the floor, knees up close to his chest, unseeing and unseen. In this great vault of echoes, anyone coming in would be heard. He'd have time to catnap, setting his ears as an alarm clock to arouse him at the first sound.

It was no squeak that awakened him, but one great clang. His watch, luminous, told him it was three A.M. Stealthily, he hauled himself upward until his eyes could peer over the pulpit sides. The church was dark, but he could hear shuffling and, reverberating now in his awakening brain, the echo of the angry whispers that had followed the clang. Someone had dropped something, someone else had cursed. The footpads came not from the street entrance but from the squeaking door that opened to the garden. Saturnino recalled that the back of that garden faced an alley and there had been a gate in its wall; an unobtrusive route, to be sure, providing either that Brother Camillo was not walking in his garden or, if he was, that he would not be perturbed by the visitors. It was likely the latter. Who else would have known and allowed the use of the crypt?

Kerbumph. Someone had slammed into something in the transept—probably the wooden table.

"Idiot," whispered an angry voice, to which there came no reply. Suddenly and surprisingly, a flashlight turned on, its owner standing just beneath Saturnino's pulpit. The light swept the church at eye level and blinked off.

"See? No one. Why are you so nervous?" The second whisper was quarrelsome, coming from near the trapdoor.

"You noisy fool. All we need is one mistake and everything is over. Haven't I told you to be more careful?" There was something odd about that loud whisper, its enunciation almost too perfect.

"The great Che is afraid, eh? A little bump and he gets upset like an old woman." The other one was talking louder now. The whining tone showed it was bravado.

"You disgust me," the other was still whispering. "If you ever drink again on a mission, I'll kill you. Do you understand that? I'll kill you." The tone was level. Steel Whisper seemed to mean what he said.

"That's no way to talk to a comrade. Who do you think you are, anyway? This is my territory, comrade, and don't you forget it."

"Your territory? Your stupidity, you mean! If I hadn't been there tonight you'd have had us all dead, opening fire before the signal. I seem to be fighting with children, not soldiers, for comrades." As Steel Whisper spoke, he was moving silently, slowly, around the back of the church toward the transept's rear side instead of directly toward the crypt. Saturnino wondered why.

"You suck your own cock, you do, Spaniard. What are you complaining about? Fifteen of us tonight ambushed a regiment and not one soldier got away. Think how that will read when their colonel makes his report tomorrow."

"A company is not a regiment, you foul-mouthed idiot. Fifty men surprised in the dark while sleeping in an arroyo. It would have been two hundred if that stupid scout hadn't missed the others up the canyon two miles. From now on it will be harder; their sentries won't be asleep. You are a rabble, not a military force."

"We're guerrillas, you Spaniard with your balls stuffed in your mouth, not tin soldiers, and I'm the general here, not you. You stick to your advising, like the orders say. What would Comrade Teran do if he knew you spend half the night at Anita's cathouse when we're in town? Wouldn't that upset his delicate little system? A political commissar, my ass; the old man is half crazy. He'd like to be general instead of me, I bet. Thinks he's big, he does, cursing me out for that police station bombing just because we had a little too much bang."

"A political officer is to be spoken of with respect, especially that one. He's organized this entire district so fools like you can come in safely from Guerrero with your unwashed, undisciplined bandits. In the last year he's recruited more supporters than you've put together in your area in five years. And that bungling at the police station—you told me you were an explosives and demolitions expert, but you're an amateur. Lucky you didn't blow yourself up. Comrade Teran is right. We want to win these people over, not kill them all off. You don't like the priest because he was right to criticize you. That's the political officer's job." Saturnino knew now why

Steel Whisper was moving so slowly, at the same time projecting his voice almost as a ventriloquist from the nave, trying to conceal his location in the apse. He had flashed his light under cover of an alcove for only a second, looking at his own leg, and Saturnino, from his vantage point, had seen the blood oozing onto the trousers of that leg—that and the automatic with the silencer on it in his hand.

Suddenly the gun sounded. *Phhhtt.* Steel Whisper shone his light on the dead man. Saturnino could see that the latter had been large, stout, and dressed in dirty peasant clothes. Nothing of Steel Whisper could be seen. For some minutes Che pulled at the body, dragging it to the little door that opened on the garden. He gasped from time to time; it was probably not the weight but the pain from his wound that made it such a slow business. He propped the door open. Saturnino crept down from his perch, made his way out the church front door, took a long detour around the block to the back alley behind the church garden, and, finding a rubbish heap—that no difficulty in Madre Dolorosa—climbed up carefully, for the pile was unstable, to look over the wall. He did so, far from the garden gate, snug between a tree and a dilapidated shack jutting into the alley, so that he was invisible from the alley.

A burial team was at work; in the light of the half moon, Brother Camillo and Steel Whisper, joined now by a third, Silent Shovel, who said nothing. With the scrape of shovels and the thud of earth, Saturnino could not hear what they said, for they were at least sixty feet away and whispering. It was a shallow grave and the soil not too hard, thanks to José's watering and gardening; within an hour they had dug and dumped the body and covered it. Faced with a pile of excess dirt, Teran made his way to the tool shed built out from the back wall near where Saturnino hid. He got out a rake and returned, handing it to Silent Shovel, who spread the dirt over the cultivated area, raking it so that it would blend unnoticeably with the topsoil. The work done, the three stood there whispering: the same voices that had awakened the Reverend York that night while he lay abed in the little cottage—the same less one, the late, departed. It took no effort now to reconstruct that conversation; the Spaniard and his now-dead companion must have been furious at Brother Camillo for taking in a Yankee, giving him hospitality and a sick bed no more than fifty feet from the side door leading to their secret hideaway. Lucky for York he'd not been strong enough to be curious, for had he gone outside to check those voices, those voices would have checkmated him. There was plenty of room in the garden for more graves.

Well, here in front of him was the leadership of the insurgency. One dead import from Guerrero; one angry, dogmatic, rebellious, sincere, idealistic, good-natured, bad-natured, fanatical priest, who would find that the political demons of Mexico could not be exorcised with a censor, incantations, or guerrillas in the hills. Who Che was, Saturnino did not know. Well traveled, tough, controlled, competent, careful, ruthless, and superior—an elitist of some sort. And foreign; why not Spanish? Che would be the one with the U.S.-made toothpaste, the cologne, the lomotil, and the hospital corners on his bed. Silent Shovel was a question mark. He'd said nothing as long as Saturnino had been watching them in the garden.

The three were hurrying now toward the tool shed, a corrugated, tin-roofed adobe hut near Saturnino. They were carrying two shovels, a pick, and a rake. There was faint light in the eastern sky and cocks were beginning to crow; Saturnino's watch said four forty-five A.M.

Che turned to Silent Shovel. "Manuel."

Manuel looked up, saying nothing. He was about thirty, thin-nosed and thick-lipped, pock-scarred, a gold tooth in front, armed with a U.S. Army .45 at his waist and now, slung over his back from where it had been standing against the building wall while he dug —Saturnino had not seen it behind the bushes—an ungleaming M16, with a new U.S. Army nightscope, all rubbed dark for night fighting. Good weapons. Saturnino wondered where they'd come from.

Che said, "I think we ought to change camps tomorrow night; the cave is fine, but it's too long a march from there to our next action." He checked his watch. "There's no point in your staying here now. You go back and see to it that the men get a good sleep today, then polish up on handling the mortars and grenade launchers. About ten tonight, I want you to move out here, southwest to this valley, here." Che pointed directions on a map he held in front of him. "That'll put you in position about three hours' quick march south of town. There's an abandoned gold mine there which the scouts reconnoitered and where we can hole up for as long as we need. They report a private airstrip nearby with signs of use, but the

old mine shafts and buildings are extensive: some of the shaft entrances are a good half mile from the airstrip, so we'll have no
trouble staying under cover. Besides, some day we may want that
airstrip for ourselves. Here, I've marked it all on this map. You'll
have to move most of the night to get there, but it's worth it—a good
location, easily defended, a long way from where the Federal troops
are likely to look and within striking distance when we're ready to
hit Madre Dolorosa. The strike force from Durango will be joining
up with us by the end of the week. On the way in, they'll detour to
cut the road between here and San Ramon. The bridges will go out
easily and then the troops will be sitting ducks. There are twelve
hundred and eighty of them, a regiment. You know I've arranged
with Anita that the brothels will give the soldiers half price on the
women and liquor—cheaper if need be. I've paid her well for that.
Within four days the Federal troops will be no better than that
conscript ragtag bunch who first came in. She and the other madam,
Carmen, will keep us well supplied with tactical intelligence; her
girls know what they're doing and, for what we're paying them,
they'll do anything. The girls are accommodating. There's one captain who's already moved in at Carmen's, leaves all the staff papers
in his girlfriend's dresser drawers. The captain is accommodating,
too. We know their strength, their equipment, their orders, even
where the colonel thinks we ought to hide. So far, so good. Now,
when the Durango group takes San Ramon apart, wearing their new
Federal uniforms so that the townsfolk know whom to blame, it will
get interesting. I expect we can recruit easily after that. The
Durango unit will make it as convincing as possible, better than
Goya's drawings of the war in Spain. When they hit this town from
the west in four days, wearing the same uniforms—well, I think the
garrison here is going to be in for a surprise. After that, the local
people will understand why they should join the revolution. We
have money, which will be appealing, and we have plenty of munitions—right, Manuel?"

Manuel nodded, smiling.

"That was a job well done, Manuel, getting those guns and
without losing a man," said Che. Manuel nodded and smiled again.
"About our plans," Che went on. "As soon as the locals experience
a little rapine and pillage from those men of ours coming in from
Durango, and after we've caught the army here in a pincers, then
the town will be ours. By then, most of the people will join forces

with us. Those that don't, well, we'll see about them—right, Manuel?"

Again the smiling nod from Manuel.

Teran had been silent during the discussion, staring gloomily at the ground. Che jostled him in a friendly way, putting his arm around the older man's shoulder and hugging him. "Hey, Camillo, what's the matter? I'd expect our political officer to be rubbing his hands with glee. First the Plan of Madre Dolorosa published and now success in battle. When this town and San Ramon fall, Sonora and Durango and Guerrero will catch fire, I guarantee it. Our people there are ready to light the match to this Mexican dynamite as soon as we advance. Chihuahua will follow. Just like Pancho Villa, eh, Camillo? Why, we'll even lob a few reminders into El Paso, just for the sake of the old days. Just for the fun of it. Watch those gringos sweat as they see their investments going up in smoke."

Teran shook his head dolefully. "I'm not pleased with it, Che, not at all."

"Oh, come on, it's your revolution, you know. You've been spearheading all these years and, now it's come to pass, you're sad. I know—you're tired and the blood upsets you."

"Unnecessary bloodletting upsets me, Che. It's not killing I mind. I revel in it when the police and the soldiers get theirs, those stinking pariahs. But it distresses me that you want to terrorize San Ramon and my own Madre Dolorosa. We're fooling the people, Che, making them think it's the Federal troops attacking them, when in fact it's the People's Brigade from Durango."

"Oh, I know, Camillo, you're still an innocent. But the people require an incident to arouse them. Marxist thought comes later. History starts with matches—you light them and then there is a fire. We control that fire and it becomes a revolution. We control the revolution and then we have socialism. Then we control the socialism to educate the people and finally one arrives at the rule of the workers and the peasants. Only when that is achieved can we say our work is done. History takes time, Camillo, you know that. Read your Lenin, you'll see."

"You're tricking the people, Che, and you're tricking yourself."

"No, Camillo, I'm not." Che still had his burly arms around the thin, taut figure of the priest, hugging his shoulders as he talked to him.

Teran argued with him.

"Militarily, even, it won't work. How do you expect fifteen or twenty guerrillas, no matter how well equipped, plus maybe fifty from Durango, to beat twelve hundred Federal soldiers? Every night won't be like tonight, when they were sleeping out in the country. They'll have sentries, they'll fortify the town; who knows what they'll do? You can't turn so soon to conventional warfare, any more than you can make sense by quoting Lenin. You read your Mao, Che, and learn from him about the shallow floodwaters that slowly cover the countryside. That flood is the people, Che. We've got to win them over, not terrorize them, and they'll rise and overthrow the oppressors. What we can do is to bite at the army's heels in the meantime, making it run, giving the people the first taste of victory."

"Come, come, my old friend, don't be so modest. I didn't come here to be beaten by a moth-eaten Mexican colonel with twelve hundred ragamuffins who do their drill in whorehouses. You must have more confidence in me. Haven't we done all right so far?"

"Brilliantly, I'll admit. You brought down those American weapons. You've taken big bites out of the police and soldiers. You're a superb tactician. I grant you that. But don't be a megalomaniac, Che, and don't push either me or my people too far. It's no better to be tricked and beaten by our own red advisers than it is by tyrants in Mexico City and Washington. Don't betray the revolution, Che."

From the darkness where he hid, in the gray dawn's light, Saturnino could see Teran's nose twitching violently. His voice, nevertheless, remained calm, like a man in a quiet discussion of the merits of one brand of cigars over another.

"Camillo, I'm no adventurer and you should know it. I'm a trained man. And no Spaniard, either, in spite of what some people think. I'm from Guatemala, as I told you when you asked, but my heart is Mexican, just as my mother was Mexican. I'd die for either one. I'll tell you something. I wasn't going to, but I don't want you worrying. The truth is Manuel and I have a little surprise for the army here. Sigfredo is getting the canisters ready now."

"What surprise?"

"A bad smell for them, Camillo, a very bad smell."

"What do you mean?"

"A special something Manuel and Sigfredo brought down with them when they came from the border."

"I don't understand. What is it?"

"Gas, my friend. A little gas to quiet the soldiers. Twelve hundred, twelve thousand—it doesn't matter. Wherever they are, they won't forget our little 'hello.' "

"But gas," protested Camillo. "That's inhuman and it'll kill the people in the town, too. My God, you can't do that. It's monstrous."

"Calm yourself, dear one, calm yourself. It's only a little pinch for the nervous system, like combining too much tequila, too many peppers, and a touch of the ameba. People get sick, very sick and weak, very weak, and then they fall down. In a few hours they get up again, but then it's all over. We kill the officers and give the soldiers a chance to join us. Simple, eh?"

"You're sure, Che? Sure it's not deadly?"

"Little brother—dear, comradely brother—would I lie to you about something as important as that? We have a revolution to make. Could I start with you on such bad faith as a big lie? It makes no sense, does it? Isn't it better for us to recruit those poor peasant boys who hate the army and the government as much as you do? Isn't that what Lenin did when he won over the sailors in the Kronstadt fleet?"

Except for the rat, Saturnino would have taken the next moment to creep off the rubbish heap, slink down the alley, and think about how to send some kind of a torpedo amidships the little red party. Instead, the rat took his moment first. Its dirty yellow incisors sank deeply into Saturnino's ankle, just above the leather sandal-strap. Saturnino didn't yell out in pain, as was his first impulse; instead, he bit his lip—but he did reflexively kick out. As he kicked, the lopsided mound on which he stood gave way and Saturnino, off balance, began to fall. He tried to right himself, but the rubbish heap was sliding now, a small avalanche of the broken, stinking midden of unclean and impoverished mankind. Irrevocably, he fell with it and, though he kept his silence, there was the jangle of the broken glass, the clatter of pieces of metal, and the thud of his own body into the garbage. It was half soft and at first he couldn't find a purchase to push against. Lying on his stomach he started to roll over, only to feel the shock of a heavily booted foot thud into his belly. Again reflexively, retching in pain, he vomited. Flat on his back in the alley, heaving, he looked up. The muzzle of an automatic rifle was burrowing into his throbbing guts, burrowing hard.

"Who are you?" Che asked menacingly.

Manuel's rifle seemed to push against his backbone through his stomach. Fighting nausea and breathlessness to speak, he could only say, taking care to slur his speech as drunkenly as possible, "Saturnino, sir."

"And what are you doing here, little Saturnino?"

"Where?"

"Here in the garbage."

Saturnino looked around in dazed, drunken confusion. "What garbage?"

"You pig," said Che, angrily. Manuel's rifle came out of Saturnino's stomach and hovered over his face. Saturnino felt wetness on his lips and, tasting it, realized it was his own blood. He must have opened his head wound in the slide. "Tell me," Che repeated, "why are you here?"

"Looking for food, sir." Saturnino's hand crept protectively to the tattered right-hand coat pocket in which sat his half bottle of rum. Caressing it, showing how glad he was that it wasn't broken, he said nothing. The others' eyes followed his hand to the bottle. Manuel reached down, pulled it out, opened the cork, smelled it, and raised his hand to dash the bottle to the ground.

"Quiet, Manuel," Che commanded him. "It's all right now. We want no attention."

Manuel lowered his hand slowly and tossed the bottle into the rubbish heap.

Saturnino grimaced and, rolling over, reached longingly for the bottle, just beyond his reach. He began to whimper.

Manuel drew his foot back to kick the whining body as it lay, rum-soaked, garbage-bedecked, bloody, and vomit-covered. Che put his hand against the other's chest. "No, we haven't time for sport, Manuel. It's too light. We don't know what this animal has heard and now that he's seen us—or we've seen him—it doesn't matter anyway. We'll kill him as soon as we can. But not now, it's getting light. Someone might come along any minute. We'll have to wait until tonight. Damn. What stupid luck. Where can we put him, Camillo?"

Teran, his face blanched and his hands shaking, said quietly, "In the tool shed. Drag him there. You can tie him up and I'll lock it. You can decide later what to do with him."

"I've decided already. We'll kill him. Then we can worry about where to dump his maggoty corpse. Let's get on with it."

Che picked up one foot and Manuel the other; hurrying together, they sledded the body over the garbage and the dirt of the
alley, through the gate, and toward the tiny tool shed. Saturnino, his
head knocking against the ground and his back torn by rocks, could
only note one glad thing over his weakness and pain. They had not
yet opened his buttoned jacket to find the 357 magnum neatly
holstered under his armpit.

"Hurry." Teran's voice was behind them as Saturnino slid over
the mercifully smooth grass of the garden. "I heard José's gate
opening down the alley. He'll be here any minute. You can't take
any more time. I'll tie him up and lock the tool shed door, while you
get into the church, Che. Manuel, you run for the front gate. You've
both got to be out of sight by the time José gets here. Hurry!"

Saturnino's body was dumped head over heels in the shed.
Manuel waited only a moment, saying to Teran, "I'll quiet him for
you so you can tie him well." That was the last Saturnino heard as
the barrel of the gun slammed against the side of his head.

He regained consciousness slowly in the intense heat of the
shed. But unlike the occasion several days before, after the explosion, everything now seemed immensely clear, every detail of mem-
ory and of place. He remembered Che and Manuel and his once-
kind host, Brother Camillo. Would Brother Camillo say the last
unction for the squalid, vomitous, drunken Saturnino tonight before that charming Manuel put a bullet or a knife through him?
That, too, would be a traditional touch, reassuring in a world so full
of change. Saturnino's stomach felt as though someone had poked
a steel rod through it to his backbone. His wrist hurt. Why was that?
Ah, yes, Brother Camillo had intended to tie him up. Had he done
a good job? Saturnino tried to rub his wrists together, tried to curl
his fingers down, tried to saw the rope on a protruding tool behind
him. Nothing happened. Camillo had done a good job.

The door of the shed was ill-fitting—a large slit of light showed
through. Perhaps if he raised himself up, he could throw his weight
against it and force it open. Once in the garden, once in the daylight,
perhaps he could wriggle to the gate and get out. Perhaps. Or
perhaps, if he could get the door open, he could see the tools; one
ought to be sharp against which he could fray the binding ropes
around his wrists, arms, and ankles. Slowly, slowly, he pushed his

girdled body upward against one wall of the shed until, after fifteen minutes of exhausting labor, the sweat pouring over his body, he leaned against the door. Sliding his ankles outward from it, his back to it, he rocked away from the door and then into it. It shook but held. The effort was not easy, his balance insecure. He tried again. The door shook but held. He tried again. Nothing. He was breathing hard now, not good for many more tries in this hotbox before heat exhaustion took him. He was bracing himself for a last try when he heard footsteps approaching the door. His heart raced. Brother Camillo had heard him and was coming to secure the baggage. As the door opened from the outside, Saturnino could not brace himself. He fell outward with the door, sprawling on his back. Thanks, at least, to José for having kept the garden grass so thick, the fall had not hurt.

"Who are you?" It was José inquiring. Saturnino looked up to see the old man's face full of surprise and curiosity.

"Please untie me. I've been robbed. I'm hurt. Please."

José, his expression now one of sympathetic concern, knelt over the stinking body and, with his gardener's knife, quickly slit the cords. Gratefully, Saturnino moved his hands and feet, then his arms and legs. There was an ugly, dead-lump feeling and then the tingling; so tight had been the ropes that his limbs had gone to sleep. "Thank you, sir, thank you very much. You've saved my life. I would have died in there." Saturnino meant every word of it. There was no point now in pretending drunkenness.

"Yes, that's true, you would have died. A terrible thing. Who did that to you?"

"I don't know. Someone beat me up and put me there."

"You said they robbed you?"

"Yes, they robbed me first."

"Terrible. And here, next to the church and in the priest's garden, too. A bad thing."

Saturnino was sitting up; his head ached from the blow. "Very bad," Saturnino agreed. "Well, thank you once again. I've got to get away from here, got to get home."

"You can't leave like that," protested José. "Why, you're a mess. I doubt if you can walk."

Saturnino tried his legs. They wobbled at first but found strength soon. "Don't worry, I can walk."

"Don't go away. Let me clean you up first. Why, if you went on the streets like that, you'd frighten the children. And the soldiers would arrest you on suspicion. Do you want that to happen?"

Saturnino hadn't thought of that. Bless José. "No," he replied.

"All right then, come with me. I'll take you into the priest's house and clean you up there."

"No," said Saturnino, emphatically. "Somewhere else."

"Why not?" asked José. "The priest is a good man. He'd help you, but he's out now."

"No priests. Either I leave by myself or you take me someplace else. How about your house?"

"Yes, we can go there, but you'll frighten my wife and children."

"I'm sorry. I don't need to go in. I'll stay outside; just take me down the alley and we can go in your back gate."

José looked at him quizzically. "All right. Here, let me help you." José grabbed him under the arm and helped him through the back gate, down the alley, and in through his own gate.

A neat little yard with oleanders and bougainvillea testified to his gardener's skill. José sat Saturnino down on a chair in a shade arbor. "Wait here," he commanded, and he went inside, returning quickly. A large pitcher of water came, along with soap, a towel, a glass, and a clean shirt. "Now, let me clean you up." Unmindful of vomit, of blood, of filth, of poverty, José scrubbed and anointed the wounded flesh of the face and, through the rent cloth, the back. "Here," he said, "I can't do more if you keep that dirty jacket on, I've got to clean your back better than that. It looks like somebody dragged you across the stones. Don't worry, I've brought you a better shirt, a clean one. You can have it. I give it to you. Take yours off."

"No," said Saturnino, obstinately, thinking of the 357 magnum hiding there.

"You're a strange man," said José, in an odd tone.

"Why?" Saturnino looked up.

"I offer you something that you badly need, free, and you don't take it."

"I'm sorry. I appreciate it. I just don't want it."

"Sure." The tone was skeptical. "How come you let them rob you when you carry a gun?" José asked the question mildly.

"A gun?"

"Yes, under your cotton jacket. I saw the leather strap when I was sponging off your back."

"Oh." Saturnino reflected for a moment and then replied, "Well, in that case, I might as well enjoy the new shirt you brought for me."

"Why not?" said José, without expression.

Saturnino took off his ruined undershirt, torn shirt, and frayed cotton jacket, put on the clean khaki one José offered, and re-strapped his 357 in place. The old jacket went back on. "There— I feel a lot cleaner now."

"You look better, too, but that wound you got from the explosion the other day, that opened up badly. Too bad you can't have it stitched. I suppose you are afraid to visit the doctor?"

"What are you talking about?" Saturnino looked up at José, puzzled.

"The wound I dressed for you when you were in Father Teran's house, wearing your padre suit."

"Oh." A long pause, then, "You recognized me."

"Yes."

"My face?"

"No, only the wound and the fact that on our way over here you knew where my house was and that your watch was on. It wouldn't be there if you'd been robbed."

"I see. Well, now that you know, what are you going to do about it?"

"You have the gun, my friend; how can I tell you what I would do? It's not my choice."

"Don't be silly. I wouldn't use the gun on you, José. I owe you my life. Besides, that's not what my gun is for."

"No?" The old man looked dubious.

"No. Not for pointing at good friends."

"That's good news, my friend, good news for me. I thought when I saw that gun I'd made a bad mistake helping you. One never knows. My wife would miss me. She is old, I am old, but she would miss me. We love each other."

"You're a good man, José, a very good man. She ought to appreciate you."

"She does. And she cooks, as you know. Now that you are clean, you won't frighten her. Let's go inside and have something to eat. It's been a long time since you ate, I think."

"Not too long. I had dinner last night." Saturnino looked at his watch. It now was eleven A.M. "Well, I would enjoy some beans for breakfast."

"Fine," said José, smiling. "And we have some good goat cheese, some fresh-baked bread, and some fruit. She gives us the cheese." The old man pointed along the garden wall to where a nanny goat was tethered, chewing her cud.

Inside, over the table, the old woman served: a gracious old lady, fat and motherly, clucking over her guest like one of the chickens that ran through the dining room. Saturnino ate while José watched. Saturnino would start a conversation, but José put him off. "Later," he said, "when you've finished. Your body has not been so lucky these days. Feed and water it first, then you can talk if you want to." Saturnino did as he was told. When he finished, the old man said to his wife, "Marta, go down to the store, will you? Bring my friend here some cold beer for lunch. Would you like that?"

"I would."

The old woman left.

"Now," said the old man, master at his own table, even though that was but a packing crate on a dirt floor. "What would you like to tell me, my friend of many faces?"

"What must I tell you, José?"

"Must? Nothing at all."

"And if I tell you nothing, what will you do?"

"You worry too much. I'll say nothing and I'll do nothing. You may stay here, if you like. My wife will feed you. You can sleep with us in the other room." He pointed to the second room of the adobe house; on its floor was a straw mat. "You'll be safe, for a little while, anyway."

"José, can you guess why I'm here?"

"No. Why should I trouble my imagination? A Yankee padre studies the church, then he comes into the priest's house full of an explosion. Later, a Mexican—well, almost a Mexican, except for the accent—presents himself all tied up in the priest's tool shed. And it's the same man, only this time he carries a gun inside his coat, like a gangster or a detective. Why should I try to guess what he's doing, except making enemies so as to leave his children as orphans."

"Well, then, José, I'll try not to lie to you."

"If it is so difficult that you can only try, why bother? How could I tell? It's not my business, anyway. You stay here and rest. When you're ready to get in trouble again, you go out. I only ask that once you leave, you don't come back, because your enemies might follow you here. I don't want to leave my children as orphans. I'm only seventy-five and too young to die. Ask my wife, she'll tell you I'm still the man she wants around."

"I'm sure you are, José. I'll do as you ask. I won't let you get into trouble."

"Won't let me? Ho! There's pride for you. You can hardly stay alive yourself and here you are, bragging how you'll protect me. No, thank you, stay as you like and go when you will, but please, please don't try to protect me." The old man was laughing at him and Saturnino had to smile.

"I didn't mean it that way, really."

"I know. Now, do you want to sleep? You look worn out."

"I am. I will take a siesta. But first, do you mind if I ask you a few questions?"

"Please. I may not tell you the truth, but I'll answer you."

"That's fair. Now, first, what do you think of Father Teran?"

"He's my employer. He's a priest. He's always treated me very well."

"Anything else?"

"Sometimes I think he dreams too much. He has a bad temper and, like you, he's sensitive. And he hates the bishop. And these days he's upset. That's what I think."

"Why is he upset?"

"I have no idea."

"None?" Saturnino pushed the query.

"None." The old man was firm and impassive.

"I see. Now is there anything you think I should know about the priest?"

"If I knew who you were, perhaps I could say, but it doesn't matter. Remember that he has a good heart, but his eyes don't see clearly. He forgets sometimes much that he has learned. That is too bad."

"I see. Anything more?"

"I will tell you nothing more about the priest." The old man was adamant.

"About the town, José, is there anything I should know about the town?"

"You already know that many people are not fond of gringos. They are also afraid of the guerrillas. There is talk in the bars that the Yankee padre is a Russian spy, that he may have brought the guerrillas. Most people don't believe it, some people do. Those ones are dangerous."

"José, do you know Lieutenant Rosales of the police?"

"Yes, I know him. He comes from here. I've known him since he was born."

"What do you think of him?"

"He is poor, a little greedy, kinder than most policemen."

"Is there any chance he is a guerrilla?"

José stared at Saturnino in displeasure. "None!"

"How can you be sure?"

"He is my second cousin. I know his family. I know him. He is no bandit and he is no insurgent. He is a patriot."

"Good. I'm glad to hear that. Now, tell me, do you know anything about an airplane that leaves here at night and flies north? I imagine it does it fairly regularly."

"An airplane? No, I've never heard it. What you say can't be true. We would have seen or heard it."

"I spoke inaccurately. The plane leaves from near here, to the west, and then goes north. It doesn't fly over the town. Has anyone ever talked about it?"

"I know nothing." Again that barrier of silence.

"All right. Now, do you know of any large caves north or west of here that are big enough to store things in and in which men may hide?"

"There are many caves around Madre Dolorosa."

"Yes, but any special ones? They would have to be close to a road so that equipment could be carried near, yet remote enough not to be seen or thought about. What do you think? Do you know caves like that?"

"There are many caves. Perhaps some are larger than others, perhaps some are nearer to roads than others. A few are even near water."

"Thank you. I'd not thought of that. Which are the caves near water?"

"Ask the cows."

Saturnino suppressed his annoyance. He had, after all, no right to interrogate the old man. Anything he learned was gravy; the old man had warned him not to expect too much. Wise ignorance was a deep habit. Saturnino returned, respectfully, to the inquiry. "Why should I ask the cows?"

"The cows go to water. Follow them. Any rancher will know where the caves near the water are. It's not my affair."

"I appreciate what you've told me."

"I haven't told you much."

"What you have said is important."

"Good," said the old man, "and what I've kept to myself is very important. As I told you, I am only seventy-five and still young."

Saturnino smiled. "May you live to be a hundred."

"I am trying to do just that. Now, why don't you nap?"

Saturnino agreed.

Fourteen

IT WAS FIVE THIRTY P.M. WHEN Saturnino, freshened by his nap and a late lunch of cheese, enchiladas, and beer, took leave of José and his wife. The street outside was the same sunbathed, dusty run that he knew so well. The sombrero that José had insisted on his taking gave welcome shade to his face. Tilted low on his forehead, it also held his forelock in place to conceal his newly dressed laceration. Dressed as he was, he could move without attracting attention; none in town looked poorer than he and there were many as disreputable. He walked slowly, for natives of this town didn't speed. Some soldiers were stationed about, but the main force would be out in the hills looking for guerrillas. With the temperature at a hundred in the shade, they would not be looking very hard. He could already see the signs of military disrepair as the garrison soldiers settled in: a few unshaven, the heavy smell of alcohol as he passed close to others, uniforms unkempt, hangover-plowed furrows between some brows. Anita and—what was her name? Oh, yes —Carmen were being hospitable—full glasses, generous loins, how could a poor soldier boy resist?

Saturnino heard a car rattling along the street behind him. As it drew abreast, he saw that it was a dirty white van with Arizona plates and a homemade astrodome on top. Its rear bumper was half off and tied down with bailing wire; that was what made the noise, bumper against the rear fenders—crash, bam, bang. The side of the truck was badly caved in. The fresh dent went in two feet deep. What was an American car doing here? Saturnino swept his eyes to the driver's seat. A hippie with long blond hair and a snub nose sat grimly behind the wheel. Who the hell? wondered Saturnino, Who the hell is he? And then the bell rang. He knew the profile. Bill! Saturnino hadn't seen him since he'd left Washington and so didn't know what vehicle he had or how he was disguised. Now he knew. The wrecked side of the truck told him what had happened to the radio, too. The accident had junked it. Bill, unable to make radio contact, had taken off on his own to Madre Dolorosa to find Barber. As if there weren't enough troubles, now this. A gringo hippie in a backwater Mexican town, a town gripped with hatred and fear, soon to be cut off from everywhere, soon to be besieged and gased, xenophobia rampant, and Bill Hickock only fresh out of training. Saturnino muttered under his breath, took note of the van moving into the plaza under the hostile eyes of the soldiery, and crossed his fingers.

Should he make contact? If he didn't, there was no telling what Billie would do. He could hardly let him sit and stew, especially since he wouldn't know the risks. The same crazies who'd be out to get the good pastor York would be tempted to make a meal of the boy.

Bill parked the van in front of the town hall. Why not? Now he had gone inside. A long wait. Out now, looking unhappy. Had they told him he couldn't have a permit to paint or that he must leave? The young man started walking slowly around the square. Why not? Sooner or later, he'd expect York to pass by; in a Mexican town everyone touches on the square, sooner or later. Then it would be up to York to make the contact. Bill would know how to act, his tradecraft would be pat. Saturnino slouched along into the square and, finding one of the old buildings with a wooden porch and veranda, he squatted there, back against the wall, haunches up, waiting. Around the square, every day, for hundreds of years, men had done the same. To live was to wait, to wait was to be alive; in Mexican-Spanish the same word expressed hope and wait and fear.

Billie was walking slowly around the square, pretending to rubberneck. It was hardly New York City; the tallest building here was the cathedral. Billie walked and watched and was walked by and was watched by all as if no one noticed anyone. It was getting cooler now and more people were in the square, walking close enough at times to jostle or touch in passing; sometimes greeting, or looking away from one another, depending upon the history of their acquaintance, and their families, and their families' families before them. Billie now sat on a bench, reading. No one sat near him. He got up and walked again, coming near a tamale dealer's cart. One could see he was tempted to buy but, probably remembering about bugs in the belly, turned away. For the fourth time his path would take him in front of Saturnino and Saturnino this time got up in advance of his coming. He moved slowly into his friend's path, not looking back but sensing like a lead horse in a race another closing behind him, and managed to block his way. Billie, unnoticing, for he was certainly expecting some Yankee apparition, began to pass around him. Gringos take a while to notice how fast they walk compared with the local amble. As Billie hurried along, Saturnino's hand brushed his, palm upward, pushing paper into Bill's unexpecting hand. Good boy, good training; the other's hand grasped automatically while he kept on walking—no look, no shift in pace, no change in his expression. Saturnino, pleased, ambled on a few hundred yards and then turned out of the square, heading toward the shed where his car waited. The note had told his comrade to set up his easel and to expect a parson to approach him there before dark.

It was about six P.M. when Father York climbed up the low steps of the Palacio Hotel and went into the lobby. There were two soldiers there now, slouching. They eyed him carefully as he went to the desk. The old man nodded an indifferent greeting. York knew the signs: any muscle of the old man's face that might betray feeling might also betray the old man, for this black-dressed stranger was dangerous. He wore the smell of it on him now; what had been someone's rumor had become everyone's knowledge. The gringo religious was set apart, exiled, so that his passage from them to death might be as from strangers.

"There are two men upstairs in your room, waiting for you, sir." The old man wouldn't have told him unless it was safe to tell. The two men were very bold to have allowed the warning.

"Thank you," York said, politely. "Do you know who they are?"

"Certainly. Lieutenant Rosales is one. He said you wouldn't mind if I gave him the key. He also said for me to tell you he was there with a friend of yours."

"Oh, how nice. Thank you." York went upstairs, unhurriedly. Reaching the door, he paused. This was a moment of trust. If anyone wanted to kill him, he was a perfect target as he opened the door. On the other hand, Lieutenant Rosales was to be trusted, if it were Lieutenant Rosales, if he were to be trusted. York opened the door and walked in, smiling. Lieutenant Rosales sat on the battered wicker chair. Standing by the open window, looking out on the street below, was an olive-skinned man, dressed in city clothes. He didn't turn when York came in. The profile was of a handsome face. Except for one thing: the tip of his nose, for about half an inch, was missing.

"Padre, how nice to see you," exclaimed Rosales. "I hoped we hadn't missed you."

"Good day, lieutenant, how nice of you to pay a call. Have you been waiting long?"

"Oh, no, we are in no hurry. On a hot day there is no hurry."

York realized they had been waiting a long time. "I'm sorry. I was out, rechecking some measurements in the church, when I did a stupid thing. I slipped and fell." York put his hand on the side of his head where Manuel had slammed him with the gun barrel; there was an ugly bruise there. "Stupid, wasn't it? Well, it put me out of commission for a while. I just sat in a cool spot and rested most of the afternoon."

"Oh, I am sorry. You're sure you fell, that it was not someone who did it? I'm worried about you."

"Oh no, I fell all right, although I appreciate your worrying. Believe me, I'm worried about me, too, after what you told me yesterday. I stayed out of sight all last night, you can be sure of that. But I'm not invisible, you know, I just can't disappear, although I'm sure I did fall, although I am still a bit dazed, probably couldn't give a good accounting of myself; sorry."

"Think nothing of it, padre. That is an ugly blow there, ugly. Well, I'm glad you're still all right. I do worry." The lieutenant was genuinely solicitous. "But see, I told you I'd find you a friend to keep you company, I brought him along. Padre, I want you to meet Pedro, your new bodyguard."

Pedro turned toward York, presenting that face with only half a nose. His eyes were without luster or expression. They did not see; they only registered. A wooden mask with a bullet-nibbled nose, otherwise perfectly featured: fine, delicate, even feminine—smooth skin, glistening clean hair, a neat tie harmonizing with the gray-striped seersucker suit. Only the shoes were dusty, and that beyond help in summer in Madre Dolorosa. A slight man, lithe, no more than five feet seven and 140 pounds, sinuous, feline, a cat in seersucker. When he walked, there was no noise. Sponge-rubber soles on his shoes, or was he substanceless? Formal, almost courtly, he held out a hand to York. It was cool and dry. The cat didn't sweat.

The lieutenant was smiling, saying to York, "There is luck, you see—not everything goes badly. I woke up this morning wondering what I could do for you, padre, just wondering. Who could have imagined what happened? I was walking on the square this morning —some errand, I can't remember what—and I saw this man in front of me. I know that back, I said to myself, I know that walk—like a cat, isn't it so? Where do I know that man, where do I know that walk? So, I walked faster to catch up. That Pedro, he walks very fast, you know, very quiet and fast. He was coming this way, in fact. Imagine that man here in Madre Dolorosa. We don't see his kind very often here, and that is not such a bad thing in itself, either. What are you doing here, I asked myself about him, what would bring Pedro here? Nothing good, I thought, but who can say? I caught up with him and we talked about this, and we talked about that, and we had a cup of coffee, and I asked him. 'Pedro,' I said, 'what brings you here to Madre Dolorosa?' Well, now, I know Pedro fairly well over the years: I was stationed for a while in Durango, and then in Hermosillo, and then in Tijuana, and then in Nuevo Laredo, that was before I came home to be a lieutenant. And, everywhere I was, there was someone who knew Pedro, or knew of Pedro, or wanted to meet Pedro, or never wanted to meet Pedro, or did meet Pedro and was sorry he'd met Pedro—oh, my, that Pedro was always on my mind. And then I met him—professionally, you might say— and I came to see why many people knew Pedro. Eh, Pedro?" The lieutenant nodded toward the cat. Pedro stared at him, his eyes not even registering. Somewhere, behind that forehead, another Pedro was far away.

The lieutenant went on, "Pedro, you see, is a professional. Some days he is a professional bodyguard, some days he changes sides." The lieutenant raised his hands as if to protest a statement never made. "Oh, no, he is an honorable man, he only changes sides for money and, if he does, he tells you. People trust Pedro. I trust Pedro, because he is always very clear about what he does. Others are very clear about it, too, eh, Pedro?" But York could see that Pedro was far away and only his substanceless body, which left no sound when it walked, was here in the room.

"Anyway, Pedro and I came to an agreement this morning, otherwise Pedro would not be welcome in Madre Dolorosa, other- wise he wouldn't be here this minute. He came here, he told me, to collect an old debt—a very old debt, he said, a great deal of money.

I explained to him that money isn't everything and that now is not
the time to settle old debts in Madre Dolorosa. The people are too
upset, there is too much happening. To collect an old debt would
only trouble people more. I'm sure you understand, padre, we have
enough excitement here these days without Pedro collecting debts.
Isn't that right, Pedro?" Pedro only appeared to look at the lieutenant. He tasted something richer somewhere far away.

"So I explained to Pedro," said the lieutenant, "what the situation was and that I had a good friend who needed him, more
than Pedro needed to settle that debt. Pedro is a busy man and
has things to do, but I explained to him that this was important to
me, important to Madre Dolorosa, that our reputation was at
stake. We had an important visitor who, through no fault of his
own, was in danger; Pedro could help us help him by protecting
the visitor. You see, Pedro owes me something, Padre York, it
isn't only that people owe Pedro, but sometimes Pedro owes people. I am one of those. And so I decided to collect one of Pedro's
debts to me and, because he is very much a gentleman and a very
wise man, he saw my point and agreed. He and I are in complete
agreement: he can stay here in Madre Dolorosa as long as you
need protection, padre—that is, until you get your papers back
and can leave, or this unpleasantness goes away. As long as he
stays, he's paying my debt back. Were he to change his mind and
leave, well, I'd say his debt wouldn't be paid and then it wouldn't
be so good for Pedro, not very good at all, eh, Pedro?" The lieutenant was still smiling and this time Pedro Cat had returned from
his inner travels to listen; one eyelid flickered, showing that he'd
heard.

"So it's all arranged. I've done my duty, Pedro pays a debt, you,
padre, are safer than you were, Madre Dolorosa is saved some
needless excitement, and if we are all lucky tomorrow, we shall each
be alive and well for a long time to come, the two of you far away
from here and poor me, the country boy, wasting my days in this
little town."

"Well," said York, "that's certainly quite a story. I am indebted to you, lieutenant, very indebted, and indebted to you, to
Mr. . . ."

"Pedro," said the lieutenant. "That is the only name he has."

"Ah, yes," York acknowledged. "Well, I am indebted to you,

Pedro. I've never been in a situation like this, never even thought of a bodyguard, except in some wild story I might read. I hardly know what else to say, except . . ."

The lieutenant interrupted. "Say nothing, padre. Pedro understands everything. He will keep you good company, rest assured."

"But what about payment? I think we ought to settle that, don't you? I mean, he just can't be my nursemaid—well, that is the way I feel about it—really, he can't do that without some salary arrangement." York spoke quickly.

"Of course. You can pay him something, if you like, but it isn't necessary. Pedro is a professional. He does a good job with or without pay, when it's a special case like this. And I assure you, in my case, this is special. I suggest you give him a gift when it is done —a few hundred pesos is plenty. Pedro is a rich man; he's collected many debts over the years, and I'm sure he'll not begrudge a few days here as his charity."

Pedro, handsome cat Pedro, wraithlike, seersucker, noseless Pedro, the dreamer, acknowledged the speech with a graceful low bow. "It will be my pleasure," he said, in a silken, educated voice. "I am at your service, Reverend York."

York had expected that Rosales had not seriously intended to find a bodyguard but only wished to express his friendly concern through the offer. But he had been wrong. It would have been suspect for York to have turned down the offer originally, but now that this unexpectedly urbane, gun-packing genie had materialized from the shimmering heat waves of the desert, what was to be done? It was another complication.

"If you will excuse me, sir." The two were standing now in the doorway of York's room, watching the lieutenant disappear down the stairs. "I'll go to my room until you are ready to leave. I took one right down the hall, around the corner from you. I'll be reading until you need me. And, please, don't go out without me. That is the lieutenant's wish."

"Yes, I appreciate that, very kind of you both," said York, "although there will be times, I'm sure, when I'll feel very silly about all of this. I mean, to be so much trouble. And not to be able to go out alone—it'll be hard to get used to."

"These things take time, sir, but I find my clients get used to it. You are the boss, of course. If you want to be by yourself, it's entirely up to you. But, if you do, you realize I can't take any responsibility, I can't help you."

"You sound like a doctor warning his patient about taking medicine."

"Yes, something like that. Like medicine, you can never be sure; if you do what I think wise, there is still no guarantee. If you don't, everything might turn out all right, anyway. One never knows in this world—so much is a matter of luck."

"Yes, it seems to be, doesn't it?" mused York.

Ten minutes later, York, wanting to be sure to get his business done in the daylight, knocked on Pedro's door. Pedro answered, an English-language book in his hand. It was *The History of the English Hand Gun.*

"Oh, you read English, then?" asked York, looking at it.

"Oh, yes. We can speak English, if you prefer. I like to read, although this—" He patted the book. "—is just background reading for my profession. To relax, I like drama, poetry. Do you know Garcia Lorca's work? I have three of his tragedies with me; *The Blood Wedding* is one—an astonishing piece. I'm proud to be Spanish when we have writers like that."

"I haven't read Lorca," confessed York.

"Oh, you should. Do you know Baudelaire's *Flowers of Evil?* I've got that with me, too, although I don't read the French."

"Oh, yes, I read him when I was at school."

"Carrion and cats, bitterness, the delicious richness of warped sex. So discreetly despairing. For all his syphilis, he was a gentleman to the end, to that miserable, unloved end. I read him first when I was a boy and never tire of him. Do you feel that way, too?" asked Pedro.

"Well, hardly. I . . ."

Pedro interrupted York's stumbling reply.

"No, I wouldn't expect you would. Obligation of the cloth, I suppose, to disapprove of anything that delicious. But you don't have to disapprove of it all, your bishop isn't watching you all the time, is he, Reverend?" The mocking, the amused hostility, played through Pedro's voice, for all the blandness on his face.

York was annoyed. "I don't think that's called for, really I don't. If you want to insult me, why . . ."

Again Pedro interrupted, "Oh, no, don't take me seriously. I say things I don't mean. After all, what are words? They can smile or sting, but there's no substance to them, not like lead, or a good enchilada, for that matter. I'm careless about words." Pedro raised his eyebrows nonchalantly.

"I fear they're my stock-in-trade."

"Are they? Are they really? I think there's more to you than that, sir. Don't sell it short. No, anyone who would come down here to study, putting up with all you've faced—Lieutenant Rosales told me about it—no, there's substance there."

"Thank you, Pedro, that's kind of you to say."

"Kind? Oh, no, I see things through my own lenses, but I see them just the same. Still, that's not what you want, is it? You want to go out. Here, let me get my things." Pedro walked back inside and a moment later appeared with a fine leather case, polished by long wear, about thirty inches long, ten inches deep, and eighteen inches high. He also had an automatic in his hand which, with a theatrical gesture, he slipped into a shoulder holster. "Do you want to see my case?" he asked York.

"Oh, no, take along what you want, it's not my business."

"Oh, but it is. A lovely beast of a submachine gun broken down: stock and clip and extra clip and the barrel, of course, all encased in silk, snuggled up against the silk like a girl's leg in a stocking." Pedro's tongue flicked his lips.

"Oh." York appeared distressed.

"Shocks you, does it?"

"Perhaps. I'm not sure. After what's happened these days here, I'm not sure there's much left of the conventional New England preacher."

Pedro eyed him impassively. "Who can say? Never mind. Where is it we're going?"

"Nowhere special. I'm hungry, that's all, and before it gets dark, I thought I'd grab a bite. There's a little place on the plaza that's not too bad."

When they reached the square, less crowded these uncertain days than before, but still the center for social encounter, they both saw a long-haired American sitting before his easel, beneath a tree. He was doing an oil painting of the cathedral.

"Well, what would bring a tourist here?" Pedro asked.

"I wonder." said York. "I'm curious. Let's see if he can paint."

York led the way as the two walked toward the American. The painting, although just begun, suggested competence.

"Not too bad," said York to the American.

"Oh, thanks," said the painter. "I didn't expect a fellow countryman around here. I thought I'd gotten off the beaten path."

"Oh, you did that, all right," commented York.

"Did I? Good. Hope there's not a whole colony of Americans retired here, bitching about the servants and driving up prices in the market."

"Hardly," York replied, a bit acidly. "Where are you from?"

"Arizona, recently, but New England before that."

"How nice. I'm from Connecticut, myself," offered York.

"I left," said the artist, a bit brusquely. "Couldn't stand it."

"Oh," said York. "Well, now that you're here, I think I owe you an introduction to Madre Dolorosa. You'll find it quite a spot. It's not without excitement."

"What excitement?"

York, showing pleasure at being with a countryman, chattered rapidly about the guerrillas and the army.

"Oh, shit!" said the artist.

"I don't think that kind of language is called for."

"Oh, no? With my van on its last legs—some drunken bastard rammed me while I was parked taking a snooze up the road—and I'm looking for peace, quiet, and a place to paint, and you tell me I'm in the middle of *For Whom the Bell Tolls*. I say shit."

"I think, young man, a bit of restraint wouldn't hurt you. Here I was going to offer to buy your dinner, but not if you go on like that."

The artist was sullen for a moment but then he smiled. "Okay, you win. You buy dinner and I'll be a good Mr. Clean. Is it a deal?"

"Of course. Here, let me introduce you to my friend, Pedro. Pedro, this is . . . uh, what is your name?" York asked, turning to the artist.

"Mark—Mark Walski." Mark put out his paint-stained hand to shake York's and then turned to Pedro, hand extended. Pedro nodded, his expression unchanged, but didn't offer his hand. Annoyed and embarrassed, Mark shrugged.

Through dinner, York pumped the boy about his travels, learning what one usually learns about the wandering young generation. Mark was broke, curious, footloose, dropped-out, future-free, artistic, and probably smoked pot. Except for the scenery to paint, he didn't know a thing about Mexico. The dinner—enchilada, refried beans, rice with grated cheese, and beer—was tasty. York chattered amiably about his studies in Madre Dolorosa, only at the end of the meal telling Walski about the warning he had had from the police about his own safety, explaining now, with what sounded like pleasure, about his being assigned Pedro as a bodyguard.

"Why, I feel like a president with a Secret Service man," he said. He advised Walski himself to leave town as soon as he could. "I would, myself, but those Hermosillo police took my papers and haven't returned them, can you imagine? And I've been ordered to stay here until they do. But you, well, you can leave. And, if I were you, I would, now. Those guerrillas stop at nothing. I wouldn't be surprised if they attacked the town itself—no, not a bit surprised. Anytime now—what do you think, Pedro?"

Pedro, smoking, idly blew a ring upward and watched it disappear. "Who knows? But, no doubt, they'll attack."

"But you're so calm," protested York.

"Yeah, man," said Walski. "I don't dig how you're so cool."

"Will they not attack were I to be excited?" Pedro blew another ring and stared indifferently out the window. Obviously, any conversation with the unwashed young American was not of interest to him.

Dinner over—and no thank you for it from Walski, either—the three got up to leave.

"I'll see you around," said Walski, breezily. "Come by tomorrow evening when I've done a watercolor of the cathedral. I'll give you a good deal on it."

"I thought I warned you to leave," said York, surprised. "This is no place for any foreigner—don't you understand that?"

"I'm cool, man. Ain't nothin' goin' to happen. Besides, I'm here and my van won't go ten miles more. I don't want to spend all my bread on a mechanic. I'll paint. That cathedral there is quite something, must be older'n hell. Good for ten, twenty watercolor studies, I'd bet. And that oil is going to take time. Now that I'm here, I'll see how it goes. Sometimes the locals in these towns turn on to my stuff; they do and I eat. So, like I say, see you around." Walski walked away toward his ramshackle van. York and Pedro began the short walk back to the hotel.

Fifteen

THEY HAD SAID GOOD NIGHT. York, entering his room, waited to hear Pedro's footsteps disappear down the hall, but Pedro made no footfalls, no more than a Siamese cat walking over a satin bedspread. There was nothing for it; Barber would have to assume he'd gone. He lay down on the bed, not undressing. He was tired and his head ached where Manuel had slammed him. A two-hour nap, and then up again; he was to meet Billie at ten P.M. At dinner, he'd slipped him a map with the garage location on it, noting the time. After Barber had slept, he would think about Pedro.

At nine forty-five his wristwatch alarm went off and Barber, still York, got up, not turning on the lights. He slid the barricading bureau away from the door and opened it quietly. One dim light lit the hall; no sign of anyone. He would have to be fast, down the corridor, out the back window, over the shed room, which extended from the rear of the hotel into an alley, down into the alley itself and to the garage. The night belonged to the crazies, and as long as York was out he'd be anyone's target. And someone's target: Guillermo's hit man from the border would be out there somewhere now, too.

York was fast, quiet, and lucky. Unnoticed, he arrived at the old stable just before ten, checked the building perimeter, opened the padlock on the door, and slipped in. In the garage he waited, listening for any intruder's breathing or movement, but he heard nothing. Reassured, he relaxed and waited. A few minutes later, at ten exactly, there was a knock on the rear door. It was Bill Hickock.

"Welcome to Madre Dolorosa," said Barber, as he closed the stable door, sliding a strong bolt into place.

"Am I glad to see you!" exclaimed his friend.

"Thanks and likewise. Since time is what we've not got, we'd better get to work. First, tell me what happened."

Bill did and it was as Barber had surmised. The parked van had been hit hard by a drunken driver. The radio was ruined. It had taken Bill some time to get the van running again and it was not running well; the gas line had makeshift repairs, the steering assem-

162

bly was loose, the transmission wailed like a banshee.

"I didn't know what to do," Bill was saying, "so I called Mexico City. This time—" He looked at Barber, remembering the chewing-out he'd had for his earlier unauthorized telephone call there. "— this time it was an emergency. I told them about the accident—told them to tell my folks and all that. They said they'd see if they could get recommendations for a good mechanic and they'd call me back in four hours. I waited at that damn phone booth, Lee, and when they did call, it was only to tell me that Mother was very worried about me and she would send me money by Western Union if she could. That was all. Headquarters obviously couldn't make up its mind to get off the pot. Anyway, I didn't want to spend my life waiting there, so I came over here instead. I couldn't leave you in the lurch without commo and no one at all to give you backup."

"Didn't they teach you that a case officer in the field is supposed to be under headquarters control at all times?" Barber's voice was calm.

"Yeah, that's what they said." Bill spoke glumly.

"Well, don't believe it. You're not the first one to go off on your own when the bureaucracy leaves you hanging. Headquarters will be pissed green, but I agree with you. With us both out of contact, maybe headquarters will begin to get as nervous as we are. That's the least they can do for us." Barber then told Bill about the planned assault on Madre Dolorosa with poison gas.

"They wouldn't dare!" Bill exclaimed.

"Want to bet? Che said it was only crowd control stuff but, if I can still read tea leaves, he was doing a number on Brother Camillo. Those citizens here who don't join up with Che's jolly band are going to end up very dead. And with all the junk headquarters put in the back of my car, no one ever considered a gas mask. So, dear friend, we either get them first or we're got for good. And so is everybody else. *Sabe?*"

"Oh, man, this is a real bummer. Poison gas is the downest of all downers."

"To be sure."

"So what do we do?"

"The million-dollar question. But first, bring me up to date on your last words with headquarters before you were put out of the radio business."

"You won't like it."

"No?"

"Neither did I. The truth is they're letting us stew in their juices."

"You mean *our* juice, don't you?"

"I wish. No. You remember your backup on the Reverend show, that New England religious magazine's special edition, showing you as a contributing editor, and how important you said it was to follow up all the inquiries coming in about the magazine?"

"Right. That was the drill."

"Well, they screwed up. Listen, Lee, that's the reason I came. I had to warn you that Washington blew your cover. It wouldn't have mattered what Mexico City or headquarters ordered me to do; if they weren't going to tell you, I was." Bill's face was grim.

Barber sighed. "Thanks, Bill, I appreciate it. That accounts for de Lemos's knowing, of course, and all the rest. That's just what we needed. Well, give me the gory details. What really happened?"

"All I know is the outline. It seems that Parks sent someone up to Connecticut from the Tiburon Committee, to oversee things, so he says. And they did, or so he says. But the guy had his annual leave time coming. And, since they thought they had it all grooved, it was business as usual in the funny factory. Our committee man took his vacation and Parks didn't send in anybody else to mind the store. When the secretary in the magazine office got sick and the editor—why the hell should he give it a thought? He was just doing the Bureau a favor—he brought in somebody from a temporary help agency—after all, they do have to publish a magazine—and he forgot to brief her, or so headquarters says. Or something. So the magazine gets a call from Mexico, somewhere—the girl didn't log when and she didn't ask where or who. The caller asked if you were on the editorial board, or if you wrote for them, and the new girl just gets out the regular journal—hell, she didn't even know about the phony copies and the backup spiel—and she says no, the journal had never heard of you. Then they called again, said they were sending in money for a subscription, and they asked again about you. Same girl, same stupid answer. And, so, you're blown sky high."

Barber nodded. "Either de Lemos or his secretary could have done it. No wonder Guillermo went hustling his butt up to the border to recruit a hit man."

"What do you mean, recruit a hit man?"

"Oh, yes, I haven't told you about that, have I? That was when I couldn't reach you. Well, Dolores gave me the word that she overheard her uncle discussing a contract on me with Guillermo. The poor girl thought it was some business deal between her uncle and me that I was hiding from her. They'll have flown the hit man into town last night on Air Narcotics. If I'm right, there's somebody looking for the good Reverend York right now, so he can blow him wide open."

"Holy mackerel, Lee, I didn't know it was that bad."

"It's bad, at least for York, thanks to those bastards in headquarters. First they deny me the man I want sent in to work Rosales and then the clowns don't even get the lines read straight when the script is on the desk in front of them. With luck they can ruin the operation and get us killed."

"I don't know what you think, Lee, but to me they're no better than the hit man."

"Well, I'll admit they are not exactly on my Christmas card list, Bill, but that's the way the Bureau is. When you're in the field working with a team, it's tops. When you're in the field and need headquarters, it's misery some of the time and once in a while catastrophe. That's the system. But say you want to do it right. Let's take the ten best case officers we've got and put them in charge of country desks or regions. Then a big guy with 'promotions board' written on his hat sits down next to them with a nice, sharp, nickel-plated emasculator and tells them that the first guy to move gets his balls cut off, but the first guy to say meow sweetly gets promoted to the tame kitten department. Then they put them in a windowless, airless room with twelve committee meetings each day and tell them that's the real world, that there is no world outside, that anything outside is illusion. Finally, they teach them through punishment that they have no merit, only failure, failure that they're allowed to hide by doing nothing, saying nothing. There's only one way to avoid it: stay out in the field, never coming home, never getting in out of the rain. That's what I do, Bill, I keep standing out here in the rain. I'm wet, Bill, through and through, and I'm tired, and one day I'm going to want to go home. I want to give it all back to them one day."

Bill looked at him. "Jesus, you are bitter. You've got a right to be, but you are a bitter, bitter man."

"Am I? A hit man on my tail, the committee sending out invitations to the funeral, and you, my poor innocent, not realizing that you, too, are on the roster of the damned. You can be sure that Parks is building up a case to defend himself, no matter what happens."

"Yeah, he has to, especially now that the whole shop is looking over his shoulder because of Hernandez."

Lee was puzzled. "Hernandez? Why any special flap about him? I mean, other than as a target for investigation or, in our case, the bad man in the big black hat."

"You know why. Not just because he's in charge of Home Ministry liaison with the Bureau—the whole covert side—but because he's our agent. Hell's bells, as I heard it, he's been one of our top agents in the Mexican government for years."

Lee's voice was cold. "Hernandez is what?"

Bill Hickock repeated his words, adding, "Why are you so surprised? He's handled out of the branch in Mexico: kid gloves, money, whatever he wants. I can see why. The deputy home minister as a Bureau agent is no small thing."

"No, no small thing. And no small thing that no one told me, either."

"You didn't know? I can't imagine. Parks told me when he was briefing me after you left; Groat was there, too. Said at the time I should keep it in mind, so as not to blow Hernandez out of the water if anything came up."

"Parks told you that?"

"Sure."

"Which means that this whole time it's been cover your ass, because everything we come in with that implicates Hernandez makes the branch and the area look more stupid for not having found out years before. Their prize agent and we tell them he's Mr. Big for narcotics in Mexico. So, first Parks and company are busy protecting Hernandez from us, then they're busy protecting Groat and themselves from security, counterintelligence, inspections, and Lord-knows-who, in case we do turn out to be right, and, last in line, they worry about protecting us."

"I guess so," said Bill, glumly.

"Not to mention the little problem it poses in verification. As liaison chief, Hernandez feeds us official baloney for years, protecting his operation from us. As agent, he confirms what his liaison boys tell us, selling us lead balloons. I grant you it can't be that stupid, nothing can be, but then again . . . well, that's the way Hernandez has to play it and, if Parks told you to protect Hernandez from being blown, someone in the Bureau trusts him. Protect Hernandez from us, nuts! Hernandez has had them all with their heads up a dark place, while he's laughing all the way to the heroin factory."

"It couldn't be that stupid, Lee. The analysts would have caught it."

"Only if branch identified the agent as the same channel as liaison; which they wouldn't have, since he was a clandestine source."

"I still don't believe it."

"No? Well, it sure as hell makes it easier to account for why no one has made any really big narcotics organizations down here, doesn't it? By the way, the story you gave me the other day about the arms rhubarb, that Hernandez was so upset about the armory theft and had asked us to put men on it: was that story ladled out to you by someone in liaison in our branch or was it out of headquarters, which means via Hernandez qua agent?"

"No, that was real," Bill replied. "It came from our liaison and you've got to give branch credit for keeping the security lid on."

"I do and will, until I hear worse," said Barber.

"Anyway," Bill went on, "maybe that's why headquarters wasn't getting anything at all on the guerrillas. Hernandez keeps it out of official liaison channels and, as agent, keeps mum. I imagine he'll do everything he can to make it look like the guerrillas don't exist until he has a chance to make sure they don't exist. Boy, if they hijacked those U.S. weapons from the Fernandez outfit and are using them for an insurrection, and if anybody in the Mexican government finds out that Hernandez let that happen, his head will be on a pole, just like you said."

"My bet," said Lee, "is that the guerrillas did and they didn't."

"What do you mean?" asked Bill.

"I've seen some of the weapons. No question the guerrillas have them and they are U.S. of A., fresh out of the packing cases. But the whole Fernandez bit still doesn't make sense; my bet is he never pulled the heist at all."

"I don't get it," replied Bill.

"I think Che and Manuel and maybe Sigfredo, whoever he is, planned the whole show. I know Manuel and Sigfredo brought the arms down. Why hijack them if they stole them originally?"

"But one of Fernandez's men was shot by the sentries at the time of the robbery," protested Billie.

"He was shot, all right, but how do you know the sentries did it? These boys here are pros. They may have some clowns working for them, but Che could have come right out of a top-flight shop, my friend, and he's been polished by experience. There was nothing to stop his boys from making a few inquiries on their way to the store, learning that there's a big narcotics ring run by some mysterious figure named Fernandez. Why not hire one of those cheap border peddlers linked to Fernandez, take him for a boat ride, and dump him overboard on the way out? Or, just as good, don't hire him at all; just pick him up, lace him up, prop him in the back of the wagon until someone conveniently blows his head off—the army or Manuel—and away they go. In either event, they've left a fine red herring behind. Fernandez strikes again and the whole thing looks like a typical bandit hijack. Which it did. And it gave Che and his boys all the time in the world to mobilize their little army."

"Does that tell us why Hernandez is so upset?" asked Hickock.

"It makes much more sense. Manuel and those boys were in a much better position to stage an armory robbery than they were to hijack stuff being run by hoods, the so-called Fernandez ring. In the first place, as military-trained guerrillas, they'd think armories— they don't think bandit. And the armory is a sitting duck, a nice quiet undefended Arizona duck. If the Mexican baddies had had those arms, I'm not sure Manuel had the clout to take them away, not without losing lots of bodies. And he didn't lose any, that I know of, because Che congratulated him for a clean operation—'no losses,' he said. That's why the hood that got wasted in Huachuca couldn't have been their man. That's why it wasn't a hijack. My bet is that there isn't any Fernandez or, if there is, he's a junior patsy set up to take a pratfall when the time comes. The operation is owned by de Lemos and Hernandez, with Guillermo managing the daily affairs. Probably other regional managers around, too, certainly where they're growing the stuff, at the laboratory and probably on the border, managing sales. Fernandez is their myth, their front: an operation like this will have hundreds, perhaps thousands, of small fry drifting in and around it. When they get set up by Che, with the result that one of their Christmas elves gets bagged at Fort Huachuca, the Fernandez ring gets a bad name with the Mexican government, a very bad name indeed. Drugs are half okay as long as they don't get consumed here—foreign exchange coming in and all that, and let the gringos worry. But arms coming into Mexico— no, siree, that threatens the government itself and you just don't do that here. Hernandez knows that Fernandez didn't rob the armory, because he is Fernandez—or owns him. If any other two-bit thugs had done it, he'd know that. As deputy minister, Hernandez's job is to know the dirt. Were it his own dirt, he'd sure know. He doesn't like to be framed and Che has just hung the big square right around his neck. Besides, who else in the government also knows that Hernandez is really managing the Fernandez business? Maybe some of the other big boys are getting a little *mordita* too, a friendly taste. But, if they think that Hernandez is stealing munitions to bring into Mexico to sell to insurgents, the pack will have him up against a firing squad quicker than he can say 'tilt.' Even if his friends in government don't know about his drug business, the fact that the arms got here and the guerrillas are using them is still a lot of heat. Either way, the frame and the threat to his legitimate job as deputy minister add injury to insult. Hernandez has reason to worry about being hung high. No wonder he's trying to keep this guerrilla thing out of the papers, denies the Bureau information via liaison, lies to us about it as our agent, and tries to keep his own minister and president from getting excited. He tries to suppress the Fernandez slander, sends in the army under his control, keeps the Justice Ministry out of Madre Dolorosa, and keeps his fingers crossed that he wipes out the guerrillas before they embarrass him right out of office. Simple."

"Yeah, simple," said Bill dubiously as he tried to sort it all out.

"Okay. Now that we know, what do we do next?" asked Barber.

"You tell me," said Billie.

"I wish I could be sure. One irony is that we're on Hernandez's side as far as the guerrillas are concerned. If we could get him zeroed in on Che and company before they blow this town apart, that's fine. But we've got to do it without showing that you and I are here without the Mexican blessing, that is, unilaterally, or that we're really here to get Hernandez. Neither of us can walk up to the local army commander and tell him about Teran, Che, and the rest; the army would lock us up on suspicion in a minute and they'd be right, they'd have made us out as Uncle Samuel's uninvited dabblers in local affairs. If York goes to Lieutenant Rosales with the same story, Rosales will either think York has flipped his lid or he, too, will arrest York as some kind of spy, who knows what variety? Nor could we be sure Rosales has the clout with the local army to get them to listen to him even if he believed York. At best, my very good friend York would be in the jailhouse. If Rosales arrests him, the local crazies will have carte blanche to throw a lynching party. All in all, York *would* lose."

"Alas, poor York!"

Barber made a wry face. "I fear the good pastor is expendable. Poor fellow, nobody loves him. His bodyguard insults him, the crazies want to kill him, and de Lemos's hit man has a contract on him. I think he must disappear."

"Fine, but doesn't Dolores love him?" asked Billie.

Barber reflected. "I don't know, friend, maybe she does. But you're right, it would be a dirty trick on her who least deserves it were we to kill off York leaving her genuinely bereft. And another point—no one else can drive this little Olds around, because whoever does, if it's not York, will be presumed to have stolen it and find himself arrested. We can only risk one trip in that Olds, Wild Bill, one fast run out of this town back on that sole road out, back to Hermosillo. That assumes, of course, the Durango mob hasn't blown up the bridges by then or Che gased us all."

"But you aren't going to tell Dolores, are you?" asked Bill, perturbed. "I mean, you haven't fallen for her, have you, that you'd chance blowing it just to keep her from getting a jolt?"

"Ah, Billie, you're beginning to talk like an intelligence officer now; that's the cruel rule—if the poor girl loves you, but you've sucked her dry, dump her. Yet, Bill, the thought has come to my mind, unprofessional as it is, that perhaps I should not cheat and betray her. It's dark in here, lad, dark enough so that I can tell you without your seeing me blush. I have fallen for her. There's no denying it. But no, I'm not going to expose the operation to her, not that it would be a favor to her, anyway. I've seen the movies and I know what I'm supposed to do. That's my business, I'll do that, but I insist on my own rule in this dirty business; you don't have many friends and you protect the ones you've got. Dolores has been the key to this whole Hernandez business; without her, I'd still be on square two, not counting her timely warning to me about the contract. We're in this together, friend, so you've got a vote and a veto. I may fail."

"Lee, if anybody can wiggle us out of this mess, you can. You call the shots."

"Okay. We'll give York a short reprieve before he departs these shores—have to, anyway, if we want to set up his passing so it doesn't raise too many question marks. As for Hernandez, our route to him is through de Lemos. If we're clever, maybe we can work it out."

York, person reprieved, left the stable garage as he had arrived: tense, charcoal-faced, stealthy. He entered the hotel as surreptitiously as he'd left it, via the low shed at the back. He noted that the piece of cardboard he'd slipped between the door and the jamb, near the latch, had not fallen to the floor. He'd had no secret visitors, unless, of course, they'd come in by the windows. Some eventualities are not readily defended against. He entered, taking care, nevertheless, that his 357 magnum was cradled in his hand.

He had just settled down in front of his basin and mirror, preparing to remove the wig, wax moustache, glasses, and other appurtenances of the soon-to-be-lamented Reverend York, when there was a hesitant knock at his door.

"Who is it?" he inquired, smoothing his wig and picking up his pistol.

It was the tired voice of the old clerk. "Sir, you have a telephone call downstairs, a young lady."

"All right, tell her I'll be right down." His first phone call in all the time he'd been in town. A woman. Dolores? Or no phone call at all, just a twenty-peso tip to the clerk to get him downstairs in the quiet of the deserted lobby? One bet was as good as the other—no, the second was a better one. He had, nevertheless, little choice. If it was Dolores, she must have something very important to say. He turned off his room light, pushed the door open, and, kneeling, looked outside. Someone waiting to blow his head off, as he came out, would find his head too low; that moment was all York would need. No one there. Quickly to the stairs and down, keeping to the side and moving quietly. The lobby was empty and so was the doorway. Someone could be waiting on the veranda outside or with the clerk, behind the reception desk. Nothing in sight. He jumped the last four steps of the staircase, hit the floor in a crouch and was running low around the stair post to the adjacent reception counter, through its swinging door, still keeping low. Luck. No one. The clerk had his back to him and the old phone was off the hook. Maybe someone had called, then again, maybe not. He grabbed the phone, his head still below the level of the desk, so that he was no target from anywhere except the clerk's cubbyhole living quarters behind the desk—no target, unless, of course, someone simply walked to the counter, looked over, and plugged him. He kept the gun out ready to swing in either direction.

"Hello?" He spoke abruptly into the mouthpiece. What happened in the next second would tell the tale.

"Al? Is it you? Oh, thank God." It was Dolores's voice. He slipped his gun back into its holster, the sweat streaming down his face. The clerk turned with surprise; most guests don't arrive at the phone so abruptly, or talk sitting on the floor. Gringos!

"Yes, Dolores, I'm here. What is it?"

Her voice was broken, near tears or already crying softly. "Al, oh, I'm so glad. I called you earlier and you weren't there. I—I— I was afraid you might be dead."

"Why?"

"I can't tell you over the phone. Guillermo or my uncle could come by any minute. I'm in his office, it's the only phone in the house, I've never understood why—but, oh, I'm just so glad you're all right. Listen, Al, I've got to see you immediately, there's something terrible afoot. Someone is going to try to kill you."

"I know."

"You know? But how could you? I mean, how did you find out?" Her voice shook with nervousness and amazement.

"I'll tell you later, but remember you said you're in a hurry."

"Yes. Oh, yes, I am." Her voice was desperate. "If anyone comes in here and finds me, I don't know what will happen."

"I do," said York, grimly. "Look, can you get up here right now? Take your car and get out of there?"

"I suppose I could. It would be strange, though—they'd wonder. I guess you can't come this way. What shall I tell them—I mean, at this hour?"

"Shock them. Tell them that it's your monthly period, you're bleeding too much, that you're coming to the pharmacy. They won't challenge it. No man would. And when you hang up, call the pharmacist and tell him the same story. Tell him you'll meet him at the store. Don't take no for an answer. Tell him you'll pay him well. Okay?"

"Okay. Yes, I'd not thought of that. How odd you did. Your voice is so different, Al, like that one time down here."

"Fine. Now, hang up, call the pharmacist, and drive up to the front of the hotel. I'll be waiting for you. When I see you, I'll come out, not before. And keep your car door locked. Open it only when you see me and then be prepared to drive off like a bat out of hell. I'll expect you in about forty-five minutes. And if, for any reason that you can't help, there's someone—anyone—in the car with you when you arrive, step on the dimmer switch twice as you stop in front of the hotel. Got it?"

"Yes, I've got it."

"Okay. Hurry. Good-bye." He put down the phone. The clerk was looking at him oddly. He hadn't understood, for York and Dolores had spoken in English.

"Is everything all right, sir?" The old man's faded voice went beyond courtesy. He was afraid.

"Fine, just fine," answered York. He got out his wallet and peeled off a hundred-peso note. "Here, take this."

"Why?" said the old man.

"Because I like you and I want you to do me a favor."

The clerk kept his hands at his side. "Perhaps, sir. What is it?"

"I want you to tell me the truth."

"Certainly, sir."

York offered him the note. The old man took it warily.

"Has anyone else called me today?"

"No, sir."

"Did this woman call me earlier this evening?"

"Yes, sir, about an hour ago. I went upstairs to call you, but you didn't answer when I knocked."

"That's all right. I was sleeping."

"Yes, sir."

"Has anyone asked for me? Has anyone come in looking for me? Has anyone been hanging around here who doesn't belong

here? Tell me the truth." York's tone was stern, brooking no eva-
sion.

"No, sir, no one asked for you, no one looked, I've seen no one
strange around the hotel. That is the truth, sir. I've no reason to
lie."

"Haven't you?" York pulled out another hundred-peso note.
"Now, who has paid you to say anything, report anything, or not to
say something in connection with me? Who has been interested in
me?"

The old man looked at York strangely and this time took the
money without hesitation. "No one, sir, no one at all. That's the
truth, sir."

York pulled out a third hundred-peso note. It was not the time
to be miserly; he was buying life. "All right. This is for the future.
Tell me if anyone does ask for me or give you any instructions
concerning me, or if you see anyone here who's a stranger. You'll
tell me, do you understand?" York's eyes bored into the frightened
ones of the withered desk clerk.

The old man took the third bill, staring at it with amazement,
"Yes, sir, you have my promise."

York watched the old man retreat to his tiny one-cot, newspa-
per-filled living quarters. The clerk had sounded straight. And it
didn't make sense. Where was the assassin that Guillermo had
brought down? That Dolores somehow had learned about the contract was certain, that the assassin had left the de Lemos compound
to come to town looking for him was also certain, otherwise Dolores
wouldn't have feared he was dead. Tonight was the time. Flanagan
had gotten his at night. The assassin should have come poking
around by now, looking, inquiring, trying to set him up for the fall.
He might be waiting to try the room while he slept, of course, but
that was the hard way; any hit man would know that doors and
windows lock and that an alert quarry holed up in his own dark room
had an advantage. A professional hit man would assume alertness.
So where was the contractor? The phone call had not been a setup.
What could the setup be? Was it Dolores? Had he fallen for an old
trick again? Had she called under duress? Had someone been with
her on that call, someone who'd be with her in the car or, easier,
be waiting as he made for the car when she arrived? Ugly. To be in
love and to realize one might be a fool. Well, there was nothing for
it. He would have to wait and hope.

He got up carefully, scanned the empty lobby, listened for telltale noises from the old wood planks of the veranda—for the night was quiet now, nothing stirred outside—but he heard only his own breathing. He ran upstairs, zigzagging up the staircase as he went. Once upstairs, he checked the still-empty hall, wondering as he did so how many hours of his life Pedro spent reading while his other clients wandered about without their guardian. York was getting to know the back window well. Again he went through it and down, over the sagging roof to the dark alley. Gun out, he detoured down the alley, across the street, right-angling through one passageway and then another alley, all in the ominous stillness of this town, besieged without its knowing. Cautious minutes later, he was across the street from the hotel, in the darkness, peering at the dim lights of the lobby from behind a wooden taco stand. There were no lights on in any of the upstairs rooms. There was nothing, no one near, and he had not been followed, of that he was sure. Ears alert, he settled down to wait.

About twenty minutes later the lights of a car swept down the lonely street. They illuminated only a slinking cat. Dolores came in fast and to a quick halt. Her car was dark but he could see her silhouetted against the lobby lights. The car lights didn't dim. No one appeared. He moved quickly out of hiding into the darkness behind her car. From behind the car he looked in the rear window to the floor of the rear seat; there was enough light from the hotel to show him that no one was there. He could see that Dolores was looking desperately toward the hotel. He moved to the passenger side, on her right, and knocked quickly on the door. She turned, frightened, but, seeing him, the shock dissipated and quickly she leaned over to unlock the door. He slipped inside and she gunned the engine while he slammed the door. No car lights followed, although that was no guarantee that no automobile was behind them.

"Thank God," she said. "You scared me to death. I thought you would come out of the hotel."

"Just a precaution." He reached out and took her right hand from the wheel, gently, and squeezed it. Her hand was wet with perspiration. She squeezed his in return.

"Where shall we go?" she asked softly.

"Just drive slowly around. Keep away from any lighted areas— no bars, no plaza. Just around this block and then the one behind it. Talk to me while you drive. Or would you rather I drove?" He hated to test her.

"Yes, I'd rather you drove." So far, so good, she'd passed another test. She stopped the car.

"I don't want to get out," he said. "Here, you slide over my lap and I'll get to the wheel." She moved toward him, raising her lithe body, and, as she moved over his lap, her arms went around his neck, tightly. She was sobbing.

"Oh, Al, I'm so scared."

He put his arms around her and kissed her, kissed her violently until their lips burned, until their tongues, touching and searching each other frantically, languorously, in their warm mouths, withdrew. Both felt the sudden desire upon them; the pulsing yet known surge must be thwarted, at least for now.

He drove with one hand; his other hand held hers. She was next to him, her body pressed close to his.

"Oh, Al, I'm so confused, there's so much happening to me. I don't understand. What will I do? What will we do?"

"Take it easy," he said, reassuringly. "Just start in with why you called me, then we'll take it from there."

He could feel how she took possession of herself, her torso stiffening in discipline, her hand still clutching his.

"Last night—no, early this morning—I wasn't sleeping. Everything that's been happening, well, I think you can understand, it's not been easy to sleep. I was thinking of you, and my uncle, and Guillermo, wondering, trying to figure it out. It must have been about three or four A.M. I guess I should have looked at my watch to check but I didn't—not that it matters, really. Well, I heard a car drive in. At first I couldn't imagine who it could be. No one has ever come in at that time. My bedroom is upstairs on the side and the window was open; it was easy to hear it, the night was so still. The car went to the garage and I heard the door close. And, later, I heard one of the back doors open, probably the one to the kitchen. It's near the garage; you may remember the garage is detached. Since my uncle was home, it had to be Guillermo, but why that hour, where had he been? I tried to go back to sleep, but I couldn't. I guess I was too upset and his coming in at that hour, well, after what you'd said, it was all so mysterious. So, I put on my dressing gown and went downstairs to the kitchen. If anybody had met me I was going to say I was getting some milk. I do that sometimes, anyway, when I can't sleep, they all know that. But I didn't meet anyone. I tried not to. I was ashamed of myself, creeping like a burglar through my own house—well, through my uncle's house, but I feel it's my home, too. It was so late, I was sure Guillermo had gone right to bed, but I wasn't really sure, I sensed something, I don't know what. I was right. I prowled, a glass of milk in my hand, and there were voices coming from Guillermo's office—you know, the outer office to my uncle's. The door was closed but I crept up to listen. I was ashamed but I had to do it. I could barely make out what they said, Guillermo and someone else. I hadn't heard the other voice before. Guillermo was telling him that he'd drive him up to town in the morning, that if they saw me, they were to say that this other man was a cattle broker come in to talk to my uncle about the Agua Prieta cattle, that it was urgent because of the drought and they had to sell the cattle to the States. Then the other man asked where you were staying and Guillermo said you must be in the hotel, that it was the other's man's business to find out. I remember he said, 'You've got the contract, you do the work.' I was so puzzled when I heard about the contract again. For a moment I thought you must some-how be in the cattle-buying business, too. Then Guillermo said that the other man was to telephone him when he'd killed you—yes, he used that word, *killed,* and they'd arrange to fly him back to the border the same night. 'I don't want you going out of Madre Dolorosa on a bus this time,' I heard him say. 'This time someone may remember seeing you last time you were here and we don't want that.' Then they talked about flying back when it was over and I just couldn't stay to listen any more. Al, I tell you, I was shaking so, I thought I'd drop the milk glass on the floor. I kept shaking all the way back to my room. I locked the door and cried, I couldn't help it. I didn't sleep at all. I had to be sure that I'd see that man in the morning, so I could tell you what he was like. I must have looked a wreck. I told them at breakfast I'd been sick; funny how your advice tonight over the telephone fitted, about my having a difficult period—I've never talked to a man about that before. We Mexican girls are brought up rather narrowly, I guess. The man didn't come to breakfast and I could tell Guillermo was pretending there was no one there. He looked pretty tired, too, but he didn't give any excuse. I suppose the man slept in one of the guest rooms.

I went outside after breakfast and picked flowers, sat on the lawn, did anything just to be close to the garage. I guess they waited as long as they could and then gave up. Guillermo brought the man out the front door and told me he was a cattle broker who'd come down on urgent business, just like I'd heard them plan it. Oh, it was a nightmare, like having a nightmare come true. And then they drove off. It was awful. I wanted to call you but my uncle spent the day in his office and since that's the only telephone we have, there was nothing I could do. Guillermo had taken the car I use; this car isn't mine, you see, my uncle simply lends it to me. I don't keep a car here. He has his own car, but I hesitated to ask for it. He never lets anyone drive it. I asked, anyway, told him I wanted to come to town to shop. Uncle was in a bad mood, hardly civil to me, said he was sorry but he might need the car and I could wait until Guillermo came back with the other one. I waited and waited but Guillermo didn't come back until almost dark. I was desperate, Al, I've never spent a day like that in my life, it was a nightmare. Oh, I'm so glad you're alive!"

"Poor Dolores, poor baby, you did have a rough time. And on my behalf, too. I'm sorry but I'm grateful, I really am." He squeezed her hand.

"Oh, Al, what can we do?"

"Well, for a start, you can tell me the visitor's name."

"Oh, Lord, yes, how stupid of me. He was introduced as Ramon Morales. Do you know anyone by that name?"

"No, but it doesn't matter. What did he look like?"

"Oh, an odd man, frightening. I'll never forget his face. He was well dressed, almost debonair, really, he would have been handsome, but, oh, he was frightening. I shivered. Part of his nose was missing. You won't believe it, but it was gone, as if it had been bitten off—just gone.

York felt the chill run up his spine. Now he had no trouble imagining how Ramon Morales looked.

Sixteen

YORK HAD NOT EVER RULED IT out, not completely, not the possibility that the discovery of Pedro by the well-intentioned Lieutenant
Rosales might, just might, also be the introduction of Guillermo's
hit man to Madre Dolorosa and his intended victim. A stranger seen
in town the very same morning that Guillermo's contractor should
have arrived, a stranger handy with guns, one the lieutenant made
clear had a reputation. No, Pedro had never been ruled out as
contractor, but surely not ruled in, either. Crafty—he'd given no
sign. Even with York's suspicious 357 on call, Pedro could probably
have hit him any time. But it wouldn't have been professional: noise,
witnesses, unknown risks. Pedro had been waiting until the professional moment.

"Al, what do you think? You're so quiet." Next to him Dolores
was beseeching his response.

"Yes, I was just thinking about Ramon. He has a room on my
floor of the hotel, his name is Pedro, I've spent part of the evening
with him, and Lieutenant Rosales has hired him as my bodyguard."

"Oh, no!" Dolores cried out. "That's horrible, Al, horrible.
How could that happen?"

York told her how it had happened.

"And of course, you'd have no idea," Dolores went on. "He was
just playing with you, cat and mouse."

"No, my darling, it's not quite that bad. I did have an idea, but
it was only a hunch. I couldn't be sure."

"Yes, I forgot, you did have an idea, didn't you?" Dolores's
voice was cooler, doubtful, almost accusing. "Over the telephone
you told me you knew that someone was trying to kill you. And
there's all that you hinted at when you saw me at dinner. When was
it? It seems so long ago, but it was only last night. I was so worried
about you that I'd completely forgotten that you're in this, somehow, yourself. You always have been and I still don't know why.
What a fool I am to go crazy with worry and you knew it all along

and now you tell me you've gone strolling with your assassin, almost as if you don't care, as if you're the cat and he's the mouse. Is that it? Damn it, Al York, you tell me what this whole stupid, dirty, secret mess is right now or I'll never see you again, do you understand? I can't stand any more of it, can't stand liking you and distrusting you, worrying for your sake and then worrying about who you are for my sake. Who is the criminal, anyway—Pedro, Guillermo, my uncle, or you? Who?" Dolores had started shouting, tears running down her cheeks. She was glaring at him. He could imagine that she might even hit him while he was driving. He should have been more realistic. She did hit him. Her palm whistled through the air and with a resounding WHAAACK she had slapped him on the cheek.

"Damn you, you sneaking, lying beast, I hate you, do you understand? I hate you, hate you." Dolores's head was in her hands.

"You have every right to," said York calmly, his stinging right cheek but a minor complement to Manuel's earlier rifle-barrel blow to his left one.

"Oh, you Anglo-Saxons and your calm voices and straight faces! Don't you ever feel anything? What are you—a machine?"

"No, I'm not a machine." York knew that all right; inside, he was shaking. Dolores got to him.

"Well, what are you, then? Who are you, then? Tell me, who? Why did you imply my uncle was doing something bad—why? Why does Guillermo want to kill you? How did you come to know that yourself? And why would Lieutenant Rosales want to give you a bodyguard?"

He had to tell her something. He owed her that. Besides, he still needed her; she was his route to de Lemos and Hernandez. Did it make any difference that he loved her? He didn't know.

"Well, Al?"

"If I told you I was kind of a cop—not really a cop, but something like one, an investigator—would you believe me?"

"And not a minister at all, no kind of minister, and no student of churches and funerals—none of that?"

"That's right, none of that. Or rather, some of that but all of it on the surface—an interest to be sure, but not the raison d'être. A convenience."

"A disguise."

"Yes."

"A lie."

"Yes."

"A living lie, a lie to me, a lie to the Church, a lie to Father Teran, a lie to everyone so you could trick them. Who'd distrust a minister, who'd think he was a spy? Is that it?"

"That's it."

"And you visited me, pretended to like me, used me, wanted to use me to find out something about my uncle or Guillermo. You suspected them of something, thought perhaps they were criminals, is that it?"

"No. I do like you, more than like you. But the rest is right."

"I see," Dolores's voice was soft, menacingly soft. "And you are an American, you don't work for Mexico, you're here in my country on your business, not our business. It doesn't even concern Mexico, whatever it is you're doing. Perhaps my government doesn't even know you're here. Perhaps if they did they wouldn't even allow it. Is that it?"

"Yes, and no, and maybe. The trilogy. I am an American, but the business concerns both countries equally and on business of this sort I'm usually working with both governments. Only this trip is an exception. It wasn't intended to be, it's just turned out that way; we didn't anticipate the situation."

"I see. 'We' it is: so you work for someone else, probably your government?"

"I can't tell you that."

"I see. Very discreet of you, to be noncommittal. And you think my family are criminals, then?"

"I made a promise to you, Dolores, that I would never say anything derogatory about your family. You asked me to and I mean to keep that promise."

"But you think so, nevertheless."

"Don't push me, Dolores."

"No, you push others, they don't push you. Is that your rule? Very convenient. All right, I relieve you of your promise. How's that?" Dolores waved her hands, giving a Latin snap of the fingers. Her eyes were bright. She was once again in command of herself. "There, you are absolved, father. Now tell me what's on your filthy rotten mind."

"Dolores, I'm trying to be reasonable, trying to work this out.

Be insulting if you like, but don't think it will improve matters." His voice was firm.

"Do you think matters can be improved? Ah, the eternal Yankee optimist. Lies, masquerades, assassins, guerrillas, criminals, conspiracies, and you think things are just fine, eh? And maybe can get better, eh? Oh, what a garbage pile you have for a mind. You pig! I don't even know your name. Do you have a name? Is it Pedro? Or are you the Scarlet Pimpernel? What name would you like to use today, father?"

"I can't tell you my real name yet, Dolores. When this is over, then I can."

"Ah, very discreet, Mr. No-name. It matches your honor, Mr. No-honor. You will forgive me if I call you 'Pig,' then, or let me see —" She hesitated, her finger pricking the air, her head nodding in theatrical cogitation. "—in Orwell, I think there was a Saint Pig of some sort, in the barnyard. Yes, that was where everyone was equal but Saint Pig was more equal than any of the others, for he was the monster. Yes, Saint Pig—do tell me what you think is wrong with my family. Please, I want to hear a pig talk." She glared at him, daring him.

"What's wrong with your family is that they produce daughters and nieces with bad tempers and tousled hair. Beautiful, sensitive daughters who want to hurt those who've hurt them. Hammurabi emotions—an eye for an eye, a hurt for a hurt. And their daughters and nieces are very loyal, very brave, very loving. Visiting American tourists fall in love with them too readily. That's what's wrong with your family."

She stared at him for a moment, gulped, clenched her teeth, shook her head fiercely, and began to bawl, throwing her arms around him, her head against his chest. He braked to a sudden halt. He had been driving very slowly.

"Oh God, I hate you!" she sobbed. "How can I be in love with someone who's so awful?"

"Poor taste," he said, smiling, his arm around her, hugging her tight. "Happens in the best of families."

"Saint Pig, what are we going to do? Please tell me, what can we do?"

"First things first," he said and, saying it, kissed her again, the kiss of love and reconciliation, tenderness, hope, and promise. A long kiss and a commitment. When they released, he said, "And now to the prosaic, like staying alive a few minutes longer and keeping your appointments."

"Appointments?"

"Sure. Didn't you call the pharmacist and tell him he had to open up his store? I told you to do that, remember?"

"Oh, heavens, I completely forgot. I did call him, as you told me to."

"Good girl. Was he difficult?"

"No. Sleepy maybe, but that kind of thing happens here. And, besides, I'm the niece of the richest man in the area. He'd never dare say no. But what does it matter? I made the call just for the excuse. We can forget it now."

"No, we can't. We've got to keep your skin intact, my love, which means we keep your story straight and consistent. You came here for a reason and you'll act on it and return home on it and, with a little caution, they won't suspect you."

"Suspect me? Guillermo, that snake in the grass? I'd scratch his eyes out."

"Dolores, you're new to this business, but let me assure you, if Guillermo thought you were a danger to him, he'd either turn you over to your uncle for a heart-to-heart talk or he'd have you killed. Probably the former, and if your uncle loves you and trusts you as you love and trust him, no harm would come to you; he'd simply ask you to be silent, which I'm sure you would be, anyway, out of loyalty. But I can't take the chance that Guillermo might act on his own. I just don't know him, that's all, and so we have to limit the risk to you. Do you understand?"

"It's preposterous. Guillermo wouldn't dare," she said, indignantly.

"Probably, but there's no need to be foolish. Now let's go to the pharmacy. And while you're there, will you do me a favor? Ask the pharmacist how his mortuary business is doing. I want to know if he's finished working on all the corpses around here or if he's still embalming some of them. And ask him if they're all identified. I suspect some killed in that bar bombing might not be."

"What crazy questions. Why do you want to know?"

"The morbid funereal interests of Reverend York, remember? No, I'll tell you that later, too, if it works out, but right now I'm just

curious. Will you do it?" The car by now had reached the corner of
the block on which the pharmacy stood. The street was dark, except
for the lone light of the pharmacy, where the owner would be
waiting, waiting with his prized polished hearse in the back that
York had admired so long ago, it seemed. "I'll drive up and stop just
short, so that he won't see in the car; when you come out, get in on
the driver's side. I'll be in the back seat by then. That way he won't
suspect anything. Okay?"

"Crazy, but okay." She hugged him tightly as he swung the car
down the street.

It was twenty minutes before she returned. No transactions in
a small Mexican town are hurried, not even in a mortuary/pharmacy
at midnight. As he waited in the back seat, Barber, now York resid-
ual only in disguise, scanned the streets and doorways like a border
guard expecting a surprise attack, but there was nothing to see.
When Dolores returned, she drove off, not looking right or left.

"You there, Saint Pig, in the back seat. What do I do now?"

"Stop around the corner and let me get up front."

"Gladly. Do you want to drive?"

"No, you're going to have to go home fairly soon, and there's
something important I have to ask you to do. But first, how's business in the mortuary?"

"Booming. He's down to the last five corpses. I could hardly get
him to stop talking about it, he's such an enthusiast. Ooh, it curdled
my blood to hear him rave on. You were right. There were unclaimed bodies from the bombing; he saved them for last. The
town's paying him too little, he said, so why hurry, who cares if they
get a little ripe? What a delicate way to put it. 'Ripe,' indeed. There
are lots of drunken derelicts around these country towns, you know
—we have a big problem with alcoholism in Mexico. Sometimes half
of the men in a town will be drunks; no wonder we're so poor and
violent. I'm not surprised there are abandoned corpses in that
morgue—lonely men who meant nothing to themselves or anyone
else. It's the real Mexican tragedy."

"Yes, I suppose it is."

"Oh, I'm quite serious," said Dolores gravely. "You may want
to pursue crime all you want, or whatever it is you claim to do for
a living, my not-so-saintly pig, but what do those ordinary crimes
mean compared to what alcoholism is to Mexico? Think of the loss
in lives, in families, in work, and in crime, too, for that matter. I'll

bet as much as one-fourth of our total adult peasant population are lost and forgotten people."

"For a musician, my sweet, you have a profound social conscience."

"Why not? I'm Mexican, I have to care. It's my responsibility, isn't it?"

"Yes, I guess it is."

"If not mine, whose? If I don't care, who does? Some little bureaucrat in the health department working for one hundred and fifty dollars a month and struggling to keep his family alive? No. If Mexico is to progress, it will only be because those of us who can, care to help others who can't." Her face, her voice, were earnest.

"You know what?"

"What?"

"I love you," he said.

She nodded without surprise. "It's stupid, isn't it, loving? We don't even know each other and here we are talking like adolescents."

"I love you, regardless," Barber replied. "But now you've got to get home. There's something terribly important I have to ask you to do—and it's very delicate."

"You want to use me, is that it, because you know I love you and would do anything—well anything decent, anyway—just for you? Is that it?"

"Yep, that's it."

"Okay. I trust you. I'm glad you didn't try to give me a nice rational ideological reason for whatever it is. I wouldn't have liked that. Now, Saint Pig, what is it you want me to do—steal the plans for the atom bomb factory from Fu Manchu?"

"No, I want you to tell your uncle a very disturbing truth and I want you to do it with a lie."

"Oh. Well, now then, I'm not so sure I can do what you want. I told you I will not conspire against my uncle. I love him, he's my family. I thought you understood that."

"I do. Hear me out and then you decide."

"All right, tell me." She folded her hands on her lap.

"It's about the guerrillas who have attacked the soldiers and the police here, the ones who set off that bomb that killed so many in the street and in that bar. Those guerrillas are not my business, Dolores. That's your business, Mexico's. How the people want to be governed is up to them. Anyway, quite by accident I've learned through someone else that they are hiding out on your uncle's land, in that old mine you told me about. I haven't been there, I haven't seen them, but I'm confident that it's true. Your hacienda isn't the target, but the town is. It's my understanding that they intend to attack this town in two or three days and it will be a deadly attack. Some of them are going to attack San Ramon, too, maybe as soon as the day after tomorrow. And they'll blow up the bridges between here and San Ramon so there will be no way for reinforcements to come in. I don't think the soldiers here will be much help. You may have noticed that discipline is deteriorating, they're whoring and drinking too much and their officers aren't first class. The guerrillas are probably well trained and very well equipped. The problem is that I can't tell anyone what I know because if they believed me they'd arrest me on suspicion, and if they don't believe me, what good is that? The local army commander is not going to believe anyone who tells him his regiment is going to be had by a gang of what he probably thinks are ragamuffin bandits. I don't think there's any question that if I could get him to surround that old goldmine of your uncle's and to attack it, his men could take the place; they'd sober up long enough for that. But, after last night's debacle up north, when a platoon was ambushed and wiped out, I imagine he'll be scouring the mountains up there, which is the wrong place. I don't think a gringo divine is going to make him change his mind, especially when the gringo can't tell him how he came to know where those guerrillas are. I don't know if you know it, Dolores, but a lot of people around here think I'm a Russian spy who brought those guerrillas here; that's why Lieutenant Rosales gave me Pedro as a bodyguard, to protect me from getting killed by some of those drunks you're so concerned about. The town is scared, suspicious, and angry. If I talk to the commander, he'll be suspicious enough to think it's a trick. If he's a fool, he'll send a patrol out to your uncle's mine to check and they'll all get killed. Then he'll blame me for having set up an ambush. No, if he goes he'll have to go in force and if I try to persuade him of that he's bound to think I have a purpose—for example, to take pressure off the guerrillas or to leave the town itself open to another bomb attack, or something. He'll have heard those rumors about me, too, and if I open my mouth he'll be convinced. Lieutenant Rosales is easier to talk to, but he's powerless. One acting police chief, with one man left alive on his force. He's got no reason to believe me either, but if he did he'd have to persuade the army commander to act, using me as his source, and we'd be back where we were, with the added problem that Lieutenant Rosales would be in trouble. The commander would certainly think him a fool and might even think he was in league with the famous Russian spy. So you see, I haven't any hope of convincing the army to get those insurgents now before their group gets larger and before they take the offensive."

"But what's this got to do with me? No one would believe me, either, even if you are right. I can't go to that army colonel. You said I should tell my uncle, but he won't go to the commander, either, not on my say-so."

"That's true. But your uncle can telephone his brother-in-law, the deputy home minister. These guerrillas are the responsibility of the Home Ministry; the army here is under its direction. And Mr. Hernandez will take some action, because he'll believe your uncle."

"But why should my uncle believe me? I can't tell him that you, of all people, told me."

"Of course not, absolutely not. But what you can tell him is that one of the families who live in the valley near you came to you and said they'd seen a group of fifteen or twenty armed men moving into the mine last night. Tell your uncle that the people made you swear you wouldn't say who told you because they were afraid they'd get into trouble; they knew they shouldn't be out there then, but they'd been poaching, poaching for gold in the mine with a pick and shovel. Your uncle will understand that all right. Tell him that your family said they saw the men carrying rifles, new machine guns, and some heavy funny-looking arms, they didn't know what they were but even in the night they looked new and very military."

"Okay, I could tell him that, I guess. But even if he thinks I'm sincere, he could still think the family who told me was crazy. That's what he's likely to think."

"No, because the clincher is this. You tell him the family said they saw the guerrillas come into the mine and its buildings just before the airplane without lights landed at the landing strip there. If you tell your uncle that, I guarantee you'll get his attention. That is, unless I'm totally crazy myself."

"What airplane? There is no airplane there. I told you that when we talked about it before."

"No? Well, how do you think Guillermo got Pedro back here so fast? If you think of the time that elapsed between when you heard your uncle talking to Guillermo over the phone, when Guillermo was on the border and when you heard them arrive at your house, you'll realize they couldn't have taken the plane from Nogales to Hermosillo. That plane leaves from Tucson only once a day; that and the drive from the border to Tucson and from Hermosillo here. No, they couldn't have made it before late this afternoon, yet you yourself saw them—well, at least heard them—in the wee hours of this morning. Isn't that so?"

Dolores pondered. "Yes, I guess that's right—yes, yes it is. But that means there is an airplane out there somewhere—and, of course, that's what you were suspecting all along, isn't it? But, if there's a plane using that field, how can my uncle not know about it?"

"I don't know if he knows about it or not, I really don't. Either way, when he hears that some peasant family was over there in the mine and saw an airplane land, you'll get his attention. My bet is, if you suggest to him that he call your uncle Hernandez, he'll do it."

"Well, yes, I guess he might, at that."

"One more thing, Dolores. It got my attention and I'm sure it will get his."

"What's that?"

"I think the guerrillas intend to use poison gas."

"Oh, no!" cried Dolores, horrified.

"I'm not sure. I think so, though. Tell your uncle that the family thought they overheard one of the insurgents saying something about poison gas. And tell him that the leader of the group was called Che."

"Oh, Al—I mean, whoever you are—this is just awful."

"Yes, it is."

"Are you really sure, I mean that it isn't some nightmare again? Everything is touched with poison today—this town, my uncle, and you somehow still. Each time I get to feeling close to you again, lying to myself it's all going to be all right, then you throw in a new thunderbolt. First it was my intuition that you weren't what you said, and I was right. And then you against my uncle. I've tried to keep you from making me doubt him, but it's insidious, the way you keep dropping things in, like etching metal with drops of acid. And then there are all those lies about yourself which you now admit to ever so calmly—blandly, as much as if to say, 'Yes, Dolores, of course I'm a sneak and a liar and have never told you the truth, but so what, does that matter?' And now this—guerrillas, poison gas, right on our own estate. And I'm supposed to be the one who does something about it, me of all people."

"It's your country. You were the one who said just a minute ago that if you weren't responsible for it there was no one who would be. I think you still mean that. It's awesome, I know, but someone has got to get the army to act on this thing before it's too late and the only channel is you to your uncle to Hernandez."

"I see your point, but what if you are wrong? I mean, could that be?"

"Possibly, I wish it were so. If I were wrong, the worst that it could be is that I'm simply crazy and there are no guerrillas in that mine. I'd prefer that to what I know."

"There's only one other thing. I'll do it, of course, but I won't be able to keep from wondering."

"What's that?"

"You said there's a rumor you're a Russian spy. What if you are? What if you are using me to do just what you said the army commandant would suspect?"

Barber smiled. "Well, I'd have been very clever, that's all."

"That's all," she said indignantly. "Aren't you going to deny it?"

"If you like. Sure, I'm not a Russian spy. But I don't need to say that. We both know it."

"How do we both know it?"

"Because we both know you have a very fine intuition. So far, it's not been wrong once—not about me, not about Guillermo, and, I suspect, not about your uncle, whatever it is that you've decided about him. My guess is that you're going to stay right about things, me included, no matter what I say."

"I hope so, and then again I hope not."

"Why? What do you mean?"

"I've always trusted my intuition and it works. If my own instincts aren't friendly, aren't in harmony with myself, I'd be in terrible trouble. As it is, I trust them and I trust me; and that means I can trust you, too. That is, I trust what my intuition says about you, never what you say about you, although sooner or later I think that will all come out all right, too."

"What's wrong, then?"

"Well, before I say, I have to ask you if you believe in premonitions?"

"No, can't say I do."

"Okay. It doesn't matter. What I want to know is how Guillermo or my uncle, if it was him, decided that you were a spy and not a minister and that you ought to be killed. Who told them what you were never willing to tell me, that you were a fake?"

"No one told them, I suspect. I think someone probably forgot to tell them that I wasn't a fake."

"Something to do with that religious magazine? I ask because my uncle was remarkably interested in that. Sending in the subscription that fast and all—it wasn't like him."

"Probably. I don't know for sure."

"So someone on whom you were counting let you down. They didn't lie for you when they were supposed to and the result is that you're to get killed. Did that person—those persons—did they want you to get killed?"

"I don't know. I don't think so. I think it was just carelessness."

"That careless? I doubt it. Do the people you work with use assassins?"

"No, not in that sense, anyway. I won't say, though, that they're always peaceful."

"But someone was so careless that what he did, or failed to do, meant that you were to be killed by someone else?"

"Yes, it turns out that way."

"But those people had no idea it would turn out that way?"

"No, I didn't say that. They should have."

"That's what I mean, Saint Pig, I don't like your friends. I don't trust them. And you shouldn't. They'd have you murdered through indifference as Guillermo would out of fear. I think you may have as many enemies there—wherever there is—as you do here."

"Oh, that's normal enough."

"But enemies willing to get you killed? Don't you understand, my love, those people you work with aren't your friends? A friend would never let a friend die, ever, no matter what, if he could help it. But they're viciously responsible. Don't you see? I want you to quit working with them once we get married. They're not good people."

Barber was flabbergasted and showed it. "Married?"

She replied matter-of-factly, this mercurial beauty, "Of course. We love each other and I'm not one for dalliances. If you don't marry me, of course that's your business. Then you will stay with those friends of yours and let them kill you any time they want. If you do marry me, I don't want to be widowed by some miserable petty bureaucrat who's jealous of you and so gets you shot. It's that simple."

"Your intuition is working overtime and, besides, I never said anything about marriage."

Dolores leaned over and kissed him gently on the cheek.

"Look at you—a wound on your forehead, a great welt on your head, slap marks where I hit you on the cheek, guerrillas and assassins all around you, drunks who want to shoot you as a Russian spy, and you have the nerve to tell me that my worrying about you is baseless, just my intuition. Saint Pig, you are not a reasonable man. As for marriage, there's no hurry. Take your time to decide, my love, I'll wait for you a little while. And now, where do you want to go, now that you're no longer the Reverend York? I have to go home myself to turn the insurgents out of Sonora. As for you, whoever you are, I imagine you'll be burying the Reverend York, won't you, now he's gone out of style? And let me know, my Proteus, when and in what form I shall see you again."

It is difficult for a man to decide, when he has fallen in love with a woman at least as clever as himself, whether to be proud or humiliated when her flights oversoar his. A true philosopher might not even notice, but Barber had no such illusions about himself. He was, in the meantime, both proud and humble. A girl that sharp would do well in the Bureau. Were they these days, he wondered, an equal-opportunity employer? Or would they fire him, as they had so many others, because he married a foreigner? Their loss, his gain. He would, he had told her, find her at home as soon as he could, warning her to urgency in seeing her uncle tonight. It was already near midnight. Her uncle must call Hernandez tonight as well. There was so little time. What he didn't tell her was that he worried for her as well, because of Guillermo, and because of the guerrillas.

He stopped the car in the dark around the corner from the back alley to the hotel, the hotel from which the Reverend York would be moving out before morning, never, he said, to be seen again. She held his hand, pressed her lips hard, told him to take care, and kissed him passionately. She then drove off, in a tearing hurry. York took his usual back-alley course to the hotel and safely clambered back to the decrepit rear roof. As he moved close to the window, keeping himself against the outside wall, so as not to form a silhouette against the dim light, his eyes saw that light cut by a shadow. Someone was inside the dead-ended hall, having walked near the window. Since the one toilet on the floor was on the other end of the U-shaped hall—a full L-leg from his room, which was at the front at the other end of this hall facing this window—it was no nighttime visitor to the bathroom. Moving very slowly, very quietly, York changed course and made for the other rear window, the one next to the toilet. As a precaution, he had earlier made sure that both windows opened easily, soaping up their old weight ropes and wooden sides, the smoother and more quietly to slide. No sounds came from the bathroom, the windows of which also faced rear. The hall that led to them, the other leg of the U, was empty when he peered inside. Pedro's room was on this leg, midway between the window and the base of the U, which ran along parallel to the front of the building. Like his, it was an outside room, not one facing the skywell. The shadow he'd seen might have been that of another guest, someone coming in from a cantina. Or it could be Pedro prowling. That cat, if he had done the Flanagan job, as York now knew, given what Dolores had overheard Guillermo saying about not chancing Pedro being seen a second time, that cat would like midnight. York slipped the window, entered with his 357 magnum in hand, tried the bathroom door, found it open, went in, flushed the toilet, and came out again. There'd been a newspaper inside, Hermosillo's news of a week before. He took it with him held open in his left hand so that, behind it, his right hand, with its 357 pointed directly forward, would not be seen. He walked down the hall, past Pedro's room, turned left, passed the stairway that came upstairs at this point, and continued almost to his room, stopping before exposing himself to the hallway leading to the rear window he'd just avoided. Why Pedro should be down there he couldn't say; an easy shot, of course, should York open his door and walk out. But so close to home? Why not? Flanagan had been close to home. All Pedro need do was shoot, crash through the rear window for noticeable exit, slide quietly over the roof to the same window York had just entered, and be down the hall and into his own room while the old clerk, if he dared, came upstairs to check the gunshot noise. If he dared not, the clerk would wait for someone else to go look. All neat enough, but why would Pedro assume York would come out at midnight? Or had Pedro simply been planning the execution, checking his shadows and angles for another time? If so, he would be there still or might have returned to his room already, for York had proceeded slowly from one window to the other, low, not liking the exposure as he'd crossed the roof open to the windows that faced the skywell, not wanting any noise to attract attention. He would chance it. Newspaper casually flapping and his trigger finger very ready, York emerged suddenly around the corner, facing left and not to his door. Pedro was kneeling halfway down the hall, an assembled submachine gun dangling idly from his hand, testing the strength with his left hand of a table that stood near him in the hallway. Such tables were scattered along its length, each holding a kerosene lamp. Electricity had not come to Madre Dolorosa in full confidence. In the rainy season, especially, the kerosene lamps were lit at least weekly as the power failed.

"Good evening," said York.

Pedro looked up. "Good evening," he said unconcernedly, his face pleasantly bland. "You were out?"

"No," said York. "I was in the bathroom, reading."

"Oh," said Pedro, his machine gun moving slowly from side to side at arm's length, unserviceable, held by the stock. Not that he would have used it, anyway, not now. York presumed Pedro knew he'd lied; would have checked the toilet doors to be sure no one would return to his room to surprise him. Probably, but not certainly. The man was so casually confident, one couldn't be sure. A bodyguard, after all, had an excuse to be out with a gun in the hall near his client.

"I think we should have a talk," said York pleasantly, slipping his magnum into its holster without Pedro's having seen it. "Do you mind if we go to your room? I'm sick of looking at the four walls of mine."

"By all means, be my guest," said Pedro affably. York waited for him to come abreast and side by side they walked to his room. York would be safe there. What assassin with a reputation to keep would kill a man in his own hotel room? They entered and sat down, two affable cats back from a stroll.

"I've been thinking, Pedro, that it's time we came to an understanding."

"Yes, sir, if there's something on your mind." Pedro was looking at him carefully, for the voice and manner of York had disappeared and there was the blunter Barber talking from the pastoral guise and garb.

"You're a professional, right?"

"That is right, sir, I consider myself that."

"Fine. How much did Guillermo give you on my contract?" Barber spoke in a businesslike manner, no animosity or drama.

Pedro scrutinized him. "One thousand dollars. Five hundred up front, five hundred on completion."

"And what did Lieutenant Rosales threaten to do if you didn't act as my bodyguard?"

"Something unpleasant. He mentioned jail. I offered him money, but he has a singular turn of mind. I don't know why he's so interested in your welfare. But he was persuasive. You have a friend there, although I don't think he would be happy knowing you deceived him." There was no malice in Pedro's tone.

"Oh, I don't think he'd mind too much. What reason did Guillermo give you for wanting me hit?"

"Sir, I'm a professional. I don't reveal confidences between myself and my clients. You should know that."

"Not even for money?" inquired Barber gently.

"No, there are things other than money. But, in fact, Guillermo couldn't tell me anything on that point. It's not revealing a confidence to say he didn't know who it was he was having killed, just that whoever it was was not who he said he was and that was quite enough. Do you see that?"

"Yes, I'm aware of Don de Lemos's problems."

"Are you? Well, that would be awkward for them; you can see they didn't have much choice. I'm sure that, as a professional yourself, you don't take it personally. Sometimes, with the others—with laymen, I should say—well, sometimes they take it so personally. It's as if I were killing them for their sins or something. The stories you hear at those times, they embarrass me. I don't know how a priest can stand the pleas and confessions. And some are so undignified about dying, I blush for them."

"You're a sensitive man," agreed Barber.

"Isn't that odd? From the start, I thought you'd understand. It makes it all the more interesting, don't you think? I think you may understand me and, perhaps, when that last hour draws close, I'll understand you better, too. That's what I meant: there's something quite special about a relationship like that. In preparing the sacrifice, the high priest and the victim are both part of a larger drama and they're drawn together by their complementary parts. In the sacrifice they are both consenting, you see." For a moment, Pedro paused and then, as if a blind had been removed from his eyes, there was a sparkle in them; he allowed himself a grin. "What do you think, will the next liberal movement in the States be to legalize sacrifice between consenting adults? Wouldn't that be avant garde?" He laughed softly.

"You're wasting your time, trying to needle me. I'm here on business, just like you. I think we should see if we can deal. If we can't, one of us dies tonight; if we can, well, neither of us does, or at least not at one another's hands. Right now, I'm so tired and pissed off generally, I can't say I much care, but we have to talk about it. Am I right about you, that you're the kind of guy who can talk about this sort of thing up front?"

"You flatter me. By the way, do you have a name?"

"Bryan, Bryan Harwood," replied Barber.

"My pleasure, BH," said Pedro, "although, to point out one small difference between us, my name really is Pedro. I've a last name, too, but I don't use it professionally. Family names shouldn't be involved in private business, don't you agree?"

"I don't really give a hang. I think we should talk." Barber bulldozed his way through the conversation.

"All right, BH. Talk."

"I'd prefer not to shoot you. It complicates things for me. But, if I'm not to have a go at you, you have to agree to shelve the contract. It's a gentlemen's agreement any way you look at it. I don't expect you to throw your gun away. The way I look at it, neither of us is under duress. We're sitting here like gentlemen and no one is trying to outdraw the other, like in some third-rate Western. That's a start, isn't it?"

"Yes, a start, but maybe not the finish. You see, I have a problem. I've taken that contract on you and unless I return the money it would be dishonorable. To return the man his money after talking to you would look as if I'd been bought by you or I was a coward. No man would do that. I'm not going to be dishonored."

"Fair enough," replied Bryan. "But you've got another problem. His name is Lieutenant Rosales. He can probably book you on any one of a dozen murder raps and you both know it. Even if someone else gets me, Rosales would hang you for not being a diligent bodyguard. But if he cottons to the fact that you were the one who hit me, I think you could count on a very unpleasant future. By the way, does Rosales know that you're the one who hit Flanagan?"

"MGF, that cloaca? You knew I hit him?"

"I used my intuition."

"Very good for you, you're better than I thought. I don't think Rosales knows and I don't think he wants to know about MGF. He and the chief weren't the best of friends. MGF amused himself once with a little second cousin of Rosales's. Poor little girl's never been the same, physically or mentally, if you know what I mean. I think Rosales would have killed MGF himself one day if I hadn't done it first."

"May I prevail on professional courtesy to learn why Flanagan was hit?"

"Don't you know? Why don't you try your intuition?"

"It tells me that Flanagan was greedy and that small-timers are very unwise to blackmail big men. Is that close?"

"Close enough. You might tell your intuition that Flanagan wasn't very bright, either. He thought there was competition where there was already a family partnership. It was a fatal error."

"He thought the home minister wanted to move in on de Lemos? That would have been stupid," said Barber thoughtfully.

"There's no need to be cute with me, BH. We agreed to a gentlemanly talk and you're the one being provocative now. Deputy minister, as you know."

"My apologies. I've got bad habits. You're right, as usual. But if Flanagan didn't know that, it seems to me that it was a rather quiet partnership. I admit we just ran onto it ourselves recently."

"Oh, 'we,' is it? Then you have friends? You know, I think Guillermo's asthma is going to act up again. It does when he's under stress. I'm sure he thought, with you blown away, things would be quiet again."

"Too bad. But, Pedro, how do you know about Hernandez and de Lemos if Flanagan didn't? I don't mean to be insulting, but you do live far away from all of this and usually people take care to keep hit men rather uninformed, when they can. You must play a very special role." Barber was feeding Pedro's vanity as best he could.

"My friend, BH, I'd like to tell you, but I can't. Someday, perhaps, if there's no tearing out of thudding hearts tonight and feeding them to jaguars, which still remains to be seen."

"But you are willing to deal if we can figure an honorable solution?"

"I suppose, why not? I don't care when I die and I certainly don't give a damn when you do, so there's certainly no pressure to agree, I don't like pressure anyway, I like to take my time—rituals, as I said. Indeed, that's why you caught me so awkwardly out in the hall just now. I enjoy staking the ground out, like a professional golfer walking over the course before he plays a match. I didn't know where you were and I didn't care much, I was going to set you up for a wake-up call about three A.M.; a lot of people die then, it's a very tired hour. But, for myself, I rather like it, especially when the moon is pale."

"How were you going to get me outside?"

"That's a professional secret. Don't worry, if I don't get you that way, there'll be another. But now it's your turn to answer me, isn't it? After all, a conversation must be two-way. A play must have actors and an audience. Remember, we watch each other. Now tell me, BH, who do you work for?"

"I'm forbidden to tell you, but if you guessed that it was big, official, and to the north of here, you'd do well."

"I see. And do you have many friends with you?"

"Enough to give me and my executioner a decent burial, with lots of wailers and a big wake."

"Good, I'd hate for us to be unlamented. And if, for some reason, we both stay alive, how do I return the money honorably to Guillermo or, failing that, how do I avoid a blow to my reputation so severe that even retirement far away will not be far enough?"

"I suggest you join me in a murder." Bryan said it with a smile.

"Splendid, two priests officiate. Will it be a maiden? Shall you rape her first, while I hold her down? I like that sort of thing, I like it immensely."

"Sorry, nothing as sweet as that. No. I want us to kill off York. I have my own reasons to get him out of the way. You might say I've got problems at home that would be solved. And it would get those crazies here off my back, the ones who think I'm a Russian spy. And you, depending on your definition of contract fulfillment, can either keep the money and go or give it back later. As long as your client thinks York is dead, he should be satisfied."

"Interesting." Pedro allowed himself facial movement in his mask. "Yes, it might work. On the other hand, I'm not sure. Why don't we do it conditionally? That is, we'll try your experiment, get rid of your York, and, if I like the looks of the job, I'll go along with you. After that, if I don't like it, I'll tell you, cat to cat and mouse to mouse. How's that?"

"Fair enough." Bryan Harwood got up and walked to Pedro, his hand outstretched. Pedro rose languorously and shook the proffered hand. It was Pedro then who walked toward his rickety chest of drawers and, taking a thin box from the top under Bryan's watchful eye, pulled out two cigars.

"Havana, my friend, although our Mexican two-dollar Orozcos are also very good. Still, Mr. Castro hasn't ruined everything. How I hate meddling politicians. The cigars are excellent. Please." He handed Bryan a cigar.

"Brandy, BH?" asked Pedro, taking a bottle of Pedro Domecq from the dresser top and pouring generously into a water tumbler on a tray next to it.

"Thanks, don't mind if I do." Barber took a sip. "Not bad, not bad at all."

Pedro eyed him speculatively. "There you sit, BH, the gentleman on the grand tour, brandy, cigars, and worldly talk. But there's more to you than that, my friend, that Yankee face is disingenuous. I wonder how many other faces you wear, my friend? And wearing so many faces, I wonder, can you ever know who you really are? Do you understand what I'm getting at, my friend?"

Bryan shook his head, lying. "No, you're too complicated for me, Pedro. I'm just an ordinary guy, trying to make a buck the only way he knows how."

"Really?" Pedro studied Bryan while they drank and smoked.

"I will tell you one thing, though." Bryan, the brandy relaxing him, spoke more expansively. "I sure envy you in some ways. You're set up here like a civilized man." He tapped the glass appreciatively. "And you haven't been doing this undercover gig I've had. Can you imagine what it's been for me to play Little Lord Fauntleroy all this time? I couldn't even keep a bottle in my room; had to pretend I didn't like to drink." Bryan shifted weight to be more comfortable, draping his shoulder over the back of the chair, hand dangling behind. "Christ, Pedro, but I think you and I have got ourselves into one crazy racket."

Pedro again reached for the bottle from his bureau top and again poured two more healthy glasses. *"Salud,"* and he took a deep gulp. Another gulp, empty, and another glass. Two, both had drained theirs. In a man's world, men drink.

"All right, I'll tell you what it is." Bryan was talking loudly, a bit drunk. "I'm in just a little bit of trouble back home, you understand? Not the wife, nothing that simple, not even the office, not yet, but that's coming soon. A few checks, you see—not so bad in itself but one of the banks I used doesn't have an account in my name. It's a lot of money, in fact. I'm sorry about that, but you know how it is. I like to play the horses a little—say, Pedro, how about a little more brandy here. My God, that's good stuff and I am tired of York, I want to kill him worse than you do, the goddamn priggish bore. Isn't that something?"

Pedro nodded and allowed himself a smile, even a giggle. "Friend, that is something. You and I are in one crazy business. Tell me something, BH, are you really a Federale or not—I mean U.S. Federale?"

"Pedro, buddy, I told you I couldn't tell you, but don't worry about it. I've got my job and I've got my friends and the twain shall never meet. Anyway, I've got to kill off York because that son of a bitch is going to get thrown in jail when he gets home, even if he is a Federale. Do you realize that, Pedro, buddy? Jail!" Bryan walked over to Pedro and put his arm around the other's shoulder. Pedro put his arm around Bryan's waist. They were both drinking and laughing. "So, I've got some money and I think I'll stay here where the climate is nice and there ain't nothing to trouble me. And you, well, Pedro, the only nice climate for you is out of town, because if Rosales thinks you killed York or even let him get iced, you're for it—oh, man, I mean you are for it!" He said the last noisily.

"Yes, yes, you are right. It is a dilemma. If I win, I lose; if I lose, I still don't win. I agree we will kill York and you will stay here in my nice Mexico and I will go back to where I live in the block of the assassins in Nogales, next door to your nice Arizona. And we shall live happily ever after, eh?"

"Right." Bryan stomped gleefully on the floor. "Hey, Pedro, do you mind if I take this damn wig off? It itches."

"Be my guest. A man must go uncovered to the sacrifice. Take off the wig. What do I care?"

Bryan pulled York's gray wig off his head, showing the auburn hair underneath.

"Ah," said Pedro, "you are young, then, BH. As I thought, it was too easy, Guillermo giving me an old man to kill. Well, there was no challenge to it, anyway. But you—" Pedro's face was cocked drunkenly. "—you, my friend—I think that is a challenge."

"Sure enough, buddy, we are both a challenge, Pancho Villa and Fierro, how's that? The twin terrors of Sonora." Bryan was laughing noisily and then they both laughed. Pedro poured another glass and drank. Bryan took a sip from his and, as he had done before when Pedro hadn't looked, emptied the rest into the metal wastebasket. "Well, now," Bryan was saying, "I say it's time to go out and kill that damn York. Right?"

"Right," Pedro nodded, laughing so, he could hardly walk.

"Buddy, now don't you forget your little old chatter gun there, you bring that along, that and its nice little old case."

"Oh, yes, I'll bring her along. She's my scissors, she's my knife, I like her chatter, she's my wife. You like that, Bryan? It rhymes."

"I like that fine. Okay, old buddy, let's us two baddies get going. Poor world, what will you do when Pedro and I take you on? Ah, ha, ha," Bryan roared and stomped on his way out the door, Pedro crying happily after him.

As they went out the lobby, Pancho Villa and Fierro, the night clerk wisely was not in sight. Past the veranda, down to the dark dirt street. And Bryan Fierro, as drunks will do, stumbled and fell to his knees. Apparently befuddled, he laughed as the dust of the dark street rose up around his face; he was dark, in the darkness, this dark suit of the soon-to-be-gone Yankee York. Pancho Pedro watched too, laughing at his new friend's fall, and laughing, tears in his eyes as he reached inside his jacket, easily, casually, as if to scratch himself or pull out but another cigar. Laughing and his hand might be touching the stock of his .38. When he died. Bryan, in his mock stumble, had pulled his 357 from its holster and, keeping his eye on Pedro, had stayed in a low crouch on the street, that position offering a reduced exposure in the dust and darkness.

It had not been necessary to wait for Pedro to reach for his weapon; whether or not he had done so at that moment, Bryan intended to kill him. Nevertheless, as Pedro would have preferred, there was a courtesy extended among gentlemen, that gracious acknowledgment of the privilege of the first move. It was good for the Anglo-Saxon conscience to be able to plead self-defense.

Bryan stared at Pedro. He had liked him, liked him better than many people he'd met. Pedro was all he'd said he was, sincere, complex, and competent. He took care of things personally; no committees doing his dirty work for him.

There was a moonstone stickpin carved in the shape of a human head, the fat face delicately done, stuck in his tie just above the wound. It was old-fashioned, dandyish, the kind of thing Pedro would insist on wearing, even with a seersucker suit. In winter, he'd be wearing his silk suits and patent-leather shoes. Bryan leaned over and took the stickpin, taking care not to get blood on his hands.

The street was quiet after that single shot. No one came rushing out, no one would. Alone with his business, Bryan pulled Pedro's body into an alleyway and placed it on a rubbish heap.

Seventeen

YORK'S LAST RIDE. WIG ON and keeping to the back alleys, Bryan
Harwood made for the rear of the pharmacy/mortuary. The bars
were still open and those streets were noisy; the troops were having
a rousing old time enjoying Che's hospitality in the cathouses; one
could hear the whoops and hollers blocks away. The garage door
of the hearse's house was tightly locked, but in that old building it
was no trouble to find a side window easily jimmied with a thin knife.
Up and over, into the old building and that fine shiny hearse; none
of those killed by the bomb had been prominent enough, nor their
families wealthy enough, to afford the luxury of a last ride in that.

The morgue itself was ripe. Chemicals as well as piles of ice had
helped; formaldehyde was better, only it was not a fine perfume.
Those who go to the potter's field do not care that it is not Ma
Griffe. One who was too far gone had been shoved unceremoni-
ously into one of the barrels of formaldehyde; instead of it into him,
him into it, like an embryo in a bottle.

Five unclaimed corpses and, with luck, one might do the trick.
About five feet ten, 168 pounds, fifty years old, and no scars and no
dental work would be perfect; but this was not a perfect world.
Bryan settled for five feet eight, 175 pounds, age about forty, and
hardly any teeth. There were scars aplenty—falls, breaks, knives;
there were, no doubt, scars in the mind as well, but those were not
so easily read; the poor devil had had a bad life. Bryan pulled the
corpse, stiff, white, and full of solution, off the slab, opened the
garage door from the inside, and dragged it down the alley. Returning to the mortuary, he wrote a note on wrapping paper, purposely
misspelling and with a clumsy script: "We have taken our beloved
Arturo home, you have no right to him here. We shall bury him
ourselves. (Signed) His wife, Teresa." A ten-peso bill was put next
to the note. The proprietor was to think the family gracious as well
as poor, loyal, and resentful of the interference of outsiders in
family affairs. Most Mexican families met that description.

The window closed, the garage door locked, Bryan dragged the corpse fifty feet at a time, stopping for frequent rests. Roller skates would have helped, or a child's wagon. Headquarters, it was turning out, had equipped him poorly for the real needs of this operation. With caution and rest, with spurts of pulling when a street was to be crossed, and with cats yowling at him and dogs kicking up a fuss from behind the falling mud walls of the courtyards, he had, by two thirty A.M., reached his destination, a wooden shed that was within a block of the stable where he kept his car and, importantly, not more than two hundred feet down a passageway from the street where were located six usually boisterous cantinas, one of which was still going strong. He dumped the naked corpse into the shed and went to the stable. Some twenty minutes later Saturnino emerged, disheveled as before, but no rum in the side-pocket pint bottle he'd picked up from a trash pile just nearby. In his hand was a burlap sack; it had been in the stables and, after shaking out the scorpions —he hadn't seen them but it was good to assume they'd be there —it was as good a suitcase as any for the Reverend York's clothes and disguise. Once in the shed, he dressed the corpse, from underwear to wig, in this latest American aid to the underprivileged Latins. Then, in an action that he didn't enjoy, he took the tire iron that he'd brought along for the purpose and beat the face of the corpse. Fortunately, it was dark and the man long dead; physically, it was no worse than hammering an abalone to tenderize it. Nevertheless, even Saturnino was squeamish. He almost threw up as he made hamburger out of what had once been the face of a man. The rest was a relief. He piled pieces of wood and tinder-dry refuse over and around the corpse. Outside in the alley, between the shack and the street, he carefully placed the broken-lens glasses—he didn't want anyone picking them up to discover there was no optical correction —and a well-worn Bible with "To Al from Mother" inscribed in it. Even nearer the cantinas he planted the wallet, empty of money but still full of York's identifying cards. The final dedication of that good wraith's spirit to another world required a shot into the body from the 357 magnum. Someone of those carousing in the cantina ought to testify to time and direction if Rosales beat him hard enough. He lit a match to the dry materials.

To the unknown wearer of that now burning clerical cloth, he murmured, "Thanks, and may you be treated better in Heaven than

on earth, Amen." Saturnino was not much on funeral orations when
it came time to leave a burning. As for the craftsmanship, he reflected, it was a disappearance that wouldn't pass muster many
places—an imperfect crime, he had no pride in it, but pragmatists
make do with what they can, and in Madre Dolorosa that would
suffice. There was no coroner here. It was unlikely the body would
ever be shipped north for autopsy. Rosales would presume what had
happened and wouldn't have time to check. If Rosales had any time
for mysteries, he'd also be worrying about who had burned Pedro.
Both kinds of burning could give his town a bad name.

Saturnino returned to the stable and curled up in the back seat
of his car to sleep. It was noon the next day before his pocket alarm
awakened him in the beastly heat of the garage. He recalled he'd
been dreaming of hellfire. There were several reasons he might,
only one of which was the heat where he was sleeping.

Saturnino had several errands; the first to get a full rum bottle,
to be half emptied on the ground somewhere, his pocket badge of
popular office, as it were. Dolores had complained of all the alcohol-
ics in Mexico; how unhappy she'd be to see him now. He would not
want to be recognized by Brother Camillo, Manuel, or Che in this
current incarnation, but the latter two ought to be keeping themselves off the streets as a matter of principle, and Camillo could be
espied from far away. Saturnino looked like one of hundreds; face
to face, not even Camillo would recognize him, except perhaps if the
protruding bottle reminded him. If he kept with the crowds and the
normal habitat of the impoverished alcoholic peons, he could not
be identified. He bought the rum and kept in the background.

The second errand was Bill Hickock, with whom a meeting had
been set at two P.M. Later they should both proceed to the de Lemos
place. He had to find out if Dolores had succeeded. Whether or not
she had, the last act would be played out there. The guerrillas were
there, Don de Lemos was there, Guillermo was there, Hernandez's
managerial ghost lurked about, and Dolores, the lovely Dolores, she
was there. He thought about the first four. He worried for her. He
must do his best to see that she wasn't hurt in whatever turmoil the
night was to bring.

The van rattled, creaked, and staggered down the bumpy
street, finally wheezing to a clattering stop on a dusty byway on
which one alley leading from the Olds stable debarked. Mark—what
was his name?—yes, Walski—got out, opened the rear doors of the

van, and ostentatiously took a set of wrenches up forward to the hood. A lot of good it would do him, Saturnino thought, recalling that Bill had been, from childhood, the world's most inept mechanic. But he'd done as instructed and parked with the van's rear door close to the alley. All that Saturnino now required as he got up from an apparently stuporous collapse in the shade of an abandoned courtyard wall at the corner of the alley was that no one pay attention to the staggering drunk who fell against the van's open doors and, finding an upright hole, crawled in.

No one noticed. As Dolores had said, county towns were full of drunks and of all the things sober citizens had to do, watching them stagger about was not a high priority. Dolores was an exception to concern herself with them, but then, if he were ever to marry again, it would have to be to an exceptional woman. What a devil, imagine her proposing to him. He might very well accept.

Billie, wiping grease off his hands, returned to the rear of the van, put the tools inside, saw the drunk on the floor, closed the doors, and returned to the driver's seat. There was the partition between front and rear, but it had a door, which Bill opened.

"Hey, boss—you all right?"

Barber, sitting up in the windowless van, said he was.

"Where to now?" asked Bill.

"Find a cool spot and park. Then come on back and we can talk. Do you have a refrigerator in this heap?"

"Sure do, up front left. Help yourself—Coke, beer, lemonade. I'm the perfect traveling host."

"Any food? I'm starved."

"Yep, lots of cans and some fresh bread, Danish butter, fresh tomatoes, and lots of cheese."

"That's the best news I've heard all week. I'm going to pitch in," replied Barber happily.

The truck lurched, chugged on noisily, and within a few blocks came to rest in the shade of a large billboard situated at the edge of town, on the main road to San Ramon and Hermosillo. Bill clambered into the back and, taking a soft drink from the refrigerator, settled down cross-legged on the floor. Saturnino, a fierce and dirty apparition, smiled at him, if a gargoyle can be said to smile.

"Man," said Bill, "I wouldn't want to meet you in the dark; you're one mean-looking *hombre*."

"Good, keeps the creditors away. Here, have some cheese."

Barber shoved a hunk of fresh goat cheese toward Billie, who refused. "Go on, take it. The incidence of brucillosis from fresh cheese is quite low; what you have to worry about here is tuberculosis. Have you been X-rayed recently?" Barber spoke cheerily.

"Oh, you're very reassuring, you are. Here I was, pleased that I'd been so healthy. No street-vendor purchases, no vegetables without washing them first in potassium permanganate, no unboiled water. Just like the tourist manual says."

"Good. I'd hate to have you taking sick leave just now. There are a couple of things to do."

"I figured."

"Here's the situation." Barber briefly reviewed the events of the evening, starting from his instructions to Dolores concerning her uncle to the passing of Pedro at Bryan's hands and the passing of York at Saturnino's. Like a boy sitting by a campfire while ghost stories are told, Bill was rapt and pale.

"I guess," he said, "I'm supposed to take this kind of thing for granted, Lee. But, frankly, it makes me sick."

"Me, too."

"But you do it. I don't know if I'm up to it."

"Any operation not conceived and executed by idiots would never require you to do it, Billie. This is the most botched-up, uncontrolled, free-style foul-up that I've ever been in. I'd be ashamed of myself if I weren't too busy keeping one jump ahead of the executioner.

We're coming up to the wire now, Bill, and we'll soon know who's won. If we only half lose, we'll get Dolores, you, and me out of here. The Olds has gas and we have guns enough to see if we can shoot our way back to Hermosillo or, as the case may be, walk if those bridges are out. That's my only contingency plan. In the meantime, before we leave for the de Lemos place, there's an outside chance we can get Che. If we do, it ought to slow his boys down considerably. We'll hit the church. If they're holed up in the crypt awaiting nightfall, I think we can take them. We've got surprise and we can rig something to smoke them out. Down in that hole they're sitting ducks. We just have to keep Camillo off our backs, because if he cottons to us he'll have some more of his friends on us. A shoot-out in the cathedral during the daytime is hardly respectful, but, hang it, we can't afford not to pursue this one."

"You're the boss," Bill replied. "But I do think I ought to remind you that headquarters told you to keep your nose out of the insurgency."

"Yeah, and they also told me to stay put in Madre Dolorosa."

"True!"

"They can't have it both ways, not with a gas attack on the town coming up. It's not our fault we're out here, hanging on for dear life. In a situation like this, a case officer has to use his own judgment, Bill. Mine is we go for broke."

"What do you want me to do?"

"Get this tin can back to town. I'll get out on the way. At fifteen hundred sharp I'll be in the church by the trapdoor. Don't show any sign of recognition of me. If the coast looks clear, I'll take a jolt out of this bottle. If not, when I see you I'll just walk out of the church and meet you here as fast as I can walk it. If it's clear, you mosey over to me and let me call the shots. You're still armed?"

"Yeah."

"That's fine. Okay, let's get under way."

At three o'clock Saturnino was in the transept of the church on his knees, praying to the saint nearby. He was sniffling, a drunk on a crying jag. The few women praying in the church ignored him. When the hippie American came in, several of the women watched. Madre Dolorosa was too far off the beaten path for people yet to have become used to their cathedral being a tourist attraction, certainly not for the unwashed, unregenerate unfaithful. Mark Walski, hands in his pocket and with an air of superior indifference, sauntered through the old building, staring at Mary while picking his nose, and scratching his crotch while scowling at Jesus. The old women frowned. He made his way to the transept and saw the drunken peasant praying there. After blowing his nose and whimpering, the filthy derelict noisily invoked the panoply of powers to find him money for another drink, and then, in most un-Christian sentiments, called on the powers to visit a series of curses, each more graphic and vulgar than the next, on his brothers, Raoul, Frederico, and Rudolfo, and on his sisters, Carlotta, Angelina, Belen, Tita, Tina, and . . . but before the list got longer or the graphics stronger, the women praying in the front of the church had walked away in shock. The drunk, taking offense, followed their footsteps with a few unhallowed insults, interspersed with slurping swigs from the bottle in his side pocket. The women, like dark chickens in the first moment of a rainstorm, gathered their black skirts and, clucking, ran to the rear of the church. The hippie had reached the drunk, who, seeing him, let loose a string of husky epithets that curled the terra-cotta ears of a nearby plaster angel.

"Well, that got them out of the line of fire, anyway. Poor old girls won't be interfering when they see us pull up the trapdoor," Saturnino whispered to Mark.

"I don't know Spanish, so I don't know what you said, but from the looks on their faces there ain't no intercession that would save your plagued soul now, my bottle-worn friend."

"Oh, I can put a string of oaths together running head to tail and mean enough to etch gold if I put my mind to it," whispered Saturnino proudly. "But now, cross your fingers. I've got a bunch of rags here soaked in soot and kerosene. That ought to make a jim-dandy smoke bomb if Che is down there. I also bought three glass bottles of ammonia, which is the nearest I can come to tear gas. I figure the smell and the smoke, along with the noise, ought to scare him out. I want to avoid shooting. In the first place, it's sacrilegious; in the second, it'll bring troops and Teran on our back; and in the third, I want Che alive. If we get him, or if we have to get out, we go through that door there—" Saturnino pointed to the door connecting to the rectory garden. "—and through the gate in the rear wall. Got that?"

"Yep."

"Okay, you stand by out of the line of fire as I pull the trapdoor up. Take this flashlight and start sweeping from your side there as soon as it's up high enough—I'm going to prop it with this." Saturnino had a three-foot-long board. "If he's there, or they are, it will blind them. They'll probably shoot, but if we both stay to the side they can't hit us. Ready?"

Mark Walski moved to the side of the trapdoor, flashlight in one hand and .38 Colt automatic in the other. Saturnino, a gunny sack filled with the soaked rags on the floor near him, next to it three ammonia bottles, and, in his hand, his 357. Keeping low to the floor, only his arm a target as he pushed upward, Saturnino raised the trapdoor. Darkness and silence. One foot, two feet, three feet: darkness and silence. The flashlight poked about aggressively, like a physician's fingers in a sore spot, unrelenting. Tension, darkness, probes of light, and nothing. The crypt was empty.

"Nuts," said Saturnino. "They must have figured their go-pher's safe house was blown and didn't come back. Maybe Che missed his pills. I should have known. Ah, well."

"That's it, eh?"

"I don't know. Look, Mark—shine that light of yours down there once again on the floor by the foot locker." Mark shone the light; an empty medicine bottle lay on the floor.

"Well, who knows, one chance in a million, but it's worth a stake-out. We've got nothing to do until tonight, anyway."

"What's the idea?" asked the hippie.

"You see that empty bottle? When I was down here day before yesterday, I found that one of them—it must have been Che—was having stomach troubles; he had antacid tablets and antidiarrhea medication. He'd used most of it up and so, to help him along, I removed some more. I left a little so he wouldn't get suspicious, but no one counts pills, you know—he'd just run out sooner. His tummy and Moctezuma have met, and Moctezuma has won."

"Why did you take the pills—pure meanness?" asked Mark.

"There's that. But a sick man is always a better choice of enemy than a well one. Nothing like a searing case of the dribbles to take a commander's mind off the action. The medical history of warfare theory, but it's so. But now, since he's used up the medication, he's going to want more. If we're lucky, he either doesn't or hasn't had time to get to it. Anyway, it's worth our spending a few hours staking out the pharmacy, just in case. We haven't anything else we can do, anyway, until dark, when we'll go on down to the de Lemos place. We can take turns going native, sleeping in the sun, our backs against a building, sombreros over our eyes, mariachis playing, se-ñoritas dancing—just like the travelogues. How's that?"

"Jim-dandy, but I don't have a sombrero," complained Mark.

"Don't take me seriously, friend, I have my moments of mad-ness. You just roll that wheeled junk heap of yours right in front of his store. Go in and buy yourself some aspirin and go back and sit inside and wait. No one will pay you any mind, not unless the soldiers arrest you as a Yankee on general principles or one of those crazies decides you're a Russian spy, too. But failing that, in the daylight you ought to be okay. I'll lounge across the street—I will have a sombrero—and if I spot Che I'll amble on over and when he walks out of the store I'll poke a small invitation in his back and we load him into the back of your truck. Like taking the lambs to market."

"What if he brings a friend?" asked Mark.

"Then we invite his friend, too. Two lambs to market. If he has two friends, though, I think I'll just pass the opportunity by. There's a chance that his friends will be backing him up with a tail. If it's Manuel, I'll recognize him, and if it's any of the guys I saw at the drop in the church, I ought to recognize them, too. Otherwise, you keep your eyes on your mirror and out the front and see if there's a backup party behind Che. Now here's how Che looks." Saturnino gave a detailed description. "So, if you see somebody like that, signal me across the street by dropping your arm out of your car window. If you see he's brought friends, make your hand into a fist. Make as many fists as you see friends. I doubt if he'll bring a whole war party in, not when they want to stay in seclusion until the Durango boys take care of San Ramon. But he's clever, a pro, so we can't underrate him. One thing is sure, this is a bonus operation and we don't want to take any chances on it. If it looks easy, we go; if not, we walk away. Okay?"

"Okay."

It was six in the evening. Saturnino had been snorting from his rum bottle ever since he'd settled into an Indian squat across from the pharmacy several hours before. The rum was vile, even though his snorts had been limited to wetting his lips and not swallowing. His lips had been parched by the cheap alcohol and the smell of it almost gave him a hangover. Across the street from him, not quite directly in front of the store, the van was parked. The hippie in it was reading a magazine taken from the great stack of them he kept at hand. This one—Saturnino could sometimes see the cover—was *The National Lampoon.* Dirty humor was just what this operation needed.

Saturnino saw him first, the Spaniard. Peasant dress, but walking too fast for a local; perhaps his stomach hurt. He was by himself. But Mark's arm, now dropping out the driver's window, was making a fist. Che had come from the direction the car faced; both Saturnino and Mark had a good view of the street. Saturnino's eyes moved behind Che. On the same side, nothing. No one moving, except two old men walking in the opposite direction. In the middle of the street, a mule pulled a wagon loaded with pottery; there was one man on the seat. On his own side of the street, and fifty feet behind, also walking too fast, limping stiff-legged and being unhappy about it—Manuel. Awkward! Manuel would stop right in front of him to cover Che while Che went in the pharmacy, if that was where he was going. The sombrero was big, there were a few other peasants down the street in the same chronic squat, so Manuel would not notice at once. But while waiting, he would be looking around and he might look down. The rum bottle, that filthy hair, the lock still down over the forehead to cover the much-healed hole in his head—no, it was awkward. It had been brazen putting Mark up front, the kind of obviousness that usually works. If Che's belly was running, he might not notice, but Manuel was no tourist bureau, and he didn't like foreigners, anyway. Awkward! If Che went into the store, Saturnino could not get up to cross the street; it would be a dead giveaway, and Manuel would be at his back. Manuel had no weapon visible, but he had limped; perhaps a light automatic rifle up his leg? In any event, there would be a pistol inside that loose blouse of his. Nor could Saturnino get up now. Manuel would be looking for just that kind of thing and would be bound to recognize him; Manuel's calling card, the gun-barrel welt, still showed on his left side, the one Manuel would see. Che had come up and gone into the store and Manuel had pulled abreast. He wasn't five feet from Saturnino, his eyes fixed on the hippie in the van and his back to the lolling drunk whose sombrero covered his face. Awkward, but no time to make it easy. If Manuel made him first, Saturnino sitting down, it would be no contest. In his mirror Mark was watching them both. It was good to have a partner around.

Saturnino carefully pulled the 357 from its holster and, remaining in his seated position, slithered forward until he was immediately behind and beneath Manuel's back. Using an old wrestling trick, he extended his right foot forward, ahead of Manuel's ankle, and, as he suddenly brought his foot sideways, pulling back against Manuel's right ankle, pushed his left leg forward in a powerful jab against the back of Manuel's leg, just below the knee. It was the stiff leg, and under the pressure it pitched forward, working like a catapult to send Manuel's body pitching headlong into the street. By the time he'd hit the ground, Saturnino was on top of him, with his magnum pressed against Manuel's neck, Manuel's left arm in a hammerlock and Saturnino's knee grinding into the small of his back. Manuel groaned in pain, surprise, fury.

"Okay, up, and up fast, or you're dead." Saturnino spoke in a low venomous tone, keeping the hammerlock on Manuel and the nose of the pistol hard into the back of his neck. As Manuel got up, were he alert he could be expected to try to break the hammerlock with a fast, clubbing stomp of his foot down to Saturnino's arch, ducking and turning to the right and coming up with a knee to Saturnino's groin. To counter, Saturnino held himself angled with all the pressure upward and forward against Manuel's cinched wrist, propelling the latter hastily ahead; he had to run to keep from falling on his face as he got up. He could respond by making a running fall to break the hammerlock; if Saturnino didn't shoot him then, Manuel would have time to reach for his pistol and, turning, fire. Manuel didn't have time, for as he stumbled across the street, heading directly for the back of the van as Saturnino had propelled him, Saturnino shifted his magnum and with a vicious blow brought the gun stock crashing down on Manuel's head. He crumpled into a ball on the street side of the truck, next to the rear fender, out of sight of the door of the pharmacy opposite.

"Get back here, quick!" said Saturnino to Walski as the hippie put his head out of the driver's window. "Open the right-hand side door first, look to see that there's no chance of Che seeing this clown. Dump him in the back and then just look busy when Che comes out. Keep your gun out behind the door. I'll steer him to you. We're into it now, so if Che makes a break for it, shoot him." Sweat pouring off his face, Saturnino ran to the front of the pharmacy, crouching behind the side toward which the door opened. He could not be seen through the one dirty window of the store, which was piled high with ancient displays of medicaments, household cleaners, trusses, patent medicines, and the like. The episode with Manuel had not taken more than two minutes. Saturnino waited nervously behind the pharmacy door, hoping that Che had not got the wind up and fled through the mortuary rear of the store. One minute and nothing. Two minutes and nothing. Three minutes—four, five. If Che came up behind him, he could take them both by surprise. "Cover the street behind me," Saturnino whispered loudly, for Mark could see behind his partner if he looked around the truck. Likewise, Saturnino could cover Mark's back, looking in the other direction. Six minutes, and there were footsteps inside the pharmacy coming toward the door. Seven, and the door opened. Che looked immediately across the street toward where Manuel should have been and, not seeing him, instantaneously began to retreat into the store. Saturnino brought the hot nose of the gun deep into his back.

"Freeze, Spaniard, or you're dead."

The Spaniard grew rigid; Saturnino could sense his muscles gathering, poised for some explosive response. Saturnino had no time to play. While the man's back was still to him, he shifted the gun and brought it crashing down on Che's skull. The Spaniard dropped like a lead weight on the sidewalk, his lungs wheezing air and two large bottles of medicine clattering to the dirt sidewalk. "Tough tummy, buddy," Saturnino murmured as he dragged the body to the rear of the van and, with Walski, dumped it like a sack of potatoes into the rear. He climbed in and, closing the doors behind him, told Mark to drive off.

Had there been soldiers in the street, nothing could have been done. As it was, there had been people—the few men sitting on the shady side of the street, some of them drunk, others asleep, some Indians impassively waiting, an undernourished, snotty-nosed child walking idly with a stick in its hand, an old woman on her way to an unhurried somewhere, an old man hobbling under a load of precious firewood strapped to his back, a man riding a mule sideways, two sacks of grain lashed behind the wooden saddle, and two idle storekeepers standing in doorways catching the air. All of these had seen one man trip, attack, and viciously hit another. They had seen the hippie come to the rear of his truck to load the body. They had seen the same attacker waiting at the pharmacy door, and they had seen him hit the customer as he emerged, with the hippie once again assisting in the kidnapping and then driving off. They had seen with eyes that had seen many troubles before and would see many troubles again. Those who could do so unobtrusively had moved inside —the storekeepers, for example, and the child. The mule rider had stopped his mule and turned around before reaching the truck; the old man with the wood stopped, too, resting cautiously in the shadow of a doorway. And the others who could not escape sat quietly and heard not and saw not. Later, when Lieutenant Rosales questioned them, Saturnino knew they might retrieve their memories if assured the villains were foreigners who would never return again. Otherwise, the wisdom of Madre Dolorosa was in its silence.

In the back of the bumping, rattling, rasping van, Saturnino disarmed and tied up his two victims. They were blindfolded, their mouths taped, with wads of oil-soaked cotton taped over their ears to deafen them. Manuel had a sidearm and a light, short-barreled automatic rifle, U.S. Army, the one that had made his leg so stiff. Che carried a U.S. Army Colt .45 automatic. Neither man had any identification.

"Where to, boss?" yelled Bill from the front of the truck.

"I think we're going to have to hide the truck for a while, Bill. I can't be sure Rosales won't be after us. Now you're in this thing publicly, you stand out like a crocodile in the wading pool and so does the truck. Stupid of me not to have planned better for this. Frankly, I don't think I ever expected to find Che at the pharmacy or, if I did, to pull it off this easily. Stupid."

"Well, round one was a lulu. Now that we've captured the general staff, their little army is going to be distraught. I think I know a place we might hide the van if you're scared to chance it in the stables where the Olds is. I hate to take that chance myself— putting all our wheels in one basket, so to speak."

"What do you have in mind?"

"There's what seems to be an abandoned brick yard and kiln about a mile east of the town square. I checked it out yesterday, just in case. There's a wall around it and the approach road is on the edge of town, not much going on out there and with luck nobody will see us turn in. There are a couple of old buildings inside, with truck or wagon entrances and plenty of room to get the van in and hole up. There was even an old wagon, if you can find the mules to pull it; we could go down to the de Lemos place in style, providing you're in no hurry. Of course, if somebody does come along and finds this van with that big shortwave radio rig in it, the balloon is up. But what the heck? It is, anyway, as far as I can see."

"Okay, any old hole in a storm. Let's try your brickworks, Bill. I'm glad your brain is working. I think mine is just plumb tuckered out."

They drove in silence to the outskirts of town, taking an indirect route, and approached the walled-off brick factory from an area of abandoned tumbledown shacks and untended, unirrigated gardens.

They passed a few people on the way in, people who could have identified them, but to conduct a search requires personnel and organization and at the moment Lieutenant Rosales, should he have been notified, which was unlikely, had neither. He had one old bailing wire–girdled police car, without radio, and one man. The army had trucks and personnel, but since midafternoon almost none had been in evidence in town. A few sentries had remained by the central plaza and city hall, but the rest had disappeared. Barber had taken that as a good sign; if Dolores had persuaded her uncle to call Hernandez, Hernandez's orders would have got the regiment moving south, toward the de Lemos hacienda. Barber hoped that was it. If so, the drama was fast approaching its finale. The van turned into the deserted yard. An old kiln sagged precariously sideways and piles of faulty bricks had brushwood poking out of the cracks. Several old buildings teetered on the verge of collapse; one had already given up, relaxing itself into a pile of rotting beams and toppled brick walls. Bill drove the van past a freight wagon with steel-rimmed, wooden, spoked wheels to the back of the yard and into a two-story building, roofless but its walls intact. A rabbit scurried across the yard and, in the building, the scamper of rats was heard as the engine stopped. In the van Che was stirring.

"Maybe our friend is waking up," Barber said to Bill. "Let's see how he is." As he looked closely at the mummy's head, so bandaged he was, he noticed something he'd missed earlier in his hurry. "Hey, Bill, come take a look at the Spaniard here. What do you think?" Bill came and knelt beside the unconscious man.

"What do you mean? Is he going to die?" Bill spoke worriedly and not without reproach.

"No. Just take a look at his hair."

"It's black."

"No, look at the roots."

"Well, bless my soul—they're blond."

"Yep," said Barber. "You know, when I saw that hair conditioner in his toilet kit, I assumed it was the middle-aged vanities, guy keeping the gray out. That's what the label said it was for. Clever. He must have refilled the bottle with strong dye, not that fifteen-days-to-your-youth stuff. So our Spaniard is a blond."

"Brown eyes, dark skin, though," said Bill. "Just like you, Lee."

"Yeah. Maybe we go to the same beautician. Probably long-lasting skin dyes in his case and the usual contact lenses. But what is a blond who uses a professional makeup artist doing down here? What do you think, Bill?"

"Maybe the Bureau sent him in and didn't tell us. Wanted to be on top whichever side won the revolution. They do it all the time."

"No," replied Barber, "although maybe the pictorial computer file would tell who he was if we could telephoto it in. No, if anybody on our side sent him in, he was sure doing his best to convince me it wasn't so. Hell, he might have won the revolution for them."

"Well, the Bureau's had that happen, too, or so I've heard."

"Well, whoever he is, I don't suppose he'll volunteer to tell us. I guess the only way we'll find out is to take him home with us."

"Home with us! Haven't we got enough troubles? Aren't you going to turn him over to the Mexicans?"

"I'd planned to," Barber agreed. "But that's when I thought he was a Guatemalan red. But, this way, if we turn him over, we'll never find out."

"Won't liaison tell us—I mean, assuming there is a new liaison control after Hernandez is gone?"

"I doubt it. They'll probably just shoot him. I don't think they're in the mood for niceties, after all the Cain these boys have raised. But if we take Sven here, or Siegfried or Ivan whatever his name is . . ."

Bill interrupted. "You're being funny, I know, but Ivan—do you think there's any chance that . . ."

Barber interrupted. "There's always a chance, Bill. Detente or otherwise, the big boys are out to take care of themselves, devil take the hindmost. I'll tell you one thing—the way it looks now it's more likely to be Ivan than Sven. I mean, those Swedes were rightfully mad at us during the Vietnam mess, but I don't think they're mad enough to want to take over Mexico to put a hostile government right on our doorstep. On the other hand, what does Ivan lose by trying? I don't really believe it, of course, Bill. This guy is probably some two-bit mercenary out of Austria by way of Katanga, being paid by Castro's slush fund. Anyway, there's no use worrying about it. He won't tell us. Now, what about Manuel? Does he look like a genuine article or is he a Martian?"

Bill was examining Manuel. "He's an ugly S.O.B. His teeth look like a ring of volcanic craters; Lord, his mother should have made him stop eating candy. With a mouth like that, he has to have grown up poor, real poor. No, he's a country boy, dirt under his fingernails, hair filthy, hasn't bathed in a month, and his black hair is his own. He's local."

"Okay, so he doesn't come home with us. I don't want the border patrol stopping us for smuggling in wetbacks."

"Now that you've got it all set in your mind, how do you figure that the four of us are going to spend our evening? Sitting here throwing rocks at the rats?"

"You're right. It'll be dark in an hour. If we're right, the army ought to be in position around the mine now. All that's left is to watch the fireworks and make sure Dolores is okay."

"What about de Lemos and Hernandez—what are you going to do about them?"

"Nothing more than I've done," said Barber. "We're not in a position to gather evidence on them here. Someone in Washington or Mexico is going to have to put on political pressure to set Hernandez up. The way it is now, nobody can even put anything those two boys run under surveillance, not even his Air Narcotics runways. They've got it locked up. No, someone is going to have to get to the ministers themselves—Home, Justice, you name it. Making a case with evidence for a trial is second; the politics comes first."

Lee looked at his watch. "We'd better get hopping if we want to get down to de Lemos's for the fireworks. Look, do you have anything else in the truck you can use as a disguise? Did they document you as anything besides Walski when they sent you in?"

"No, nothing," replied Bill.

"Too bad. Well, we've got to get rid of us as well as this van, and I've just had an idea. When it turns dark, I want to trade this for the Olds, leaving this buggy in the stable."

"But you can't take the Olds out. You said so yourself, everybody in town knows it belonged to York. Why, there aren't more than twenty cars in the whole place. It stands out."

"Agreed, but we've got to take a chance. As I said, we're down to the line now."

When darkness fell, the van crept out of its brick yard and, circling the town center through side streets and byways, arrived at the stable. All the houses stood with their back walls to the alley, which, as usual, was deserted, except for a few urchins and the ever-present rats, cats, and mongrel dogs. Inside, the two men made a complete change of clothes, using the limited wardrobe that lay in the hidden steel storage locker.

"Okay, let's get going," Lee said as they locked the stable door, leaving the van inside. The rear of the Olds had two concealed passengers, one flat on the floor, the other flat across the seat, both covered with a blanket, their heads cushioned by blankets beneath them. The car stopped in an alley. A man emerged and walked the remaining distance to the hotel. He entered the hotel lobby and approached the desk clerk. He spoke in English but held a Spanish-English dictionary in his hand.

"Sir, I'm looking for the Reverend Alfred York."

The desk clerk looked at the visitor uncomprehendingly. Leafing through the dictionary, the visitor put together the question in pidgin Spanish.

"He's gone, sir." The desk clerk was not going to tell the visitor that York was dead. Let others carry bad news.

"I'm his brother, Harold York."

"Yes, sir," said the clerk.

Harold knew the clerk would appreciate the resemblance: height, weight, and voice the same, only Harold was forty, auburn-haired, only touched with gray at the sideburns, blue eyes, not brown, eyebrows bushy red, not gray, and of course no moustache. Harold had not been able to conceal the wound in his forehead but, using the medical kit in the Olds, had found some skin-colored tape that, when extended fully across his forehead, gave the appearance of a long, narrow injury, not the centered one that York had covered with his locally procured white bandages. Perhaps the clerk would think the family was accident-prone.

"He's not here, then?" Harold spoke aggressively, unlike the diffident nervousness of his elder brother. The clerk would notice the difference in manner. Harold was tough, unpleasant.

"No, sir."

"I'm a police officer. Did my brother tell you that?" The question was ridiculous, of course, but a tough Jersey cop would spit it out, anyway. It accomplished what was intended. The frail desk clerk was intimidated.

"My brother's room—I want the keys." Harold spoke English.

"Yes, sir." The desk clerk spoke in Spanish.

"Damn it, give them to me." Angrily, Harold didn't wait for an answer but strode behind the counter and, scanning the seven keys hanging on the board, pointed at one and then another until he paused at what he knew to be Alfred's. "This one?"

"Yes, sir."

A few minutes later, Harold York came running down the stairs. He spoke accusingly. "There's not a sign of him. The bed wasn't slept in last night."

"Yes, sir," said the clerk apologetically.

"I've got his car keys." Harold dangled them in front of the clerk's eyes. "Where's his car?"

"Yes, sir."

"He must have kept it nearby."

"Yes, sir."

"Well, damn it, if you don't know anything, I'll find it myself. I need a car. I came here on that crummy bus from Hermosillo. My brother didn't even respond to my telegram. He told me he'd meet me." The tone was accusatory.

"Yes, sir," apologetically. The old man shifted his weight nervously.

"If I find that car, I'm going to use it. You tell him that when he comes in, do you hear?"

"Yes, sir."

"And another thing." Harold was speaking loudly. "My brother wanted me to meet Lieutenant Rosales of the local police. Do you know him?"

"Yes, sir."

"Good. Well, I'm a busy man, lots to do. I'll go see Rosales after I find my brother. Now, you go tell Lieutenant Rosales that Harold York is in town—you tell him who I am—and you tell him I look forward to meeting him. Tell him I'll see him tomorrow, if I can find my scatterbrained brother and his car. Here." Harold took out a piece of paper from his suit coat pocket—he was perspiring in his overdressed state—and scribbled a note. "Here, you get this to Lieutenant Rosales right away, you understand?"

"Yes, sir."

"And here." Harold rifled through a pack of notes in his wallet and pulled out one hundred pesos for the clerk. The casual way he treated the bills suggested that he thought it all worthless. "For Lieutenant Rosales, you understand?"

"Yes, sir."

"Understand?" Taking his dictionary, Harold leafed through it for the Spanish and repeated his message. "Take this to Lieutenant Rosales now."

"Yes, sir." The clerk, of course, had not understood a word, but it was, after all, courteous to say yes.

Harold rushed into the street and disappeared down an alley. A few minutes later he pushed the car's nose into a different street and made off for the de Lemos estate. Beside him sat a freckled, snub-nosed, clean-cut young American with short brown hair—very short. He had just had the crew cut he'd worn under his wig trimmed by Harold York.

Eighteen

IF THE TROOPS HAD MOVED south, they'd left no sign of their passage. Not that there should be signs, but it was worrisome, not knowing. It was one thing to be bringing two guerrilla leaders into an area controlled by a governmental regiment; it was another to be bringing them near the guerrilla hideout with the army far away. In that case, the road, the hacienda, was theirs any time the insurgents chose to take it. It was not just a gamble, it was *the* gamble. Everything had depended on Dolores, on her believing him.

Barber stopped the car, having run it off the main road into the desert behind a thick clump of shrubs. They were about a mile and a half from the de Lemos compound. He'd been driving without lights for several miles and had seen, from time to time, the lights of the house flickering behind the trees. They pulled out their two passengers, mute still, blind, and deaf, thanks to rope, tape, gauze, and cotton. Barber lashed them separately to heavy mesquite brush. They would not get away on their own. Were Barber and Hickock not to return, they would drift drying, indistinguishably, into death, for they were already conveniently mummified.

Barber and Hickock hiked toward the de Lemos place, keeping to the bushes. There was a half-moon that gave sufficient light. When they came in sight of the side road that ran to the house, Barber felt an ominous load depart. There were army trucks silhouetted near the house and the talk of soldiers could be heard. Dolores had done it, the regiment had been dispatched. They had been using the area outside the compound for staging; it appeared as they walked closer that only sentries had been left behind.

The same men who had been carousing in the bars and whorehouses the night before, used to easy discipline, could not be expected to be too alert as perimeter guards. Coming upon the compound from the rear, Barber could see a cluster of five men lounging about, one fool leaning on his rifle. About one hundred yards beyond, there were another five soldiers. Either they'd not

221

been assigned a walking post or had no officer of the guard. What would have been to the advantage of the guerrillas, had they chosen to attack the place, now stood Barber and Hickock in good stead. From brush clump to cactus to shallow arroyo, they stealthily moved to the rear wall and, where spindly trees hugged the wall to give cover, prepared to make their way over. Barber gave Hickock a hand boost until Hickock stood on his shoulders. The wall, about eight feet high here, had the usual broken glass on top. They had prepared for that with a thick mat of woven reeds, the torn-off roof of a shed that they'd passed on their way out of town. The reeds, doubled and redoubled, were nearly a foot thick, deep enough to absorb the shards which, in turn, sunk as they were in the wall's cement, stabilized the matting.

When Hickock was over the wall, he threw a rope to Barber and, bracing himself on the interior surface, held fast while his partner pulled himself up and over. Inside it was dark and no sign of sentries in the back garden. They kept low, nevertheless, enjoying the cover of the plantings as they approached the house itself. It was a big house and Barber had been in only the reception and dining areas and the office. What the various dark windows opened to, he could not be sure. One lighted window revealed a hallway, which, with crocks and food sacks in it, suggested a pantry or kitchen access. It was better to chance entry there than try a dark room where some frightened sleeping servant might cry out at the intruders. The lock was not prey to the thin knife that had worked so well in the mortuary only the night before. Barber motioned to Hickock to try it; just out of training school, his burglary skills ought to be first rate. A kit had come with the car. To start it, Hickock taped glass to the window, cut the glass deeply with a glazier's diamond, pulled the circle of glass out with the suction cup he'd placed on it before the surgery, reached his hand in to the casement lever, turned it, and the window opened. Fortunately, electronic burglar alarms had not made their way to Sonora, even in the house of a crime king.

Inside, the footsteps were soft. The cushioned rubber overshoes that they'd brought along—again, the standard kit of the recent Bureau trainee—assured that. The first door to the left proved to be a pantry, across a cellar entrance, at the end a kitchen. Through the kitchen, its lights still bright, and the smell of dinner cooking, although it was ten thirty P.M., suggested that de Lemos, as Dolores once had told him, would be having a late dinner. Voices from a room next to the kitchen—and the sound of low laughter and eating—allowed the lucky inference that the servants ate first and had their own dining area. From the kitchen they went next to a linen, plate, and silver storage area and through a swinging door from there to the dining room, the table set for six. Six! De Lemos, Guillermo, Dolores, and . . . Barber wondered who the others might be. Outside the dining room another hall, long. At one end it ought to meet the foyer. A door prevented checking that hunch out. If correct, then the parlor would be near there, too, across the courtyard, then, perhaps the formal reception or living room, in which he'd once sat with Dolores. He remembered a library off of that. To the left, across the courtyard, there also ought to be the office sector. To their right, toward the parlor, there ought to be a front staircase. Behind them, near the kitchen somewhere, there was probably a rear staircase as well.

Where would Dolores be? He had to make sure that she was and would remain safe. He would worry later about his second task, the minor one of dumping sweet Manuel into the army's lap. To do that, Barber had to be credible to the soldiery, a little matter he had yet to work out.

He would try upstairs first. She'd said her bedroom was on the side of the house. She'd been able to hear Guillermo swing his car in with Pedro, to hear the garage doors close. The best bet, then, although by no means sure, was the west side, nearer the garages. The front of the house and its drive were on the north. It was a big house to be a sneak thief in and no ease in the doing of it, either. They had their guns holstered. Were, for instance, a maid to chance upon them, she would scream more if she saw a gun, unless they bluffed her into silence. And if they met de Lemos? It was too boorish to consider. Shoot him down in his own house? Not if they could help it. Especially with the sentries posted close outside.

They found the main staircase off the reception hall, an ornate, winding affair, its well hung high with tapestries, fine French and Spanish pieces, for de Lemos was a man of taste. Upstairs, they proceeded along the front hall, only the light of the chandelier from the stairwell to guide them. It was much too early for bedtime—unless, of course, there were members of the household about whom he'd not heard. Dolores, de Lemos, Guillermo, and the unknown dinner guests; at most, six bedrooms in use, whereas there must be twelve such rooms upstairs. He reached a turning that brought the hall to the western rooms. Three doors to a side, some perhaps bathrooms, linen closets, sewing rooms—who knew what? It was an old house in the grand style, rooms also opening to the central courtyard, a fountain in its center.

At each door he stopped and listened, Bill behind him. Hearing nothing, he tried the knob. The first two on the right and left were locked. The second on the right proved to be a study: dusty, feminine—perhaps de Lemos's wife, when she lived, had made it hers. The knob second left, facing outward west, responded to his grasp. He opened the door quietly and listened. Silence. And the smell of perfume. Odd, he'd not thought about Dolores and perfume, but it was hers—no, this was her. "Dolores," he whispered. No response. He pulled his pen flashlight out and probed the darkness. The room was delicately done: Florentine silk draperies, a Nain hunting scene rug, Louis XIV furniture, the vanity, with cut-glass bottles on its lace-covered top, a single bed. He resented his own intrusion here in her boudoir.

He gestured to Bill to follow and, guessing a rear stairway to be safer, he led the way to the end of the hall where, in the darkness, a narrower stairway led down. It should land them near the courtyard and near the pantryway where they had broken in. It did and, once downstairs, heading right instead of left, toward the kitchen, they dared not go near again, for those servants must be in and out. The two men kept to an inner veranda. They were getting the hang of the place. Into the parlor now, their flashlights guiding them, and from there by the route he'd been taken before, when Guillermo had escorted him on that first visit. And here it was—first the hallway crossing, then the waiting room, and . . . the sound now of voices. They were not loud enough to be in Guillermo's office immediately behind the door in front of them, that the forequarters of the de Lemos business precinct. If the door to the latter's office was open, they'd be in trouble as they entered Guillermo's. If, on the other hand, it was closed, they would be able to listen and, if necessary, conceal themselves behind a right-angled nest of four drawer files that Barber remembered made a sheltered corner.

Barber opened the door cautiously. Luck was still with them. The inner door to de Lemos's office was closed and now the voices were louder, loud enough to be heard. Bill, not understanding Spanish, positioned himself as lookout listening at the hall door to the waiting room, which they had closed behind them. Barber drew himself close to the inner office door. Just as he moved, he heard the sound of distant firing. Turning his head, he saw that the office window, this one facing south toward the rear, was half open. Small arms, machine guns; a mortar burp, blomph, smack, crackle, and, far away, chatter. It was happening. The troops were hitting the guerrillas in the mine over the ridge in the next valley west. Score one for the visiting team of Barber and Hickock. Important business was being done.

"It's started." Barber heard de Lemos's voice. "Well, thank goodness for that. It's one worry off our minds. Thank you, Raphael, you've reason to be pleased."

Raphael? Who was that? wondered Barber.

"It's little enough, considering the trouble they've been. I told General Sanchez they were to be wiped out to a man, no prisoners —I mean none after they finish the interrogations." That was Raphael, then, just a good-natured delegate from the Geneva Convention on the treatment of prisoners of war. Raphael went on, "I can't stay in here much longer, now that they're attacking. It was awkward, leaving General Sanchez and Sigua in the living room at a time like this. Family conference, indeed, all over this fool child here. What a mess. An army general and a justice deputy minister in the living room while our little war starts over there and we've got stupidity to deal with. I don't see how you could have done it, Dolores, opening our house to an American agent."

"I tell you, Uncle Raphael, he's no agent. How can you all insist he's anything but a pastor, just as he said? And if he weren't, I still don't understand what difference it would make. What do you care? You've never made any sense on that, any of you. What's it all about? I mean, I can understand you rushing up here with your little airplane, with your generals and your justice ministers, to fight the rebels. But what are you browbeating me for about that poor American? Ever since we came in here fifteen minutes ago, I've heard nothing but protests and accusations. Are you all mad? If I invite an American down here for dinner, what's wrong with that?"

"I've tried to tell you, Dolores." It was Don de Lemos speaking. "We're an old family and we can't have you taking up with just anyone. As your Uncle Raphael has told you, he has reasons to believe York is an impostor, no doubt a criminal. There's no telling what he's after. You're not safe with him and certainly we're not safe with him around. At best, he's a confidence man; at worst—well, I shouldn't have to tell you about the world, you're old enough."

"I tell you, Uncle Francisco, he's an honorable man. Oh, I don't pretend to know all about him. After all, he's a complicated person. But I'm absolutely sure he's decent and honest."

"And in the face of contrary information from the Home Ministry that your Uncle Raphael has just faced you with, what is your evidence, my dear?"

"My intuition." Dolores spoke indignantly.

"Good heavens, girl, you can't just ignore what we tell you on the grounds of your female intuition." Raphael, Barber realized, was Raphael Hernandez, having arrived courtesy of a ministry helicopter, probably parked in the desert in front of the house. Uncle Raphael was remonstrating with her. "No, you just can't do that. I'll have to insist. I want your promise you'll never see him again. Never correspond, never mention him. Do you understand?"

"Raphael!" Her voice was angry now. The man had suddenly lost his avuncular title. "I am not a child. I am a grown woman with a life of my own and I shall do in this matter as I please. Do you understand *that?*"

"You place us in a difficult position, my child," said de Lemos, his voice soft.

"Oh, and why is that, pray tell?"

"There is much that I'm not at liberty to divulge, my dear. Raphael here has told me much more that I can't bring myself to discuss. You simply must have faith in us this time. It's a matter of family loyalty."

"I am sorry, Uncle Francisco, you know I love you and don't want to upset you, but I can't make promises to you that don't make sense. Frankly, I think, were you to push it, there might be some explaining to do on your part." She was speaking reasonably but there was a warning edge to her voice.

"Oh, and what might you mean by that?" asked Raphael.

"I think you'd better ask Guillermo here."

"Ask him what, my dear?" said de Lemos.

"Ask him who that man was he brought here the other night,

the one without a nose. Ask him how he managed to arrive here at
the hour he did. Ask him why the police are looking for a man
without a nose in the killing of Chief Flanagan last month. Ask him
that."

There was a long silence behind the door. Finally Don de
Lemos spoke. "What are you talking about, Dolores? The man
you're talking about is a cattle broker, you know that. And about the
police, well, your imagination is working overtime. How could you
know? Are you sure you're feeling well?"

"Oh, Uncle Francisco, stop it. We're family, I love you no
matter what it is you've done. Why must we have all these lies?" Her
voice was serious, pleading.

Raphael's tone was cold. "I think you've made a very serious
accusation, Dolores. I think we deserve an apology from you. I'm
not going to stand for much more in the way of your insults, young
lady."

"Raphael, I'm not going to argue with you. It's all so stupid.
Maybe you're right, maybe you don't know anything about it, maybe
it's some private dirty business that Guillermo is up to. Lord knows
I wouldn't put it past him. He's sitting here like a bump on a log but
I can imagine what's on his mind, can't I, Guillermo?" There was
no reply. "Go ahead, Guillermo—I suppose you're going to tell me
that you didn't bring that noseless man down to kill the Yankee
minister." Again silence. "Raphael, why don't you go ahead and tell
Guillermo to tell me the truth? Why not? You're the deputy home
minister, you ought to be interested. Aren't you?"

"Why, of course. All right, Guillermo, answer Dolores."

The sullen, irritable voice of the secretary was heard. "I'm your
employee, of course, I'm at your service. But, really, don't you think
we should stop playing? It's clear enough your niece knows what's
going on—the gringo spy probably told her. For all we know, she's
been spying on us here for him. I don't want to play the fool any
longer. She knows. After all, last night she told you, Don de Lemos,
that she knew of the airplane. Tonight, we find she knows about
Pedro, Flanagan, and the contract on York. Why fool ourselves? If
she knows these things, she also knows that the Yankee is a government agent, a Bureau man, and if she lies it's to protect herself.
There's no need for her to protect him. She must know, as we do,
that Pedro's dead and so's the Yankee. She's very clever, this young

woman. But she's not my business, she's your niece. If you trust her, fine. I'm at your service in all matters. Tell me to do so and I'll give her the flight plan to Arizona. She can manage the heroin labs, as far as that goes. If she's going to know the operation, she might as well come in all the way. She's either in or out, it seems to me. Now that the Yankee's dead, maybe she'll think twice."

"What makes you say the Yankee is dead?" Dolores's voice was tense.

Guillermo replied, "Oh, there is something you don't know about? He was burned to death last night. Lieutenant Rosales has it that some of those town barflies rumored it that he was a Russian spy heading those lousy guerrillas. So sometime around two A.M. someone beat him and then they shot him and then they burned him to a crisp. But Rosales identified him all right: glasses, Bible, wallet, all right there. No question about it. There, what do you say to that?" Guillermo's voice was hostile, challenging, sadistic. But she surprised him.

"Well, so there you are. Why are you worried about me, then? If he's dead it's clear I won't be seeing him again, Raphael. Now aren't you satisfied?"

Raphael was surprised, "He's dead? Why didn't you tell me, Francisco?"

"How could I? You just flew in a little while ago and we've been with your colleagues. I hardly want to talk in front of them. But Guillermo's right—the assassin is dead and so is York, although who hit the assassin I've no idea. Maybe someone with an old score to settle. The town is full of old scores aching to become new scores."

"Well, that does put a new light on it. I confess I'm pleased and surprised, Dolores, about how you're taking it. I respect you for that. I'd have expected you to go to pieces. Well, maybe I was pushing things too hard. What do you think, Francisco?"

"I think perhaps we were too hard on Dolores. My dear, I'm not sure how much you knew or guessed, but, as Guillermo says, we have to assume now that you know everything. If you didn't before, my indiscreet secretary Guillermo here certainly saw to it just now that you learned quickly. I know it must come as a shock to you, dearest, and I'm sorry. We would have all preferred to keep you from worrying. But these things happen. The mines were failing, the cattle business was having bad years, I was foolish and failed to diversify. I didn't invest well in industry. We old landowners aren't always as clever as we like to pretend. So, with things pressing in on us, I had to look for a better crop. The estates in Cuilican simply made more money growing drugs. First it was marijuana, but that's a child's drug and too bulky for profit; opium is a cash crop and we've found nothing can compete with it. With Raphael here in his position in the ministry, we saw we had an ideal arrangement. The business just grew. I must say I have no regrets; we've made a fortune. Organized as it is, as long as Raphael can protect it at a federal level, well, I see no reason that we can't continue to prosper. You may not like it, my dear, but that money sent you to college. It pays for your travel and has bought you your apartments in Paris and wherever else it is you have them. Now do you understand just a little bit? We're not vicious criminals or anything of the sort. We're just businessmen taking advantage of the opportunities we have. It's not so serious—nothing like these guerrillas with their killings and revolutions. No, drugs are greatly overplayed. There's not that much difference between heroin and sleeping pills, as far as that's concerned. The whole effect is psychological, really. I mean, those people who use it want to. Frankly, I think alcohol is worse, much worse. I don't mean to run on, but I want you to understand. Raphael and I love you. Now, can we count on you to be loyal, not running off in a state of shock or saying something embarrassing to outsiders?"

"Yes, uncle. You know I wouldn't betray you, any more than I'd betray anyone I loved. I don't approve of what you're doing. In fact, I think it's terrible. But we're family. I'll be quiet about it. But for my own pride, I hope you understand if I take a job somewhere. I just couldn't face myself, taking money that I knew was made dishonestly. Perhaps I'll move north for a while. Is that all right?"

"Of course it is, my dear. Whatever you want. You see, Raphael," Francisco was talking happily, "we had nothing to worry about. Good girl."

"Yes, Dolores," agreed Hernandez. "I want to say I think you've behaved very well about this, in view of the circumstances. Well, perhaps we've gone on enough about this business. I can't keep my colleagues waiting forever in the living room. General Sanchez gets nervous sitting too long. And Sigua, well, he might drink too much if we leave him there with the Scotch. No, I think we'd better forget all of this and join them. Dinner should be soon. That will mollify them."

Barber had realized that the group would leave the office soon and, rather than chance a noisy retreat down the hall, had signaled to Hickock to join him behind the tall file cabinets in the corner. These were quite bulky. There should be no problem; Bill and he could leave through the window afterward. The two of them were well concealed before the group in the inner room had even come near the door. As he waited with Bill, Barber marveled at Dolores —her cleverness in guessing about the Flanagan affair and provocatively throwing it out like a live grenade on the dining-room table. When he married her, he might have to leave the Bureau, although he wouldn't tell her why. She'd be pleased enough, given her forebodings, that he had quit. But to be in the Bureau and have as uncles-in-law one of the Western Hemisphere's major narcotic traffickers was probably pushing the security boys too far. On the other hand, it would be droll to stay on. He could give it a try; after all, what did he care? He was not Crusader Rabbit. He'd keep an open mind. Barber was musing to himself, glad Dolores was safe, while waiting for the inner door to open and the group to pass by, when he felt Bill go tense. It was electric. Barber himself became frightened, a sympathetic vibration in response to something Bill had sensed. What was it?

He turned to look at Hickock. The man's face was ashen and his eyes, staring at his leg, were bulging. Barber's glance followed. His, too, paled. A gigantic scorpion, pale white with brown legs and stinger, was slowly crawling up Hickock's thigh. It was three inches long at least and the tail, turned upward and over its back, must have been four. A monster. And deadly. It could only have come in from the desert, probably scuffed up from a rock as they walked, riding in Hickock's trouser cuff. Now, as he had been standing still, it was trying to escape. One awkward move from Bill and he was in for it, the poison whip would lash. All either man could do was to wait and pray, until de Lemos and company had passed by, watching the exoskeletal demon crawl slowly upward. The sweat was pouring from Bill's brow and his fist was clenched so tightly that the tendons stood out to make his hand a claw.

"Wait, Bill, it'll be all right. I'll get it as soon as they're gone." Barber whispered it ever so softly just as the door was opening.

Once in the outer office, Guillermo ambled over to his desk and turned the lamp on. The other two men walked along, smiling; Dolores was somber. Brave girl, but near tears. Barber watched them through the safety of a crack between the cabinets. Next to him, Barber heard a low clacking noise. Bill's muscles had become so stiff with fear that, overly contracted, they began to shiver in tetanylike spasms. He couldn't help it—his teeth began to chatter. Under the stress, knowing the noise he was making by his unbidden spasm, and knowing its source in that pale venomous creature moving slowly, swaying, up his thigh, Bill surrendered to instinct. Swiftly, violently, as quietly as he could, his fist swept in a semicircle, hitting the scorpion to send it whirling in the air, its tail whipping out. By no more than a hair's breadth, the stinger missed Bill's hand, his life measured in micromillimeters.

The noise he'd made was measured in larger units. Guillermo at his desk heard it. He'd taken his gun while Barber's eyes had been on his friend. Now Guillermo was next to them behind the files, his automatic leveled at their hearts.

Nineteen

"MOVE AND YOU'RE DEAD." Guillermo meant it.

Both men stood still. In the corner the scorpion, its tail swinging, scurried into a crack in the floor. "All right—hands on your heads. Out." He spoke in Spanish, but Bill didn't need an interpreter. Cold-eyed, the uncles watched the two men come out from behind the cabinets; Dolores was pale but controlled. She, like the others, seemed not to recognize Barber as Harold York.

"Okay, feet apart, lean, hands against the wall. Lean, I said, damn it." Viciously, Guillermo poked the gun into Hickock's back, hard enough to injure the kidney. Bill grunted. Guillermo frisked them. Two guns, two wallets without identification, the burglary tools, flashlight, and miscellany. "Okay, who are you and what are you doing here?"

The older of the two intruders looked at the group nonplussed. "Hey," he said, his accent a Midwestern twang, his voice nasal, "I hope somebody here speaks English, because my Spanish stinks. You speak English?" He looked at Guillermo who, glowering, turned to Don de Lemos. The Don, in perfect English, repeated Guillermo's questions. Looking relieved, and with a disarming smile on his face, the auburn-haired American looked at de Lemos.

"My name's Jimmy the Gopher and this here—" He gestured toward his partner. "—this is Churchyard Mike. Ask anyone up north, they'll tell you who we are, they know us. We're houseworkers. We admit it, that's what we are—burglars. I guess you want to know why we're here. Well, we heard you all had a stash of nuggets and gold silt from the mine. Everybody on the border knows about it, how de Lemos struck it rich. They say you fly it out directly to beat the taxes. Lots of people up north seen that plane at night. Not bad, I got to hand it to you all, very smooth. Anyway, we thought we'd have a sweat at it. We got past that private army you've got outside and came through this window here—nothing to it, didn't even need the jimmy. This office looked like a good place to start.

We saw the can over there in the corner." Jimmy nodded toward the large floor safe behind Guillermo's desk. "But just as we got here, you started to come in through the door. We ducked into here. That's it. We're spiflicated."

De Lemos's eyes were hard. "Well, Raphael, what shall we do with them? If they are burglars, I suppose Lieutenant Rosales should handle it. Or we could ask Sigua out there to send someone down from the Justice Ministry to pick them up. The soldiers can hold them in the meantime. That is, if they are burglars. I don't like it."

Raphael Hernandez spoke. "Guillermo, check the files. See if they've been tampered with." Guillermo pulled at the locked drawers but found them secured.

"No, sir, everything's in order."

"Check the safe."

Guillermo went to the corner of the room behind his desk, where a large floor safe stood. He examined the dials and door. "No, sir, untouched. Whoever they are, we got them in time. They couldn't have been here long. I only opened the window just before we all came in here."

Hernandez pondered. "Well, that's something, anyway. They haven't stolen anything yet. If that's what they came for. Guillermo!"

"Yes, sir?"

"I've an idea," Hernandez said in English. "Take their shirts off." Under the nose of the pistol, the two took off their shirts, Mike's a flowered, Hawaiian-type sport shirt, Jimmy's a neat dark blue summer rayon. "Hand them to me, Guillermo." The deputy minister looked at the maker's tags inside the rear collar. There was none in Jimmy the Gopher's, but Churchyard Mike's read "Garfinkel's." "Garfinkel's—now where would that be?" asked Hernandez. De Lemos was the one to reply.

"In Washington, D.C., Raphael. I've been there. A good store."

Hernandez nodded, his lips pursed. "So, our Arizona burglar buys a new shirt in Washington, D.C.? Interesting. You travel a great deal, don't you?" He was staring hostilely at Mike. "Churchyard Mike, is it? Well, Mike, I think you'd better begin praying. Guillermo, I'll hold the gun on them while you tie their hands. Hobble their feet as well. Then take them out back and around beneath this window outside. We'll wait until you get them there."

"Yes, sir." Guillermo left the room for a moment and returned with rope. Expertly, he tied their hands and hobbled their ankles so that one foot couldn't move more than eight inches ahead of the other.

"Good. All right, get them on their way."

"What are you going to do?" protested Jimmy the Gopher. "You've got to turn us over to the cops."

"Oh, do we now? How convenient for you. Two American agents turned in to the good Lieutenant Rosales and within a day your liaison with the Justice Ministry will have you free and on your way home. Or do you have enough evidence already to stay down here to bring a case against us? Or perhaps you're looking for your advance party, the good Reverend York? Well, in case you haven't heard, he's now a deceased party."

"I tell you," Jimmy the Gopher was insisting, agitation and fear written over his face, "we're good, honest burglars—professionals. Ask anybody."

"Stop the clowning, my friend," said Raphael coldly. "Your little theater has reached its last act. I've no time for you. Guillermo, take them outside."

Guillermo prodded Jimmy with his gun.

Dolores, having surveyed the scene, spoke quietly. "Surely, Uncle Raphael, you're not going to kill them?"

"Yes, my dear, that is exactly what we're going to do. They are guerrillas. They were trying to break into the house. They fired at us. We shot them in defense. They'll have their discharged guns in their hands as evidence when we bring Sanchez and Sigua back here to show them. Guillermo will untie them as soon as they're safely dead. A homeowner's right, Dolores, and in these troubled times a heroic action on our part. It will read well in the papers. Can't you see the headlines? 'Deputy Minister Hernandez shoots attacking guerrillas, his family saved.'"

"But that's foolish. You said they were Yankee agents. I take that to mean U.S. police. There will be an incident, an investigation, you'll be found out, we'll all be found out. Isn't that right, Uncle Francisco?" She was calm, calculating. Jimmy, listening, wondered what was on her mind.

"Dolores is right, Raphael. As corpses, they'll be identified and there could be trouble. Still, we can't let them live. Not now. Perhaps if we could shoot them quietly somewhere and bury them without a fuss, that might do it."

"No!" said Hernandez. "I think the bolder approach is best. With Sanchez and Sigua as witnesses, there won't be any question. I'm serious about the publicity. The minister retires soon and I'm under strong consideration by the president for the post. Can you imagine what it would mean for all of us if I were home minister? No, it's too good an opportunity to miss. But Dolores, you're right about the investigation. You've a good brain in that head." He turned to Guillermo. "We'll listen to Dolores. Before you take these spies outside, find some black shoe polish and cooking oil, and some brown liquid shoe dye. We'll give them a quick makeup so that they'll be as dark as Indios. Dirty their clothes up, too. In the night outside they'll be dark enough. I'll arrange for the soldiers to take the bodies away to bury them in the common grave with the rest of the guerrillas. Perhaps we can just dump them all down one of the abandoned mine shafts. What do you think, Francisco?"

"Excellent!"

"All, right, Guillermo, we'll hold them. Get the shoe polish and dye." Hernandez spoke peremptorily.

Guillermo hurried off.

"The girl is right." Barber had dropped his slangy nasal twang. "You can't get away with it. You don't need a murder charge, Hernandez, you're in enough trouble."

Hernandez smiled grimly. "Ah, so the charade ends. Jimmy the Gopher was an inspiration, but short-lived, you might say. Don't worry, my friend, there'll be no murder charge, not with a volley of shots, two dead guerrillas, and all of these fine witnesses. But now that we're being frank, tell us, how long have you been visiting our area?"

"We came in on the bus this afternoon. We were supposed to make contact with our man Harwood, your Reverend York, but we couldn't find him. We didn't know he was dead. What happened to him?"

"Something unfortunate. A beating, a bullet, an incineration. A shame, isn't it? An older fellow like that, so near to retirement, ought to be careful where he travels, don't you agree?"

"You're all bastards." Bill Hickock spat out the words.

"I'd rather hoped, now that the play is over, that you two would at least be gentlemen. I hate to see the Bureau lose its style."

Barber turned toward Dolores. "Miss, surely you can't allow this to happen? It just won't work. They're destroying themselves; it'll destroy you. It's cold-blooded murder—think of that, think of it on your conscience." He looked at her, his eyes boring into hers. She gave no hint of recognition.

"I agree. I don't like it. My uncles know that. But I can't stop them. Ours is a very close family. It's all I have. What I don't like, I'll have to ignore." As she spoke, her lovely face was troubled, but not sad. Barber wondered how she could do it. She really was going along with them. As she had told him, she was loyal and she didn't betray those whom she loved. And she had no idea that Al York stood before her. There was no point in telling her now. She couldn't help, anyway, and if she'd been so insensitive, after all, as not to know him, he'd misread her. To countenance cold-blooded murder in her own house, in front of her eyes . . . And he'd wanted to marry her. What an intuition he had. What an idiot he'd been.

Guillermo returned and began smearing black shoe grease in Barber's hair, staining his face with brown dye. Barber tossed and turned his head, resisting Guillermo as best he could.

"Do you mind, Uncle Francisco?" It was Dolores's voice. "I really can't watch you do it. I'll go into the living room and entertain General Sanchez and Mr. Sigua. Someone ought to look after them. They can only drink so much Scotch by themselves and the maid has probably forgotten them."

"Of course, my dear. Quite right, you do that. This is nothing for you to see. I am sorry, you do appreciate that I am?"

"Yes, Uncle, I understand."

She left before Guillermo finished, not even flicking an eye toward Barber.

Guillermo enjoyed his work, heavily smearing their faces and black-oiling their hair. He punished them with his hands; both men were bleeding from the scratches on their cheeks. Finished with his handiwork, Guillermo kicked them toward the french window. He'd tied them together for a stumble-walk and slowly they were forced back to stand outside. They stood there, mouths taped, watching. Inside, Barber could see that Hernandez had Barber's 357 ready to fire; de Lemos handled Bill's .38. They were going to shoot into the wall of the office. Another .38, this one from de Lemos's desk, lay on the table ready to deliver the sentence.

Hernandez got off the first round and de Lemos the second, chunking into the wall, as the anteroom door burst open. Three soldiers, with automatic rifles at the ready, walked uneasily through the doorway. Behind them was a uniformed man with great golden epaulettes, green-tinted glasses, a gray moustache, and very even, white teeth. Next to him was a very thin man in a fashionable—once old-fashioned, now new-fashioned—off-white linen suit. He was balding. Sigua, Luis Sigua: Barber had known him in earlier times when he was third deputy in the ministry—an ordinary man and no great friend, but very welcome now. If he knew what to do.

"Please, General Sanchez," Dolores was saying, "you can see for yourself. That's all I ask you to do. Look with your own eyes. There they are, my uncles. There are the guns. Outside the window, go ahead, look. You see? Guillermo with a gun and those two men bound and gagged, ready to be shot. Now do you believe me?"

Hernandez and de Lemos were staring at the girl in disbelief. Behind Barber, the realist Guillermo had turned and was running away across the garden toward the back wall. Both Hernandez and de Lemos held pistols in their hands. The general, stunned, continued to stare. The soldiers, without a cue, averted their weapons away from the deputy minister and the famous landowner.

"General, please," pleaded Dolores. "At least order your men to take those pistols away. Mr. Sigua, will you order my uncles to lay down their guns?"

His face showed the dilemma. To walk in on one's hosts and colleagues accompanied by armed soldiers was outrageous. But it was exactly as the girl had said. Firing, guns, two bound men waiting outside the window. There was no protocol for handling it. Obviously, General Sanchez had the same difficulty. No order issued from his lips and his soldiers wavered even more. A soldier could get in trouble holding a gun on a deputy minister.

De Lemos spoke first, trying to bluff it out. "Good evening, general. Good evening, Luis. I am embarrassed. We were testing these guns that my secretary seized from those two guerrillas. It was a very close call. If we hadn't surprised them outside we'd all be dead by now."

Barber watched Hernandez, a man whose face showed he'd

resolved to take a greater gamble. "Look out," he shouted, pointing to the window. "There's another guerrilla out there. Look out, I say!" Their attention diverted, the soldiers swung their weapons toward the window, toward Barber and Hickock standing there. Hernandez shouted again: "Yes, I see him. No, look, there are two of them. Look out! Well, good heavens, shoot them before they get away. Shoot, you fools!" His tone demanded obedience. The soldiers, peasants on temporary duty, crouched ready to fire at invisible enemies. The barrels of their guns pointed well over the heads of the two prisoners. They would fire into the air. But Hernandez wouldn't. He lowered Lee's 357 magnum, aiming out the window, lowering the barrel to fire into Lee's chest. Only Dolores appreciated what was happening.

"No!" she cried and lunged for Hernandez, hitting his arm. The 357 fired. Its second round of the evening whistled between Lee and Hickock.

"Stop it! I order you to put your gun down." General Sanchez at last had understood. "Put it down, I tell you."

Dolores was clinging to Hernandez's wrist, trying to wrestle the gun away.

"Damn you, damn you, you witch!" Hernandez with his free hand hit her full force across the face. The impact spun the girl backward, toppling her to the floor. "Damn you!" he said again. With his gun hand now free, he swung it on the helpless girl, who lay stunned on the floor. He squeezed the trigger and the magnum bullet tore a gaping hole in her chest. Lee watched as a portion of her breast disintegrated under the impact and her body, under the force of the bullet, bounced and recoiled and was pushed across the floor. Blood and noise and the shattered, torn flesh of the breast of his beloved, a breast uncaressed, a nipple unkissed. On her face, that lovely face, in her eyes, a look of the most profound hurt and shock, lips wide open as though to speak. Barber could hear the words she would have spoken, those intended words, "love and trust, my darling, forget me not, good-bye."

Twenty

LEE BARBER WAS IN THE HALLS of the mighty, before the throne of kings, deep on plush carpet. Here, let the trumpets ring out the empire of Groat. Barber had stopped to talk to Elise in the outer office. This time, he was the one who was sad and she had taken his hand and held it. No words, just a hand squeezed. Back in the kingdom of black and white, Elise, faithful secretary, would always be with the angels.

Groat had been waiting, but success had taught him patience. Why not? He had everything he wanted. Like hell. Lee glared at the big man as he entered the opulent office and settled down in the overstuffed chair. Groat handed him a cigar.

"Go on—Havana, Castro's best. Don't be shy. Fidel would want you to have it."

"Thanks."

They both smoked for a while, saying nothing. Groat blew smoke rings.

"I understand you're back," said Groat, his eyes drifting about the high ceiling.

"Congratulations. Another triumph of Bureau intelligence. Yeah, I'm back."

Groat fondled the gold watch. "Some people are saying you did a good job."

"Are they? And what are you saying?" Barber's tone was sarcastic, his expression suspicious. He had a wound on his forehead that still hurt when he frowned.

"I'd say it was a goddamn bloody disaster. What were you trying to do—open a second front to the Mexican War of 1846? I mean, are there any of those greasers left down there?"

"Mexicans, Julius, not greasers. Mexicans."

"Spicks. I never did go for them much. Christ, what a lot of trouble they've been to me."

"You ought to choose your agents down there with more care,

Julius. Hernandez had you tied up in knots. What did you assess him with when you recruited him, a Girl Scout running a Ouija board?"

"You choose to hurt me, Lee. You have no appreciation for all I've done for you, and now you hurl nasty words." Groat's big face took on an injured look. "How the hell was I to know Hernandez was a crook? Besides, they're all thieves down there. But, all right, it was a bit hairy, I grant. But don't worry, I've got the paper in the mill. When I find out who recruited him I'll have that guy picking grains of salt out of the Great Salt Lake, one by one."

"Julius, what I find so lovable about you, aside from your sense of personal responsibility when things go wrong here, is your sense of charity and forgiveness."

"More barbs. You take a little trip among the unbenighted heathen and you come back worse than the worst. I'll have to keep you here, Lee. I can't have your own noble character ruined by travel."

"Benighted, Julius, not 'unbenighted.' "

"Oh, all right, I'll be big about that—'benighted.' "

"Thank you, Julius."

"You're welcome, Lee. A little education around here might do this place some good. That's why I'm keeping you home for a while."

"You've said that twice, Julius, and I don't like it. Nobody, not you, not anybody, is keeping me around here."

"That's no way to show your appreciation for a promotion. A big promotion. I persuaded the big chief that you had it coming. It was better than firing you, wasn't it?"

"I'm not so sure."

"You're difficult today. What will my wife say tonight when you come to dinner in such a bad mood? You've got a responsibility to her, you know. She's in love with you. Why don't you do me a favor, Lee; run away with Alice and I'll be rid of you both. Will you do that for me?"

"I haven't accepted your invitation. I may be busy tonight. I've got a lot of things to straighten out. This is my first day back."

"Oh, what a treacherous type we hire for this lousy outfit. Lies, lies. You got back day before yesterday."

"That was Saturday. I came in Saturday night. Yesterday was Sunday; today is my first duty day. I should have called in sick."

"Don't be defensive, my boy, I didn't say I dislike liars; on the contrary, I just don't want you to lie to me. Dinner is at seven thirty. Billie is bringing the wine."

"Billie Hickock is coming?"

"That's right. So is his old man. The big boss is coming to dinner in your honor. Now, will you come?"

Lee nodded a suspicious assent.

"I thought so. You see the light sooner or later, Lee, but you're slow, as usual. I don't know how you'll manage as boss of this unit. These Byzantine types around here will run rings around you."

"Did I hear you, Julius?"

"You always hear me, you just never listen. I said 'boss of this unit.' This chair, this office, and, when I go, I'm going to lend you my personality, too. God knows, you're going to need some assets."

"Area chief! Are you crazy? That's three steps up. And besides, what happens to you?"

"Oh, don't you worry about me. I've got mine, Jack, as they say. In fact, everything changes, nothing changes—French proverb, you know. I'm going to be your boss, just like now."

"What do you mean?"

"You hear and you don't listen. Boss! Spelled t-y-r-a-n-t. I'm moving up to deputy chief, next to Hickock. When he retires next year, who can say? Maybe I'll own the goodies. Keep on my good side, little man, or I'll have you on the rack every Monday, just to test the ropes. You like that?"

"Who the hell would promote you, Julius?"

"Same people who have so far, same people who promote you. They can't be all crazy, can they?"

"But why?"

"Oh, Lee, you will never make it as area chief. You are an idiot. You just don't comprehend government. The reason I'm promoted is that you did so well in Mexico; that and the moment. That there is an opening, a friendly heart attack above me. That and the fact that I managed to fix about ten other people's wagons who were competing with me. They're lucky not to be picking salt grains, too. And they are—I mean, I am promoting you as part of the deal. Because I like you. I like liars and fools, or rather a knave just like the rest, but I can predict exactly what you'll do. That's your advantage to me. Besides, no one else would have done what you did in

Madre Dolorosa. Nobody. All their necks would have been tucked
in neatly like turtle's heads. And then where would we be? Exactly
where we are supposed to be, a nice, smooth-running, well-con-
trolled, well-audited, no-flap, no-action, well-appreciated government bureau. And, believe me, if it weren't for me and Hickock,
that's exactly what we'd have; hell, that's what we have, anyway. You
won't last, Lee, not as area chief, not as deputy. When it's all reviewed on judgment day, you won't have come in third, let alone
second. But this outfit is having its one last gasp of lunacy before
we turn it all over to the clerks and the management-and-budget
hatchet men. You're the last of the humanoids, Lee, all confused
about what's real. After you the computer takes over."

Lee Barber was genuinely surprised. "Julius, I'm amazed. 'Hu-
manoid'—that's the first kind word you've said about me."

"Don't let it go to your head. When you're area chief and I'm
your boss, we stick together. It's not admiration, believe me, it's
survival. Unless, of course, you're out to get me, in which case I will
get you first. Understand that?"

"Oh, Julius, it's your trusting nature that endears you most to
me."

"Never mind, you get the point. Now, I suppose you'd like to
hear the wrap-up on Tiburon before you sit down to spend the rest
of your life at committee meetings?"

"Okay."

"They got Hernandez cold. Murdering his niece in front of
unshutupable witnesses, can you imagine? General Sanchez was so
upset, he lost his upper plate; I'm not kidding, Sigua told us about
it. Too bad about the girl; I hear she saved your lives."

"Yeah, she did. Too bad about her." Barber stared ahead.

Groat went on, taking no notice of the expression on his colleague's face. "De Lemos fell with Hernandez. He'll buy his way out
in time—they all do, down there—but the fall's the thing. Now the
other big boys won't touch him. He's tainted. Being seen with him
could ruin their acts. He'll get out all right, but he's no longer big
time. That's what we want. Harass the bastards, make their lives
miserable, make them pay through the nose. They all get tired.
Keeps new faces coming into the drug trade that way, gives everybody a chance. Gives us a good press, too, we get to bust new faces.
The newspapers like that."

"I suppose they do," murmured Barber. "What about Father Teran?"

"Who's that?"

"The priest, Brother Camillo, the idealist who fell in with evil companions."

"Oh, yeah, him. Yeah, they got him."

"Who? How?"

"Oh, the Mexicans got him, who else? They shot him trying to escape, you know how those things go."

"Yeah, I know. And Manuel, the one we turned over to General Sanchez?"

"Shot while trying to escape. I guess that they just had a rash of those breakouts, huh?" Groat smiled grimly.

"Yeah," said Barber, not smiling.

"You'd think a priest would have more sense, wouldn't you?"

"Oh, I don't know that it was a matter of sense. He was on the road, searching. Perhaps he was sidetracked somewhere and got desperate. Salvation wasn't inconsequential to him. I admired him in some ways."

Groat grunted.

"Well, anyway, maybe you'll be glad to know we got the arms back that those chumps stole out of Huachuca. The army owes us one for that. Oh, they're missing some stuff, but down there what can you expect? What are a few machine guns, more or less? Maybe General Sanchez is building his own private army for the day when he can start his own revolution. The big thing is, the army owes us Brownie points. We'll be collecting for years."

"Why, just for returning some stolen weapons?"

"Oh, no, not that. You were the one who picked up on the poison gas; I read your report. Well, it was true. The chumps stole that from Fort Huachuca, too. Only Huachuca wasn't supposed to have any, not the X_4. C_2 maybe, crowd control, who cares? But we got the army with their britches down, buddy boy. They were storing a brand-new deadly chemical—deadly, I say—and they weren't supposed to have it there at all. We won't say anything, of course. We returned it to army with hardly a word. Well, maybe just a teensy-weensy word, so they'd understand we understood. We've got Defense where we want them now. I can play with those chips starting next week when I get close to the big man's chair. Oh, yes,

old buddy, I owe you a lot on that one. That and the other big one
you brought me. That one puts State over a barrel."

"What one?"

"I love your naïveté, Lee, it's so refreshing. It'll be all over your
face as they sail your ass out of here, those subordinates of yours
around here with the long knives."

"Thank you, Julius, for the warning. But what other big one did
I give you?"

"Che. You brought us back a real present. We made him out
as KGB. The Soviets were trying to set up one of their friendly little
people's socialist federated republics out there in Sonora. They'd
gone to lots of trouble, too. Money—you never saw so much money.
Documents—Christ, you could pave Pennsylvania Avenue. All for
nothing. Che, alias Grigor Kuzmanich, blew it. You remember saying in your report it might be so. You were dead right. He didn't
talk a whole lot, but some. Enough. We got him and we got State."

"You recruited him?"

"Damned if I know. He may double, he may just retire, then
again he may belong to us, his whole sweet KGB body and soul.
We'll see. We couldn't keep him, in any event. He was too big a fish.
Had to throw him back. It would have been a hell of a stink if we'd
kept him. International repercussions and all that. He was no second lieutenant, no, sir. You caught yourself a bird colonel, Lee. I
can do business with chips like that."

"With State?"

"Right. Oh, you'll learn, but slowly, ever so slowly. I can see
that. We told State we had him but were going to have to release
the whole story. Tell the Mexicans, tell the Latins, tell NATO, tell
everybody. We'd have to rev up a few of our covert action programs,
we told State, just to pay the Ruskies back. Retaliatory, like a few
counterrevolutions in Soviet client states—Africa, maybe, and some
dead KGB in New York City. Lord, you would have loved to see
their faces in Foggy Bottom. They're into détente this week, very big
on détente. Fashionable. I've nothing against it myself, you understand, but I played it cold bluff all the way. 'No choice,' I said, 'too
big. Can't keep it covered. A Soviet military operation in Sonora,'
I said, 'and you want us not to respond? Missile silos in Nogales,'
I said, 'atomic field weapons on the border would permanently
destroy our whole national deterrent credibility. SALT treaties I

through X down the tubes. Soviet first-strike capability assured and the only way to beat it is to invade Mexico now.' Can you hear it? That's what I told State and they damn near died. Paroxysms. Spastic. But I've a sweet nature, I let them persuade us not to invade Mexico, and not to start any private wars. Christ, they really thought we would. Can you imagine that? As if they don't know that we're all gentlemen together in this game. I bet they had visions of Colonel Kuzmanich being tortured in the basement while I was talking to them. The iron maiden, cattle prods, the rack, hot irons, thumbscrews, the whole bit. Do you know that Parks had Kuzmanich as his house guest the whole time? Golf, swimming, tennis, you name it. Parks never had it so good and an unlimited per diem for entertainment. Damn fool couldn't find a whore in Washington, though; I had to get one for Kuzmanich myself. That Parks is a useless pansy. Anyway, we got our points, and Kuzmanich is back home, happy as a clam. State's going to agree to anything we want: the posts we need abroad, communications control, precedence at diplomatic parties, our choice for the titles our boys get under Foreign Service cover. They even take over paying for the limousine service between the Bureau building and theirs. Talk about sweet, oh my; and we've got Kuzmanich on tape and tapes play back for years. So you see, Lee, we owe you lots. I'm a hard man, but I'm not ungrateful. I'm giving you your chance. You're moving upstairs. After that, play it as you will. The game doesn't change, only the players."

"I know one player who's changing."

"Yeah, who's that, not that I care?"

"Bill Hickock."

"You're kidding? The old man won't like that. Is the boy mad about something? Is he beefing about anything in my unit?"

"I don't suppose he's too happy about Parks. The way that committee damn near got us assassinated by themselves."

"Yeah, that was a booboo all right. Those damn vacation schedules. Look, you think if we cut Parks down, it would buy Bill Hickock back?"

"I doubt it, why do you care?"

"Why do I care? Lord, when his old man finds out the boy's quitting because he doesn't like the way Parks's committee ran Tiburon, the old man will be down on my neck. I could lose that promotion I just sewed up. And if I lose it, you don't get to sit in this big chair, either. Think about that, Barber."

"That, Julius, is one of the happier prospects you've held out to me today."

"Be serious, Lee. If I burn Parks—I mean, if I really cut him down to where he'll be grateful to see a light bulb and a folding chair in his office from now to the day he retires—do you think that will buy Bill Hickock back?"

"No, I don't think so."

"Well, then, the hell with it. Parks stays where he is, that useless scheming S.O.B. Bill can't influence the play unless he stays in the game. I'll just have to sweat it out with the old man, eh? Would you be willing to say a good word for me, Lee? Explain to him that his son is quitting because he wants to go to college or something?"

"Bill's been to college, Julius."

"Hell's bells, I know that. Just lay a story on the old man at dinner tonight, that's all. Cover my ass for me. Until now I didn't know it was hanging out."

"I don't think it is. The old man doesn't play it like that. He's the old school. If his son wants to quit, he'll understand. Why should he blame you when you're indistinguishable from the rest of the establishment, except maybe you're smarter and uglier. Don't feel bad, though. Around here, ugliness pays. Anyway, don't worry about the old man. He's glad that Bill's getting out, before it's too late. He didn't want him to join in the first place."

Groat looked up, surprised. "What do you know about how the old man thinks? What does he do, invite you to tea with him to talk about family problems?"

"Sometimes. It's mostly tennis and dinner, though. My family and his were friends, I've known him for years."

"You're kidding!" Groat was genuinely shocked.

"No!"

"You had a hook like that and you never threw it?"

"No, why should I?"

Groat was shaking his head. "I will never understand you. You've known the old man for years and I never knew about it."

"I don't know what you know and don't know, Julius. What's my business I keep to myself. It's no secret, though. All you have to do is play tennis on the courts next to me."

"I thought I ran an intelligence outfit," Groat was still shaking his head, "and I missed the important pieces."

"No you didn't, Julius, it was inconsequential and that's why you missed it. You were on the money, as always. You always will be. Primitive cunning, I suppose. I don't have it."

"No?" asked Groat dubiously. "If you don't, why the hell are you the hero around here and not me? Why are you friends with the big boss and not me? Why are you going to be area chief ten years younger than me? Answer me that. And how did you stay alive in Mexico when Sam Parks had you set up for the final fall? Oh, yeah, we're grown up around here, we can say it all out loud. And Grigor —he almost got you. And de Lemos—he nearly did. And that clown Manuel whom you gave away to the spicks like you throw itsy birds to kitty cats, and Hernandez and Teran, who wanted you dead, no doubt, in spite of your mystico-religious prayer-meeting affinities? You not cunning? The hell you're not. You're kinkier than a snake on a rake. What about that girl who copped out that her own family had a contract out on you and then gets herself killed saving your life? What about that bunch of drunken crazies who were out to ventilate you as their favorite Russian spy? A con man, Lee, that's what you are, and don't you forget I know it. By the way, at the party Colonel Kuzmanich nearly died laughing when we told him the Mexicans thought you were a Russian spy. I thought he'd split a gut; damn near did myself. On the strength of it, he got you a present, some Soviet Champagne from the embassy here in D.C., from them to you, one Russian spy to the next. Elise has the bottle out in the office for you. Good stuff. Man, did we all have a laugh over that one. And you're welcome to visit Moscow any time, Grigor said, and he means it. If security will let you go.

"Anyway, don't tell me any more jokes, you slippery bastard. You make me look like a Sunday school teacher. You've got more tongues than a butcher shop. Oh, don't frown at me, the Reverend Alfred Saturnino Bryan Harold Jimmy the Gopher lover-boy Lee Barber, don't give me that. I don't mind liars, I just don't want you lying to me. I know you, buddy boy. You are one cold-blooded player. And you've got more lives than a cat."

Barber glanced down at his necktie. The moonstone face of the stickpin glistened complacently under the light. Barber eyed Groat, imagining how he would look behind that big desk and a gold watch in his vest pocket. As Groat had said, Lee and the business were as one. Pedro had seen that, too. Well, why not? Barber looked at Groat and smiled. Everything was working out just fine.

F   7-3-78

Hartshorne
   The Mexican assassin